PENGUIN ENGLISH LIBRARY
A BOOK OF ENGLISH ESSAYS

Sir William Emrys Williams, C.B.E., D. Litt., who has edited this selection of *English Essays*, was literary adviser to Penguin Books from its earliest years. In 1934 he initiated the 'Art for the People' plan which a few years later stimulated the formation of the Arts Council. During the war he created the Army Bureau of Current Affairs (A.B.C.A.). He was for several years the Radio Critic of the *Observer* and Television Critic of the *New Statesman*, and, before he took to criticism, was himself a successful broadcaster and televiser. He was Secretary-General of the Arts Council of Great Britain from 1951 to 1963 and ended a thirty-year directorship at Penguin Books in 1965. From 1963 to 1970 he was Chairman of the Arts Council Theatre Enquiry. In 1964 he was given the American Medal of Freedom. Sir William Emrys Williams died in 1976.

A BOOK OF
ENGLISH ESSAYS

SELECTED BY
W. E. WILLIAMS

PENGUIN BOOKS

Penguin Books Ltd, Harmondsworth, Middlesex, England
Penguin Books, 625 Madison Avenue, New York, New York 10022, U.S.A.
Penguin Books Australia Ltd, Ringwood, Victoria, Australia
Penguin Books Canada Ltd, 2801 John Street, Markham, Ontario, Canada L3R 1B4
Penguin Books (N.Z.) Ltd, 182–190 Wairau Road, Auckland 10, New Zealand

—

First published in Pelican Books 1942
Reprinted 1948
New and enlarged edition 1951
Reprinted 1952, 1954, 1956, 1957, 1959, 1962, 1963, 1964, 1965, 1967,
1970, 1973, 1976, 1977
Reissued in the Penguin English Library 1980

—

—

Made and printed in Great Britain by
C. Nicholls & Company Ltd
Set in Monotype Baskerville

CONTENTS

CONTENTS

ACKNOWLEDGEMENTS

FOR permission to reprint the essays specified we are indebted to:

The late Lloyd Osbourne for Robert Louis Stevenson's 'Walking Tours', 'An Apology for Idlers', and 'A Plea for Gas Lamps' from *Virginibus Puerisque*;

Messrs J. M. Dent & Sons for G. K. Chesterton's 'A Defence of Nonsense', and 'A Defence of Penny Dreadfuls' from *The Defendant*;

Messrs Methuen & Co. for G. K. Chesterton's 'A Piece of Chalk' from *Tremendous Trifles*, for E. V. Lucas's 'A Funeral' from *Character and Comedy*, 'The Town Week' from *Fireside and Sunshine*, and 'A Door-plate' from *Twixt Eagle and Dove*, for Arthur Clutton-Brock's 'The Defects of English Prose' from *More Essays on Books*, and for Robert Lynd's 'On Not Being a Philosopher' from *It's a Fine World*, 'Why We Hate Insects' and 'The Pleasures of Ignorance' from *The Pleasures of Ignorance*;

The late Hilaire Belloc and Messrs Methuen & Co. for 'The Crooked Streets' from *This and That*, and Messrs Cassell for 'A Conversation with a Cat' from the book of this title;

Mrs Welby-Everard for Maurice Hewlett's 'The Maypole and the Column' from *Extemporary Essays* (Oxford University Press);

Messrs Duckworth & Co. for Edward Thomas's 'Broken Memories' from *Horae Solitariae*;

The late A. A. Milne and Messrs Methuen & Co. for 'A Village Celebration' from *If I May*, and 'Golden Fruit' from *Not that it Matters*;

Mr J. B. Priestly and Messrs Wm Heinemann for 'On Doing Nothing' from *Open House*, and 'My First Article', 'Seeing the Actors', 'Money for Nothing', 'Quietly Malicious Chairmanship' from *Delight*;

Mr Ivor Brown for 'A Sentimental Journey' from *Masques and Phases* (Cobden-Sanderson);

The late James Agate for 'Likes and Dislikes' from *Responsibility* (Richards);

The late Aldous Huxley and Messrs Chatto & Windus for 'Tragedy and the Whole Truth' and 'Selected Snobberies' from *Music at Night*; and V. S. Pritchett and Messrs Chatto & Windus for 'The First Detective' and 'The Dean' from *In My Good Books*;

The late Neville Cardus and The Richards Press for 'W. G.' from *A Cricketer's Book*;

The late Robert Lynd for 'The Darkness';

The late Harold Nicolson, Messrs Constable & Co., and Messrs Harcourt Brace & Co. for 'Men's Clothes', 'Food', and 'A Defence of Shyness' from *Small Talk*.

INTRODUCTION

A Minimum Definition

No elaborate definition of the Essay is necessary for those who read the following selection. The English Essay has a multitude of forms and manners, and scarcely any rules and regulations. A minimum definition would be to say that the Essay is a piece of prose, usually on the short side, which is not devoted to narrative. The essayist may use anecdotes to make his point; he may even take a leaf out of the novelist's book and create characters to illustrate his own opinions. But his chief interest is not that of the story-teller. The essayist's usual role is that of the social philosopher, the critic, the annotator.

But before we are lured any farther in this attempt to identify the special interests of the essayist, let us look over a few of the many types of Essay included in this selection. First, Bacon, the father of the English Essay, who would fail to recognize most of his descendants. Bacon's compact, laconic style suggests the kinship between the word 'essay' and the mineralogist's word 'assay'; for the handful of carefully-washed words which come out in one of Bacon's Essays puts one in mind of the prospector sluicing away the grit until a few clear specks of gold are left in the bottom of his pan. Bacon brooded over some topic of social custom or behaviour until he could reduce his conclusions upon it to an almost aphoristic brevity. That is why he so often reads like a string of mottoes and proverbs – except that he has the Elizabethan power of illuminating a bare truth by a brilliant image: when, for example, he likens the ill-natured man 'to the thorn or briar which prick or scratch because they can do no other'.

The early English Essay made no bones about its deliberate moral purpose. Many of Bacon's are homilies on conduct; and many of the divines who wrote Essays in the seventeenth century were preoccupied with a similar purpose: Jeremy Taylor, for example, one of whose finest testimonies will be found in this selection.

A form so handy as the Essay – so short, so free from literary convention – was bound to produce variants of Bacon's or Taylor's manner. Thus during the seventeenth century there developed a popular literary exercise called the 'Character' – a kind of still-life composite portrait of various familiar 'types' – the Undergraduate, the Poet, the Yeoman, and so on. Few of those character-studies would interest the modern reader, but they are worth referring to here because they brought a new interest into Essay-writing, and set the fashion by which such essayists as Addison, Steele, and Goldsmith so often introduced into their Essays fictional characters like Sir Roger de Coverley or Beau Tibbs.

The Eighteenth-century Essay

The eighteenth century produced a galaxy of essayists and here we should note a factor which so often determines the form literature shall take. Thus, the complex shape of a Shakespearean play, with its alternating intimate and crowd scenes, was prescribed by the peculiar architecture of the Elizabethan stage – with its balconies, alcoves, and platforms. In a similar way, the length and tone of that spate of Essays which appeared in the eighteenth century were determined by the swift contemporary development of the Press. It was the eighteenth-century periodical and newspaper which made the eighteenth-century Essay. By the end of that century there were sixty daily or weekly papers published in London. Most of them supplemented the news with an article of comment upon literature, manners or politics; some of them, like the famous *Spectator*, left the news to others and concentrated upon the job of criticism. In these periodicals, then, the Essay found a new scope; and such masters as Addison and Steele gave the Essay a new charter. Henceforth it was free to air any topic of public interest; and as the Press developed into the many forms we know today, the Essay found many lengths and many levels for its business of comment and criticism. In our modern dailies, weeklies, monthlies or quarterlies we can find so many moods, themes, styles, and sizes of the Essay that we realize how broad any definition of that form must be nowadays.

It is an agreeable exercise to compare the varieties of the Essay during the eighteenth, nineteenth, and twentieth centuries. Addison, for instance: meticulous and elaborate. His paragraphing is a model of precision, the balance and antithesis of his sentences are as carefully contrived as a stonemason's or a carpenter's. His diction, again, is as formal as the costume of his day: never relapsing into a full-blooded colloquialism, never robust in its humour. Yet his is a style to be analysed and respected – absorbed and forgotten – by anyone who wishes to master the mechanics of good English. Goldsmith, too, can make sentences as elegant and correct as a peruke, but his favourite manner is more supple and coloured; and although he is as willing as Addison to comment on social behaviour, he does it less pontifically, more humanely. Addison does not 'receive' until he is dressed and powdered; Goldsmith will talk to you in his dressing-gown.

Hazlitt represents a more searching kind of Essay than Addison or Goldsmith – the critical analysis of an exacting literary theme – and in our own age he has his counterpart in such a critic as Aldous Huxley. Lamb, again, is the sharpest possible contrast to Hazlitt. His themes call for no precise terms of definitions, not even for logic. Lamb is involved always in a mood rather than a topic, and what he writes is a kind of ode in prose. His 'subject' is a pretext rather than an assignment. It moves him as a wind flutters the thousand bits of glass which hang from the ridges of a Japanese temple; it sets him off on an excursion as liable to land him into the fanciful as anywhere else. Yet anyone who examines an Essay of Lamb's will see that he is no mere bubble-blower. His fancy and his responsiveness to moods are disciplined into a pattern of progress and development.

Take, for example, *In Praise of Chimney Sweepers*. The Essay begins with a panegyric to the 'matin lark' – the young sweep. Immediately afterwards, Lamb is recalling the thrill he felt as a boy when he saw a sweep's brush suddenly emerge from a chimney-top. The fifth paragraph is a parenthetic exhortation to the reader to give a penny to a sweep when he sees one. In the next paragraph, the maze takes what seems an incomprehensible turn, for it does nothing but describe a shop which sells sassafras tea; but soon we discover that this is the favourite beverage of sweeps. Then the Essay takes a fresh turn, to mention those other stalls where the early workman gets his herbal beer. The following paragraph comes back to the sweep at the stall, where you are invited to stand him a drink and a snack. There we come into a new section of the maze, which begins most disconcertingly: 'I am by nature extremely susceptible to street affronts', but which leads us on to consider the mischievous nature of sweeps. No sooner do we feel our way along than we come across a fresh and startling line: 'I am by theory obdurate to the seductiveness of what are called a fine set of teeth', – but it directs us eventually to a consideration of the possibility that many sweeps are mislaid lordlings. We are led on to a pleasant story of one such romance. On the heels of that, we are without warning introduced to 'my pleasant friend, Jem White', who, however, turns out to be a kind of patron saint of sweeps. One of his annual feeds for them is next described; and, just afterwards, we emerge unexpectedly to find that, Jem now dead, the sweeps lament his lost bounty.

From first to last the thread is there, and the shocks we get as we fancy ourselves lost from time to time, serve to heighten our pleasure at the constant return to the central idea.

Further comparisons between the themes and methods of the English Essayists can be left for the reader to explore for himself. When he has done so he may feel capable of expanding the tentative definition with which this Introduction began. Yet perhaps he will be disposed to add no more than this – that throughout the manifold variety of the English Essay there runs in one form or another a sense of moral purpose: a zeal to edify and clarify our thought upon a thousand different themes; sometimes that purpose is boldly revealed, sometimes it is camouflaged with humour or irony, sometimes it is so implicit that it discloses itself to you only after a long reflexion. But it is consistent enough and clear enough to leave no doubt that the English Essay is a 'serious' mode of literature, and that whether he is writing about behaviour or books or science or politics, the essayist is out to edify rather than to entertain. And even when, in fulfilling that intention, he manages also to be amusing, the fact remains that he still conforms to the purpose which Bacon was the first to practise.

With these few pointers in mind the reader is now advised, before dipping into this selection, to turn first to Maurice Hewlett's *The Maypole and the Column* (on page 235), for it is one of the best essays ever written on the English Essay.

W. E. WILLIAMS

LONDON, 1951

FRANCIS BACON

Of Studies

STUDIES serve for delight, for ornament, and for ability. Their chief use for delight, is in privateness and retiring; for ornament, is in discourse; and for ability, is in the judgement and disposition of business; for expert men can execute, and perhaps judge of particulars, one by one: but the general counsels, and the plots and marshalling of affairs come best from those that are learned. To spend too much time in studies, is sloth; to use them too much for ornament, is affectation; to make judgement wholly by their rules, is the humour of a scholar: they perfect nature, and are perfected by experience: for natural abilities are like natural plants, that need pruning by study; and studies themselves do give forth directions too much at large, except they be bounded in by experience. Crafty men contemn studies, simple men admire them, and wise men use them; for they teach not their own use; but that is a wisdom without them and above them, won by observation. Read not to contradict and confute, nor to believe and take for granted, nor to find talk and discourse, but to weigh and consider. Some books are to be tasted, others to be swallowed, and some few to be chewed and digested; that is, some books are to be read only in parts; others to be read but not curiously; and some few to be read wholly, and with diligence and attention. Some books also may be read by deputy, and extracts made of them by others; but that would be only in the less important arguments and the meaner sort of books; else distilled books are, like common distilled waters, flashy things. Reading maketh a full man; conference a ready man; and writing an exact man; and, therefore, if a man write little, he had need have a great memory; if he confer little, he had need have a present wit; and if he read little, he had need have much cunning, to seem to know that he doth not. Histories make men wise; poets, witty; the mathematics, subtle; natural philosophy, deep; moral, grave; logic and rhetoric, able to contend: *Abeunt studia in mores;* nay, there is no stand or impediment in the wit, but may be wrought out by fit studies: like as diseases of the body may have appropriate exercises; bowling is good for the stone and reins, shooting for the lungs and breast, gentle walking for the stomach, riding for the head and the like; so if a man's wit be wandering, let him study the mathematics; for in demonstrations, if his wit be called away never so little, he must begin again; if his wit be not apt to distinguish or find difference, let him study the schoolmen; for they are *Cymini sectores.* If he be not apt to beat over matters, and to call up one thing to prove and illustrate another, let him study the lawyers' cases: so every defect of the mind may have a special receipt.

Of Ambition

AMBITION is like choler; which is an humour that maketh men active, earnest, full of alacrity, and stirring, if it be not stopped. But if it be stopped, and cannot have his way, it becometh adust, and thereby malign and venomous. So ambitious men, if they find the way open for their rising, and still get forward, they are rather busy than dangerous; but if they be checked in their desires, they become secretly discontent, and look upon men and matters with an evil eye, and are best pleased when things go backward; which is the worst property in a servant of a prince or state. Therefore it is good for princes, if they use ambitious men, to handle it so as they be still progressive and not retrograde: which because it cannot be without inconvenience, it is good not to use such natures at all. For if they rise not with their service, they will take orders to make their service fall with them. But since we have said it were good not to use men of ambitious natures, except it be upon necessity, it is fit we speak in what cases they are of necessity. Good commanders in the wars must be taken, be they never so ambitious: for the use of their service dispenseth with the rest; and to take a soldier without ambition is to pull off his spurs. There is also great use of ambitious men in being screens to princes in matters of danger and envy: for no man will take that part, except he be like a seeled dove, that mounts and mounts because he cannot see about him. There is use also of ambitious men in pulling down the greatness of any subject that overtops: as Tiberius used Macro in the pulling down of Sejanus. Since therefore they must be used in such cases, there resteth to speak how they must be bridled, that they may be less dangerous. There is less danger of them if they be of mean birth, than if they be noble; and if they be rather harsh of nature, than gracious and popular; and if they be rather new raised, than grown cunning and fortified in their greatness. It is counted by some a weakness in princes to have favourites; but it is of all others the best remedy against ambitious great ones. For when the way of pleasuring and displeasuring lieth by the favourite, it is impossible any other should be over great. Another means to curb them, is to balance them by others as proud as they. But then there must be some middle counsellors, to keep things steady; for without that ballast the ship will roll too much. At the least, a prince may animate and inure some meaner persons to be, as it were, scourges to ambitious men. As for the having of them obnoxious to ruin, if they be of fearful natures, it may do well; but if they be stout and daring, it may precipitate their designs, and prove dangerous. As for the pulling of them down, if the affairs require it, and that it may be done with safety suddenly, the only way is the interchange continually of favours and disgraces; whereby they may not know what to expect, and be, as it were, in a wood. Of ambitions, it is less harmful, the ambition to prevail in great things, than that other, to appear in everything; for that breeds confusion, and mars business. But yet it is less danger to have an ambitious man stirring in business, than great in dependences. He that seeketh to be eminent amongst able men hath a great task; but that is ever good for the public. But he that plots to be the only figure amongst ciphers is the decay of an whole age. Honour hath three things in it: the vantage ground to do good; the approach to kings and principal persons; and the raising of man's own fortunes. He that hath the best of these intentions, when he aspireth, is an honest man; and that prince that can discern of these intentions in another that aspireth, is a wise prince. Generally, let princes and states choose such ministers as are more sensible of duty than of rising; and such as love business rather upon conscience than upon bravery: and let them discern a busy nature from a willing mind.

Of Travel

TRAVEL, in the younger sort, is a part of education; in the elder, a part of experience. He that travelleth into a country, before he hath some entrance into the language, goeth to school, and not to travel. That young men travel under some tutor or grave servant, I allow well; so that he be such a one that hath the language, and hath been in the country before; whereby he may be able to tell them what things are worthy to be seen in the country where they go, what acquaintances they are to seek, what exercises or discipline the place yieldeth; for else young men shall go hooded, and look abroad little. It is a strange thing, that in sea voyages, where there is nothing to be seen but sky and sea, men should make diaries; but in land travel, wherein so much is to be observed, for the most part they omit it; as if chance were fitter to be registered than observation: let diaries, therefore, be brought in use. The things to be seen and observed are, the courts of princes, especially when they give audience to ambassadors; the courts of justice, while they sit and hear causes; and so of consistories ecclesiastic; the churches and monasteries, with the monuments which are therein extant; the walls and fortifications of cities and towns; and so the havens and harbours, antiquities and ruins, libraries, colleges, disputations, and lectures, where any are; shipping and navies; houses and gardens of state and pleasure, near great cities; armories, arsenals, magazines, exchanges, burses, warehouses, exercises of horsemanship, fencing, training of soldiers, and the like: comedies, such whereunto the better sort of persons do resort; treasuries of jewels and robes; cabinets and rarities; and, to conclude, whatsoever is memorable in the places

where they go; after all which the tutors or servants
ought to make diligent inquiry. As for triumphs, masks,
feasts, weddings, funerals, capital executions, and such
shows, men need not to be put in mind of them: yet
are they not to be neglected. If you will have a young man
to put his travel into a little room, and in short time to
gather much, this you must do: first, as was said, he must
have some entrance into the language before he goeth;
then he must have such a servant, or tutor, as knoweth
the country, as was likewise said: let him carry with him
also some card, or book, describing the country where
he travelleth, which will be a good key to his inquiry;
let him keep also a diary; let him not stay long in one
city or town, more or less as the place deserveth, but not
long; nay, when he stayeth in one city or town, let him
change his lodging from one end and part of the town
to another, which is a great adamant of acquaintance;
let him sequester himself from the company of his countrymen, and diet in such places where there is good company
of the nation where he travelleth: let him, upon his
removes from one place to another, procure recommenda-
tion to some person of quality residing in the place
whither he removeth, that he may use his favour in those
things he desireth to see or know; thus he may abridge his
travel with much profit. As for the acquaintance which
is to be sought in travel, that which is most of all profitable,
is acquaintance with the secretaries and employed men
of ambassadors; for so in travelling in one country he
shall suck the experience of many: let him also see and
visit eminent persons in all kinds, which are of great name
abroad, that he may be able to tell how the life agreeth
with the fame; for quarrels, they are with care and
discretion to be avoided; they are commonly for mistresses,
healths, place, and words; and let a man beware how he

keepeth company with choleric and quarrelsome persons; for they will engage him into their own quarrels. When a traveller returneth home, let him not leave the countries where he hath travelled altogether behind him, but maintain a correspondence by letters with those of his acquaintance which are of most worth; and let his travel appear rather in his discourse than in his apparel or gesture; and in his discourse let him be rather advised in his answers, than forward to tell stories: and let it appear that he doth not change his country manners for those of foreign parts; but only prick in some flowers of that he hath learned abroad into the customs of his own country.

JEREMY TAYLOR

On Death

THE autumn with its fruits provides disorders for us, and
the winter's cold turns them into sharp diseases, and the
spring brings flowers to strew our hearse, and the summer
gives green turf and brambles to bind upon our graves.

The wild fellow in Petronius that escaped upon a
broken table from the furies of a shipwreck, as he was
sunning himself upon the rocky shore, espied a man rolled
upon his floating bed of waves, ballasted with sand in
the folds of his garment, and carried by his civil enemy
the sea towards the shore to find a grave: and it cast
him into some sad thoughts: that peradventure this man's
wife in some part of the continent, safe and warm, looks
next month for the good man's return; or it may be his
son knows nothing of the tempest; or his father thinks of
that affectionate kiss which still is warm upon the good
old man's cheek ever since he took a kind farewell, and
how he weeps with joy to think how blessed he shall be
when his beloved boy returns into the circle of his father's
arms. These are the thoughts of mortals, this the end and
sum of all their designs: a dark night and an ill guide, a
boisterous sea and a broken cable, and hard rock and a
rough wind dashed in pieces the fortune of a whole
family, and they that shall weep loudest for the accident
are not yet entered into the storm, and yet have suffered
shipwreck. Then looking upon the carcase, he knew it,
and found it to be the master of the ship, who the day
before cast up the accounts of his patrimony and his

trade, and named the day when he thought to be at home. See how the man swims who was so angry two days since; his passions are becalmed with the storm, his accounts cast up, his cares at an end, his voyage done, and his gains are the strange events of death.

It is a mighty change that is made by the death of every person, and it is visible to us who are alive. Reckon but from the sprightfulness of youth and the fair cheeks and the full eyes of childhood, from the vigorousness and strong flexure of the joints of five and twenty, to the hollowness and dead paleness, to the loathsomeness and horror of a three days' burial, and we shall perceive the distance to be very great and very strange. But so I have seen a rose newly springing from the clefts of its hood, and at first it was fair as the morning, and full with the dew of heaven as a lamb's fleece: but when a ruder breath had forced open its virgin modesty, and dismantled its too youthful and unripe retirements, it began to put on darkness, and to decline to softness and the smyptoms of a sickly age; it bowed the head, and broke its stalk; and at night having lost some of its leaves and all its beauty, it fell into the portion of weeds and outworn faces.

When the sentence of death is decreed, and begins to be put in execution, it is sorrow enough to see or feel respectively the sad accents of the agony and last contentions of the soul, and the reluctances and unwillingnesses of the body: the forehead washed with a new and stranger baptism, besmeared with a cold sweat, tenacious and clammy, apt to make it cleave to the roof of his coffin; the nose cold and undiscerning, not pleased with perfumes, nor suffering violence with a cloud of unwholesome smoke; the eyes dim as a sullied mirror, or the face of Heaven when God shews his anger in a prodigious storm; the feet cold, the hands stiff; the physicians despairing, our friends weeping, the room dressed with darkness and sorrow; and the exterior parts betraying what the violences which the soul and spirit suffer.

Then calamity is great, and sorrow rules in all the capacities of man; then the mourners weep, because it is civil, or because they need thee, or because they fear: but who suffers for thee with a compassion sharp as is thy pain? Then the noise is like the faint echo of a distant valley, and few hear, and they will not regard thee, who seemest like a person void of understanding, and of a departing interest.

JOSEPH ADDISON

The Tombs in Westminster Abbey

Pallida mors aequo pulsat pede pauperm tabernas
  Regumque turres, o beate Sexti.
Vitae summa brevis spem nos vetat inchoare longam.
  Jam te premet nox, fabulaeque manes,
Et domus exilis Plutonia –

HOR., 1 *Od.* iv. 13.

WHEN I am in a serious humour, I very often walk by
myself in Westminster Abbey; where the gloominess of
the place, and the use to which it is applied, with the
solemnity of the building, and the condition of the people
who lie in it, are apt to fill the mind with a kind of
melancholy, or rather thoughtfulness, that is not disagreeable. I yesterday passed a whole afternoon in the
churchyard, the cloisters, and the church, amusing myself
with the tombstones and inscriptions that I met with in
those several regions of the dead. Most of them recorded
nothing else of the buried person but that he was born
upon one day and died upon another: the whole history
of his life being comprehended in those two circumstances
that are common to all mankind. I could not but look
upon these registers of existence, whether of brass or
marble, as a kind of satire upon the departed persons;
who had left no other memorial of them, but that they
were born and that they died. They put me in mind of
several persons mentioned in the battles of heroic poems,
who have sounding names given them for no other reason
but that they may be killed, and are celebrated for
nothing but being knocked on the head.

Γλαύκου τε Μέδοντά τε θερσιλοχὸν τε. – Hom.
Glaucumque, Medontaque, Thersilochumque. – Vir.

The Life of these men is finely described in Holy Writ by
the path of an arrow, which is immediately closed up and
lost.

Upon my going into the church, I entertained myself
with the digging of a grave; and saw in every shovelful of
it that was thrown up, the fragment of a bone or skull
intermixed with a kind of fresh mouldering earth that
some time or other had a place in the composition of a
human body. Upon this I began to consider with myself
what innumerable multitudes of people lay confused
together under that pavement of that ancient cathedral;
how men and women, friends and enemies, priests and
soldiers, monks and prebendaries, were crumbled amongst
one another, and blended together in the same common
mass; how beauty, strength, and youth, with old age,
weakness, and deformity, lay undistinguished in the same
promiscuous heap of matter.

After having thus surveyed this great magazine of
mortality, as it were in the lump, I examined it more
particularly by the accounts which I found on several of
the monuments which are raised in every quarter of that
ancient fabric. Some of them were covered with such
extravagant epitaphs that, if it were possible for the dead
person to be acquainted with them, he would blush at
the praises which his friends have bestowed upon him.
There are others so excessively modest that they deliver
the character of the person departed in Greek or Hebrew,
and by that means are not understood once in a twelvemonth. In the poetical quarter, I found there were poets
who had no monuments, and monuments which had no
poets. I observed indeed that the present war had filled

the church with many of these uninhabited monuments, which had been erected to the memory of persons whose bodies were perhaps buried in the plains of Blenheim, or in the bosom of the ocean.

I could not but be very much delighted with several modern epitaphs, which are written with great elegance of expression and justness of thought, and therefore do honour to the living as well as to the dead. As a foreigner is very apt to conceive an idea of the ignorance or politeness of a nation from the turn of their public monuments and inscriptions, they should be submitted to the perusal of men of learning and genius before they are put in execution. Sir Cloudesley Shovel's monument has very often given me great offence. Instead of the brave, rough English admiral, which was the distinguishing character of that plain, gallant man, he is represented on his tomb by the figure of a beau, dressed in a long periwig, and reposing himself upon velvet cushions under a canopy of state. The inscription is answerable to the monument, for instead of celebrating the many remarkable actions he had performed in the service of his country, it acquaints us only with the manner of his death, in which it was impossible for him to reap any honour. The Dutch, whom we are apt to despise for want of genius, show an infinitely greater taste of antiquity and politeness in their buildings and works of this nature, than what we meet with in those of our own country. The monuments of their admirals, which have been erected at the public expense, represent them like themselves, and are adorned with rostral crowns and naval ornaments, with beautiful festoons of seaweed, shells, and coral.

But to return to our subject. I have left the repository of our English kings for the contemplation of another day, when I shall find my mind disposed for so serious an amusement. I know that entertainments of this nature are apt to raise dark and dismal thoughts in timorous minds and gloomy imaginations; but for my own part, though I am always serious, I do not know what it is to be melancholy, and can therefore take a view of nature in her deep and solemn scenes, with the same pleasure as in her most gay and delightful ones. By this means, I can improve myself with those objects which others consider with terror. When I look upon the tombs of the great, every emotion of envy dies in me; when I read the epitaphs of the beautiful, every inordinate desire goes out; when I meet with the grief of parents upon a tombstone, my heart melts with compassion; when I see the tomb of the parents themselves, I consider the vanity of grieving for those whom we must quickly follow; when I see kings lying by those who deposed them, when I consider rival wits placed side by side, or the holy men that divided the world with their contests and disputes, I reflect with sorrow and astonishment on the little competitions, factions, and debates of mankind. When I read the several dates of the tombs – of some that died yesterday, and some six hundred years ago – I consider that great day when we shall all of us be contemporaries, and make our appearance together.

A Vision of Justice

Jam redit et Virgo, redeunt Saturnia regna.
VIRG., *Ecl.* iv. ver. 6.
Returning justice brings a golden age. – R.W.
Sheer Lane, November 28.

I WAS last week taking a solitary walk in the garden of Lincoln's Inn (a favour that is indulged me by several of the benchers, who are my intimate friends, and grown old with me in this neighbourhood) when, according to the

nature of men in years, who have made but little progress
in the advancement of their fortune or their fame, I was
repining at the sudden rise of many persons who are my
juniors, and indeed, at the unequal distribution of wealth,
honour, and all other blessings of life. I was lost in this
thought, when the night came upon me, and drew my
mind into a far more agreeable contemplation. The
heaven above me appeared in all its glories, and presented
me with such a hemisphere of stars as made the most
agreeable prospect imaginable to one who delights in the
study of nature. It happened to be a freezing night, which
had purified the whole body of air into such a bright
transparent ether, as made every constellation visible;
and, at the same time, gave such a particular glowing
to the stars, that I thought it the richest sky I had ever
seen. I could not behold a scene so wonderfully adorned
and lighted up, if I may be allowed that expression, without suitable meditations on the author of such illustrious
and amazing objects; for, on these occasions philosophy
suggests motives to religion, and religion adds pleasure to
philosophy.

As soon as I had recovered my usual temper and serenity
of soul, I retired to my lodgings, with the satisfaction of
having passed away a few hours in the proper employ-
ments of a reasonable creature; and promising myself
that my slumbers would be sweet, I no sooner fell into
them, but I dreamed a dream, or saw a vision, for I know
not which to call it, that seemed to rise out of my evening
meditation, and had something in it so solemn and serious,
that I cannot forbear communicating it; though, I must
confess, the wildness of imagination, which, in a dream,
is always loose and irregular, discovers itself too much in
several parts of it.

Methought I saw the same azure sky diversified with the

same glorious luminaries which had entertained me a little before I fell asleep. I was looking very attentively on that sign in the heavens which is called by the name of the Balance,* when, on a sudden, there appeared in it an extraordinary light, as if the sun should rise at midnight. By its increasing in breadth and lustre, I soon found that it approached towards the earth; and at length could discern something like a shadow hovering in the midst of a great glory, which, in a little time after, I distinctly perceived to be the figure of a woman. I fancied at first, it might have been the angel, or intelligence that guided the constellation from which it descended; but, upon a nearer view, I saw about her all the emblems with which the goddess of justice is usually described. Her countenance was unspeakably awful and majestic, but exquisitely beautiful to those whose eyes were strong enough to behold it; her smiles transported with rapture, her frowns terrified to despair. She held in her hand a mirror, endowed with the same qualities as that which the painters put into the hand of truth.

There streamed from it a light, which distinguished itself from all the splendours that surrounded her, more than a flash of lightning shines in the midst of daylight. As she moved it in her hand, it brightened the heavens, the air, or the earth. When she had descended so low as to be seen and heard by mortals, to make the pomp of her appearance more supportable, she threw darkness and clouds about her, that tempered the light into a thousand beautiful shades and colours, and multiplied that lustre, which was before too strong and dazzling, into a variety of milder glories.

* *The Balance*, Libra, or the Balance, is next the sign Virgo, into which Astraea, the goddess of justice, was translated, when she could no longer stay on earth.

In the meantime, the world was in an alarm, and all the inhabitants of it gathered together upon a spacious plain; so that I seemed to have the whole species before my eyes. A voice was heard from the clouds declaring the intention of this visit, which was to restore and appropriate to every one living what was his due. The fear and hope, joy and sorrow, which appeared in that great assembly, after this solemn declaration, are not to be expressed. The first edict was then pronounced, 'That all titles and claims to riches and estates, or to any part of them, should be immediately vested in the rightful owner.' Upon this, the inhabitants of the earth held up the instruments of their tenure, whether in parchment, paper, wax, or any other form of conveyance; and as the goddess moved the mirror of truth which she held in her hand, so that the light which flowed from it fell upon the multitude, they examined the several instruments by the beams of it. The rays of this mirror had a particular quality of setting fire to all forgery and falsehood. The blaze of papers, the melting of seals, and crackling of parchments, made a very odd scene. The fire very often ran through two or three lines only and then stopped. Though I could not but observe that the flames chiefly broke out among the interlineations and codicils; the light of the mirror, as it was turned up and down, pierced into all the dark corners and recesses of the universe, and by that means detected many writings and records which had been hidden or buried by time, chance, or design. This occasioned a wonderful revolution among the people. At the same time, the spoils of extortion, fraud, and robbery, with all the fruits of bribery and corruption, were thrown together in a prodigious pile, that almost reached to the clouds, and was called, 'The Mount of Restitution'; to which all injured persons were invited, to receive what belonged to them.

One might see crowds of people in tattered garments come up, and change clothes with others that were dressed with lace and embroidery. Several who were *Plums*,* or very near it, became men of moderate fortunes; and many others, who were overgrown in wealth and possessions, had no more left than what they usually spent. What moved my concern most was to see a certain street† of the greatest credit in Europe, from one end to the other, become bankrupt.

The next command was 'that all the posts of dignity and honour in the universe should be conferred on persons of the greatest merit, abilities, and perfection.' The handsome, the strong, and the wealthy immediately pressed forward; but, not being able to bear the splendour of the mirror, which played upon their faces, they immediately fell back among the crowd: but as the goddess tried the multitude by her glass, as the eagle does its young ones by the lustre of the sun, it was remarkable, that every one turned away his face from it, who had not distinguished himself either by virtue, knowledge, or capacity in business, either military or civil. This select assembly was drawn up in the centre of a prodigious multitude, which was diffused on all sides, and stood observing them, as idle people use to gather about a regiment that are exercising their arms. They were drawn up in three bodies: in the first, were the men of virtue; in the second, men of knowledge; and in the third, the men of business. It is impossible to look at the first column without a secret veneration, their aspects were so sweetened with humanity, raised with contemplation, emboldened with resolution, and adorned with the most agreeable airs, which are those that proceed from secret habits of virtue. I could not but take notice,

* *Plums.* Those having a fortune of £100,000.
† *A certain street.* A reference to the bankers in Lombard Street.

that there were many faces among them which were unknown, not only to the multitude, but even to several of
their own body.

In the second column, consisting of the men of knowledge, there had been great disputes before they fell into
the ranks, which they did not do at last without the positive command of the goddess who presided over the
assembly. She had so ordered it, that men of the greatest
genius and strongest sense were placed at the head of the
column. Behind these were such as had formed their
minds very much on the thoughts and writings of others.
In the rear of the column were men who had more wit
than sense, or more learning than understanding. All
living authors of any value were ranged in one of these
classes; but, I must confess, I was very much surprised to
see a great body of editors, critics, commentators, and
grammarians meet with so very ill a reception. They had
formed themselves into a body, and, with a great deal of
arrogance, demanded the first station in the column
of knowledge; but, the goddess, instead of complying
with their request, clapped them all into liveries, and bid
them know themselves for no other but lackeys of the
learned.

The third column were men of business, and consisting
of persons in military and civil capacities. The former
marched out from the rest, and placed themselves in the
front; at which the others shook their heads at them, but
did not think fit to dispute the post with them. I could not
but make several observations upon this last column of
people; but I have certain private reasons why I do not
think fit to communicate them to the public. In order to
fill up all the posts of honour, dignity, and profit, there
was a draft made out of each column of men, who were
masters of all three qualifications in some degree, and

were preferred to stations of the first rank. The second draft was made out of such as were possessed of any two of the qualifications, who were disposed of in stations of a second dignity. Those who were left, and were endowed only with one of them, had their suitable posts. When this was over, there remained many places of trust and profit unfilled, for which there were fresh drafts made out of the surrounding multitude, who had any appearance of these excellencies, or were recommended by those who possessed them in reality.

All were surprised to see so many new faces in the most eminent dignities; and, for my own part, I was very well pleased to see that all my friends either kept their present posts, or were advanced to higher.

Having filled my paper with those particulars of my vision which concern the male part of mankind, I must reserve for another occasion the sequel of it, which relates to the fair sex.

Ladies' Head-dress

Tanta est quaerendi cura decoris.
JUV. *Sat.* vi. 500.
So studiously their persons they adorn.

THERE is not so variable a thing in nature as a lady's head-dress. Within my own memory, I have known it rise and fall above thirty degrees. About ten years ago it shot up to a very great height, insomuch that the female part of our species were much taller than the men.* The women were of such an enormous stature that 'we appeared as

* *Taller than men.* This refers to the commode, a kind of head-dress worn by the ladies at the beginning of the eighteenth century, which, by means of a wire, bore up their hair and the fore part of their cap, consisting of many folds of fine lace, to a great height. On this subject see the *Lively Lady Townshend,* by Mr Erroll Sherson.

grasshoppers * before them.' At present the whole sex is in a manner dwarfed, and shrunk into a race of beauties that seems almost another species. I remember several ladies, who were once very near seven foot high, that at present want some inches of five. How they came to be thus curtailed I cannot learn; whether the whole sex be at present under any penance which we know nothing of; or whether they have cast their head-dresses in order to surprise us with something in that kind which shall be entirely new; or whether some of the tallest of the sex, being too cunning for the rest, have contrived this method to make themselves appear sizeable – is still a secret; though I find most are of opinion, they are at present like trees new lopped and pruned, that will certainly sprout up and flourish with greater heads than before. For my own part, as I do not love to be insulted by women who are taller than myself, I admire the sex much more in their present humiliation, which has reduced them to their natural dimensions, than when they had extended their persons and lengthened themselves out into formidable and gigantic figures. I am not for adding to the beautiful edifices of nature, nor for raising any whimsical superstructure upon her plans: I must therefore repeat it, that I am highly pleased with the coiffure now in fashion, and think it shews the good sense which at present very much reigns among the valuable part of the sex. One may observe that women in all ages have taken more pains than men to adorn the outside of their heads; and indeed I very much admire, that those female architects, who raise such wonderful structures out of ribands, lace, and wire, have not been recorded for their respective inventions. It is certain there have been as many orders in these kinds of building, as in those which have been made

* *As grasshoppers.* Numbers xiii. 33.

of marble. Sometimes they rise in the shape of a pyramid, sometimes like a tower, and sometimes like a steeple. In Juvenal's time the building grew by several orders and storeys, as he has very humorously described it:

> *Tot premit ordinibus tot adhuc compagibus altum*
> *Aedificat caput; Andromachen a fronte videbis;*
> *Post minor est; aliam credas.* —
>
> JUV. *Sat.* vi. 501.

> *With curls on curls they build her head before,*
> *And mount it with a formidable tow'r;*
> *A giantess she seems; but look behind,*
> *And then she dwindles to the pigmy kind.*
>
> DRYDEN.

But I do not remember in any part of my reading, that the head-dress aspired to so great an extravagance as in the fourteenth century; when it was built up in a couple of cones or spires, which stood so exceedingly high on each side of the head, that a woman, who was but a pigmy without her head-dress, appeared like a colossus upon putting it on. Monsieur Paradin says, 'that these old-fashioned fontanges rose an ell above the head; that they were pointed like steeples, and had long loose pieces of crape fastened to the tops of them, which were curiously fringed, and hung down their backs like streamers.'

The women might possibly have carried this Gothic building much higher, had not a famous monk, Thomas Conecte by name, attacked it with great zeal and resolution. This holy man travelled from place to place to preach down this monstrous commode; and succeeded so well in it, that, as the magicians sacrificed their books to the flames upon the preaching of an apostle, many of the women threw down their head-dresses in the middle of the sermon, and made a bonfire of them within sight of the pulpit. He was so renowned as well for the sanctity of his life as his manner of preaching, that he had often a congregation of twenty thousand people; the men placing themselves on the one side of his pulpit, and the women on the other, that appeared (to use the similitude of an ingenious writer) like a forest of cedars with their heads reaching to the clouds. He so warmed and animated the people against this monstrous ornament that it lay under a kind of persecution; and whenever it appeared in public, was pelted down by the rabble, who flung stones at the persons that wore it. But notwithstanding this prodigy vanished while the preacher was among them, it began to appear again some months after his departure, or, to tell it in Monsieur Paradin's own words, 'the women that like snails in a fright, had drawn in their horns, shot them out again as soon as the danger was over. This extravagance of the women's head-dresses in that age is taken notice of by Monsieur d'Argentre in his history of Bretagne, and by other historians, as well as the person I have here quoted.

It is usually observed, that a good reign is the only proper time for making laws against the exorbitance of power; in the same manner an excessive head-dress may be attacked the most effectually when the fashion is against it. I do therefore recommend this paper to my female readers by way of prevention.

I would desire the fair sex to consider how impossible it is for them to add anything that can be ornamental to what is already the master-piece of nature. The head has the most beautiful appearance, as well as the highest station, in a human figure. Nature has laid out all her art in beautifying the face; she has touched it with vermilion, planted in it a double row of ivory, made it the seat of smiles and blushes, lighted it up and enlivened it with the brightness of the eyes, hung it on each side with curious organs of sense, given it airs and graces that cannot be described, and surrounded it with such a flowing shade of hair as sets all its beauties in the most agreeable light. In short, she seems to have designed the head as the cupola to the most glorious of her works: and when we load it with such a pile of supernumerary ornaments, we destroy the symmetry of the human figure, and foolishly contrive to call off the eye from great and real beauties, to childish gew-gaws, ribands, and bone-lace.

The Exercise of the Fan

I DO not know whether to call the following letter a satire upon coquettes, or a representation of their several fantastical accomplishments, or what other title to give it; but as it is I shall communicate it to the public. It will sufficiently explain its own intentions, so that I shall give it my reader at length, without either preface or post-script.

'MR SPECTATOR, Women are armed with fans as men with swords, and sometimes do more execution with them. To the end, therefore, that ladies may be entire mistresses of the weapon which they bear, I have erected an academy for the training up of young women in the exercise of the Fan, according to the most fashionable airs and motions that are now practised at court. The ladies who carry fans under me are drawn up twice a day in my great hall, where they are instructed in the use of their arms, and exercised by the following words of command:

> Handle your fans,
> Unfurl your fans,
> Discharge your fans,
> Ground your fans,
> Recover your fans,
> Flutter your fans.

'By the right observation of these few plain words of command, a woman of tolerable genius, who will apply herself diligently to her exercise for the space of but one half-year, shall be able to give her fan all the graces that can possibly enter into that little modish machine.

'But to the end that my readers may form to themselves a right notion of this exercise, I beg leave to explain it to them in all its parts. When my female regiment is drawn up in array, with every one her weapon in her hand, upon my giving the word to "handle their fans", each of them shakes her fan at me with a smile, then gives her right-hand woman a tap upon the shoulder, then presses her lips with the extremity of her fan, then lets her arms fall in an easy motion, and stands in a readiness to receive the next word of command. All this is done with a close fan, and is generally learned in the first week.

'The next motion is that of "unfurling the fan", in which are comprehended several little flirts and vibrations, as also gradual and deliberate openings, with many voluntary fallings asunder in the fan itself, that are seldom learned under a month's practice. This part of the exercise pleases the spectators more than any other, as it discovers on a sudden an infinite number of cupids, garlands, altars, birds, beasts, rainbows, and the like agreeable figures that display themselves to view – whilst every one in the regiment holds a picture in her hand.

'Upon my giving the word to Discharge their fans, they

give one general crack that may be heard at a considerable distance when the wind sets fair. This is one of the most difficult parts of the exercise: but I have several ladies with me, who at their first entrance could not give a pop loud enough to be heard at the farther end of a room, who can now discharge a fan in such a manner, that it shall make a report like a pocket-pistol. I have likewise taken care (in order to hinder young women from letting off their fans in wrong places or on unsuitable occasions) to shew upon what subject the crack of a fan may come in properly: I have likewise invented a fan, with which a girl of sixteen, by the help of a little wind which is enclosed about one of the largest sticks, can make as loud a crack as a woman of fifty with an ordinary fan.

'When the fans are thus discharged, the word of command, of course, is to Ground their fans. This teaches a lady to quit her fan gracefully when she throws it aside in order to take up a pack of cards, adjust a curl of hair, replace a falling pin, or apply herself to any other matter of importance. This part of the exercise, as it only consists in tossing a fan with an air upon a long table (which stands by for that purpose), may be learned in two days' time as well as in a twelvemonth.

'When my female regiment is thus disarmed, I generally let them walk about the room for some time; when, on a sudden (like ladies that look upon their watches after a long visit), they all of them hasten to their arms, catch them up in a hurry, and place themselves in their proper stations upon my calling out "Recover your fans." This part of the exercise is not difficult, provided a woman applies her thoughts to it.

'The "fluttering of the fan" is the last, and indeed the masterpiece of the whole exercise; but if a lady does not misspend her time, she may make herself mistress of it in three months. I generally lay aside the dog-days, and the hot time of the summer, for the teaching this part of the exercise; for, as soon as ever I pronounce "Flutter your fans", the place is filled with so many zephyrs and gentle breezes, as are very refreshing in that season of the year, though they might be dangerous to ladies of a tender constitution in any other.

'There is an infinite variety of motions to be made use of in the flutter of a fan. There is the angry flutter, the modest flutter, the timorous flutter, the confused flutter, the merry flutter, and the amorous flutter. Not to be tedious, there is scarce any emotion in the mind which does not produce a suitable agitation in the fan; insomuch that if I only see the fan of a disciplined lady, I know very well whether she laughs, frowns, or blushes. I have seen a fan so very angry, that it would have been dangerous for the absent lover who provoked it to have come within the wind of it; and at other times so very languishing, that I have been glad, for the lady's sake, the lover was at a sufficient distance from it. I need not add, that a fan is either a prude or a coquette, according to the nature of the person who bears it. To conclude my letter, I must acquaint you that I have, from my own observations, compiled a little treatise for the use of my scholars, entitled "The Passions of the Fan"; which I will communicate to you, if you think it may be of use to the public. I shall have a general review on Thursday next; to which you shall be very welcome if you will honour it with your presence.

'I am, etc.

'P.S. I teach young gentlemen the whole art of gallanting a fan.

'N.B. I have several little plain fans made for this use, to avoid expense.'

Sunday in the Country

I AM always very well pleased with a country Sunday, and think, if keeping holy the seventh day were only a human institution, it would be the best method that could have been thought of for the polishing and civilizing of mankind. It is certain the country people would soon degenerate into a kind of savages and barbarians, were there not such frequent returns of a stated time, in which the whole village meet together with their best faces, and in their cleanliest habits, to converse with one another upon indifferent subjects, hear their duties explained to them, and join together in adoration of the Supreme Being. Sunday clears away the rust of the whole week, not only as it refreshes in their minds the notions of religion, but as it puts both the sexes upon appearing in their most agreeable forms, and exerting all such qualities as are apt to give them a figure in the eye of the village. A country fellow distinguishes himself as much in the churchyard, as a citizen does upon the 'Change, the whole parish-politics being generally discussed in that place either after sermon or before the bell rings.

My friend Sir Roger, being a good churchman, has beautified the inside of his church with several texts of his own choosing. He has likewise given a handsome pulpit-cloth, and railed in the communion-table at his own expense. He has often told me, that at his coming to his estate he found his parishioners very irregular: and that in order to make them kneel and join in the responses, he gave every one of them a hassock and a common-prayer book: and at the same time employed an itinerant singing-master, who goes about the country for that purpose, to instruct them rightly in the tunes of the Psalms; upon which they now very much value themselves, and indeed outdo most of the country churches that I have ever heard.

As Sir Roger is landlord to the whole congregation, he keeps them in very good order, and will suffer nobody to sleep in it besides himself; for if by chance he has been surprised into a short nap at sermon, upon recovering out of it he stands up and looks about him, and if he sees any body else nodding, either wakes them himself or sends his servants to them. Several other of the old knight's particularities break out upon these occasions. Sometimes he will be lengthening out a verse in the singing Psalms half a minute after the rest of the congregation have done with it; sometimes, when he is pleased with the matter of his devotion, he pronounces amen three or four times to the same prayer; and sometimes stands up when everybody else is upon their knees, to count the congregation, or see if any of his tenants are missing.

I was yesterday very much surprised to hear my old friend, in the midst of the service, calling out to one John Matthews to mind what he was about and not disturb the congregation. This John Matthews it seems is remarkable for being an idle fellow, and at that time was kicking his heels for his diversion. This authority of the knight, though exerted in that odd manner which accompanies him in all the circumstances of life, has a very good effect upon the parish, who are not polite enough to see any thing ridiculous in his behaviour; besides that the general good sense and worthiness of his character make his friends observe these little singularities as foils that rather set off than blemish his good qualities.

As soon as the sermon is finished, nobody presumes to stir till Sir Roger is gone out of the church. The knight walks down from his seat in the chancel between a double row of his tenants, that stand bowing to him on each side; and every now and then inquires how such a one's wife, or mother, or son, or father do, whom he does not see at church; which is understood as a secret reprimand to the person that is absent.

The chaplain has often told me that, upon a catechizing day, when Sir Roger has been pleased with a boy that answers well, he has ordered a Bible to be given to him next day for his encouragement; and sometimes accompanies it with a flitch of bacon to his mother. Sir Roger has likewise added five pounds a year to the clerk's place; and that he may encourage the young fellows to make themselves perfect in the church service, has promised upon the death of the present incumbent, who is very old, to bestow it according to merit.

The fair understanding between Sir Roger and his chaplain, and their mutual concurrence in doing good, is the more remarkable because the very next village is famous for the differences and contentions that arise between the parson and the squire, who live in a perpetual state of war. The parson is always preaching at the squire; and the squire, to be revenged on the parson, never comes to church. The squire has made all his tenants atheists and tithe-stealers; while the parson instructs them every Sunday in the dignity of his order, and insinuates to them, in almost every sermon, that he is a better man than his patron. In short, matters are come to such an extremity, that the squire has not said his prayers either in public or private this half year; and the parson threatens him, if he does not mend his manners, to pray for him in the face of the whole congregation.

Feuds of this nature, though too frequent in the country, are very fatal to the ordinary people, who are so used to be dazzled with riches, that they pay as much deference to the understanding of a man of an estate, as of a man of learning; and are very hardly brought to regard any truth, how important soever it may be, that is preached to them, when they know there are several men of five hundred a year who do not believe it.

On the Cries of London

Linguae centum sunt, oraque centum,
Ferrea vox . . .

VIRG. *Aen.* vi. 625.

A hundred mouths, a hundred tongues,
And throats of brass inspir'd with iron lungs.

DRYDEN.

THERE is nothing which more astonishes a foreigner, and frights a country squire, than the Cries of London. My good friend Sir Roger often declares that he cannot get them out of his head or go to sleep for them, the first week that he is in town. On the contrary, Will Honeycomb calls them the *Ramage de la Ville*, and prefers them to the sound of larks and nightingales, with all the music of fields and woods. I have lately received a letter from some very odd fellow upon this subject, which I shall leave with my reader, without saying anything further of it.

'SIR,

'I am a man out of all business, and would willingly turn my head to anything for an honest livelihood. I have invented several projects for raising many millions of money without burdening the subject, but I cannot get the parliament to listen to me, who look upon me, forsooth, as a crack, and a projector; so that despairing to

enrich either myself or my country by this public-spirited-
ness, I would make some proposals to you relating to a
design which I have very much at heart, and which may
procure me a handsome subsistence, if you will be pleased
to recommend it to the cities of London and Westminster.

'The post I would aim at, is to be comptroller-general of
the London Cries, which are at present under no manner
of rules or discipline. I think I am pretty well qualified
for this place, as being a man of very strong lungs, of great
insight into all the branches of our British trades and
manufactures, and of a competent skill in music.

'The Cries of London may be divided into vocal and
instrumental. As for the latter, they are at present under a
very great disorder. A fireman of London has the privilege
of disturbing a whole street for an hour together, with a
twanking of a brass kettle or frying-pan. The watchman's
thump at midnight startles us in our beds as much as the
breaking in of a thief. The sowgelder's horn has indeed
something musical in it, but this is seldom heard within
the liberties. I would therefore propose, that no instrument of this nature should be made use of, which I have
not tuned and licensed, after having carefully examined in
what manner it may affect the ears of her majesty's liege
subjects.

'Vocal cries are of a much larger extent, and indeed so
full of incongruities and barbarisms, that we appear a dis-
tracted city to foreigners, who do not comprehend the
meaning of such enormous outcries. Milk is generally sold
in a note above E-la, and in sounds so exceedingly shrill,
that it often sets our teeth on edge. The chimney-sweeper
is confined to no certain pitch; he sometimes utters himself in the deepest bass, and sometimes in the sharpest
treble; sometimes in the highest, and sometimes in the
lowest, note of the gamut. The same observation might be

made on the retailers of small-coal, not to mention broken glasses, or brick-dust. In these, therefore, and the like cases, it should be my care to sweeten and mellow the voices of these itinerant tradesmen, before they make their appearance in our streets, as also to accommodate their cries to their respective wares; and to take care in particular, that those may not make the most noise who have the least to sell, which is very observable in the vendors of card-matches, to whom I cannot but apply that old proverb of "Much cry, but little wool".

'Some of these last-mentioned musicians are so very loud in the sale of these trifling manufactures, that an honest splenetic gentleman of my acquaintance bargained with one of them never to come into the street where he lived. But what was the effect of this contract? Why, the whole tribe of card-match-makers which frequent that quarter passed by his door the very next day, in hopes of being bought off after the same manner.

'It is another great imperfection in our London Cries, that there is no just time nor measure observed in them. Our news should indeed be published in a very quick time, because it is a commodity that will not keep cold. It should not, however, be cried with the same precipitation as fire. Yet this is generally the case. A bloody battle alarms the town from one end to another in an instant. Every motion of the French is published in so great a hurry, that one would think the enemy were at our gates. This likewise I would take upon me to regulate in such a manner, that there should be some distinction made between the spreading of a victory, a march, or an encampment, a Dutch, a Portugal, or a Spanish mail. Nor must I omit under this head those excessive alarms with which several boisterous rustics infest our streets in turnip season; and which are more inexcusable, because they are wares which are in no danger of cooling upon their hands.

'There are others who affect a very slow time, and are in my opinion much more tunable than the former. The cooper in particular swells his last note in a hollow voice, that is not without its harmony; nor can I forbear being inspired with a most agreeable melancholy, when I hear that sad and solemn air with which the public are very often asked if they have any chairs to mend? Your own memory may suggest to you many other lamentable ditties of the same nature, in which the music is wonderfully languishing and melodious.

'I am always pleased with that particular time of the year which is proper for the picking of dill * and cucumbers; but alas! this cry, like the song of the nightingale, is not heard above two months. It would therefore be worth while to consider whether the same air might not in some cases be adapted to other words.

'It might likewise deserve our most serious considerations, how far, in a well-regulated city, those humourists are to be tolerated, who, not contented with the traditional cries of their forefathers, have invented particular songs and tunes of their own: such as was, not many years since, the pastry-man, commonly known by the name of the Colly-Molly-Puff†: and such as is at this day the vendor of powder and wash-balls, who, if I am rightly informed, goes under the name of Powder-Wat.

'I must not here omit one particular absurdity which runs through this whole vociferous generation, and which renders their cries very often not only incommodious, but

* *Dill.* A herb with scented seeds.

† *Colly-Molly-Puff.* This little man was just able to support the basket of pastry which he carried on his head, and sang in a very peculiar tone the cant words which passed into his name, Colly-Molly-Puff.

altogether useless to the public. I mean that idle accomplishment which they all of them aim at, of crying so as not to be understood. Whether or no they have learned this from several of our affected singers, I will not take upon me to say; but most certain it is, that people know the wares they deal in rather by their tunes than by their words; insomuch that I have sometimes seen a country boy run out to buy apples of a bellows-mender, and ginger-bread from a grinder of knives and scissors. Nay, so strangely infatuated are some very eminent artists of this particular grace in a cry, that none but their acquaintance are able to guess at their profession; for who else can know, that "work if I had it" should be the signification of a corn-cutter?

'Forasmuch, therefore, as persons of this rank are seldom men of genius or capacity I think it would be very proper that some men of good sense and sound judgement should preside over these public cries, who should permit none to lift up their voices in our streets that have not tunable throats, and are not only able to overcome the noise of the crowd, and the rattling of coaches, but also to vend their respective merchandises in apt phrases, and in the most distinct and agreeable sounds. I do therefore humbly recommend myself as a person rightly qualified for this post; and if I meet with fitting encouragement, shall communicate some other projects which I have by me, that may no less conduce to the emolument of the public.

'I am, Sir, &c.

'RALPH CROTCHET.'

A Citizen's Diary

Fruges consumere nati. – HOR. I *Ep.* ii. 27.
Born to drink and eat. – CREECH.

AUGUSTUS, a few minutes before his death, asked his
friends who stood about him, if they thought he had acted
his part well; and upon receiving such an answer as was
due to his extraordinary merit, 'Let me then,' says he,
'go off the stage with your applause'; using the expression*
with which the Roman actors made their exit at the conclusion of a dramatic piece. I could wish that men, while
they are in health, would consider well the nature of the
part they are engaged in, and what figure it will make in
the minds of those they leave behind them, whether it was
worth coming into the world for; whether it be suitable
to a reasonable being: in short, whether it appear
graceful in this life, or will turn to advantage in the next.
Let the sycophant or the buffoon, the satirist or the good
companion, consider with himself, when his body shall be
laid in the grave, and his soul pass into another state of
existence, how much it will redound to his praise to have
it said of him, that no man in England ate better, that
he had an admirable talent at turning his friends into
ridicule, that nobody outdid him at an ill-natured jest,
or that he never went to bed before he had dispatched
his third bottle. These are, however, very common
funeral orations, and eulogiums on deceased persons
who have acted among mankind with some figure and
reputation.

But if we look into the bulk of our species, they are such
as are not likely to be remembered a moment after their

* Vos valete et plaudite.

disappearance. They leave behind them no traces of their existence, but are forgotten as though they had never been. They are neither wanted by the poor, regretted by the rich, nor celebrated by the learned. They are neither missed in the commonwealth, nor lamented by private persons. Their actions are of no significancy to mankind, and might have been performed by creatures of much less dignity than those who are distinguished by the faculty of reason. An eminent French author speaks somewhere to the following purpose: I have often seen from my chamber-window two noble creatures, both of them of an erect countenance and endowed with reason. These two intellectual beings are employed from morning to night in rubbing two smooth stones one upon another: that is, as the vulgar phrase is, in polishing marble.

My friend, Sir Andrew Freeport, as we were sitting in the club last night, gave us an account of a sober citizen, who died a few days since. This honest man, of greater consequence in his own thoughts than in the eye of the world, had for some years past kept a journal of his life. Sir Andrew shewed us one week of it. Since the occurrences set down in it mark out such a road of action as that I have been speaking of, I shall present my reader with a faithful copy* of it; after having first informed him, that the deceased person had in his youth been bred to trade, but finding himself not so well turned for business, he had for several years past lived altogether upon a moderate annuity.

* *Faithful copy*. This journal was, it may be, genuine, but certainly was published here as a banter on a gentleman who was a member of a congregation of Dissenters, commonly called Independents, where a Mr Nesbit officiated at that time as minister. Of him an account is given in John Dutton's *Life, Errors, and Opinions*.

Monday, eight o'clock. I put on my clothes, and walked into the parlour.

Nine o'clock, ditto. Tied my knee-strings and washed my hands.

Hours ten, eleven, and twelve. Smoked three pipes of Virginia. Read the Supplement and Daily Courant. Things go ill in the north. Mr Nisby's opinion thereupon.

One o'clock in the afternoon. Chid Ralph for mislaying my tobacco-box.

Two o'clock. Sat down to dinner. Mem. Too many plums and no suet.

From three to four. Took my afternoon's nap.

From four to six. Walked into the fields. Wind S.S.E.

From six to ten. At the club. Mr Nisby's opinion about the peace.

Ten o'clock. Went to bed, slept sound.

Tuesday, being holiday, eight o'clock. Rose as usual.

Nine o'clock. Washed hands and face, shaved, put on my double-soled shoes.

Ten, eleven, twelve. Took a walk to Islington.

One. Took a pot of Mother Cobb's mild.

Between two and three. Returned, dined on a knuckle of veal and bacon. Mem. Sprouts wanting.

Three. Nap as usual.

From four to six. Coffee-house. Read the news. A dish of twist. Grand vizier strangled.

From six to ten. At the club. Mr Nisby's account of the Great Turk.

Ten. Dream of the grand vizier. Broken sleep.

Wednesday, eight o'clock. Tongue of my shoebuckle broke. Hands but not face.

Nine. Paid off the butcher's bill. Mem. To be allowed for the last leg of mutton.

Ten, eleven. At the coffee-house. More work in the

north. Stranger in a black wig asked me how stocks went.

From twelve to one. Walked in the fields. Wind to the south.

From one to two. Smoked a pipe and a half.

Two. Dined as usual. Stomach good.

Three. Nap broke by the falling of a pewter dish. Mem. Cook-maid in love, and grown careless.

From four to six. At the coffee-house. Advice from Smyrna that the grand vizier was first of all strangled, and afterwards beheaded.

Six o'clock in the evening. Was half an hour in the club before anybody else came. Mr Nisby of opinion that the grand vizier was not strangled the sixth instant.

Ten at night. Went to bed. Slept without waking until nine the next morning.

Thursday, nine o'clock. Stayed within until two o'clock for Sir Timothy: who did not bring me my annuity according to his promise.

Two in the afternoon. Sat down to dinner. Loss of appetite. Small beer sour. Beef over-corned.

Three. Could not take my nap.

Four and five. Gave Ralph a box on the ear. Turned off my cook-maid. Sent a messenger to Sir Timothy. Mem. I did not go to the club to-night. Went to bed at nine o'clock.

Friday. Passed the morning in meditation upon Sir Timothy, who was with me a quarter before twelve.

Twelve o'clock. Bought a new head to my cane, and a tongue to my buckle. Drank a glass of purl to recover appetite.

Two and three. Dined and slept well.

From four to six. Went to the coffee-house. Met Mr Nisby there. Smoked several pipes. Mr Nisby of opinion that laced coffee is bad for the head.

Six o'clock. At the club as steward. Sat late.

Twelve o'clock. Went to bed. Dreamt that I drank small beer with the grand vizier.

Saturday. Waked at eleven. Walked in the fields, wind N.E.

Twelve. Caught in a shower.

One in the afternoon. Returned home and dried myself.

Two. Mr Nisby dined with me. First course, marrow-bones; second, ox-cheek, with a bottle of Brooks and Hellier.

Three. Overslept myself.

Six. Went to the club. Like to have fallen into a gutter. Grand vizier certainly dead.

I question not but the reader will be surprised to find the above-mentioned journalist taking so much care of a life that was filled with such inconsiderable actions, and received so very small improvements; and yet if we look into the behaviour of many whom we daily converse with, we shall find that most of their hours are taken up in those three important articles of eating, drinking, and sleeping. I do not suppose that man loses his time, who is not engaged in public affairs, or in an illustrious course of action. On the contrary, I believe our hours may very often be more profitably laid out in such transactions as make no figure in the world, than in such as are apt to draw upon them the attention of mankind. One may become wiser and better by several methods of employing one's self in secrecy and silence, and do what is laudable without noise or ostentation. I would, however, recommend to every one of my readers, the keeping a journal of their lives for one week, and setting down punctually their whole series of employment during that space of time. This kind of self-examination would give them a true state of themselves, and incline them to consider seriously what they are about. One day would rectify the omissions of another, and make a man weigh all those indifferent actions, which, though they are easily forgotten, must certainly be accounted for.

RICHARD STEELE

Recollections of Childhood

THERE are those among mankind, who can enjoy no relish of their being, except the world is made acquainted with all that relates to them, and think everything lost that passes unobserved; but others find a solid delight in stealing by the crowd, and modelling their life after such a manner, as is as much above the approbation as the practice of the vulgar. Life being too short to give instances great enough of true friendship or good will, some sages have thought it pious to preserve a certain reverence for the names of their deceased friends; and have withdrawn themselves from the rest of the world at certain seasons, to commemorate in their own thoughts such of their acquaintance who have gone before them out of this life. And indeed, when we are advanced in years, there is not a more pleasing entertainment, than to recollect in a gloomy moment the many we have parted with, that have been dear and agreeable to us, and to cast a melancholy thought or two after those, with whom, perhaps, we have indulged ourselves in whole nights of mirth and jollity. With such inclinations in my heart I went to my closet yesterday in the evening, and resolved to be sorrowful; upon which occasion I could not but look with disdain upon myself, that though all the reasons which I had to lament the loss of many of my friends are now as forcible as at the moment of their departure, yet did not my heart swell with the same sorrow which I felt at the time; but I could, without tears, reflect upon many pleasing adventures

I have had with some, who have long been blended with common earth. Though it is by the benefit of nature, that length of time thus blots out the violence of afflictions; yet, with tempers too much given to pleasure, it is almost necessary to revive the old places of grief in our memory; and ponder step by step on past life, to lead the mind into that sobriety of thought which poises the heart, and makes it beat with due time, without being quickened with desire, or retarded with despair, from its proper and equal motion. When we wind up a clock that is out of order, to make it go well for the future, we do not immediately set the hand to the present instant, but we make it strike the round of all its hours, before it can recover the regularity of its time. Such, thought I, shall be my method this evening; and since it is that day of the year which I dedicate to the memory of such in another life as I much delighted in when living, an hour to two shall be sacred to sorrow and their memory, while I run over all the melancholy circumstances of this kind which have occurred to me in my whole life.

The first sense of sorrow I ever knew was upon the death of my father, at which time I was not quite five years of age; but was rather amazed at what all the house meant, than possessed with a real understanding why nobody was willing to play with me. I remember I went into the room where his body lay, and my mother sat weeping alone by it. I had my battledore in my hand, and fell a-beating the coffin, and calling Papa; for, I know not how, I had some slight idea that he was locked up there. My mother caught me in her arms, and, transported beyond all patience of the silent grief she was before in, she almost smothered me in her embraces; and told me in a flood of tears, Papa could not hear me, and would play with me no more, for they were going to put him under ground, whence he could never come to us again. She was a very beautiful woman, of a noble spirit, and there was a dignity in her grief amidst all the wildness of her transport, which, methought, struck me with an instinct of sorrow, that, before I was sensible of what it was to grieve, seized my very soul, and has made pity the weakness of my heart ever since. The mind in infancy is, methinks, like the body in embryo; and receives impressions so forcible, that they are as hard to be removed by reason, as any mark with which a child is born is to be taken away by any future application. Hence it is, that good nature in me is no merit; but having been so frequently overwhelmed with her tears before I knew the cause of any affliction, or could draw defences from my own judgement, I imbibed commiseration, remorse, and an unmanly gentleness of mind, which has since ensnared me into ten thousand calamities; and from whence I can reap no advantage, except it be, that, in such a humour as I am now in, I can the better indulge myself in the softnesses of humanity, and enjoy that sweet anxiety which arises from the memory of past afflictions.

We, that are very old, are better able to remember things which befell us in our distant youth, than the passages of later days. For this reason it is, that the companions of my strong and vigorous years present themselves more immediately to me in this office of sorrow. Untimely and unhappy deaths are what we are most apt to lament; so little are we able to make it indifferent when a thing happens, though we know it must happen. Thus we groan under life, and bewail those who are relieved from it. Every object that returns to our imagination raises different passions, according to the circumstance of their departure. Who can have lived in an army, and in a serious hour reflect upon the many gay and agreeable men that might long have flourished in the arts of peace, and not join with the imprecations of the fatherless and widows on the tyrant to whose ambition they fell sacrifices? But gallant men, who are cut off by the sword, move rather our veneration than our pity; and we gather relief enough from their own contempt of death, to make that no evil, which was approached with so much cheerfulness, and attended with so much honour. But when we turn our thoughts from the great parts of life on such occasions, and instead of lamenting those who stood ready to give death to those from whom they had the fortune to receive it; I say, when we let our thoughts wander from such noble objects, and consider the havoc which is made among the tender and the innocent, pity enters with an unmixed softness, and possesses all our souls at once.

Here (were there words to express such sentiments with proper tenderness) I should record the beauty, innocence, and untimely death, of the first object my eyes ever beheld with love. The beauteous virgin! how ignorantly did she charm, how carelessly excel! Oh death! thou hast right to the bold, to the ambitious, to the high, and to the haughty; but why this cruelty to the humble, to the meek, to the undiscerning, to the thoughtless? Nor age, nor business, nor distress, can erase the dear image from my imagination. In the same week I saw her dressed for a ball, and in a shroud. How ill did the habit of death become the pretty trifler! I still behold the smiling earth – A large train of disasters were coming on to my memory, when my servant knocked at my closet-door, and interrupted me with a letter, attended with a hamper of wine, of the same sort with that which is to be put to sale on Thursday next, at Garraway's coffee-house. Upon the receipt of it, I sent for three of my friends. We are so intimate, that we can be company in whatever state of mind we meet, and can entertain each other without expecting always to rejoice. The wine we found to be generous and warming, but with such a heat as moved us rather to be cheerful than frolicsome. It revived the spirits, without firing the blood. We commended it until two of the clock this morning; and having to-day met a little before dinner, we found, that though we drank two bottles a man, we had much more reason to recollect than forget what had passed the night before.

A Prize Fight

BEING a Person of insatiable Curiosity, I could not forbear going on *Wednesday* last to a Place of no small Renown for the Gallantry of the lower Order of *Britons*, namely, to the Bear-Garden at *Hockley in the Hole*; where (as a whitish brown Paper, put into my Hands in the Street, inform'd me) there was to be a Tryal of Skill to be exhibited between two Masters of the Noble Science of Defence, at two of the Clock precisely. I was not a little charm'd with the Solemnity of the Challenge, which ran thus:

'*I* James Miller, *Serjeant, (lately come from the Frontiers of* Portugal) *Master of the Noble Science of Defence, hearing in most Places where I have been of the great Fame of* Timothy Buck *of* London, *Master of the said Science, do invite him to meet me, and exercise at the several Weapons following, viz.*

Back-Sword,	*Single Falchon,*
Sword and Dagger,	*Case of Falchons,*
Sword and Buckler,	*Quarter-Staff.*

If the generous Ardour in *James Miller* to dispute the Reputation of *Timothy Buck*, had something resembling the old Heroes of Romance, *Timothy Buck* return'd Answer in the same Paper with the like Spirit, adding a little Indignation at being challenged, and seeming to condescend to fight *James Miller*, not in regard to *Miller* himself, but in that, as the Fame went out, he had fought *Parkes of Coventry*. The Acceptance of the Combat ran in these Words:

' *I* Timothy Buck, *of* Clare-Market, *Master of the Noble Science of Defence, hearing he did fight Mr* Parkes *of* Coventry, *will not fail (God willing) to meet this fair Inviter at the Time and Place appointed desiring a clear Stage and no Favour.*

Vivat Regina.'

I shall not here look back on the Spectacles of the *Greeks* and *Romans* of this Kind, but must believe this Custom took its Rise from the Ages of Knight-Errantry; from those who lov'd one Woman so well, that they hated all Men and Women else; from those who would fight you, whether you were or were not of their Mind; from those who demanded the Combat of their Contemporaries, both for admiring their Mistress or discommending her. I cannot therefore but lament, that the terrible Part of the ancient Fight is preserved, when the amorous Side of it is forgotten. We have retained the Barbarity, but lost the Gallantry of the old Combatants. I could wish, methinks, these Gentlemen had consulted me in the Promulgation of the Conflict. I was obliged by a fair young Maid whom I understood to be called *Elizabeth Preston*, Daughter of the Keeper of the Garden, with a Glass of Water; whom I imagined might have been, for Form's sake, the general Representative of the Lady fought for, and from her Beauty the proper *Amarillis* on these Occasions. It would have ran better in the Challenge; I James

Miller, *Serjeant, who have travelled Parts abroad, and came last
from the Frontiers of* Portugal, *for the love of* Elizabeth
Preston, *do assert, That the said* Elizabeth *is the Fairest of
Women.* Then the Answer; *I* Timothy Buck, *who have
stay'd in* Great Britain *during all the War in Foreign Parts for
the Sake of* Susanna Page, *do deny that* Elizabeth Preston *is
so fair as the said* Susanna Page. Let *Susanna Page* look on,
and I desire of *James Miller* no Favour.

This would give the Battel quite another Turn; and a
proper Station for the Ladies, whose Complexion was disputed by the Sword, would animate the Disputants with
a more gallant Incentive than the Expectation of Mony
from the Spectators; though I would not have that neglected, but thrown to that Fair One whose Lover was
approved by the Donor.

Yet, considering the Thing wants such Amendments, it
was carried with great Order. *James Miller* came on first;
preceded by two disabled Drummers, to shew, I suppose,
that the Prospect of maimed Bodies did not in the least
deter him. There ascended with the daring *Miller* a
Gentleman, whose Name I could not learn, with a dogged
Air, as unsatisfied that he was not Principal. This Son of
Anger lowred at the whole Assembly, and weighing himself as he march'd around from Side to Side, with a stiff
Knee and Shoulder, he gave Intimations of the Purpose
he smothered till he saw the Issue of this Encounter.
Miller had a blue Ribband tyed round the Sword Arm;
which Ornament I conceive to be the Remain of that
Custom of wearing a Mistress's Favour on such Occasions
of old.

Miller is a Man of six Foot eight Inches Height, of a
kind but bold Aspect, well-fashioned, and ready of his
Limbs; and such Readiness as spoke his Ease in them, was
obtained from a Habit of Motion in Military Exercise.

The Expectation of the Spectators was now almost at its Height, and the Crowd pressing in, several active Persons thought they were placed rather according to their Fortune than their Merit, and took it in their Heads to prefer themselves from the open Area, or Pit, to the Galleries. This Dispute between Desert and Property brought many to the Ground, and raised others in proportion to the highest Seats by Turns for the Space of Ten Minutes, till *Timothy Buck* came on, and the whole Assembly giving up their Disputes, turned their Eyes upon the Champions. Then it was that every Man's Affection turned to one or the other irresistibly. A judicious Gentleman near me said, *I could, methinks, be* Miller's *Second, but I had rather have* Buck *for mine. Miller* had an audacious Look that took the Eye; *Buck* a perfect Composure, that engaged the Judgement. *Buck* came on in a plain Coat, and kept all his Air till the Instant of Engaging; at which Time he undress'd to his Shirt, his Arm adorned with a Bandage of red Ribband. No one can describe the sudden Concern in the whole Assembly; the most tumultuous Crowd in Nature was as still and as much engaged, as if all their Lives depended on the first blow. The Combatants met in the Middle of the Stage, and shaking Hands as removing all Malice, they retired with much Grace to the Extremities of it; from whence they immediately faced about, and approached each other. *Miller* with an Heart full of Resolution, *Buck* with a watchful untroubled Countenance; *Buck* regarding principally his own Defence, *Miller* chiefly thoughtful of annoying his Opponent. It is not easie to describe the many Escapes and imperceptible Defences between two Men of quick Eyes and ready Limbs; but *Miller's* Heat laid him open to the Rebuke of the calm *Buck*, by a large Cut on the Forehead. Much Effusion of Blood covered his Eyes in a Moment, and the

Huzzas of the Crowd undoubtedly quickened the Anguish. The Assembly was divided into Parties upon their different ways of Fighting; while a poor Nymph in one of the Galleries apparently suffered for *Miller*, and burst into a Flood of Tears. As soon as his Wound was wrapped up, he came on again with a little Rage, which still disabled him further. But what brave Man can be wounded into more Patience and Caution? The next was a warm eager Onset which ended in a decisive Stroke on the left Leg of *Miller*. The Lady in the Gallery, during this second Strife, covered her Face; and for my Part, I could not keep my Thoughts from being mostly employed on the Consideration of her unhappy Circumstance that Moment, hearing the Clash of Swords, and apprehending Life or Victory concerned her Lover in every Blow, but not daring to satisfy herself on whom they fell. The Wound was exposed to the View of all who could delight in it, and sewed up on the Stage. The surly Second of *Miller* declared at this Time, that he would that Day Fortnight fight Mr *Buck* at the same Weapons, declaring himself the Master of the renowned *Gorman*; but *Buck* denied him the Honour of that courageous Disciple, and asserting that he himself had taught that Champion, accepted the Challenge.

There is something in Nature very unaccountable on such Occasions, when we see the People take a certain painful Gratification in beholding these Encounters. Is it Cruelty that administers this Sort of Delight? or is it a Pleasure which is taken in the Exercise of Pity? It was methought pretty remarkable, that the Business of the Day being a Trial of Skill, the Popularity did not run so high as one would have expected on the Side of *Buck*. Is it that People's Passions have their Rise in Self-love, and thought themselves (in Spite of all the Courage they had) liable to the Fate of *Miller*, but could not so easily think themselves qualified like *Buck*?

Tully speaks of this Custom with less Horror than one would expect, though he confesses it was much abused in his Time, and seems directly to approve of it under its first Regulations, when Criminals only fought before the People. *Crudele Gladiatorum spectaculum & inhumanum nonnullis videri solet; & haud scio annon ita sit ut nunc fit; cum vero sontes ferro depugnabant, auribus fortasse multa oculis quidem nulla, poterat esse fortior contra dolorem & mortem disciplina. The Shows of Gladiators may be thought barbarous and inhumane, and I know not but it is so as it is now practised; but in those Times when only Criminals were Combatants, the Ear perhaps might receive many better Instructions, but it is impossible that anything which affects our Eyes, should fortify us so well against Pain and Death.*

OLIVER GOLDSMITH

The Man in Black

THOUGH fond of many acquaintances, I desire an intimacy only with a few. The Man in Black, whom I have often mentioned, is one whose friendship I could wish to acquire, because he possesses my esteem. His manners, it is true, are tinctured with some strange inconsistencies; and he may be justly termed a humorist in a nation of humorists. Though he is generous even to profusion, he affects to be thought a prodigy of parsimony and prudence; though his conversation be replete with the most sordid and selfish maxims, his heart is dilated with the most unbounded love. I have known him profess himself a man-hater, while his cheek was glowing with compassion; and, while his looks were softened into pity, I have heard him use the language of the most unbounded ill-nature. Some affect humanity and tenderness, others boast of having such dispositions from Nature; but he is the only man I ever knew who seemed ashamed of his natural benevolence. He takes as much pains to hide his feelings, as any hypocrite would to conceal his indifference; but on every unguarded moment the mask drops off, and reveals him to the most superficial observer.

In one of our late excursions into the country, happening to discourse upon the provision that was made for the poor in England, he seemed amazed how any of his countrymen could be so foolishly weak as to relieve occasional objects of charity, when the laws had made such ample provision for their support. 'In every parish-house,' says he, 'the poor are supplied with food, clothes, fire, and a bed to lie on; they want no more, I desire no more myself; yet still they seem discontented. I'm surprised at the inactivity of our magistrates in not taking up such vagrants, who are only a weight upon the industrious; I'm surprised that the people are found to relieve them, when they must be at the same time sensible that it, in some measure, encourages idleness, extravagance, and imposture. Were I to advise any man for whom I had the least regard, I would caution him by all means not to be imposed upon by their false pretences; let me assure you, sir, they are imposters, every one of them; and rather merit a prison than relief.'

He was proceeding in this strain earnestly, to dissuade me from an imprudence of which I am seldom guilty, when an old man, who still had about him the remnants of tattered finery, implored our compassion He assured us that he was no common beggar, but forced into the shameful profession to support a dying wife and five hungry children. Being prepossessed against such false-hoods, his story had not the least influence upon me; but it was quite otherwise with the Man in Black; I could see it visibly operate upon his countenance, and effectually interrupt his harangue. I could easily perceive that his heart burned to relieve the five starving children, but he seemed ashamed to discover his weakness to me. While he thus hesitated between compassion and pride, I pretended to look another way and he seized this opportunity of giving the poor petitioner a piece of silver, bidding him at the same time, in order that I should hear, go work for his bread, and not tease passengers with such impertinent falsehoods for the future.

As he had fancied himself quite unperceived, he continued, as we proceeded, to rail against beggars with as much animosity as before; he threw in some episodes on his own amazing prudence and economy, with his profound skill in discovering impostors; he explained the manner in which he would deal with beggars, were he a magistrate, hinted at enlarging some of the prisons for their reception, and told two stories of ladies that were robbed by beggarmen. He was beginning a third to the same purpose, when a sailor with a wooden leg once more crossed our walks, desiring our pity, and blessing our limbs. I was for going on without taking any notice, but my friend, looking wistfully upon the poor petitioner, bade me stop, and he would show me with how much ease he could at any time detect an impostor.

He now, therefore, assumed a look of importance, and in an angry tone began to examine the sailor, demanding in what engagement he was thus disabled and rendered unfit for service. The sailor replied in a tone as angrily as he, that he had been an officer on board a private ship of war, and that he had lost his leg abroad, in defence of those who did nothing at home. At this reply, all my friend's importance vanished in a moment; he had not a single question more to ask; he now only studied what method he should take to relieve him unobserved. He had, however, no easy part to act, as he was obliged to preserve the appearance of ill-nature before me, and yet relieve himself by relieving the sailor. Casting, therefore, a furious look upon some bundles of chips which the fellow carried in a string at his back, my friend demanded how he sold his matches; but not waiting for a reply, desired in a surly tone to have a shilling's worth. The sailor seemed at first surprised at his demand, but soon recollecting himself, and presenting his whole bundle – 'Here, master,' says he, 'take all my cargo, and a blessing into the bargain.'

It is impossible to describe with what an air of triumph my friend marched off with his new purchase; he assured me that he was firmly of opinion that these fellows must have stolen their goods who could thus afford to sell them for half value. He informed me of several different uses to which those chips might be applied; he expatiated largely upon the savings that would result from lighting candles with a match instead of thrusting them into the fire. He averred, that he would as soon have parted with a tooth as his money to those vagabonds, unless for some valuable consideration. I cannot tell how long this panegyric upon frugality and matches might have continued, had not his attention been called off by another object more distressful than either of the former. A woman in rags with one child in her arms, and another on her back, was attempting to sing ballads, but with such a mournful voice that it was difficult to determine whether she was singing or crying. A wretch who in the deepest distress still aimed at good-humour, was an object my friend was by no means capable of withstanding; his vivacity and his discourse were instantly interrupted; upon this occasion his very dissimulation had forsaken him. Even in my presence, he immediately applied his hands to his pockets, in order to relieve her; but guess his confusion, when he found he had already given away all his money he carried about him to former objects. The misery painted in the woman's visage was not half so strongly expressed as the agony in his. He continued to search for some time, but to no purpose, till, at length, recollecting himself, with a face of ineffable good-nature, as he had no money, he put into her hands his shilling's worth of matches.

Beau Tibbs

THOUGH naturally pensive, yet I am fond of gay company, and take every opportunity of thus dismissing the mind from duty. From this motive I am often found in the centre of a crowd; and wherever pleasure is to be sold, am always a purchaser. In those places, without being remarked by any, I join in whatever goes forward; work my passions into a similitude of frivolous earnestness, shout as they shout, and condemn as they happen to disapprove. A mind thus sunk for awhile below its natural standard, is qualified for stronger flights, as those first retire who would spring forward with greater vigour.

Attracted by the serenity of the evening, a friend and I lately went to gaze upon the company in one of the public walks near the city. Here we sauntered together for some time, either praising the beauty of such as were handsome, or the dresses of such as had nothing else to recommend them. We had gone thus deliberately forward for some time, when my friend, stopping on a sudden, caught me by the elbow, and led me out of the public walk. I could perceive by the quickness of his pace, and by his frequently looking behind, that he was attempting to avoid somebody who followed; we now turned to the right, then to the left; as we went forward, he still went faster, but in vain; the person whom he attempted to escape, hunted us through every doubling, and gained upon us each moment; so that at last we fairly stood still, resolving to face what we could not avoid.

Our pursuer soon came up, and joined us with all the familiarity of an old acquaintance. 'My dear Charles,' cries he, shaking my friend's hand, 'where have you been hiding this half a century? Positively I had fancied you were gone down to cultivate matrimony and your estate in the country.' During the reply I had an opportunity of surveying the appearance of our new companion. His hat was pinched up with peculiar smartness; his looks were pale, thin, and sharp; round his neck he wore a broad black ribbon, and in his bosom a buckle studded with glass; his coat was trimmed with tarnished twist; he wore by his side a sword with a black hilt, and his stockings of silk, though newly washed, were grown yellow by long service. I was so much engaged with the peculiarity of his dress, that I attended only to the latter part of my friend's reply, in which he complimented Mr Tibbs on the taste of his clothes, and the bloom in his countenance. 'Psha, psha, Charles,' cried the figure, 'no more of that if you love me; you know I hate flattery, on my soul I do; and yet, to be sure, an intimacy with the great will improve one's appearance, and a course of venison will fatten; and yet, faith, I despise the great as much as you do; but there are a great many honest fellows among them; and we must not quarrel with one half because the other wants breeding. If they were all such as my Lord Mudler, one of the most good-natured creatures that ever squeezed a lemon, I should myself be among the number of their admirers. I was yesterday to dine at the Duchess of Piccadilly's. My lord was there. "Ned," says he to me, "Ned," says he, "I'll hold gold to silver I can tell where you were poaching last night." "Poaching, my lord?" says I; "faith, you have missed already; for I stayed at home, and let the girls poach for me. That's my way; I take a fine woman as some animals do their prey; stand still, and swoop, they fall into my mouth."'

'Ah, Tibbs, thou art an happy fellow,' cried my companion, with looks of infinite pity; 'I hope your fortune is as much improved as your understanding in such

company?' 'Improved,' replied the other; 'you shall know
– but let it go no further – a great secret – five hundred a
year to begin with. My lord's word of honour for it. His
lordship took me down in his own chariot yesterday, and
we had a *tête-à-tête* dinner in the country; where we
talked of nothing else.' 'I fancy you forgot, sir,' cried I;
'you told us but this moment of your dining yesterday in
town.' 'Did I say so?' replied he coolly. 'To be sure, if I
said so it was so. Dined in town: egad, now I do remember,
I did dine in town; but I dined in the country too; for
you must know, my boys, I eat two dinners. By the bye,
I am grown as nice as the devil in my eating. I'll tell you
a pleasant affair about that: We were a select party of
us to dine at Lady Grogram's, an affected piece, but let
it go no further; a secret. "Well," says I, "I'll hold a
thousand guineas, and say done first, that – " But, dear
Charles, you are an honest creature, lend me half-a-crown
for a minute or two, or so, just till – But, harkee, ask me
for it the next time we meet, or it may be twenty to one
but I forget to pay you.'

When he left us, our conversation naturally turned upon
so extraordinary a character. 'His very dress,' cries my
friend, 'is not less extraordinary than his conduct. If you
meet him this day you find him in rags; if the next, in
embroidery. With those persons of distinction, of whom
he talks so familiarly, he has scarce a coffee-house acquaintance. However, both for the interests of society,
and perhaps for his own, Heaven has made him poor;
and while all the world perceives his wants, he fancies
them concealed from every eye. An agreeable companion,
because he understands flattery; and all must be pleased
with the first part of his conversation, though all are sure
of its ending with a demand on their purse. While his
youth countenances the levity of his conduct, he may thus

earn a precarious subsistence; but when age comes on the gravity of which is incompatible with buffoonery, then will he find himself forsaken by all; condemned, in the decline of life, to hang upon some rich family whom he once despised, there to undergo all the ingenuity of studied contempt, to be employed only as a spy upon the servants, or a bugbear to fright children into duty.'

A Party at Vauxhall Gardens

THE people of London are as fond of walking as our friends at Pekin of riding; one of the principal entertainments of the citizens here in summer is to repair about nightfall to a garden not far from town, where they walk about, show their best clothes and best faces, and listen to a concert provided for the occasion.

I accepted an invitation a few evenings ago from my old friend, the Man in Black, to be one of a party that was to sup there; and at the appointed hour waited upon him at his lodgings. There I found the company assembled and expecting my arrival. Our party consisted of my friend, in superlative finery, his stockings rolled, a black velvet waistcoat, which was formerly new, and a grey wig combed down in imitation of hair; a pawnbroker's widow, of whom, by the by, my friend was a professed admirer, dressed out in green damask, with three gold rings on every finger; Mr Tibbs, the second-rate beau I have formerly described; together with his lady, in flimsy silk, dirty gauze instead of linen, and an hat as big as an umbrella.

Our first difficulty was in settling how we should set out. Mrs Tibbs had a natural aversion to the water, and the widow, being a little in flesh, as warmly protested against walking; a coach was therefore agreed upon; which being too small to carry five, Mr Tibbs consented to sit in his wife's lap.

In this manner, therefore, we set forward, being entertained by the way with the bodings of Mr Tibbs, who assured us he did not expect to see a single creature for the evening above the degree of a cheesemonger; that this was the last night of the gardens, and that consequently we should be pestered with the nobility and gentry from Thames Street and Crooked Lane; with several other prophetic ejaculations, probably inspired by the uneasiness of his situation.

The illuminations began before we arrived, and I must confess, that upon entering the gardens I found every sense overpaid with more than expected pleasure: the lights everywhere glimmering through the scarcely moving trees – the full-bodied concert bursting on the stillness of the night – the natural concert of the birds in the more retired part of the grove, vying with that which was formed by art – the company gaily dressed, looking satisfaction – and the tables spread with various delicacies, – all conspired to fill my imagination with the visionary happiness of the Arabian lawgiver, and lifted me into an ecstasy of admiration.

We were called to a consultation by Mr Tibbs and the rest of the company, to know in what manner we were to lay out the evening to the greatest advantage. Mrs Tibbs was for keeping the genteel walk of the garden, where, she observed, there was always the very best company; the widow, on the contrary, who came but once a season, was for securing a good standing place to see the waterworks, which she assured us would begin in less than an hour at farthest: a dispute therefore began, and as it was managed between two of very opposite characters, it threatened to grow more bitter at every reply. Mrs Tibbs wondered how people could pretend to know the polite world, who had received all their rudiments of breeding behind a counter: to which the other replied, that though some people sat behind counters, yet they could sit at the head of their own tables too, and carve three good dishes of hot meat whenever they thought proper; which was more than some people could say for themselves, that hardly knew a rabbit and onions from a green goose and gooseberries.

It is hard to say where this might have ended, had not the husband, who probably knew the impetuosity of his wife's disposition, proposed to end the dispute by adjourning to a box, and try if there was anything to be had for supper that was supportable. To this we all consented; but here a new distress arose: Mr and Mrs Tibbs would sit in none but a genteel box – a box where they might see and be seen – one, as they expressed it, in the very focus of public view; but such a box was not easy to be obtained, for though we were perfectly convinced of our own gentility, and the gentility of our appearance, yet we found it a difficult matter to persuade the keepers of the boxes to be of our opinion; they chose to reserve genteel boxes for what they judged more genteel company.

At last, however, we were fixed, though somewhat obscurely, and supplied with the usual entertainment of the place. The widow found the supper excellent, but Mrs Tibbs thought everything detestable. 'Come, come, my dear,' cries the husband, by way of consolation, 'to be sure we can't find such dressing here as we have at Lord Crump's or Lady Crimp's; but, for Vauxhall dressing, it is pretty good: it is not their victuals, indeed, I find fault with, but their wine; their wine,' cries he, drinking off a glass, 'indeed, is most abominable.'

By this last contradiction the widow was fairly conquered in point of politeness. She perceived now that she
had no pretensions in the world to taste; her very senses
were vulgar, since she had praised detestable custard,
and smacked at wretched wine; she was therefore content
to yield the victory, and for the rest of the night to listen
and improve. It is true, she would now and then forget
herself, and confess she was pleased; but they soon brought
her back again to miserable refinement. She once praised
the painting of the box in which we were sitting, but was
soon convinced that such paltry pieces ought rather to
excite horror than satisfaction: she ventured again to
commend one of the singers, but Mrs Tibbs soon let her
know, in the style of a connoisseur, that the singer in
question had neither ear, voice, nor judgement.

Mr Tibbs, now willing to prove that his wife's pretensions to music were just, entreated her to favour the
company with a song; but to this she gave a positive
denial – 'for you know very well, my dear,' says she, 'that
I am not in voice to-day, and when one's voice is not
equal to one's judgement, what signifies singing? Besides,
as there is no accompaniment, it would be but spoiling
music.' All these excuses, however, were overruled by the
rest of the company, who, though one would think they
already had music enough, joined in the entreaty. But
particularly the widow, now willing to convince the
company of her breeding, pressed so warmly, that she
seemed determined to take no refusal. At last, then, the
lady complied, and after humming for some minutes,
began with such a voice, and such affectation, as, I could
perceive, gave but little satisfaction to any except her
husband. He sat with rapture in his eye, and beat time
with his hand on the table.

You must observe, my friend, that it is the custom of

this country, when a lady or gentleman happens to sing,
for the company to sit as mute and motionless as statues.
Every feature, every limb, must seem to correspond in
fixed attention; and while the song continues, they are
to remain in a state of universal petrifaction. In this
mortifying situation we had continued for some time,
listening to the song, and looking with tranquillity, when
the master of the box came to inform us, that the waterworks were going to begin. At this information I could
instantly perceive the widow bounce from her seat; but
correcting herself, she sat down again, repressed by
motives of good breeding. Mrs Tibbs, who had seen the
waterworks a hundred times, resolving not to be interrupted, continued her song without any share of mercy,
nor had the smallest pity on our impatience. The widow's
face, I own, gave me high entertainment; in it I could
plainly read the struggle she felt between good breeding
and curiosity: she talked of the waterworks the whole
evening before, and seemed to have come merely in
order to see them: but then she could not bounce out in
the very middle of a song, for that would be forfeiting
all pretensions to high life, or high-lived company, ever
after. Mrs Tibbs, therefore, kept on singing, and we
continued to listen, till at last, when the song was just
concluded, the waiter came to inform us that the waterworks were over.

'The waterworks over!' cried the widow; 'the waterworks over already! that's impossible! they can't be over
so soon!' – 'It is not my business,' replied the fellow, 'to
contradict your ladyship; I'll run again and see.' He went,
and soon returned with a confirmation of the dismal
tidings. No ceremony could now bind my friend's disappointed mistress. She testified her displeasure in the
openest manner; in short, she now began to find fault

in turn, and at last insisted upon going home, just at the
time that Mr and Mrs Tibbs assured the company that
the polite hours were going to begin, and that the ladies
would instantaneously be entertained with the horns.

National Prejudices

As I am one of that sauntering tribe of mortals, who
spend the greatest part of their time in taverns, coffee-
houses, and other places of public resort, I have thereby an
opportunity of observing an infinite variety of characters,
which, to a person of a contemplative turn, is a much
higher entertainment than a view of all the curiosities of
art or nature. In one of these, my late rambles, I accidentally fell into the company of half a dozen gentlemen,
who were engaged in a warm dispute about some political
affair; the decision of which, as they were equally divided
in their sentiments, they thought proper to refer to me,
which naturally drew me in for a share of the conversation.

Amongst a multiplicity of other topics, we took occasion
to talk of the different characters of the several nations of
Europe; when one of the gentlemen, cocking his hat, and
assuming such an air of importance as if he had possessed
all the merit of the English nation in his own person,
declared that the Dutch were a parcel of avaricious
wretches; the French a set of flattering sycophants; that
the Germans were drunken sots, and beastly gluttons;
and the Spaniards proud, haughty, and surly tyrants;
but that in bravery, generosity, clemency, and in every
other virtue, the English excelled all the rest of the world.

This very learned and judicious remark was received
with a general smile of approbation by all the company —

all, I mean, but your humble servant; who, endeavouring to keep my gravity as well as I could, and reclining my head upon my arm, continued for some time in a posture of affected thoughtfulness, as if I had been musing on something else, and did not seem to attend to the subject of conversation; hoping by these means to avoid the disagreeable necessity of explaining myself . . .

But my pseudo-patriot had no mind to let me escape so easily. Not satisfied that his opinion should pass without contradiction, he was determined to have it ratified by the suffrage of every one in the company; for which purpose addressing himself to me with an air of inexpressible confidence, he asked me if I was not of the same way of thinking. As I am never forward in giving my opinion, especially when I have reason to believe that it will not be agreeable; so, when I am obliged to give it, I always hold it for a maxim to speak my real sentiments. I therefore told him that, for my own part, I should not have ventured to talk in such a peremptory strain, unless I had made the tour of Europe, and examined the manners of these several nations with great care and accuracy: that, perhaps, a more impartial judge would not scruple to affirm that the Dutch were more frugal and industrious, the French more temperate and polite, the Germans more hardy and patient of labour and fatigue, and the Spaniards more staid and sedate, than the English; who, though undoubtedly brave and generous, were at the same time rash, headstrong, and impetuous; too apt to be elated with prosperity, and to despond in adversity.

I could easily perceive that all the company began to regard me with a jealous eye before I had finished my answer, which I had no sooner done, than the patriotic gentleman observed, with a contemptuous sneer, that he was greatly surprised how some people could have the conscience to live in a country which they did not love, and to enjoy the protection of a government, to which in their hearts they were inveterate enemies. Finding that by this modest declaration of my sentiments I had forfeited the good opinion of my companions, and given them occasion to call my political principles in question, and well knowing that it was in vain to argue with men who were so very full of themselves, I threw down my reckoning and retired to my own lodgings, reflecting on the absurd and ridiculous nature of national prejudice and prepossession.

Among all the famous sayings of antiquity, there is none that does greater honour to the author, or affords greater pleasure to the reader (at least if he be a person of a generous and benevolent heart), than that of the philosopher, who, being asked what 'countryman he was', replied, that he was, 'a citizen of the world'. – How few are there to be found in modern times who can say the same, or whose conduct is consistent with such a profession! – We are now become so much Englishmen, Frenchmen, Dutchmen, Spaniards, or Germans, that we are no longer citizens of the world; so much the natives of one particular spot, or members of one petty society, that we no longer consider ourselves as the general inhabitants of the globe, or members of that grand society which comprehends the whole human kind.

Did these prejudices prevail only among the meanest and lowest of the people, perhaps they might be excused, as they have few, if any, opportunities of correcting them by reading, travelling, or conversing with foreigners; but the misfortune is, that they infect the minds, and influence the conduct, even of our gentlemen; of those, I mean, who have every title to this appellation but an exemption from prejudice, which however, in my opinion, ought to

be regarded as the characteristical mark of a gentleman;
for let a man's birth be ever so high, his station ever so
exalted, or his fortune ever so large, yet if he is not free
from national and other prejudices, I should make bold
to tell him, that he had a low and vulgar mind, and had
no just claim to the character of a gentleman. And in
fact, you will always find that those are most apt to boast
of national merit, who have little or no merit of their
own to depend on; than which, to be sure, nothing is
more natural: the slender vine twists around the sturdy
oak, for no other reason in the world but because it has
not strength sufficient to support itself.

Should it be alleged in defence of national prejudice,
that it is the natural and necessary growth of love to our
country, and that therefore the former cannot be destroyed
without hurting the latter, I answer, that this is a gross
fallacy and delusion. That it is the growth of love to our
country, I will allow; but that it is the natural and
necessary growth of it, I absolutely deny. Superstition
and enthusiasm too are the growth of religion; but who
ever took it in his head to affirm that they are the
necessary growth of this noble principle? They are, if
you will, the bastard sprouts of this heavenly plant, but
not its natural and genuine branches, and may safely
enough be lopped off, without doing any harm to the
parent stock: nay, perhaps, till once they are lopped off,
this goodly tree can never flourish in perfect health and
vigour.

Is it not very possible that I may love my own country,
without hating the natives of other countries? that I may
exert the most heroic bravery, the most undaunted resolution, in defending its laws and liberty, without despising
all the rest of the world as cowards and poltroons? Most
certainly it is; and if it were not – But why need I suppose

what is absolutely impossible? – But if it were not, I must own, I should prefer the title of the ancient philosopher, viz. a citizen of the world, to that of an Englishman, a Frenchman, a European, or to any other appellation whatever.

CHARLES LAMB

Old China

I HAVE an almost feminine partiality for old china. When I go to see any great house, I inquire for the china-closet, and next for the picture-gallery. I cannot defend the order of preference, but by saying, that we have all some taste or other, of too ancient a date to admit of our remembering distinctly that it was an acquired one. I can call to mind the first play, and the first exhibition, that I was taken to; but I am not conscious of a time when china jars and saucers were introduced into my imagination.

I had no repugnance then – why should I now have? – to those little, lawless, azure-tinctured grotesques, that under the notion of men and women, float about, uncircumscribed by any element, in that world before perspective – a china tea-cup.

I like to see my old friends – whom distance cannot diminish – figuring up in the air (so they appear to our optics), yet on *terra firma* still – for so we must in courtesy interpret that speck of deeper blue, – which the decorous artist, to prevent absurdity, had made to spring up beneath their sandals.

I love the men with women's faces, and the women, if possible, with still more womanish expressions.

Here is a young and courtly Mandarin, handing tea to a lady from a salver – two miles off. See how distance seems to set off respect! And here the same lady, or another – for likeness is identity on tea-cups – is stepping into a little fairy boat, moored on the hither side of this calm garden river, with a dainty mincing foot, which in a right angle of incidence (as angles go in our world) must infallibly land her in the midst of a flowery mead – a furlong off on the other side of the same strange stream!

Farther on – if far or near can be predicated of their world – see horses, trees, pagodas, dancing the hays.

Here – a cow and rabbit couchant, and co-extensive – so objects show, seen through the lucid atmosphere of fine Cathay.

I was pointing out to my cousin last evening, over our Hyson (which we are old fashioned enough to drink unmixed still of an afternoon), some of these *speciosa miracula* upon a set of extraordinary old blue china (a recent purchase) which we were now for the first time using; and could not help remarking, how favourable circumstances had been to us of late years, that we could afford to please the eye sometimes with trifles of this sort – when a passing sentiment seemed to overshade the brows of my companion. I am quick at detecting these summer clouds in Bridget.

‘I wish the good old times would come again,’ she said, ‘when we were not quite so rich. I do not mean that I want to be poor; but there was a middle state’ – so she was pleased to ramble on – ‘in which I am sure we were a great deal happier. A purchase is but a purchase, now that you have money enough and to spare. Formerly it used to be a triumph. When we coveted a cheap luxury (and, O! how much ado I had to get you to consent in those times!) – we were used to have a debate two or three days before, and to weigh the *for* and *against*, and think what we might spare it out of, and what saving we could hit upon, that should be an equivalent. A thing was worth buying then, when we felt the money that we paid for it.

'Do you remember the brown suit, which you made to hang upon you, till all your friends cried shame upon you it grew so thread-bare – and all because of that folio Beaumont and Fletcher, which you dragged home late at night from Barker's in Covent Garden? Do you remember how we eyed it for weeks before we could make up our minds to the purchase, and had not come to a determination till it was near ten o'clock of the Saturday night, when you set off from Islington, fearing you should be too late – and when the old bookseller with some grumbling opened his shop, and by the twinkling taper (for he was setting bedwards) lighted out the relic from his dusty treasures – and when you lugged it home, wishing it were twice as cumbersome – and when you presented it to me – and when we were exploring the perfectness of it (*collating* you called it) – and while I was repairing some of the loose leaves with paste, which your impatience would not suffer to be left till daybreak – was there no pleasure in being a poor man? or can those neat black clothes which you wear now, and are so careful to keep brushed, since we have become rich and finical, give you half the honest vanity, with which you flaunted it about in that overworn suit – your old corbeau – for four or five weeks longer than you should have done, to pacify your conscience for the mighty sum of fifteen – or sixteen shillings was it? – a great affair we thought it then – which you had lavished on the old folio. Now you can afford to buy any book that pleases you, but I do not see that you ever bring me home any nice old purchases now.

'When you came home with twenty apologies for laying out a less number of shillings upon that print after Lionardo, which we christened the "Lady Blanch"; when you looked at the purchase, and thought of the money – and thought of the money, and looked again at the picture

– was there no pleasure in being a poor man? Now, you have nothing to do but to walk into Colnaghi's, and buy a wilderness of Lionardos. Yet do you?

'Then, do you remember our pleasant walks to Enfield, and Potter's Bar, and Waltham, when we had a holyday – holydays, and all other fun, are gone, now we are rich – and the little hand-basket in which I used to deposit our day's fare of savoury cold lamb and salad – and how you would pry about at noon-tide for some decent house, where we might go in, and produce our store – only paying for the ale that you must call for – and speculate upon the looks of the landlady, and whether she was likely to allow us a table-cloth – and wish for such another honest hostess, as Izaak Walton has described many a one on the pleasant banks of the Lea, when he went a-fishing – and sometimes they would prove obliging enough, and sometimes they would look grudgingly upon us – but we had cheerful looks still for one another, and would eat our plain food savourily, scarcely grudging Piscator his Trout Hall? Now, – when we go out a day's pleasuring, which is seldom moreover, we *ride* part of the way – and go into a fine inn, and order the best of dinners, never debating the expense – which, after all, never has half the relish of those chance country snaps, when we were at the mercy of uncertain usage, and a precarious welcome.

'You are too proud to see a play anywhere now but in the pit. Do you remember where it was we used to sit, when we saw the Battle of Hexham, and the Surrender of Calais, and Bannister and Mrs Bland in the Children in the Wood – when we squeezed out our shilling a-piece to sit three or four times in a season in the one-shilling gallery – where you felt all the time that you ought not to have brought me – and more strongly I felt obligation to you for having brought me – and the pleasure was the

better for a little shame – and when the curtain drew up,
what cared we for our place in the house, or what mattered
it where we were sitting, when our thoughts were with
Rosalind in Arden, or with Viola at the Court of Illyria?
You used to say, that the Gallery was the best place of all
for enjoying a play socially – that the relish of such ex-
hibitions must be in proportion to the infrequency of
going – that the company we met there, not being in
general readers of plays, were obliged to attend the more
and did attend, to what was going on, on the stage –
because a word lost would have been a chasm, which it
was impossible for them to fill up. With such reflections
we consoled our pride then – and I appeal to you,
whether, as a woman, I met generally with less attention
and accommodation, than I have done since in more
expensive situations in the house? The getting in indeed
and the crowding up those inconvenient staircases, was
bad enough, – but there was still a law of civility to woman
recognized to quite as great an extent as we ever found in
the other passages – and how a little difficulty overcome
heightened the snug seat, and the play, afterwards! Now
we can only pay our money and walk in. You cannot see,
you say, in the galleries now. I am sure we saw, and heard
too, well enough then – but sight, and all, I think, is gone
with our poverty.

'There was pleasure in eating strawberries, before they
became quite common – in the first dish of peas, while they
were yet dear – to have them for a nice supper, a treat.
What treat can we have now? If we were to treat ourselves now – that is, to have dainties a little above our
means, it would be selfish and wicked. It is very little more
that we allow ourselves beyond what the actual poor can
get at, that makes what I call a treat – when two people
living together, as we have done, now and then indulge

themselves in a cheap luxury, which both like; while each apologizes, and is willing to take both halves of the blame to his single share. I see no harm in people making much of themselves in that sense of the word. It may give them a hint how to make much of others. But now – what I mean by the word – we never do make much of our-selves. None but the poor can do it. I do not mean the veriest poor of all, but persons as we were, just above poverty.

'I know what you were going to say, that it is mighty pleasant at the end of the year to make all meet, – and much ado we used to have every Thirty-first Night of December to account for our exceedings – many a long face did you make over your puzzled accounts, and in contriving to make it out how we had spent so much – or that we had not spent so much – or that it was impos-sible we should spend so much next year – and still we found our slender capital decreasing – but then, betwixt ways, and projects, and compromises of one sort or another, and talk of curtailing this charge, and doing without that for the future – and the hope that youth brings, and laughing spirits (in which you were never poor till now) we pocketed up our loss, and in conclusion, with "lusty brimmers" as you used to quote it out of *hearty cheerful Mr Cotton* (as you called him), we used to welcome in the "coming guest". Now we have no reckoning at all at the end of the old year – no flattering promises about the new year doing better for us.'

Bridget is so sparing of her speech on most occasions, that when she gets into a rhetorical vein, I am careful how I interrupt it. I could not help, however, smiling at the phantom of wealth which her dear imagination had conjured up out of a clear income of a poor – hundred pounds a year. 'It is true we were happier when we were

poorer, but we were also younger, my cousin. I am afraid
we must put up with the excess, for if we were to shake the
superflux into the sea, we should not much mend ourselves. That we had much to struggle with, as we grew
up together, we have reason to be most thankful. It
strengthened, and knit our compact closer. We could
never have been what we have been to each other, if
we had always had the sufficiency which you now com-
plain of. The resisting power – those natural dilations of
the youthful spirit, which circumstances cannot straiten –
with us are long since passed away. Competence to age
is supplementary youth, a sorry supplement indeed, but I
fear the best that is to be had. We must ride, where we
formerly walked: live better, and lie softer – and shall
be wise to do so – than we had means to do in those good
old days you speak of. Yet could those days return –
could you and I once more walk our thirty miles a day –
could Bannister and Mrs Bland again be young, and you
and I young to see them – could the good old one-shilling
gallery days return – they are dreams, my cousin, now –
but could you and I at this moment, instead of this quiet
argument, by our well-carpeted fire-side, sitting on this
luxurious sofa – be once more struggling up those inconvenient staircases, pushed about, and squeezed, and
elbowed by the poorest rabble of poor gallery scramblers –
could I once more hear those anxious shrieks of yours –
and the delicious *Thank God, we are safe*, which always
followed when the topmost stair, conquered, let in the
first light of the whole cheerful theatre down beneath us –
I know not the fathom line that ever touched a descent
so deep as I would be willing to bury more wealth in
than Croesus had, or the great Jew R— is supposed to
have, to purchase it. And now do just look at that merry
little Chinese waiter holding an umbrella, big enough for

a bed-tester, over the head of that pretty insipid half-
Madonnaish chit of a lady in that very blue summer
house.'

Imperfect Sympathies

> I am of a constitution so general, that it consorts and sympathizeth
> with all things; I have no antipathy, or rather idiosyncrasy in anything.
> Those natural repugnances do not touch me, nor do I behold with
> prejudice the French, Italian, Spaniard, or Dutch.– *Religio Medici.*

THAT the author of the *Religio Medici* mounted upon the
airy stilts of abstraction, conversant about notional and
conjectural essences; in whose categories of Being the
possible took the upper hand of the actual; should have
overlooked the impertinent individualities of such poor
concretions as mankind, is not much to be admired. It
is rather to be wondered at, that in the genus of animals
he should have condescended to distinguish that species
at all. For myself – earth-bound and fettered to the
scene of my activities, –

Standing on earth, not rapt above the sky.

I confess that I do feel the differences of mankind, national
or individual, to an unhealthy excess. I can look with no
indifferent eye upon things or persons. Whatever is, is
to me a matter of taste or distaste; or when once it becomes
indifferent it begins to be disrelishing. I am, in plainer
words, a bundle of prejudices – made up of likings and
dislikings – the veriest thrall to sympathies, apathies,
antipathies. In a certain sense, I hope it may be said of
me that I am a lover of my species. I can feel for all
indifferently, but I cannot feel towards all equally. The

more purely-English word that expresses sympathy, will better explain my meaning. I can be a friend to a worthy man, who upon another account cannot be my mate or *fellow*. I cannot *like* all people alike.

I have been trying all my life to like Scotchmen, and am obliged to desist from the experiment in despair. They cannot like me – and in truth, I never knew one of that nation who attempted to do it. There is something more plain and ingenuous in their mode of proceeding. We know one another at first sight. There is an order of imperfect intellects (under which mine must be content to rank) which in its constitution is essentially anti-Caledonian. The owners of the sort of faculties I allude to, have minds rather suggestive than comprehensive. They have no pretences to much clearness or precision in their ideas, or in their manner of expressing them. Their intellectual wardrobe (to confess fairly) has few whole pieces in it. They are content with fragments and scattered pieces of Truth. She presents no full front to them – a feature or side-face at the most. Hints and glimpses, germs and crude essays at a system, is the utmost they pretend to. They beat up a little game peradventure – and leave it to knottier heads, more robust constitutions, to run it down. The light that lights them is not steady and polar, but mutable and shifting: waxing and again waning. Their conversation is accordingly. They will throw out a random word in or out of season, and be content to let it pass for what it is worth. They cannot speak always as if they were upon their oath – but must be understood, speaking or writing, with some abatement. They seldom wait to mature a proposition, but e'en bring it to market in the green ear. They delight to impart their defective discoveries as they arise, without waiting for their development. They are no

systematizers, and would but err more by attempting it.
Their minds, as I said before, are suggestive merely. The
brain of a true Caledonian (if I am not mistaken) is
constituted upon quite a different plan. His Minerva is
born in panoply. You are never admitted to see his ideas
in their growth – if, indeed, they do grow, and are not
rather put together upon principles of clock-work. You
never catch his mind in an undress. He never hints or
suggests anything, but unlades his stock of ideas in perfect
order and completeness. He brings his total wealth into
company, and gravely unpacks it. His riches are always
about him. He never stoops to catch a glittering something in your presence to share it with you, before he
quite knows whether it be true touch or not. You cannot
cry *halves* to anything that he finds. He does not find,
but bring. You never witness his first apprehension of a
thing. His understanding is always at its meridian – you
never see the first dawn, the early streaks – he has no
falterings of self-suspicion. Surmises, guesses, misgivings,
half-intuitions, semi-consciousnesses, partial illuminations,
dim instincts, embryo conceptions, have no place in his
brain or vocabulary. The twilight of dubiety never falls
upon him. Is he orthodox – he has no doubts. Is he an
infidel – he has none either. Between the affirmative and
the negative there is no border-land with him. You cannot
hover with him upon the confines of truth, or wander in
the maze of a probable argument. He always keeps the
path. You cannot make excursions with him – for he
sets you right. His taste never fluctuates. His morality
never abates. He cannot compromise, or understand
middle actions. There can be but a right and a wrong.
His conversation is as a book. His affirmations have the
sanctity of an oath. You must speak upon the square
with him. He stops a metaphor like a suspected person in

an enemy's country. 'A healthy book!' – said one of his
countrymen to me, who had ventured to give that appellation to John Buncle – 'Did I catch rightly what you said?
I have heard of a man in health, and of a healthy state of
body, but I do not see how that epithet can be properly
applied to a book.' Above all, you must beware of indirect
expressions before a Caledonian. Clap an extinguisher
upon your irony, if you are unhappily blest with a vein
of it. Remember you are upon your oath. I have a print
of a graceful figure after Leonardo da Vinci, which I was
showing off to Mr*** After he had examined it minutely,
I ventured to ask him how he liked MY BEAUTY (a foolish
name it goes by among my friends) – when he very
gravely assured me, that 'he had considerable respect for
my character and talents' (so he was pleased to say), 'but
had not given himself much thought about the degree of
my personal pretensions.' The misconception staggered
me, but did not seem much to disconcert him. – Persons
of this nation are particularly fond of affirming a truth –
which nobody doubts. They do not so properly affirm, as
annunciate it. They do indeed appear to have such a love
of truth (as if, like virtue, it were valuable for itself) that
all truth becomes equally valuable, whether the proposition that contains it be new or old, disputed, or such as
is impossible to become a subject of disputation. I was
present not long since at a party of North Britons, where
a son of Burns was expected; and happened to drop a
silly expression (in my South British way), that I wished it
were the father instead of the son – when four of them
started up at once to inform me, that 'that was impossible,
because he was dead.' An impracticable wish, it seems, was
more than they could conceive. Swift has hit off his part of
their character, namely their love of truth, in his biting
way, but with an illiberality that necessarily confined

the passage to the margin. The tediousness of these
people is certainly provoking. I wonder if they ever tire
one another ! – In my early life I had a passionate fondness
for the poetry of Burns. I have sometimes foolishly hoped
to ingratiate myself with his countrymen by expressing it.
But I have always found that a true Scot resents your
admiration of his compatriot even more than he would
your contempt of him. The latter he imputes to your
'imperfect acquaintance with many of the words which
he uses'; and the same objection makes it a presumption
in you to suppose that you can admire him. – Thomson
they seem to have forgotten. Smollett they have neither
forgotten nor forgiven, for his delineation of Rory and
his companion, upon their first introduction to our metropolis. – Speak of Smollett as a great genius, and they will
retort upon you Hume's History compared with *his*
Continuation of it. What if the historian had continued
Humphrey Clinker?

I have, in the abstract, no disrespect for the Jews. They
are a piece of stubborn antiquity, compared with which
Stonehenge is in its nonage. They date beyond the
pyramids. But I should not care to be in habits of familiar
intercourse with any of that nation. I confess that I have
not the nerves to enter their synagogues. Old prejudices
cling about me. I cannot shake off the story of Hugh of
Lincoln. Centuries of injury, contempt, and hate, on the
one side, – of cloaked revenge, dissimulation, and hate,
on the other, between our and their fathers, must and
ought to affect the blood of the children. I cannot believe
it can run clear and kindly yet; or that a few words, such
as candour, liberality, the light of the nineteenth century,
can close up the breaches of so deadly a disunion. A
Hebrew is nowhere congenial to me. He is least distasteful
on 'Change – for the mercantile spirit levels all distinctions,

as all are beauties in the dark. I boldly confess that I do not relish the approximation of Jew and Christian, which has become so fashionable. The reciprocal endearments have, to me, something hypocritical and unnatural in them. I do not like to see the Church and Synagogue kissing and congeeing in awkward postures of an affected civility. If *they* are converted, why do they not come over to us altogether? Why keep up a form of separation, when the life of it is fled? If they can sit with us at table, why do they keck at our cookery? I do not understand these half convertites. Jews christianizing – Christians judaizing – puzzles me. I like fish or flesh. A moderate Jew is a more confounding piece of anomaly than a wet Quaker. The spirit of the synagogue is essentially *separative*. B— would have been more in keeping if he had abided by the faith of his forefathers. There is a fine scorn in his face, which nature meant to be of – Christians. – The Hebrew spirit is strong in him, in spite of his proselytism. He cannot conquer the Shibboleth. How it breaks out, when he sings, 'The Children of Israel passed through the Red Sea!' The auditors, for the moment, are as Egyptians to him, and he rides over our necks in triumph. There is no mistaking him. B— has a strong expression of sense in his countenance, and it is confirmed by his singing. The foundation of his vocal excellence is sense. He sings with understanding, as Kemble delivered dialogue. He would sing the Commandments, and give an appropriate character to each prohibition. His nation, in general, have not over-sensible countenances. How should they? – but you seldom see a silly expression among them. – Gain, and the pursuit of gain, sharpen a man's visage. I never heard of an idiot being born among them. – Some admire the Jewish female-physiognomy. I admire it – but with trembling. Jael had those full dark inscrutable eyes.

In the Negro countenance you will often meet with strong traits of benignity. I have felt yearnings of tenderness towards some of these faces – or rather masks – that have looked out kindly upon one in casual encounters in the streets and highways. I love what Fuller beautifully calls – 'these images of God cut in ebony'. But I should not like to associate with them, to share my meals and my good nights with them – because they are black.

I love Quaker ways, and Quaker worship. I venerate the Quaker principles. It does me good for the rest of the day when I meet any of their people in my path. When I am ruffled or disturbed by an occurrence, the sight, or quiet voice of a Quaker, acts upon me as a ventilator, lightening the air, and taking off a load from the bosom. But I cannot like the Quakers (as Desdemona would say) 'to live with them'. I am all over sophisticated – with humours, fancies, craving hourly sympathy. I must have books, pictures, theatres, chit-chat, scandal, jokes, ambiguities, and a thousand whim-whams, which their simpler taste can do without. I should starve at their primitive banquet. My appetites are too high for the salads which (according to Evelyn) Eve dressed for the angel; my gusto too excited.

To sit a guest with Daniel at his pulse.

The indirect answers which Quakers are often found to return to a question put to them may be explained, I think, without the vulgar assumption, that they are more given to evasion and equivocating than other people. They naturally look to their words more carefully, and are more cautious of committing themselves. They have a peculiar character to keep up on this head. They stand in a manner upon their veracity. A Quaker is by law exempted from taking an oath. The custom of resorting to an oath in extreme cases, sanctified as it is by all religious antiquity, is apt (it must be confessed) to introduce into the laxer sort of minds the notion of two kinds of truth – the one applicable to the solemn affairs of justice, and the other to the common proceedings of daily inter-course. As truth bound upon the conscience by an oath can be but truth, so in the common affirmations of the shop and the market-place a latitude is expected and conceded upon questions wanting this solemn covenant. Something less than truth satisfies. It is common to hear a person say, 'You do not expect me to speak as if I were upon my oath.' Hence a great deal of incorrectness and inadvertency, short of falsehood, creeps into ordinary conversation; and a kind of secondary or laic-truth is tolerated, where clergy-truth – oath-truth, by the nature of the circumstance, is not required. A Quaker knows none of this distinction. His simple affirmation being received upon the most sacred occasions, without any further test, stamps a value upon the words which he is to use upon the most indifferent topics of life. He looks to them, naturally, with more severity. You can have of him no more than his word. He knows, if he is caught tripping in a casual expression, he forfeits, for himself at least, his claim to the invidious exemption. He knows that his syllables are weighed – and how far a consciousness of this particular watchfulness, exerted against a person, has a tendency to produce indirect answers, and a diverting of the question by honest means, might be illustrated, and the practice justified by a more sacred example than is proper to be adduced upon this occasion. The admirable presence of mind, which is notorious in Quakers upon all contingencies, might be traced to this imposed self-watchfulness – if it did not seem rather an humble and secular scion of that old stock of religious constancy, which never bent or faltered, in the Primitive Friends, or gave ways to the winds of persecution, to the violence of judge or accuser, under trials and racking examinations. 'You will never be the wiser, if I sit here answering your questions till midnight,' said one of those upright Justicers to Penn, who had been putting law-cases with a puzzling subtlety. 'Thereafter as the answers may be,' retorted the Quaker. The astonishing composure of this people is sometimes ludicrously displayed in lighter instances – I was travelling in a stage-coach with three male Quakers, buttoned up in the straitest nonconformity of their sect. We stopped to bait at Andover, where a meal, partly tea apparatus, partly supper, was set before us. My friends confined themselves to the tea-table. I in my way took supper. When the landlady brought in the bill, the eldest of my companions discovered that she had charged for both meals. This was resisted. Mine hostess was very clamorous and positive. Some mild arguments were used on the part of the Quakers, for which the heated mind of the good lady seemed by no means a fit recipient. The guard came with his usual peremptory notice. The Quakers pulled out their money and formally tendered it – so much for tea – I, in humble imitation, tendering mine – for the supper which I had taken. She would not relax in her demand. So they all three quietly put up their silver, as did myself, and marched out of the room, the eldest and gravest going first, with myself closing up the rear, who thought I could not do better than follow the example of such grave and warrantable personages. We got in. The steps went up. The coach drove off. The murmurs of mine hostess, not very indistinctly or ambiguously pronounced, became after a time inaudible – and now my conscience, which the whimsical scene had for a while suspended, beginning to give some twitches,

I waited, in the hope that some justification would be offered by these serious persons for the seeming injustice of their conduct. To my great surprise not a syllable was dropped on the subject. They sat as mute as at a meeting. At length the eldest of them broke silence, by inquiring of his next neighbour, 'Hast thee heard how indigos go at the India House?' and the question operated as soporific on my moral feeling as far as Exeter.

Poor Relations

A POOR Relation – is the most irrelevant thing in nature – a piece of impertinent correspondency, – an odious approximation, – a haunting conscience, – a preposterous shadow, lengthening in the noontide of our prosperity, – an unwelcome remembrancer, – a perpetually recurring mortification, – a drain on your purse, – a more intolerable dun upon your pride, – a drawback upon success, – a rebuke to your rising, – stain in your blood, – a blot on your 'scutcheon, – a rent in your garment, – a death's head at your banquet, – Agathocles' pot, – a Mordecai in your gate, – a Lazarus at your door, – a lion in your path, – a frog in your chamber, – a fly in your ointment, – a mote in your eye, – a triumph to your enemy, an apology to your friends, – the one thing not needful, – the hail in harvest, – the ounce of sour in a pound of sweet.

He is known by his knock. Your heart telleth you 'That is Mr—.' A rap between familiarity and respect; that demands, and, at the same time, seems to despair of, entertainment. He entereth smiling and – embarrassed. He holdeth out his hand to you to shake, and – draweth it back again. He casually looketh in about dinner-time –

when the table is full. He offereth to go away, seeing you
have company, but is induced to stay. He filleth a chair,
and your visitor's two children are accommodated at a
side table. He never cometh upon open days, when your
wife says with some complacency, 'My dear, perhaps
Mr— will drop in to-day.' He remembered birthdays –
and professeth he is fortunate to have stumbled upon one.
He declareth against fish, the turbot being small – yet
suffereth himself to be importuned into a slice against his
first resolution. He sticketh by the port – yet will be
prevailed upon to empty the remainder glass of claret, if
a stranger press it upon him. He is a puzzle to the servants,
who are fearful of being too obsequious, or not civil
enough, to him. The guests think 'they have seen him
before.' Everyone speculateth upon his condition; and the
most part take him to be – a tide waiter. He calleth you
by your Christian name, to imply that his other is the
same with your own. He is too familiar by half, yet you
wish he had less diffidence. With half the familiarity he
might pass for a casual dependent; with more boldness
he would be in no danger of being taken for what he is.
He is too humble for a friend, yet taketh on him more
state than befits a client. He is a worse guest than a
country tenant, inasmuch as he bringeth up no rent – yet
'tis odds, from his garb and demeanour, that your guests
take him for one. He is asked to make one at the whist
table; refuseth on the score of poverty, and – resents being
left out. When the company break up he proffereth to go
for a coach – and lets the servant go. He recollects your
grandfather; and will thrust in some mean and quite
unimportant anecdote of – the family. He knew it when
it was not quite so flourishing as 'he is blest in seeing it
now'. He reviveth past situations to institute what he
calleth – favourable comparisons. With a reflecting sort

of congratulation, he will inquire the price of your furniture: and insults you with a special commendation of your window-curtains. He is of opinion that the urn is the more elegant shape, but, after all, there was something more comfortable about the old tea-kettle – which you must remember. He dare say you must find a great convenience in having a carriage of your own, and appealeth to your lady if it is not so. Inquireth if you have had your arms done on vellum yet; and did not know, till lately, that such-and-such had been the crest of the family. His memory is unseasonable; his compliments perverse; his talk a trouble; his stay pertinacious; and when he goeth away, you dismiss his chair into a corner, as precipitately as possible, and feel fairly rid of two nuisances.

There is a worse evil under the sun, and that is – a female Poor Relation. You may do something with the other; you may pass him off tolerably well; but your indigent she-relative is hopeless. 'He is an old humorist,' you may say, 'and affects to go threadbare. His circumstances are better than folks would take them to be. You are fond of having a Character at your table, and truly he is one.' But in the indications of female poverty there can be no disguise. No woman dresses below herself from caprice. The truth must out without shuffling, 'She is plainly related to the L—s; or what does she at their house?' She is, in all probability, your wife's cousin. Nine times out of ten, at least, this is the case. Her garb is something between a gentlewoman and a beggar, yet the former evidently predominates. She is most provokingly humble, and ostentatiously sensible to her inferiority. He may require to be repressed sometimes – *aliquando sufflaminandus erat* – but there is no raising her. You send her soup at dinner, and she begs to be helped – after the gentlemen. Mr— requests the honour of taking wine with her; she hesitates between Port and Madeira, and chooses the former – because he does. She calls the servant *Sir*; and insists on not troubling him to hold her plate. The housekeeper patronizes her. The children's governess takes upon her to correct her, when she has mistaken the piano for harpsichord.

Richard Amlet, Esq., in the play, is a noticeable instance of the disadvantages, to which this chimerical notion of *affinity constituting a claim to an acquaintance*, may subject the spirit of a gentleman. A little foolish blood is all that is betwixt him and a lady with a great estate. His stars are perpetually crossed by the malignant maternity of an old woman, who persists in calling him 'her son Dick'. But she has wherewithal in the end to recompense his indignities, and float him again upon the brilliant surface, under which it has been her seeming business and pleasure all along to sink him. All men, besides, are not of Dick's temperament. I knew an Amlet in real life, who wanting Dick's buoyancy, sank indeed. Poor W— was of my own standing at Christ's, a fine classic, and a youth of promise. If he had a blemish, it was too much pride; but its quality was inoffensive; it was not of that sort which hardens the heart, and serves to keep inferiors at a distance; it only sought to ward off derogation from itself. It was the principle of self-respect carried as far as it could go, without infringing upon that respect, which he would have every one else equally maintain for himself. He would have you to think alike with him on this topic. Many a quarrel have I had with him, when we were rather older boys, and our tallness made us more obnoxious to observation in the blue clothes, because I would not thread the alleys and blind ways of the town with him to elude notice, when we have been out together on a holiday in the streets of this sneering and prying metropolis. W— went, sore with these notions, to Oxford, where the dignity and sweetness of a scholar's life, meeting with the alloy of a humble introduction, wrought in him a passionate devotion to the place, with a profound aversion of the society. The servitor's gown (worse than his school array) clung to him with Nessian venom. He thought himself ridiculous in a garb, under which Latimer must have walked erect; and in which Hooker, in his young days, possibly flaunted in a vein of no discommendable vanity. In the depths of college shades, or in his lonely chamber, the poor student shrunk from observation. He found shelter among books, which insult not; and studies, that ask no questions of a youth's finances. He was lord of his library, and seldom cared for looking out beyond his domains. The healing influence of studious pursuits was upon him, to soothe and to abstract. He was almost a healthy man; when the waywardness of his fate broke out against him with a second and worse malignity. The father of W— had hitherto exercised the humble profession of house-painter at N—, near Oxford. A supposed interest with some of the heads of colleges had now induced him to take up his abode in that city, with the hope of being employed upon some public works which were talked of. From that moment I read in the countenance of the young man, the determination which at length tore him from academical pursuits for ever. To a person unacquainted with our Universities, the distance between the gownsmen and the townsmen, as they are called – the trading part of the latter especially – is carried to an excess that would appear harsh and incredible. The temperament of W—'s father was diametrically the reverse of his own. Old W— was a little, busy, cringing tradesman, who, with his son upon his arm, would stand bowing and

scraping, cap in hand, to anything that wore the semblance
of a gown – insensible to the winks and opener remon-
strances of the young man, to whose chamber-fellow, or
equal in standing, perhaps, he was thus obsequiously and
gratuitously ducking. Such a state of things could not
last. W— must change the air of Oxford or be suffocated.
He chose the former; and let the sturdy moralist, who
strains the point of the filial duties as high as they can
bear, censure the dereliction; he cannot estimate the
struggle. I stood with W—, the last afternoon I ever saw
him, under the eaves of his paternal dwelling. It was in
a fine lane leading from the High Street to the back of
*** college, where W— kept his rooms. He seemed
thoughtful, and more reconciled. I ventured to rally him –
finding him in a better mood – upon a representation of
the Artist Evangelist, which the old man, whose affairs
were beginning to flourish, had caused to be set up in a
splendid sort of frame over his really handsome shop,
either as a token of prosperity, or badge of gratitude to
his saint. W— looked up at the Luke, and, like Satan,
'knew his mounted sign – and fled'. A letter on his father's
table the next morning, announced that he had accepted
a commission in a regiment about to embark for Portugal.
He was among the first who perished before the walls of
St Sebastian.

I do not know how, upon a subject which I began with
treating half seriously, I should have fallen upon a recital
so eminently painful; but this theme of poor relationship
is replete with so much matter for tragic as well as comic
associations, that it is difficult to keep the account distinct
without blending. The earliest impressions which I received on this matter, are certainly not attended with
anything painful, or very humiliating, in the recalling.
At my father's table (no very splendid one) was to be

found, every Saturday, the mysterious figure of an aged
gentleman, clothed in neat black, of a sad yet comely
appearance. His deportment was of the essence of gravity;
his words few or none; and I was not to make a noise in
his presence. I had little inclination to have done so – for
my cue was to admire in silence. A particular elbow chair
was appropriated to him, which was in no case to be
violated. A peculiar sort of sweet pudding, which appeared
on no other occasion, distinguished the days of his coming.
I used to think him a prodigiously rich man. All I could
make out of him was, that he and my father had been
schoolfellows a world ago at Lincoln, and that he came
from the Mint. The Mint I knew to be a place where all
the money was coined – and I thought he was the owner
of all that money. Awful ideas of the Tower twined
themselves about his presence. He seemed above human
infirmities and passions. A sort of melancholy grandeur
invested him. From some inexplicable doom I fancied
him obliged to go about in an eternal suit of mourning;
a captive – a stately being, let out of the Tower on
Saturdays. Often have I wondered at the temerity of my
father, who, in spite of an habitual general respect which
we all in common manifested towards him, would venture
now and then to stand up against him in some argument,
touching their youthful days. The houses of the ancient
city of Lincoln are divided (as most of my readers know)
between the dwellers on the hill, and in the valley. This
marked distinction formed an obvious division between
the boys who lived above (however brought together in a
common school) and the boys whose paternal residence
was on the plain; a sufficient cause of hostility in the code
of these young Grotiuses. My father had been a leading
Mountaineer; and would still maintain the general superiority, in skill and hardihood, of the *Above Boys* (his own

faction) over the *Below Boys* (so were they called), of which
party his contemporary had been a chieftain. Many and
hot were the skirmishes on this topic – the only one upon
which the old gentleman was ever brought out – and bad
blood bred; even sometimes almost to the recommencement (so I expected) of actual hostilities. But my father,
who scorned to insist upon advantages, generally contrived to turn the conversation upon some adroit by-
commendation of the old Minster: in the general preference of which, before all other cathedrals in the island,
the dweller on the hill, and the plain-born, could meet
on a conciliating level, and lay down their less important
differences. Once only I saw the old gentleman really
ruffled, and I remembered with anguish the thought that
came over me: 'Perhaps he will never come here again.'
He had been pressed to take another plate of the viand,
which I have already mentioned as the indispensable
concomitant of his visits. He had refused with a resistance
amounting to rigour – when my aunt, an old Lincolnian,
but who had something of this in common with my cousin
Bridget, that she would sometimes press civility out of
season – uttered the following memorable application –
'Do take another slice, Mr Billet, for you do not get
pudding every day.' The old gentleman said nothing at
the time – but he took occasion in the course of the
evening, when some argument had intervened between
them, to utter with an emphasis which chilled the company, and which chills me now as I write it – 'Woman,
you are superannuated.' John Billet did not survive long,
after the digesting of this affront; but he survived long
enough to assure me that peace was actually restored!
and, if I remember aright, another pudding was discreetly
substituted in the place of that which had occasioned the
offence. He died at the Mint (anno 1781) where he had

long held, what he accounted, a comfortable independence; and with five pounds, fourteen shillings, and a
penny, which were found in his escritoire after his decease,
left the world, blessing God that he had enough to bury
him, and that he had never been obliged to any man for
a sixpence. This was – a Poor Relation.

The Convalescent

A PRETTY severe fit of indisposition which, under the
name of a nervous fever, has made a prisoner of me for
some weeks past, and is but slowly leaving me, has reduced
me to an incapacity of reflecting upon any topic foreign
to itself. Expect no healthy conclusions from me this
month, reader; I can offer you only sick men's dreams.

And truly the whole state of sickness is such; for what
else is it but a magnificent dream for a man to lie a-bed,
and draw daylight curtains about him; and, shutting out
the sun, to induce a total oblivion of all the works which
are going on under it? To become insensible to all the
operations of life, except the beatings of one feeble pulse?

If there be a regal solitude, it is a sick bed. How the
patient lords it there; what caprices he acts without control! how kinglike he sways his pillow – tumbling, and
tossing, and shifting, and lowering, and thumping, and
flatting, and moulding it, to the ever varying requisitions
of his throbbing temples.

He changes *sides* oftener than a politician. Now he lies
full length, then half-length, obliquely, transversely, head
and feet quite across the bed; and none accuses him of
tergiversation. Within the four curtains he is absolute.
They are his Mare Clausum.

How sickness enlarges the dimensions of a man's self to himself! he is his own exclusive object. Supreme selfishness is inculcated upon him as his only duty. 'Tis the Two Tables of the Law to him. He has nothing to think of but how to get well. What passes out of doors, or within them, so he hear not the jarring of them, affects him not.

A little while ago he was greatly concerned in the event of a law-suit, which was to be the making or the marring of his dearest friend. He was to be seen trudging about upon this man's errand to fifty quarters of the town at once, jogging this witness, refreshing that solicitor. The cause was to come on yesterday. He is absolutely as indifferent to the decision, as if it were a question to be tried at Pekin. Peradventure from some whispering, going on about the house, not intended for his hearing, he picks up enough to make him understand, that things went cross-grained in the Court yesterday, and his friend is ruined. But the word 'friend', and the word 'ruin', disturb him no more than so much jargon. He is not to think of anything but how to get better.

What a world of foreign cares are merged in that absorbing consideration!

He has put on his strong armour of sickness, he is wrapped in the callous hide of suffering, he keeps his sympathy, like some curious vintage, under trusty lock and key, for his own use only.

He lies pitying himself, honing and moaning to himself; he yearneth over himself; his bowels are even melted within him, to think what he suffers; he is not ashamed to weep over himself.

He is for ever plotting how to do some good to himself; studying little stratagems and artificial alleviations.

He makes the most of himself; dividing himself, by an allowable fiction, into as many distinct individuals, as he

hath sore and sorrowing members. Sometimes he medi-
tates – as of a thing apart from him – upon his poor
aching head, and that dull pain which, dozing or waking,
lay in it all the past night like a log, or palpable substance
of pain, not to be removed without opening the very
skull, as it seemed, to take it thence. Or he pities his long,
clammy, attenuated fingers. He compassionates himself
all over; and his bed is a very discipline of humanity, and
tender heart.

He is his own sympathizer; and instinctively feels that
none can so well perform that office for him. He cares for
few spectators to his tragedy. Only that punctual face of
the old nurse pleases him, that announces his broths, and
his cordials. He likes it because it is so unmoved, and
because he can pour forth his feverish ejaculations before
it as unreservedly as to his bed-post.

To the world's business he is dead. He understands not
what the callings and occupations of mortals are; only he
has a glimmering conceit of some such thing, when the
doctor makes his daily call: and even in the lines on that
busy face he reads no multiplicity of patients, but solely
conceives of himself as *the sick man*. To what other uneasy
couch the good man is hastening, when he slips out of his
chamber, folding up his thin douceur so carefully for fear
of rustling – is no speculation which he can at present
entertain. He thinks only of the regular return of the same
phenomenon at the same hour to-morrow.

Household rumours touch him not. Some faint murmur,
indicative of life going on within the house, soothes him,
while he knows not distinctly what it is. He is not to know
anything, not to think of anything. Servants gliding up
or down the distant staircase, treading as upon velvet,
gently keep his ear awake, so long as he troubles not
himself further than with some feeble guess at their

errands. Exacter knowledge would be a burthen to him: he can just endure the pressure of conjecture. He opens his eye faintly at the dull stroke of the muffled knocker, and closes it again without asking 'Who was it?' He is flattered by a general notion that inquiries are making after him, but he cares not to know the name of the inquirer. In the general stillness, and awful hush of the house, he lies in state, and feels his sovereignty.

To be sick is to enjoy monarchal prerogatives. Compare the silent tread, and quiet ministry, almost by the eye only, with which he is served – with the careless demeanour, the unceremonious goings in and out (slapping of doors, or leaving them open) of the very same attendants when he is getting a little better – and you will confess, that from the bed of sickness (throne let me rather call it) to the elbow chair of convalescence, is a fall from dignity, amounting to a deposition.

How convalescence shrinks a man back to his pristine stature! where is now the space, which he occupied so lately, in his own, in the family's eye?

The scene of his regalities, his sick room, which was his presence chamber, where he lay and acted his despotic fancies – how is it reduced to a common bed-room! The trimness of the very bed has something petty and unmeaning about it. It is *made* every day. How unlike to that wavy, many-furrowed, oceanic surface, which it presented so short a time since, when to *make* it was a service not to be thought of at oftener than three or four day revolutions, when the patient was with pain and grief to be lifted for a little while out of it, to submit to the encroachments of unwelcome neatness, and decencies which his shaken frame deprecated; then to be lifted into it again, for another three or four days' respite, to flounder it out of shape again, while every fresh furrow was an historical record of some shifting posture, some uneasy turning, some seeking for a little ease; and the shrunken skin scarce told a truer story than the crumpled coverlid.

Hushed are those mysterious sighs – those groans – so much more awful, while we knew not from what caverns of vast hidden suffering they proceeded. The Lernean pangs are quenched. The riddle of sickness is solved; and Philoctetes is become an ordinary personage.

Perhaps some relic of the sick man's dream of greatness survives in the still lingering visitations of the medical attendant. But how is he too changed with everything else! Can this be he – this man of news – of chat – of anecdote – of everything but physic – can this be he, who so lately came between the patient and his cruel enemy, as on some solemn embassy from Nature, erecting herself into a high mediating party? – Pshaw! 'tis some old woman.

Farewell with him all that made sickness pompous – the spell that hushed the household – the desert-like stillness, felt throughout its inmost chambers – the mute attendance – the inquiry by looks – the still softer delicacies of self-attention – the sole and single eye of distemper alonely fixed upon itself – world-thoughts excluded – the man a world unto himself – his own theatre:

What a speck is he dwindled into!

In this flat swamp of convalescence, left by the ebb of sickness, yet far enough from the terra firma of established health, your note, dear Editor, reached me requesting – an article. In Articulo Mortis, thought I; but it is something hard – and the quibble, wretched as it was, relieved me. The summons, unseasonable as it appeared, seemed to link me on again to the petty businesses of life, which I had lost sight of; a gentle call to activity, however trivial; a wholesome weaning from that preposterous dream of self-absorption – the puffy state of sickness – in which I confess to have lain so long, insensible to the magazines and monarchies of the world alike; to its laws and to its literature. The hypochondriac flatus is subsiding; the acres, which in imagination I had spread over – for the sick man swells in the sole contemplation of his single sufferings, till he becomes a Tityus to himself – are wasting to a span; and for the giant of self-importance, which I was so lately, you have me once again in my natural pretensions – the lean and meagre figure of your insignificant Essayist.

The Superannuated Man

If peradventure, Reader, it has been thy lot to waste the golden years of thy life – thy shining youth – in the irksome confinement of an office; to have thy prison days prolonged through middle-age down to decrepitude and silver hairs, without hope of release or respite; to have lived to forget that there are such things as holidays, or to remember them but as the prerogatives of childhood; then, and then only, will you be able to appreciate my deliverance.

It is now six and thirty years since I took my seat at the desk in Mincing Lane. Melancholy was the transition at fourteen from the abundant playtime, and the frequently intervening vacations of school days, to the eight, nine, and sometimes ten hours' a day attendance at a counting-house. But time partially reconciles us to anything. I gradually became content – doggedly content, as wild animals in cages.

It is true I had my Sundays to myself; but Sundays, admirable as the institution of them is for purposes of worship, are for that very reason the very worst adapted for days of unbending and recreation. In particular, there is a gloom for me attendant upon a city Sunday, a weight in the air. I miss the cheerful cries of London, the music, and the ballad-singers – the buzz and stirring murmur of the streets. Those eternal bells depress me. The closed shops repel me. Prints, pictures, all the glittering and endless succession of knacks and gew-gaws, and ostentatiously displayed wares of tradesmen, which make a weekday saunter through the less busy parts of the metropolis so delightful – are shut out. No bookstalls deliciously to idle over – No busy faces to recreate the idle man who contemplates them ever passing by – the very face of business a charm by contrast to this temporary relaxation from it. Nothing to be seen but unhappy countenances – or half-happy at best – of emancipated 'prentices and little tradesfolk, with here and there a servant maid that has got leave to go out, who, slaving all the week, with the habit has lost almost the capacity of enjoying a free hour; and livelily expressing the hollowness of a day's pleasuring. The very strollers in the fields on that day looked anything but comfortable.

But besides Sundays I had a day at Easter, and a day at Christmas, with a full week in the summer to go and air myself in my native fields of Hertfordshire. This last was a great indulgence; and the prospect of its recurrence, I believe, alone kept me up through the year, and made my durance tolerable. But when the week came round, did the glittering phantom of the distance keep touch with me? or rather was it not a series of seven uneasy days, spent in restless pursuit of pleasure, and a wearisome anxiety to find out how to make the most of them? Where was the quiet, where the promised rest? Before I had a taste of it, it was vanished. I was at the desk again, counting upon the fifty-one tedious weeks that must intervene before such another snatch would come. Still the prospect of its coming threw something of an illumination upon the darker side of my captivity. Without it, as I have said, I could scarcely have sustained my thraldom.

Independently of the rigours of attendance, I have ever been haunted with a sense (perhaps a mere caprice) of incapacity for business. This, during my latter years, had increased to such a degree, that it was visible in all the lines of my countenance. My health and my good spirits flagged. I had perpetually a dread of some crisis, to which I should be found unequal. Besides my daylight servitude, I served over again all night in my sleep, and would awake with terrors of imaginary false entries, errors in my accounts, and the like. I was fifty years of age, and no prospect of emancipation presented itself. I had grown to my desk, as it were; and the wood had entered into my soul.

My fellows in the office would sometimes rally me upon the trouble legible in my countenance; but I did not know that it had raised the suspicions of any of my employers, when on the 5th of last month, a day ever to be remembered by me, L—, the junior partner in the firm, calling me on one side, directly taxed me with my bad looks, and frankly inquired the cause of them. So taxed, I honestly made confession of my infirmity, and added that I was afraid I should eventually be obliged to resign his service. He spoke some words of course to hearten me, and there the matter rested. A whole week I remained labouring under the impression that I had acted imprudently in my disclosure; that I had foolishly given a handle against myself, and had been anticipating my own dismissal. A week passed in this manner, the most anxious one, I verily believe, in my whole life, when on the evening of the 12th of April, just as I was about quitting my desk to go home (it might be about eight o'clock) I received an awful summons to attend the presence of the whole assembled firm in the formidable back parlour. I thought now my time is surely come, I have done for myself, I am going to be told that they have no longer occasion for me. L—, I could see, smiled at the terror I was in, which was a little relief to me, – when to my utter astonishment B—, the eldest partner, began a formal harangue to me on the length of my services, my very meritorious conduct during the whole of the time (the deuce, thought I, how did he find out that? I protest I never had the confidence to think as much). He went on to descant on the expediency of retiring at a certain time of life (how my heart panted!), and asking me a few questions as to the amount of my own property, of which I have a little, ended with a proposal, to which his three partners nodded a grave assent, that I should accept from the house, which I had served so well, a pension for life to the amount of two-thirds of my accustomed salary – a magnificent offer! I do not know what I answered between surprise and gratitude, but it was understood that I accepted their proposal, and I was told that I was free from that hour to leave their service. I stammered out a bow, and at just ten minutes after eight I went home – for ever. This noble benefit – gratitude forbids me to conceal their names – I owe to the kindness of the most munificent firm in the world – the house of Boldero, Merryweather, Bosanquet, and Lacy.

Esto perpetua!

For the first day or two I felt stunned, overwhelmed. I

could only apprehend my felicity; I was too confused to taste it sincerely. I wandered about, thinking I was happy, and knowing that I was not. I was in the condition of a prisoner in the Old Bastile, suddenly let loose after a forty years' confinement. I could scarce trust myself with myself. It was like passing out of Time to Eternity – for it is a sort of Eternity for a man to have his Time all to himself. It seemed to me that I had more time on my hands than I could ever manage. From a poor man, poor in Time, I was suddenly lifted up into a vast revenue; I could see no end of my possessions; I wanted some steward, or judicious bailiff, to manage my estates in Time for me. And here let me caution persons grown old in active business, not lightly, not without weighing their own resources, to forego their customary employment all at once, for there may be danger in it. I feel it by myself, but I know that my resources are sufficient; and now that those first giddy raptures have subsided, I have a quiet home-feeling of the blessedness of my condition. I am in no hurry. Having all holidays, I am as though I had none. If Time hung heavy upon me, I could walk it away; but I do *not* walk all day long, as I used to do in those old transient holidays, thirty miles a day, to make the most of them. If Time were troublesome, I could read it away, but I do *not* read in that violent measure, with which, having no Time my own but candlelight Time, I used to weary out my head and eye-sight in bygone winters. I walk, read, or scribble (as now) just when the fit seizes me. I no longer hunt after pleasure; I let it come to me. I am like the man

> *that's born, and has his years come to him,*
> *In some green desert.*

'Years,' you will say; 'what is this superannuated

simpleton calculating upon? He has already told us he is past fifty.'

I have indeed lived nominally fifty years, but deduct out of them the hours which I have lived to other people, and not to myself, and you will find me still a young fellow. For *that* is the only true Time, which a man can properly call his own, that which he has all to himself; the rest, though in some sense he may be said to live it, is other people's time, not his. The remnant of my poor days, long or short, is at least multiplied for me threefold. My ten next years, if I stretch so far, will be as long as any preceding thirty. 'Tis a fair rule-of-three sum.

Among the strange fantasies which beset me at the commencement of my freedom, and of which all traces are not yet gone, one was, that a vast tract of time had intervened since I quitted the Counting House. I could not conceive of it as an affair of yesterday. The partners, and the clerks with whom I had for so many years, and for so many hours in each day of the year, been so closely associated – being suddenly removed from them – they seemed as dead to me. There is a fine passage, which may serve to illustrate this fancy, in a Tragedy, by Sir Robert Howard, speaking of a friend's death:

> *'Twas but just now he went away;*
> *I have not since had time to shed a tear;*
> *And yet the distance does the same appear*
> *As if he had been a thousand years from me.*
> *Time takes no measure in eternity.*

To dissipate this awkward feeling, I have been fain to go among them once or twice since; to visit my old desk-fellows – my co-brethren of the quill – that I had left below in the state militant. Not all the kindness with which they received me could quite restore to me that pleasant familiarity, which I had heretofore enjoyed among them. We cracked some of our old jokes, but methought they went off but faintly. My old desk; the peg where I hung my hat, were appropriated to another. I knew it must be, but I could not take it kindly. D——l take me if I did not feel some remorse – beast, if I had not, – at quitting my old compeers, the faithful partners of my toils for six and thirty years, that smoothed for me with their jokes and conundrums the ruggedness of my professional road. Had it been so rugged then after all? or was I a coward simply? Well, it is too late to repent; and I also know, that these suggestions are a common fallacy of the mind on such occasions. But my heart smote me. I had violently broken the bands betwixt us. It was at least not courteous. I shall be some time before I get quite reconciled to the separation. Farewell, old cronies, yet not for long, for again and again I will come among ye, if I shall have your leave. Farewell, Ch——, dry, sarcastic, and friendly! Do——, mild, slow to move, and gentlemanly! Pl——, officious to do, and to volunteer, good services! – and thou, thou dreary pile, fit mansion for a Gresham or a Whittington of old, stately House of Merchants; with thy labyrinthine passages, and light-excluding, pent-up offices, where candles for one half the year supplied the place of the sun's light; unhealthy contributor to my weal, stern fosterer of my living, farewell! In thee remain, and not in the obscure collection of some wandering bookseller, my 'works'! There let them rest, as I do from my labours, piled on thy massy shelves, more MSS. in folio than ever Aquinas left, and full as useful! My mantle I bequeath among ye.

A fortnight has passed since the date of my first communication. At that period I was approaching to tranquillity, but had not reached it. I boasted of a calm indeed, but it was comparative only. Something of the first flutter was left; an unsettling sense of novelty; the dazzle to weak eyes of unaccustomed light. I missed my old chains, forsooth, as if they had been some necessary part of my apparel. I was a poor Carthusian, from strict cellular discipline suddenly by some revolution returned upon the world. I am now as if I had never been other than my own master. It is natural to me to go where I please, to do what I please. I find myself at eleven o'clock in the day in Bond Street, and it seems to me that I have been sauntering there at that very hour for years past. I digress into Soho, to explore a book-stall. Methinks I have been thirty years a collector. There is nothing strange nor new in it. I find myself before a fine picture in the morning. Was it ever otherwise? What is become of Fish Street Hill? Where is Fenchurch Street? Stone of old Mincing Lane which I have worn with my daily pilgrimage for six and thirty years, to the footsteps of what toil-worn clerk are your everlasting flints now vocal? I indent the gayer flags of Pall Mall. It is 'Change time, and I am strangely among the Elgin marbles. It was no hyperbole when I ventured to compare the change in my condition to a passing into another world. Time stands still in a manner to me. I have lost all distinction of season. I do not know the day of the week, or of the month. Each day used to be individually felt by me in its reference to the foreign post days; in its distance from, or propinquity to, the next Sunday. I had my Wednesday feelings, my Saturday nights' sensations. The genius of each day was upon me distinctly during the whole of it, affecting my appetite, spirits, etc. The phantom of the next day, with the dreary five to follow, safe as a load upon my poor Sabbath recreations. What charm has washed the Ethiop white? – What is gone of Black Monday? All days are the same. Sunday itself – that unfortunate failure of a holiday as it

too often proved, what with my sense of its fugitiveness,
and over-care to get the greatest quantity of pleasure out
of it – is melted down into a week day. I can spare to go to
church now, without grudging the huge cantle which it
used to seem to cut out of the holiday. I have Time for
everything. I can visit a sick friend. I can interrupt the
man of much occupation when he is busiest. I can insult
over him with an invitation to take a day's pleasure with
me to Windsor this fine May-morning. It is Lucretian
pleasure to behold the poor drudges, whom I have left
behind in the world, carking and caring; like horses in a
mill, drudging on in the same eternal round – and what is
it all for? A man can never have too much Time to himself,
nor too little to do. Had I a little son, I would christen him
NOTHING-TO-DO; he should do nothing. Man, I verily
believe, is out of his element as long as he is operative. I
am altogether for the life contemplative. Will no kindly
earthquake come and swallow up those accursed cotton
mills? Take me that lumber of a desk there, and bowl it
down

> *As low as to the fiends.*

I am no longer —, clerk to the firm of, etc. I am
Retired Leisure. I am to be met with in trim gardens. I am
already come to be known by my vacant face and careless
gesture, perambulating at no fixed pace nor with any
settled purpose. I walk about; not to and from. They tell
me, a certain *cum dignitate* air, that has been buried so long
with my other good parts, has begun to shoot forth in my
person. I grow into gentility perceptibly. When I take up
a newspaper it is to read the state of the opera. *Opus
operatum est.* I have done all that I came into this world to
do. I have worked task-work, and have the rest of the day
to myself.

In Praise of Chimney-sweepers

I LIKE to meet a sweep – understand me – not a grown sweeper – old chimney-sweepers are by no means attractive – but one of those tender novices, blooming through their first nigritude, the maternal washings not quite effaced from the cheek – such as come forth with the dawn, or somewhat earlier, with their little professional notes sounding like the *peep peep* of a young sparrow; or liker to the matin lark should I pronounce them, in their aerial ascents not seldom anticipating the sunrise?

I have a kindly yearning toward these dim specks – poor blots – innocent blacknesses.

I reverence these young Africans of our own growth, these almost clergy imps, who sport their cloth without assumption; and from their little pulpits (the tops of chimneys), in the nipping air of a December morning, preach a lesson of patience to mankind.

When a child, what a mysterious pleasure it was to witness their operation! to see a chit no bigger than one's-self enter, one knew not by what process, into what seemed the *fauces Averni* – to pursue him in imagination, as he went sounding on through so many dark stifling caverns, horrid shades! – to shudder with the idea that 'now, surely he must be lost for ever'! – to revive at hearing his feeble shout of discovered daylight – and then (O fulness of delight) running out of doors, to come just in time to see the sable phenomenon emerge in safety, the brandished weapon of his art victorious like some flag waved over a conquered citadel! I seem to remember having been told, that a bad sweep was once left in a stack with his brush, to indicate which way the wind blew. It was an awful spectacle certainly; not much unlike the old stage direction in

Macbeth where the 'Apparition of a child crowned with a tree in his hand rises.'

Reader, if thou meetest one of these small gentry in thy early rambles, it is good to give him a penny. It is better to give him twopence. If it be starving weather, and to the proper troubles of his hard occupation, a pair of kibed heels (no unusual accompaniment) be superadded, the demand of thy humanity will surely rise to a tester.

There is a composition, the groundwork of which I have understood to be the sweet wood yclept sassafras. This wood boiled down to a kind of tea, and tempered with an infusion of milk and sugar, hath to some tastes a delicacy beyond the China luxury. I know not how thy palate may relish it; myself, with every deference to the judicious Mr Read, who hath time out of mind kept open a shop (the only one he avers in London) for the vending of this 'wholesome and pleasant beverage', on the south side of Fleet-street, as thou approachest Bridge-street – *the only Salopian house* – I have never yet adventured to dip my own particular lip in a basin of his commended ingredients – a cautious premonition to the olfactories constantly whispering to me, that my stomach must infallibly, with all due courtesy, decline it. Yet I have seen palates, otherwise not uninstructed in dietetical elegances, sup it up with avidity.

I know not by what particular conformation of the organ it happens, but I have always found that this composition is surprisingly gratifying to the palate of a young chimney-sweeper – whether the oily particles (sassafras is slightly oleaginous) do attenuate and soften the fuliginous concretions, which are sometimes found (in dissections) to adhere to the roof of the mouth in these unfledged practitioners; or whether Nature, sensible that she had mingled too much of bitter wood in the lot of these raw victims,

caused to grow out of the earth her sassafras for a sweet
lenitive – but so it is, that no possible taste or odour to the
senses of a young chimney-sweeper can convey a delicate
excitement comparable to this mixture. Being penniless,
they will yet hang their black heads over the ascending
steam, to gratify one sense if possible, seemingly no less
pleased than those domestic animals – cats – when they
purr over a new found sprig of valerian. There is something more in these sympathies than philosophy can
inculcate.

Now albeit Mr Read boasteth, not without reason, that
his is the *only Salopian house*; yet be it known to thee, reader
– if thou art one who keepest what are called good hours,
thou art haply ignorant of the fact – he hath a race of
industrious imitators, who from stalls, and under open sky,
dispense the same savoury mess to humbler customers, at
that dead time of the dawn, when (as extremes meet) the
rake, reeling home from his midnight cups, and the hard-
handed artisan leaving his bed to resume the premature
labour of the day, jostle, not infrequently to the manifest
disconcerting of the former, for the honours of the pavement. It is the time when, in summer, between the expired
and the not yet relumined kitchen-fires, the kennels of our
fair metropolis give forth their least satisfactory odours.
The rake, who wisheth to dissipate his o'er-night vapours
in more grateful coffee, curses the ungenial fume, as he
passeth; but the artisan stops to taste, and blesses the
fragrant breakfast.

This is *Saloop* – the precocious herb-woman's darling –
the delight of the early gardener, who transports his
smoking cabbages by break of day from Hammersmith to
Covent-garden's famed piazzas – the delight, and, oh I
fear, too often the envy, of the unpennied sweep. Him
shouldest thou haply encounter, with his dim visage

pendent over the grateful steam, regale him with a sump-
tuous basin (it will cost thee but three half-pennies) and a
slice of delicate bread and butter (an added halfpenny) – so
may thy culinary fires, eased of the o'er-charged secretions
from thy worse placed hospitalities, curl up a lighter
volume to the welkin – so may the descending soot never
taint thy costly well-ingredienced soups – nor the odious
cry, quick-reaching from street to street, of the *fired chimney*, invite the rattling engines from ten adjacent parishes,
to disturb for a casual scintillation thy peace and pocket!

I am by nature extremely susceptible of street affronts;
the jeers and taunts of the populace; the low-bred
triumph they display over the casual trip, or splashed
stocking, of a gentleman. Yet can I endure the jocularity
of a young sweep with something more than forgiveness.
In the last winter but one, pacing along Cheapside with
my accustomed precipitation when I walk westward, a
treacherous slide brought me upon my back in an instant.
I scrambled up with pain and shame enough – yet out-
wardly trying to face it down, as if nothing had happened
– when the roguish grin of one of these young wits en-
countered me. There he stood, pointing me out with his
dusky finger to the mob, and to a poor woman (I suppose
his mother) in particular, till the tears for the exquisiteness
of the fun (so he thought it) worked themselves out at the
corners of his poor red eyes, red for many a previous weeping, and soot-inflamed, yet twinkling through all with such
a joy, snatched out of desolation, that Hogarth – but
Hogarth has got him already (how could he miss him?)
in the March to Finchley, grinning at the pye-man – there
he stood, as he stands in the picture, irremovable, as if the
jest was to last for ever – with such a maximum of glee,
and minimum of mischief, in his mirth – for the grin of a
genuine sweep hath absolutely no malice in it – that I

could have been content, if the honour of a gentleman might endure it, to have remained his butt and his mockery till midnight.

I am by theory obdurate to the seductiveness of what are called a fine set of teeth. Every pair of rosy lips (the ladies must pardon me) is a casket, presumably holding such jewels; but methinks, they should take leave to 'air' them as frugally as possible. The fine lady, or fine gentleman, who show me their teeth, show me bones. Yet must I confess, that from the mouth of a real sweep a display (even to ostentation) of those white and shining ossifications, strikes me as an agreeable anomaly in manners, and an allowable piece of foppery. It is, as when

> *A sable cloud*
> *Turns forth her silver lining on the night.*

It is like some remnant of gentry not quite extinct; a badge of better days; a hint of nobility: – and, doubtless, under the obscuring darkness and double night of their forlorn disguisement, oftentimes lurketh good blood, and gentle condition derived from lost ancestry and a lapsed pedigree. The premature apprenticements of these tender victims give but too much encouragement, I fear, to clandestine, and almost infantile abductions; the seeds of civility and true courtesy, so often discernible in these young grafts (not otherwise to be accounted for) plainly hint at some forced adoptions; many noble Rachels mourning for their children, even in our days, countenance the fact; the tales of fairy-spiriting may shadow a lamentable verity, and the recovery of the young Montagu be but a solitary instance of good fortune, out of many irreparable and hopeless *defiliations*.

In one of the state-beds at Arundel Castle, a few years since – under a ducal canopy – (that seat of the Howards

is an object of curiosity to visitors, chiefly for its beds, in
which the late Duke was especially a connoisseur) –
encircled with curtains of delicatest crimson, with starry
coronets inwoven – folded between a pair of sheets whiter
and softer than the lap where Venus Ascanius was discovered by chance, after all methods of search had failed,
at noon-day, fast asleep, a lost chimney-sweeper. The
little creature, having somehow confounded his passage
among the intricacies of those lordly chimneys, by some
unknown aperture had alighted upon this magnificent
chamber; and, tired with his tedious explorations, was
unable to resist the delicious invitement to repose, which
he there saw exhibited; so, creeping between the sheets
very quietly, laid his black head upon the pillow, and
slept like a young Howard.

Such is the account given to the visitors at the Castle.
But I cannot help seeming to perceive a confirmation of
what I have just hinted at in this story. A high instinct was
at work in the case, or I am mistaken. Is it probable that a
poor child of that description, with whatever weariness he
might be visited, would have ventured, under such a
penalty as he would be taught to expect, to uncover the
sheets of a Duke's bed, and deliberately to lay himself
down between them, when the rug, or the carpet, presented an obvious couch, still far above his pretensions –
is this probable, I would ask, if the great power of nature,
which I contend for, had not been manifested within him,
prompting to the adventure? Doubtless this young noble-
man (for such my mind misgives me that he must be) was
allured by some memory, not amounting to full consciousness, of his condition in infancy, when he was used
to be lapt by his mother, or his nurse, in just such sheets
as he there found, into which he was now but creeping
back as into his proper *incunabula*, and resting-place. By

no other theory, than by this sentiment of a pre-existent
state (as I may call it), can I explain a deed so venturous,
and, indeed, upon any other system, indecorous, in this
tender, but unseasonable, sweeper.

My pleasant friend Jem White was so impressed with a
belief of metamorphosis like this frequently taking place,
that in some sort to reverse the wrongs of fortune in these
poor changelings, he instituted an annual feast of chimney-
sweepers, at which it was his pleasure to officiate as host
and waiter. It was a solemn supper held in Smithfield,
upon the yearly return of the fair of St Bartholomew.
Cards were issued a week before to the master-sweeps in
and about the metropolis, confining the invitation to their
younger fry. Now and then an elderly stripling would get
in among us, and be good-naturedly winked at; but our
main body were infantry. One unfortunate wight, indeed,
who, relying upon his dusky soot, had intruded himself
into our party, but by tokens was providentially discovered in time to be no chimney-sweeper (all is not soot
which looks so,) was quoited out of the presence with
universal indignation, as not having on the wedding garment; but in general the greatest harmony prevailed. The
place chosen was a convenient spot among the pens, at the
north side of the fair, not so far distant as to be impervious
to the agreeable hubbub of that vanity, but remote enough
not to be obvious to the interruption of every gaping
spectator in it. The guests assembled about seven. In
those little temporary parlours three tables were spread
with napery, not so fine as substantial, and at every board
a comely hostess presided with her pan of hissing sausages.
The nostrils of the young rogues dilated at the savour.
James White, as head waiter, had charge of the first table;
and myself, with our trusty companion Bigod, ordinarily
ministered to the other two. There was clambering and

jostling, you may be sure, who should get at the first table
– for Rochester in his maddest days could not have done
the humours of the scene with more spirit than my friend.
After some general expression of thanks for the honour the
company had done him, his inaugural ceremony was to
clasp the greasy waist of old dame Ursula (the fattest of the
three), that stood frying and fretting, half-blessing, half-
cursing 'the gentleman', and imprint upon her chaste lips
a tender salute, whereat the universal host would set up a
shout that tore the concave, while hundreds of grinning
teeth startled the night with their brightness. O it was a
pleasure to see the sable younkers lick in the unctuous
meat, with his more unctuous sayings – how he would fit
the tit-bits to the puny mouths, reserving the lengthier
links for the seniors – how he would intercept a morsel
even in the jaws of some young desperado, declaring it
'must to the pan again to be browned, for it was not fit for
a gentleman's eating' – how he would recommend this
slice of white bread, or that piece of kissing-crust, to a
tender juvenile, advising them all to have a care of crack-
ing their teeth, which were their best patrimony, – how
genteelly he would deal about the small ale, as if it were
wine, naming the brewer, and protesting if it were not
good, he should lose their custom; with a special recom-
mendation to wipe the lip before drinking. Then we had
our toasts – 'The King', – the 'Cloth', – which, whether
they understood or not, was equally diverting and flattering; – and for a crowning sentiment, which never failed,
'May the British supersede the Laurel!' All these, and
fifty other fancies, which were rather felt than comprehended by his guests, would he utter, standing upon tables
and prefacing every sentiment with a 'Gentlemen, give me
leave to propose so and so.' Which was prodigious comfort
to those young orphans; every now and then stuffing into

his mouth (for it did not do to be squeamish on these occasions) indiscriminate pieces of those reeking sausages which pleased them mightily, and was the savouriest part, you may believe, of the entertainment.

> *Golden lads and lasses must,*
> *As chimney-sweepers, come to dust —*

James White is extinct, and with him those suppers have long ceased. He carried away with him half the fun of the world when he died – of my world at least. His old clients look for him among the pens; and, missing him, reproach the altered feast of St Bartholomew, and the glory of Smithfield departed for ever.

WILLIAM HAZLITT

On Going a Journey

ONE of the pleasantest things in the world is going a journey; but I like to go by myself. I can enjoy society in a room; but out of doors, nature is company enough for me. I am then never less alone than when alone.

> *The fields his study, nature was his book.*

I cannot see the wit of walking and talking at the same time. When I am in the country I wish to vegetate like the country. I am not for criticizing hedgerows and black cattle. I go out of town in order to forget the town and all that is in it. There are those who for this purpose go to watering-places, and carry the metropolis with them. I like more elbow-room and fewer encumbrances. I like solitude, when I give myself up to it, for the sake of solitude; nor do I ask for

> *a friend in my retreat,*
> *Whom I may whisper solitude is sweet.*

The soul of a journey is liberty, perfect liberty, to think, feel, do just as one pleases. We go a journey chiefly to be free of all impediments and of all inconveniences, to leave ourselves behind, much more to get rid of others. It is because I want a little breathing space to muse on indifferent matters, where Contemplation

> *May plume her feathers and let grow her wings,*
> *That in the various bustle of resort*
> *Were all too ruffled, and sometimes impair'd.*

that I absent myself from the town for a while, without

feeling at a loss the moment I am left by myself. Instead of a friend in a post-chaise or in a Tilbury, to exchange good things with, and vary the same stale topics over again, for once let me have a truce with impertinence. Give me the clear blue sky over my head, and the green turf beneath my feet, a winding road before me, and a three hours' march to dinner – and then to thinking! It is hard if I cannot start some game on these lone heaths. I laugh, I run, I leap, I sing for joy. From the point of yonder rolling cloud I plunge into my past being, and revel there, as the sunburnt Indian plunges headlong into the wave that wafts him to his native shore. Then long-forgotten things, like 'sunken wrack and sunless treasuries', burst upon my eager sight, and I begin to feel, think, and be myself again. Instead of an awkward silence, broken by attempts at wit or dull common-places, mine is that undisturbed silence of the heart which alone is perfect eloquence. No one likes puns, alliterations, antitheses, arguments, and analysis better than I do; but I sometimes had rather be without them. 'Leave, oh, leave me to my repose!' I have just now other business in hand, which would seem idle to you, but is with me 'very stuff o' the conscience.' Is not this wild rose sweet without a comment? Does not this daisy leap to my heart set in its coat of emerald? Yet if I were to explain to you the circumstance that has so endeared it to me, you would only smile. Had I not better then keep it to myself, and let it serve me to brood over, from here to yonder craggy point, and from thence onward to the far-distant horizon? I should be but bad company all that way, and therefore prefer being alone. I have heard it said that you may, when the moody fit comes on, walk or ride on by yourself, and indulge your reveries. But this looks like a breach of manners, a neglect of others, and you are think-ing all the time that you ought to rejoin your party. 'Out upon such half-faced fellowship,' say I. I like to be either entirely to myself, or entirely at the disposal of others; to talk or be silent, to walk or sit still, to be sociable or solitary. I was pleased with an observation of Mr Cobbett's, that 'he thought it a bad French custom to drink our wine with our meals, and that an Englishman ought to do only one thing at a time.' So I cannot talk and think, or indulge in melancholy musing and lively conversation by fits and starts. 'Let me have a companion of my way,' says Sterne, 'were it but to remark how the shadows lengthen as the sun declines.' It is beautifully said; but, in my opinion, this continual comparing of notes interferes with the involuntary impression of things upon the mind, and hurts the sentiment. If you only hint what you feel in a kind of dumb show, it is insipid: if you have to explain it, it is making a toil of a pleasure. You cannot read the book of nature without being perpetually put to the trouble of translating it for the benefit of others. I am for the synthetical method on a journey in preference to the analytical. I am content to lay in a stock of ideas then, and to examine and anatomize them afterwards. I want to see my vague notions float like the down of the thistle before the breeze, and not to have them entangled in the briars and thorns of controversy. For once, I like to have it all my own way; and this is impossible unless you are alone, or in such company as I do not covet. I have no objection to argue a point with anyone for twenty miles of measured road, but not for pleasure. If you remark the scent of a beanfield crossing the road, perhaps your fellow-traveller has no smell. If you point to a distant object, perhaps he is shortsighted, and has to take out his glass to look at it. There is a feeling in the air, a tone in the colour of a cloud, which hits your fancy, but the effect of which you are unable to account for. There is then no sympathy, but an uneasy craving after it, and a dissatisfaction which pursues you on your way, and in the end probably produces ill-humour. Now I never quarrel with myself, and take all my own conclusions for granted till I find it necessary to defend them against objections. It is not merely that you may not be of accord on the objects and circumstances that present themselves before you – these may recall a number of objects, and lead to associations too delicate and refined to be possibly communicated to others. Yet these I love to cherish, and sometimes still fondly clutch them, when I can escape from the throng to do so. To give way to our feelings before company seems extravagance or affectation; and, on the other hand, to have to unravel this mystery of our being at every turn, and to make others take an equal interest in it (otherwise the end is not answered), is a task to which few are competent. We must 'give it an understanding, but no tongue'. My old friend Coleridge, however, could do both. He could go on in the most delightful explanatory way over hill and dale, a summer's day, and convert a landscape into a didactic poem or a Pindaric ode. 'He talked far above singing.' If I could so clothe my ideas in sounding and flowing words, I might perhaps wish to have someone with me to admire the swelling theme; or I could be more content, were it possible for me to still hear his echoing voice in the woods of All-Foxden. They had 'that fine madness in them which our first poets had'; and if they could have been caught by some rare instrument, would have breathed such strains as the following:

> Here be woods as green
> As any, air likewise as fresh and sweet
> As when smooth Zephyrus plays on the fleet
> Face of the curled stream, with flow'rs as many
> As the young spring gives, and as choice as any;

Here be all new delights, cool streams and wells
Arbours o'ergrown with woodbines, caves and dells;
Choose where thou wilt, whilst I sit by and sing,
Or gather rushes to make many a ring
For thy long fingers; tell thee tales of love,
How the pale Phoebe, hunting in a grove,
First saw the boy Endymion, from whose eyes
She took eternal fire that never dies;
How she convey'd him softly in a sleep,
His temples bound with poppy, to the steep
Head of old Latmos, where she stoops each night,
Gilding the mountain with her brother's light,
To kiss her sweetest.

Had I words and images at command like these, I would attempt to wake the thoughts that lie slumbering on golden ridges in the evening clouds: but at the sight of nature my fancy, poor as it is, droops and closes up its leaves, like flowers at sunset. I can make nothing out on the spot: I must have time to collect myself.

In general, a good thing spoils out-of-door prospects: it should be reserved for Table-talk. Lamb is, for this reason I take it, the worst company in the world out of doors; because he is the best within. I grant there is one subject on which it is pleasant to talk on a journey, and that is, what one shall have for supper when we get to our inn at night. The open air improves this sort of conversation or friendly altercation, by setting a keener edge on appetite. Every mile of the road heightens the flavour of the viands we expect at the end of it. How fine it is to enter some old town, walled and turreted, just at approach of nightfall, or to come to some straggling village, with the lights streaming through the surrounding gloom; and then, after inquiring for the best entertainment that the place affords, to 'take one's ease at one's inn'! These eventful moments in our lives' history are too precious, too full of solid, heartfelt happiness to be frittered and dribbled away in imperfect sympathy. I would have them all to myself, and drain them to the last drop: they will do to talk of or to write about afterwards. What a delicate speculation it is, after drinking whole goblets of tea –

The cups that cheer, but not inebriate –

and letting the fumes ascend into the brain, to sit considering what we shall have for supper – eggs and a rasher, a rabbit smothered in onions, or an excellent veal cutlet! Sancho in such a situation once fixed on cow-heel; and his choice, though he could not help it, is not to be disparaged. Then, in the intervals of pictured scenery and Shandean contemplation, to catch the preparation and the stir in the kitchen (getting ready for the gentleman in the parlour). *Procul, O procul este profani!* These hours are sacred to silence and to musing, to be treasured up in the memory, and to feed the source of smiling thoughts hereafter. I would not waste them in idle talk; or if I must have the integrity of fancy broken in upon, I would rather it were by a stranger than a friend. A stranger takes his hue and character from the time and place; he is a part of the furniture and costume of an inn. If he is a Quaker, or from the West Riding of Yorkshire, so much the better. I do not even try to sympathize with him, and he breaks no squares. (How I love to see the camps of the gypsies, and to sigh my soul into that sort of life. If I express this feeling to another, he may qualify and spoil it with some objection.) I associate nothing with my travelling companion but present objects and passing events. In his ignorance of me and my affairs, I in a manner forget myself. But a friend reminds one of other things, rips up old grievances, and destroys the abstraction of the scene. He comes in ungraciously between us and our imaginary character. Something is dropped in the course of conversation that gives a hint of your profession and pursuits; or from having some one with you that knows the less sublime portions of your history, it seems that other people do. You are no longer a citizen of the world; but your 'unhoused free condition is put into circumspection and confine'. The incognito of an inn is one of its striking privileges – 'lord of one's self, uncumbered with a name.' Oh! it is great to shake off the trammels of the world and of public opinion – to lose our importunate, tormenting, everlasting personal identity in the elements of nature, and become the creature of the moment, clear of all ties – to hold to the universe only by a dish of sweetbreads, and to owe nothing but the score of the evening – and no longer seeking for applause and meeting with contempt, to be known by no other title than *the Gentlemen in the parlour*! One may take one's choice of all characters in this romantic state of uncertainty as to one's real pretensions, and become indefinitely respectable and negatively right worshipful. We baffle prejudice and disappoint conjecture; and from being so to others, begin to be objects of curiosity and wonder even to ourselves. We are no more those hackneyed commonplaces that we appear in the world; an inn restores us to the level of nature, and quits scores with society! I have certainly spent some enviable hours at inns – sometimes when I have been left entirely to myself, and have tried to solve some metaphysical problem, as once at Witham Common, where I found out the proof that likeness is not a case of the association of ideas – at other times, when there have been pictures in the room, as at St Neot's (I think it was), where I first met with Gribelin's engravings of the Cartoons, into which I entered at once, and at a little inn on the borders of Wales,

where there happened to be hanging some of Westall's
drawings, which I compared triumphantly (for a theory
that I had, not for the admired artist) with the figure of a
girl who had ferried me over the Severn, standing up in a
boat between me and the twilight – at other times I might
mention luxuriating in books, with a peculiar interest in
this way, as I remember sitting up half the night to read
Paul and Virginia, which I picked up at an inn at Bridge-
water, after being drenched in the rain all day; and at the
same place I got through two volumes of Madame
d'Arblay's *Camilla*. It was on the 10th April 1798 that I
sat down to a volume of the *New Eloise*, at the inn at
Llangollen, over a bottle of sherry and a cold chicken. The
letter I chose was that in which St Preux describes his
feelings as he first caught a glimpse from the heights of the
Jura of the Pays de Vaud, which I had brought with me
as a *bonne bouche* to crown the evening with. It was my birth-
day, and I had for the first time come from a place in the
neighbourhood to visit this delightful spot. The road to
Llangollen turns off between Chirk and Wrexham; and
on passing a certain point you come all at once upon the
valley, which opens like an amphitheatre, broad, barren
hills rising in majestic state on either side, with 'green
upland swells that echo to the bleat of flocks' below, and
the river Dee babbling over its stony bed in the midst of
them. The valley at this time 'glittered green with sunny
showers', and a budding ash-tree dipped its tender
branches in the chiding stream. How proud, how glad I
was to walk along the high road that overlooks the delicious prospect, repeating the lines which I have just
quoted from Mr Coleridge's poems! But besides the
prospect which opened beneath my feet, another also
opened to my inward sight, a heavenly vision, on which
were written, in letters large as Hope could make them,

these four words, LIBERTY, GENIUS, LOVE, VIRTUE; which have since faded into the light of common day, or mock my idle gaze.

The beautiful is vanished, and returns not.

Still I would return some time or other to this enchanted spot; but I would return to it alone. What other self could I find to share that influx of thoughts, of regret and delight, the fragments of which I could hardly conjure up to myself, so much have they been broken and defaced? I could stand on some tall rock, and overlook the precipice of years that separates me from what I then was. I was at that time going shortly to visit the poet whom I have above named. Where is he now? Not only I myself have changed: the world, which was then new to me, has become old and incorrigible. Yet will I turn to thee in thought, O sylvan Dee, in joy, in youth and gladness as thou then wert; and thou shalt always be to me the river of Paradise, where I will drink of the waters of life freely!

There is hardly anything that shows the short-sightedness or capriciousness of the imagination more than travelling does. With change of place we change our ideas; nay, our opinions and feelings. We can by an effort indeed transport ourselves to old and long-forgotten scenes, and then the picture of the mind revives again; but we forget those that we have just left. It seems that we can think but of one place at a time. The canvas of the fancy is but of a certain extent, and if we paint one set of objects upon it, they immediately efface every other. We cannot enlarge our conceptions, we only shift our point of view. The landscape bares its bosom to the enraptured eye, we take our fill of it, and seem as if we could form no other image of beauty or grandeur. We pass on, and think no more of it; the horizon that shuts

it from our sight also blots it from our memory like a
dream. In travelling through a wild barren country I can
form no idea of a woody and cultivated one. It appears to
me that all the world must be barren, like what I see of it.
In the country we forget the town, and in town we despise
the country. 'Beyond Hyde Park,' says Sir Fopling
Flutter, 'all is a desert.' All that part of the map that we do
not see before us is blank. The world in our conceit of it is
not much bigger than a nutshell. It is not one prospect expanded into another, county joined to county, kingdom
to kingdom, land to seas, making an image voluminous
and vast; – the mind can form no larger idea of space than
the eye can take in at a single glance. The rest is a name
written in a map, a calculation of arithmetic. For instance,
what is the true signification of that immense mass of
territory and population known by the name of China to
us? An inch of pasteboard on a wooden globe, of no more
account than a China orange! Things near us are seen of
the size of life: things at a distance are diminished to the
size of the understanding. We measure the universe by
ourselves, and even comprehend the texture of our own
being only piecemeal. In this way, however, we remember
an infinity of things and places. The mind is like a mechanical instrument that plays a great variety of tunes, but
it must play them in succession. One idea recalls another,
but it at the same time excludes all others. In trying to
renew old recollections, we cannot as it were unfold the
whole web of our existence; we must pick out the single
threads. So in coming to a place where we have formerly
lived, and with which we have intimate associations, everyone must have found that the feeling grows more vivid
the nearer we approach the spot, from the mere anticipation of the actual impression: we remember circumstances,
feelings, persons, faces, names that we had not thought of

for years; but for the time all the rest of the world is forgotten! – To return to the question I have quitted above: –

I have no objection to go to see ruins, aqueducts, pictures, in company with a friend or a party, but rather the contrary, for the former reason reversed. They are intelligible matters, and will bear talking about. The sentiment here is not tacit, but communicable and overt. Salisbury Plain is barren of criticism, but Stonehenge will bear a discussion antiquarian, picturesque, and philosophical. In setting out on a party of pleasure, the first consideration always is where we shall go to: in taking a solitary ramble, the question is what we shall meet with by the way. 'The mind is its own place'; nor are we anxious to arrive at the end of our journey. I can myself do the honours indifferently well to works of art and curiosity. I once took a party to Oxford with no mean *éclat* – showed them that seat of the Muses at a distance,

With glistering spires and pinnacles adorn'd –

descanted on the learned air that breathes from the grassy quadrangles and stone walls of halls and colleges – was at home in the Bodleian; and at Blenheim quite superseded the powdered cicerone that attended us, and that pointed in vain with his wand to commonplace beauties in matchless pictures. As another exception to the above reasoning, I should not feel confident in venturing on a journey in a foreign country without a companion. I should want at intervals to hear the sound of my own language. There is an involuntary antipathy in the mind of an Englishman to foreign manners and notions that requires the assistance of social sympathy to carry it off. As the distance from home increases, this relief, which was at first a luxury, becomes a passion and an appetite. A person would almost feel stifled to find himself in the deserts of Arabia without

friends and countrymen: there must be allowed to be something in the view of Athens or old Rome that claims the
utterance of speech; and I own that the Pyramids are too
mighty for any single contemplation. In such situations, so
opposite to all one's ordinary train of ideas, one seems a
species by one's-self, a limb torn off from society, unless
one can meet with instant fellowship and support. Yet I
did not feel this want or craving very pressing once, when
I first set my foot on the laughing shores of France.
Calais was peopled with novelty and delight. The confused,
busy murmur of the place was like oil and wine poured
into my ears; nor did the mariners' hymn, which was sung
from the top of an old crazy vessel in the harbour, as the
sun went down, send an alien sound into my soul. I only
breathed the air of general humanity. I walked over 'the
vine-covered hills and gay regions of France', erect and
satisfied; for the image of man was not cast down and
chained to the foot of arbitrary thrones: I was at no loss
for language, for that of all the great schools of painting
was open to me. The whole is vanished like a shade. Pictures, heroes, glory, freedom, all are fled: nothing remains
but the Bourbons and the French people! – There is
undoubtedly a sensation in travelling into foreign parts
that is to be had nowhere else; but it is more pleasing at
the time than lasting. It is too remote from our habitual
associations to be a common topic of discourse or reference, and, like a dream or other state of existence, does
not piece into our daily modes of life. It is an animated but
a momentary hallucination. It demands an effort to
exchange our actual for our ideal identity; and to feel the
pulse of our old transports revive very keenly, we must
'jump' all our present comforts and connexions. Our romantic and itinerant character is not to be domesticated.
Dr Johnson remarked how little foreign travel added to

the facilities of conversation in those who had been abroad. In fact, the time we have spent there is both delightful, and in one sense instructive; but it appears to be cut out of our substantial, downright existence, and never to join kindly on to it. We are not the same, but another, and perhaps more enviable individual, all the time we are out of our own country. We are lost to ourselves, as well as our friends. So the poet somewhat quaintly sings:

> *Out of my country and myself I go.*

Those who wish to forget painful thoughts, do well to absent themselves for a while from the ties and objects that recall them; but we can be said only to fulfil our destiny in the place that gave us birth. I should on this account like well enough to spend the whole of my life in travelling abroad, if I could anywhere borrow another life to spend afterwards at home!

On the Ignorance of the Learned

> *For the more languages a man can speak,*
> *His talent has but sprung the greater leak;*
> *And, for the industry he has spent upon't,*
> *Must full as much some other way discount.*
> *The Hebrew, Chaldee, and the Syriac*
> *Do, like their letters, set men's reason back,*
> *And turn their wits that strive to understand it*
> *(Like those that write the characters) left-handed.*
> *Yet he that is but able to express*
> *No sense at all in several languages,*
> *Will pass for learneder than he that's known*
> *To speak the strongest reason in his own.*
>
> BUTLER.

THE description of persons who have the fewest ideas of all others are mere authors and readers. It is better to be able neither to read nor write than to be able to do nothing else. A lounger who is ordinarily seen with a book in his hand is (we may be almost sure) equally without the power or inclination to attend either to what passes around him or in his own mind. Such a one may be said to carry his understanding about with him in his pocket, or to leave it at home on his library shelves. He is afraid of venturing on any train of reasoning, or of striking out any observation that is not mechanically suggested to him by passing his eyes over certain legible characters; shrinks from the fatigue of thought, which, for want of practice, becomes insupportable to him; and sits down contented with an endless, wearisome succession of words and half-formed images, which fill the void of the mind, and continually efface one another. Learning is, in too many cases, but a foil to common sense; a substitute for true knowledge. Books are less often made use of as 'spectacles' to look at nature with, than as blinds to keep out its strong light and shifting scenery from weak eyes and indolent dispositions. The book-worm wraps himself up in his web of verbal generalities, and sees only the glimmering shadows of things reflected from the minds of others. Nature *puts him out*. The impressions of real objects, stripped of the disguises of words and voluminous roundabout descriptions, are blows that stagger him; their variety distracts, their rapidity exhausts him; and he turns from the bustle, the noise, and glare, and whirling motion of the world about him (which he has not an eye to follow in its fantastic changes, nor an understanding to reduce to fixed principles), to the quiet monotony of the dead languages, and the less startling and more intelligible combinations of the letters of the alphabet. It is well, it is perfectly well. 'Leave me to my repose', is the motto of the sleeping and the dead. You might as well ask the paralytic to leap from his chair, and throw away his crutch, or, without a miracle, to 'take up his bed and walk', as expect the learned reader to throw down his book and think for himself. He clings to it for his intellectual support; and his dread of being left to himself is like the horror of a vacuum. He can only breathe a learned atmosphere, as other men breathe common air. He is a borrower of sense. He has no ideas of his own, and must live on those of other people. The habit of supplying our ideas from foreign sources 'enfeebles all internal strength of thought' as a course of dram-drinking destroys the tone of the stomach. The faculties of the mind, when not exerted, or when cramped by custom and authority, become listless, torpid, and unfit for the purposes of thought or action. Can we wonder at the languor and lassitude which is thus produced by a life of learned sloth and ignorance; by poring over lines and syllables that excite little more idea or interest than if they were the characters of an unknown tongue, till the eye closes on vacancy, and the book drops from the feeble hand! I would rather be a woodcutter, or the meanest hind, that all day 'sweats in the eye of Phoebus, and at night sleeps in Elysium', than wear out my life so, 'twixt dreaming and awake. The learned author differs from the learned student in this, that the one transcribes what the other reads. The learned are mere literary drudges. If you set them upon original composition, their heads turn, they don't know where they are. The indefatigable readers of books are like the everlasting copiers of pictures, who, when they attempt to do anything of their own, find they want an eye quick enough, a hand steady enough, and colours bright enough, to trace the living forms of nature.

Anyone who has passed through the regular gradations of a classical education, and is not made a fool by it, may consider himself as having had a very narrow escape. It is an old remark, that boys who shine at school do not make the greatest figure when they grow up and come out into the world. The things, in fact, which a boy is set to learn at school, and on which his success depends, are things which do not require the exercise either of the highest or the most useful faculties of the mind. Memory (and that of the lowest kind) is the chief faculty called into play in conning over and repeating lessons by rote in grammar, in languages, in geography, arithmetic, etc., so that he who has the most of this technical memory, with the least turn for other things, which have a stronger and more natural claim upon his childish attention, will make the most forward schoolboy. The jargon containing the definitions of the parts of speech, the rules for casting up an account, or the inflexions of a Greek verb, can have no attraction to the tyro of ten years old, except as they are imposed as a task upon him by others, or from his feeling the want of sufficient relish or amusement in other things. A lad with a sickly constitution and no very active mind, who can just retain what is pointed out to him, and has neither sagacity to distinguish nor spirit to enjoy for himself, will generally be at the head of his form. An idler at school, on the other hand, is one who has high health and spirits, who has the free use of his limbs, with all his wits about him, who feels the circulation of his blood and the motion of his heart, who is ready to laugh and cry in a breath, and who had rather chase a ball or a butterfly, feel the open air in his face, look at the fields or the sky, follow a winding path, or enter with eagerness into all the little conflicts and interests of his acquaintances and friends, than doze over a musty spelling-book, repeat

barbarous distichs after his master, sit so many hours
pinioned to a writing-desk and receive his reward for the
loss of time and pleasure in paltry prize-medals at Christmas and Midsummer. There is indeed a degree of stupidity which prevents children from learning the usual
lessons, or ever arriving at these puny academic honours.
But what passes for stupidity is much oftener a want of
interest, of a sufficient motive to fix the attention and
force a reluctant application to the dry and unmeaning
pursuits of school-learning. The best capacities are as
much above this drudgery as the dullest are beneath it.
Our men of the greatest genius have not been most distinguished for their acquirements at school or at the
university.

Th' enthusiast Fancy was a truant ever.

Gray and Collins were among the instances of this wayward disposition. Such persons do not think so highly of
the advantages, nor can they submit their imaginations so
servilely to the trammels of strict scholastic discipline.
There is a certain kind and degree of intellect in which
words take root, but into which things have not power to
penetrate. A mediocrity of talent, with a certain slender-
ness of moral constitution, is the soil that produces the
most brilliant specimens of successful prize-essayists and
Greek epigrammatists. It should not be forgotten that the
least respectable character among modern politicians was
the cleverest boy at Eton.

Learning is the knowledge of that which is not generally
known to others, and which we can only derive at second-
hand from books or other artificial sources. The knowledge
of that which is before us, or about us, which appeals to
our experience, passions, and pursuits, to the bosoms and
business of men, is not learning. Learning is the knowledge of that which none but the learned know. He is the

most learned man who knows the most of what is farthest removed from common life and actual observation, that is of the least practical utility, and least liable to be brought to the test of experience, and that, having been handed down through the greatest number of intermediate stages, is the most full of uncertainty, difficulties, and contradictions. It is seeing with the eyes of others, hearing with their ears, and pinning our faith on their understandings. The learned man prides himself in the knowledge of names and dates, not of men or things. He thinks and cares nothing about his next-door neighbours, but he is deeply read in the tribes and castes of the Hindoos and Calmuc Tartars. He can hardly find his way into the next street, though he is acquainted with the exact dimensions of Constantinople and Pekin. He does not know whether his oldest acquaintance is a knave or a fool, but he can pronounce a pompous lecture on all the principal characters in history. He cannot tell whether an object is black or white, round or square, and yet he is a professed master of the laws of optics and the rules of perspective. He knows as much of what he talks about as a blind man does of colours. He cannot give a satisfactory answer to the plainest question, nor is he ever in the right in any one of his opinions upon any one matter of fact that really comes before him, and yet he gives himself out for an infallible judge on all these points, of which it is impossible that he or any other person living should know anything but by conjecture. He is expert in all the dead and in most of the living languages; but he can neither speak his own fluently, nor write it correctly. A person of this class, the second Greek scholar of his day, undertook to point out several solecisms in Milton's Latin style; and in his own performance there is hardly a sentence of common English. Such was Dr—. Such is Dr—. Such was not Porson.

He was an exception that confirmed the general rule, – a man that, by uniting talents and knowledge with learning, made the distinction between them more striking and palpable.

A mere scholar, who knows nothing but books, must be ignorant even of them. 'Books do not teach the use of books.' How should he know anything of a work who knows nothing of the subject of it? The learned pedant is conversant with books only as they are made of other books, and those again of others, without end. He parrots those who have parroted others. He can translate the same word into ten different languages, but he knows nothing of the *thing* which it means in any one of them. He stuffs his head with authorities built on authorities, with quotations quoted from quotations, while he locks up his senses, his understanding, and his heart. He is unacquainted with the maxims and manners of the world; he is to seek in the characters of individuals. He sees no beauty in the face of nature or of art. To him 'the mighty world of eye and ear' is hid; and 'knowledge', except at one entrance, 'quite shut out'. His pride takes par with his ignorance; and his self-importance rises with the number of things of which he does not know the value, and which he therefore despises as unworthy of his notice. He knows nothing of pictures, – 'of the colouring of Titian, the grace of Raphael, the purity of Domenichino, the *corregioscity* of Correggio, the learning of Poussin, the airs of Guido, the taste of the Caracci, or the grand contour of Michael Angelo', – of all those glories of the Italian and miracles of the Flemish school, which have filled the eyes of mankind with delight, and to the study and imitation of which thousands have in vain devoted their lives. These are to him as if they had never been, a mere dead letter, a by-word; and no wonder, for he neither sees nor understands

their prototypes in nature. A print of Rubens' Watering-
place or Claude's Enchanted Castle may be hanging on
the walls of his room for months without his once perceiving them; and if you point them out to him he will
turn away from them. The language of nature, or of art
(which is another nature), is one that he does not understand. He repeats indeed the names of Apelles and Phidias,
because they are to be found in classic authors, and boasts
of their works as prodigies, because they no longer exist;
or when he sees the finest remains of Grecian art actually
before him in the Elgin Marbles, takes no other interest in
them than as they lead to a learned dispute, and (which is
the same thing) a quarrel about the meaning of a Greek
particle. He is equally ignorant of music; he 'knows no
touch of it', from the strains of the all-accomplished
Mozart to the shepherd's pipe upon the mountain. His
ears are nailed to his books; and deadened with the sound
of the Greek and Latin tongues, and the din and smithery
of school-learning. Does he know anything more of poetry?
He knows the number of feet in a verse, and of acts in a
play; but of the soul or spirit he knows nothing. He can
turn a Greek ode into English, or a Latin epigram into
Greek verse; but whether either is worth the trouble he
leaves to the critics. Does he understand 'the act and
practique part of life' better than 'the theorique'? No.
He knows no liberal or mechanic art, no trade or occupation, no game of skill or chance. Learning 'has no skill in
surgery', in agriculture, in building, in working in wood or
in iron; it cannot make any instrument of labour, or use
it when made; it cannot handle the plough or the spade,
or the chisel or the hammer; it knows nothing of hunting
or hawking, fishing or shooting, of horses or dogs, of
fencing or dancing, or cudgel-playing, or bowls, or cards,
or tennis, or anything else. The learned professor of all arts

and sciences cannot reduce any one of them to practice, though he may contribute an account of them to an Encyclopedia. He has not the use of his hands nor of his feet; he can neither run, nor walk, nor swim; and he considers all those who actually understand and can exercise any of these arts of body or mind as vulgar and mechanical men, – though to know almost any one of them in perfection requires long time and practice, with powers originally fitted, and a turn of mind particularly devoted to them. It does not require more than this to enable the learned candidate to arrive, by painful study, at a doctor's degree and a fellowship, and to eat, drink, and sleep the rest of his life!

The thing is plain. All that men really understand is confined to a very small compass; to their daily affairs and experience; to what they have an opportunity to know, and motives to study or practise. The rest is affectation and imposture. The common people have the use of their limbs; for they live by their labour or skill. They understand their own business and the characters of those they have to deal with; for it is necessary that they should. They have eloquence to express their passions, and wit at will to express their contempt and provoke laughter. Their natural use of speech is not hung up in monumental mockery, in an obsolete language; nor is their sense of what is ludicrous, or readiness at finding out allusions to express it, buried in collections of *Anas*. You will hear more good things on the outside of a stage-coach from London to Oxford than if you were to pass a twelvemonth with the undergraduates, or heads of colleges, of that famous university; and more *home* truths are to be learnt from listening to a noisy debate in an alehouse than from attending to a formal one in the House of Commons. An elderly country gentlewoman will often know more of character, and be able to illustrate it by more amusing anecdotes taken from the history of what has been said, done, and gossiped in a country town for the last fifty years, than the best blue-stocking of the age will be able to glean from that sort of learning which consists in an acquaintance with all the novels and satirical poems published in the same period. People in towns, indeed, are woefully deficient in a knowledge of character, which they see only *in the bust*, not as a whole-length. People in the country not only know all that has happened to a man, but trace his virtues or vices, as they do his features, in their descent through several generations, and solve some contradiction in his behaviour by a cross in the breed half a century ago. The learned know nothing of the matter, either in town or country. Above all, the mass of society have common sense, which the learned in all ages want. The vulgar are in the right when they judge for themselves; they are wrong when they trust to their blind guides. The celebrated nonconformist divine, Baxter, was almost stoned to death by the good women of Kidderminster, for asserting from the pulpit that 'hell was paved with infants' skulls'; but, by the force of argument, and of learned quotations from the Fathers, the reverend preacher at length prevailed over the scruples of his congregation, and over reason and humanity.

Such is the use which has been made of human learning. The labourers in this vineyard seem as if it was their object to confound all common sense, and the distinctions of good and evil, by means of traditional maxims and preconceived notions taken upon trust and increasing in absurdity with increase of age. They pile hypothesis on hypothesis, mountain high, till it is impossible to come at the plain truth on any question. They see things, not as they are, but as they find them in books, and 'wink and

shut their apprehensions up', in order that they may discover nothing to interfere with their prejudices or convince them of their absurdity. It might be supposed that
the height of human wisdom consisted in maintaining
contradictions and rendering nonsense sacred. There is no
dogma, however fierce or foolish, to which these persons have not set their seals, and tried to impose on the
understandings of their followers as the will of Heaven,
clothed with all the terrors and sanctions of religion. How
little has the human understanding been directed to find
out the true and useful! How much ingenuity has been
thrown away in the defence of creeds and systems! How
much time and talents have been wasted in theological
controversy, in law, in politics, in verbal criticism, in
judicial astrology, and in finding out the art of making
gold! What actual benefit do we reap from the writings
of a Laud or a Whitgift, or of Bishop Bull or Bishop
Waterland, or Prideaux' *Connections*, or Beausobre, or
Calmet, or St Augustine, or Puffendorf, or Vattel, or
from the more literal but equally learned and unprofitable
labours of Scaliger, Cardan, and Scioppius? How many
grains of sense are there in their thousand folio or quarto
volumes? What would the world lose if they were committed to the flames to-morrow? Or are they not already
'gone to the vault of all the Capulets'? Yet all these were
oracles in their time, and would have scoffed at you or me,
at common sense and human nature, for differing with
them. It is our turn to laugh now.

To conclude this subject. The most sensible people to
be met with in society are men of business and of the world,
who argue from what they see and know, instead of
spinning cobweb distinctions of what things ought to be.
Women have often more of what is called *good sense* than
men. They have fewer pretensions; are less implicated in

theories; and judge of objects more from their immediate and involuntary impression on the mind, and, therefore, more truly and naturally. They cannot reason wrong; for they do not reason at all. They do not think or speak by rule; and they have in general more eloquence and wit as well as sense, on that account. By their wit, sense, and eloquence together, they generally contrive to govern their husbands. Their style, when they write to their friends (not for the booksellers), is better than that of most authors. – Uneducated people have most exuberance of invention and the greatest freedom from prejudice. Shakespeare's was evidently an uneducated mind, both in the freshness of his imagination and in the variety of his views; as Milton's was scholastic, in the texture both of his thoughts and feelings. Shakespeare had not been accustomed to write themes at school in favour of virtue or against vice. To this we owe the unaffected but healthy tone of his dramatic morality. If we wish to know the force of human genius we should read Shakespeare. If we wish to see the insignificance of human learning we may study his commentators.

On Familiar Style

IT is not easy to write a familiar style. Many people mistake a familiar for a vulgar style, and suppose that to write without affectation is to write at random. On the contrary, there is nothing that requires more precision, and, if I may so say, purity of expression, than the style I am speaking of. It utterly rejects not only all unmeaning pomp, but all low, cant phrases, and loose, unconnected, *slipshod* allusions. It is not to take the first word that offers, but the best word in common use; it is not to throw words together in any combinations we please, but to follow and avail ourselves of the true idiom of the language. To write a genuine familiar or truly English style is to write as any one would speak in common conversation who had a thorough command and choice of words, or who could discourse with ease, force, and perspicuity, setting aside all pedantic and oratorical flourishes. Or, to give another illustration, to write naturally is the same thing in regard to common conversation as to read naturally is in regard to common speech. It does not follow that it is an easy thing to give the true accent and inflexion to the words you utter, because you do not attempt to rise above the level of ordinary life and colloquial speaking. You do not assume, indeed, the solemnity of the pulpit, or the tone of stage-declamation; neither are you at liberty to gabble on at a venture, without emphasis or discretion or to resort to vulgar dialect or clownish pronunciation. You must steer a middle course. You are tied down to a given and appropriate articulation, which is determined by the habitual associations between sense and sound, and which you can only hit by entering into the author's meaning, as you must find the proper words and style to express yourself by fixing your thoughts on the subject you have to write about. Any one may mouth out a passage with a theatrical cadence, or get upon stilts to tell his thoughts; but to write or speak with propriety and simplicity is a more difficult task. Thus it is easy to affect a pompous style, to use a word twice as big as the thing you want to express: it is not so easy to pitch upon the very word that exactly fits it. Out of eight or ten words equally common, equally intelligible, with nearly equal pretensions, it is a matter of some nicety and discrimination to pick out the very one the preferableness of which is scarcely perceptible but decisive. The reason why I object to Dr Johnson's style is that there is no discrimination, no selection, no variety in it. He uses none but 'tall, opaque words', taken from the 'first row of the rubric' – words with the greatest number of syllables, or Latin phrases with merely English terminations. If a fine style depended on this sort of arbitrary pretension, it would be fair to judge of an author's elegance by the measurement of his words and the substitution of foreign circumlocutions (with no precise associations) for the mother-tongue.* How simple is it to be dignified without ease, to be pompous without meaning! Surely it is but a mechanical rule for avoiding what is low, to be always pedantic and affected. It is clear you cannot use a vulgar English word if you never use a common English word at all. A fine tact is shown in adhering to those which are perfectly common, and yet never falling into any expressions which are debased by disgusting circumstances, or which owe their signification and point to technical or professional allusions. A truly natural or familiar style can never be quaint or vulgar, for this reason, that it is of universal force and applicability, and that quaintness and vulgarity arise out of the immediate connexion of certain words with coarse and disagreeable or with confined ideas. The last form what we understand by *cant* or *slang* phrases. – To give an example of what is not very clear in the general statement. I should say that the phrase *To cut with a knife,* or *To cut a piece of wood,* is perfectly free from vulgarity, because it is perfectly common; but to *cut an acquaintance* is not quite unexceptionable, because it is not perfectly common or

---

* I have heard of such a thing as an author who makes it a rule never to admit a monosyllable into his vapid verse. Yet the charm and sweetness of Marlowe's lines depended often on their being made up almost entirely of monosyllables.

intelligible, and has hardly yet escaped out of the limits of slang phraseology. I should hardly, therefore, use the word in this sense without putting it in italics as a license of expression, to be received *cum grano salis*. All provincial or bye-phrases come under the same mark of reprobation – all such as the writer transfers to the page from his fireside or a particular *coterie*, or that he invents for his own sole use and convenience. I conceive that words are like money, not the worse for being common, but that it is the stamp of custom alone that gives them circulation or value. I am fastidious in this respect, and would almost as soon coin the currency of the realm as counterfeit the King's English. I never invented or gave a new and unauthorized meaning to any word but one single one (the term *impersonal* applied to feelings), and that was in an abstruse metaphysical discussion to express a very difficult distinction. I have been (I know) loudly accused of revelling in vulgarisms and broken English. I cannot speak to that point; but so far I plead guilty to the determined use of acknowledged idioms and common elliptical expressions. I am not sure that the critics in question know the one from the other, that is, can distinguish any medium between formal pedantry and the most barbarous solecism. As an author I endeavour to employ plain words and popular modes of construction, as, were I a chapman and dealer, I should common weights and measures.

The proper force of words lies not in the words themselves, but in their application. A word may be a fine-sounding word, of an unusual length, and very imposing from its learning and novelty, and yet in the connexion in which it is introduced may be quite pointless and irrelevant. It is not pomp or pretension, but the adaptation of the expression to the idea, that clenches a writer's meaning: – as it is not the size or glossiness of the materials, but their being fitted each to its place, that gives strength to the arch; or as the pegs and nails are as necessary to the support of the building as the larger timbers, and more so than the mere showy, unsubstantial ornaments. I hate anything that occupies more space than it is worth. I hate to see a load of bandboxes go along the street, and I hate to see a parcel of big words without anything in them. A person who does not deliberately dispose of all his thoughts alike in cumbrous draperies and flimsy disguises may strike out twenty varieties of familiar everyday language, each coming somewhat nearer to the feeling he wants to convey, and at last not hit upon that particular and only one which may be said to be identical with the exact impression in his mind. This would seem to show that Mr Cobbett is hardly right in saying that the first word that occurs is always the best. It may be a very good one; and yet a better may present itself on reflection or from time to time. It should be suggested naturally, however, and spontaneously, from a fresh and lively conception of the subject. We seldom succeed by trying at improvement, or by merely substituting one word for another that we are not satisfied with, as we cannot recollect the name of a place or person by merely plaguing ourselves about it. We wander farther from the point by persisting in a wrong scent; but it starts up accidentally in the memory when we least expected it, by touching some link in the chain of previous association.

There are those who hoard up and make a cautious display of nothing but rich and rare phraseology – ancient medals, obscure coins, and Spanish pieces of eight. They are very curious to inspect, but I myself would neither offer nor take them in the course of exchange. A sprinkling of archaisms is not amiss, but a tissue of obsolete expressions is more fit *for keep than wear*. I do not say I would not use any phrase that had been brought into fashion before the middle or the end of the last century, but I should be shy of using any that had not been employed by any approved author during the whole of that time. Words, like clothes, get old-fashioned, or mean and ridiculous, when they have been for some time laid aside. Mr Lamb is the only imitator of old English style I can read with pleasure; and he is so thoroughly imbued with the spirit of his authors that the idea of imitation is almost done away. There is an inward unction, a marrowy vein, both in the thought and feeling, an intuition, deep and lively, of his subject, that carries off any quaintness or awkwardness arising from an antiquated style and dress. The matter is completely his own, though the manner is assumed. Perhaps his ideas are altogether so marked and individual as to require their point and pungency to be neutralized by the affectation of a singular but traditional form of conveyance. Tricked out in the prevailing costume, they would probably seem more startling and out of the way. The old English authors, Burton, Fuller, Coryate, Sir Thomas Browne, are a kind of mediators between us and the more eccentric and whimsical modern, reconciling us to his peculiarities. I do not, however, know how far this is the case or not, till he condescends to write like one of us. I must confess that what I like best of his papers under the signature of Elia (still I do not presume, amidst such excellence, to decide what is most excellent) is the account of 'Mrs Battle's Opinions on Whist', which is also the most free from obsolete allusions and turns of expression –

A well of native English undefiled.

To those acquainted with his admired prototypes, these *Essays* of the ingenious and highly gifted author have the same sort of charm and relish that Erasmus's *Colloquies* or a fine piece of modern Latin have to the classical scholar. Certainly, I do not know any borrowed pencil that has more power or felicity of execution than the one of which I have here been speaking.

It is as easy to write a gaudy style without ideas as it is to spread a pallet of showy colours or to smear in a flaunting transparency. 'What do you read?' 'Words, words, words.' – 'What is the matter?' '*Nothing*', it might be answered. The florid style is the reverse of the familiar. The last is employed as an unvarnished medium to convey ideas; the first is resorted to as a spangled veil to conceal the want of them. When there is nothing to be set down but words, it costs little to have them fine. Look through the dictionary, and cull out a *florilegium*, rival the *tulippo-mania*. *Rouge* high enough, and never mind the natural complexion. The vulgar, who are not in the secret, will admire the look of preternatural health and vigour; and the fashionable, who regard only appearances, will be delighted with the imposition. Keep to your sounding generalities, your tinkling phrases, and all will be well. Swell out an unmeaning truism to a perfect tympany of style. A thought, a distinction is the rock on which all this brittle cargo of verbiage splits at once. Such writers have merely *verbal* imaginations, that retain nothing but words. Or their puny thoughts have dragon-wings, all green and gold. They soar far above the vulgar failing of the *Sermo humi obrepens* – their most ordinary speech is never short of an hyperbole, splendid, imposing, vague, incomprehensible, magniloquent, a cento of sounding common-places. If some of us, whose 'ambition is more lowly', pry a little too narrowly into nooks and corners to pick up a number of 'unconsidered trifles', they never once direct their eyes or lift their hands to seize on any but the most gorgeous, tarnished, threadbare, patchwork set of phrases, the left-off finery of poetic extravagance, transmitted down through successive generations of barren pretenders. If they criticize actors and actresses, a huddled phantasmagoria of feathers, spangles, floods of light, and oceans of sound float before their morbid sense, which they paint in the style of Ancient Pistol. Not a glimpse can you get of the merits or defects of the performers: they are hidden in a profusion of barbarous epithets and wilful rhodomontade. Our hypercritics are not thinking of these little *fantoccini* beings –

> *That strut and fret their hour upon the stage* –

but of tall phantoms of words, abstractions, *genera* and *species*, sweeping clauses, periods that unite the Poles, forced alliterations, astounding antitheses –

> *And on their pens* Fustian *sits plumed.*

If they describe kings and queens, it is an Eastern pageant. The Coronation at either House is nothing to it. We get at four repeated images – a curtain, a throne, a sceptre, and a footstool. These are with them the wardrobe of a lofty imagination; and they turn their servile strains to servile uses. Do we read a description of pictures? It is not a reflection of tones and hues which 'nature's own sweet and cunning hand laid on', but piles of precious stones, rubies, pearls, emeralds, Golconda's mines, and all the blazonry of art. Such persons are in fact besotted with words, and their brains are turned with the glittering but empty and sterile phantoms of things. Personifications, capital letters, seas of sunbeams, visions of glory, shining inscriptions, the figures of a transparency, Britannia with her shield, or Hope leaning on an anchor, make up their stock-in-trade. They may be considered as *hieroglyphical* writers. Images stand out in their minds isolated and important merely in themselves, without any groundwork of feeling – there is no context in their imaginations. Words affect them in the same way, by the mere sound, that is, by their possible, not by their actual application to the subject in hand. They are fascinated by first appearances, and have no sense of consequences. Nothing more is meant by them than meets the ear: they understand or feel nothing more than meets their eye. The web and texture of the universe, and of the heart of man, is a mystery to them: they have no faculty that strikes a chord in unison with it. They cannot get beyond the daubings of fancy, the varnish of sentiment. Objects are not linked to feelings, words to things, but images revolve in splendid mockery, words represent themselves in their strange rhapsodies. The categories of such a mind are pride and ignorance – pride in outside show, to which they sacrifice everything, and ignorance of the true worth and hidden structure both of words and things. With a sovereign contempt for what is familiar and natural, they are the slaves of vulgar affectation – of a routine of high-flown phrases. Scorning to imitate realities, they are unable to invent anything, to strike out one original idea. They are not copyists of nature, it is true; but they are the poorest of all plagiarists, the plagiarists of words. All is far-fetched dear-bought, artificial, oriental in subject and allusion; all is mechanical, conventional, vapid, formal, pedantic in style and execution. They startle and confound the understanding of the reader by the remoteness and obscurity of their illustrations; they soothe the ear by the monotony of the same everlasting round of circuitous metaphors. They are the *mock-school* in poetry and prose. They flounder about between fustian in expression and bathos in sentiment. They tantalize the fancy, but never reach the head nor touch the heart. Their Temple of Fame is like a shadowy structure raised by Dulness to Vanity, or like Cowper's description of the Empress of Russia's palace of ice, 'as worthless as in show 'twas glittering' –

It smiled, and it was cold!

THOMAS DE QUINCEY

On the Knocking at the Gate in Macbeth

FROM my boyish days I had always felt a great perplexity on one point in Macbeth: it was this: the knocking at the gate, which succeeds to the murder of Duncan, produced to my feelings an effect for which I never could account: the effect was – that it reflected back upon the murder a peculiar awfulness and a depth of solemnity: yet, however obstinately I endeavoured with my understanding to comprehend this, for many years I could never see *why* it should produce such an effect. –

Here I pause for one moment to exhort the reader never to pay any attention to his understanding when it stands in opposition to any other faculty of his mind. The mere understanding, however useful and indispensable, is the meanest faculty in the human mind and the most to be distrusted: and yet the great majority of people trust to nothing else; which may do for ordinary life, but not for philosophical purposes. Of this, out of ten thousand instances that I might produce, I will cite one. Ask of any person whatsoever, who is not previously prepared for the demand by a knowledge of perspective, to draw in the rudest way the commonest appearance which depends upon the laws of that science – as for instance to represent the effect of two walls standing at right angles to each other, or the appearance of the houses on each side of a street, as seen by a person looking down the street from one extremity. Now in all cases, unless the person has happened to observe in pictures how it is that artists produce these effects, he will be utterly unable to make the smallest approximation to it. Yet why? – For he has actually seen the effect every day of his life. The reason is – that he allows his understanding to overrule his eyes. His understanding, which includes no intuitive knowledge of the laws of vision, can furnish him with no reason why a line which is known and can be proved to be a horizontal line, should not *appear* a horizontal line: a line, that made any angle with the perpendicular less than a right angle, would seem to him to indicate that his houses were all tumbling down together. Accordingly he makes the line of his houses a horizontal line, and fails of course to produce the effect demanded. Here then is one instance out of many, in which not only the understanding is allowed to overrule the eyes, but where the understanding is positively allowed to obliterate the eyes as it were: for not only does the man believe the evidence of his understanding in opposition to that of his eyes, but (which is monstrous!) the idiot is not aware that his eyes ever gave such evidence. He does not know that he has seen (and therefore *quoad* his consciousness has *not* seen) that which he *has* seen every day of his life. But to return from this digression, – my understanding could furnish no reason why the knocking at the gate in Macbeth should produce any effect direct or reflected: in fact, my understanding said positively that it could *not* produce any effect. But I knew better: I felt that it did: and I waited and clung to the problem until further knowledge should enable me to solve it. – At length, in 1812, Mr Williams made his *début* on the stage of Ratcliffe Highway, and executed those unparalleled murders which have procured for him such a brilliant and undying reputation. On which murders, by the way, I must observe, that in one respect they have had an ill effect, by making the connoisseur in murder very fastidious in his taste, and dissatisfied with anything that has been since done in that line. All other murders look pale by the deep crimson of his: and, as an amateur once said to me in a querulous tone, 'There has been absolutely nothing *doing* since his time, or nothing that's worth speaking of.' But this is wrong: for it is unreasonable to expect all men to be great artists, and born with the genius of Mr Williams. – Now it will be remembered that in the first of these murders (that of the Marrs) the same incident (of a knocking at the door soon after the work of extermination was complete) did actually occur which the genius of Shakespeare had invented: and all good judges and the most eminent dilettanti acknowledged the felicity of Shakespeare's suggestion as soon as it was actually realized. Here then was a fresh proof that I had been right in relying on my own feeling in opposition to my understanding; and again I set myself to study the problem: at length I solved it to my own satisfaction; and my solution is this. Murder in ordinary cases, where the sympathy is wholly directed to the case of the murdered person, is an incident of coarse and vulgar horror; and for this reason – that it flings the interest exclusively upon the natural but ignoble instinct by which we cleave to life; an instinct which, as being indispensable to the primal law of self-preservation, is the same in kind (though different in degree) amongst all living creatures; this instinct therefore, because it annihilates all distinctions, and degrades the greatest of men to the level of 'the poor beetle that we tread on', exhibits human nature in its most abject and humiliating attitude. Such an attitude would little suit the purpose of the poet. What then must he do? He must throw the interest on the murderer: our sympathy must be with *him* (of course I mean a sympathy of comprehension, a sympathy by which we enter into his feelings, and are made to understand them, – not a sympathy* of pity or approbation): in the murdered person all strife of thought, all flux and reflux of passion and of purpose, are crushed by one over-whelming panic: the fear of instant death smites him 'with its petrific mace'. But in the murderer, such a murderer as a poet will condescend to, there must be raging some great storm of passion, – jealousy, ambition, vengeance, hatred, – which will create a hell within him; and into this hell we are to look. In Macbeth, for the sake of gratifying his own enormous and teeming faculty of creation, Shakespeare has introduced two murderers: and as usual in his hands, they are remarkably discriminated: but though in Macbeth the strife of mind is greater than in his wife, the tiger spirit not so awake, and his feelings caught chiefly by contagion from her, – yet, as both were finally involved in the guilt of murder, the murderous mind of necessity is finally to be presumed in both. This was to be expressed; and on its own account, as well as to make it a more proportionable antagonist to the un-offending nature of their victim, 'the gracious Duncan', and adequately to expound 'the deep damnation of his taking off', this was to be expressed with peculiar energy. We were to be made to feel that the human nature, i.e., the divine nature of love and mercy, spread through the hearts of all creatures and seldom utterly withdrawn from man, – was gone, vanished, extinct; and that the fiendish

* It seems almost ludicrous to guard and explain my use of a word in a situation where it should naturally explain itself. But it has become necessary to do so, in consequence of the unscholarlike use of the word sympathy, at present so general, by which, instead of taking it in its proper use, as the act of reproducing in our minds the feelings of another, whether for hatred, indignation, love, pity, or approbation, it is made a mere synonyme of the word *pity*; and hence, instead of saying, 'sympathy *with* another', many writers adopt the monstrous barbarism of 'sympathy *for* another'.

nature had taken its place. And, as this effect is marvellously accomplished in the dialogues and soliloquies
themselves, so it is finally consummated by the expedient
under consideration; and it is to this that I now solicit the
reader's attention. If the reader has ever witnessed a wife,
daughter, or sister, in a fainting fit, he may chance to
have observed that the most affecting moment in such a
spectacle, is *that* in which a sigh and a stirring announce
the recommencement of suspended life. Or, if the reader
has ever been present in a vast metropolis on the day
when some great national idol was carried in funeral
pomp to his grave, and chancing to walk near to the
course through which it passed, has felt powerfully in the
silence and desertion of the streets and in the stagnation
of ordinary business, the deep interest which at that
moment was possessing the heart of man, – if all at once
he should hear the death-like stillness broken up by the
sound of wheels rattling away from the scene, and making
known that the transitory vision was dissolved, he will be
aware that at no moment was his sense of the complete
suspension and pause in ordinary human concerns so full
and affecting as at that moment when the suspension
ceases, and the goings-on of human life are suddenly
resumed. All action in any direction is best expounded,
measured, and made apprehensible, by reaction. Now
apply this to the case in Macbeth. Here, as I have said,
the retiring of the human heart and the entrance of the
fiendish heart was to be expressed and made sensible.
Another world has stepped in; and the murderers are
taken out of the region of human things, human purposes,
human desires. They are transfigured: Lady Macbeth is
'unsexed'; Macbeth has forgot that he was born of woman;
both are conformed to the image of devils; and the world
of devils is suddenly revealed. But how shall this be

conveyed and made palpable? In order that a new world may step in, this world must for a time disappear. The murderers, and the murder, must be insulated — cut off by an immeasurable gulf from the ordinary tide and succession of human affairs — locked up and sequestered in some deep recess: we must be made sensible that the world of ordinary life is suddenly arrested — laid asleep — tranced — racked into a dread armistice: time must be annihilated; relation to things without abolished; and all must pass self-withdrawn into a deep syncope and suspension of earthly passion. Hence it is that when the deed is done — when the work of darkness is perfect, then the world of darkness passes away like a pageantry in the clouds: the knocking at the gate is heard; and it makes known audibly that the reaction has commenced: the human has made its reflux upon the fiendish: the pulses of life are beginning to beat again: and the re-establishment of the goings-on of the world in which we live, first makes us profoundly sensible of the awful parenthesis that had suspended them.

Oh! mighty poet! — Thy works are not as those of other men, simply and merely great works of art; but are also like the phenomena of nature, like the sun and the sea, the stars and the flowers, — like frost and snow, rain and dew, hail-storm and thunder, which are to be studied with entire submission of our own faculties, and in the perfect faith that in them there can be no too much or too little, nothing useless or inert — but that, the further we press in our discoveries, the more we shall see proofs of design and self-supporting arrangement where the careless eye had seen nothing but accident!

N.B. In the above specimen of psychological criticism, I have purposely omitted to notice another use of the knocking at the gate, viz. the opposition and contrast which it produces in the porter's comments to the scenes immediately preceding; because this use is tolerably obvious to all who are accustomed to reflect on what they read.

Getting Up on Cold Mornings

AN Italian author – Giulio Cordara, a Jesuit – has written a poem upon insects, which he begins by insisting, that those troublesome and abominable little animals were created for our annoyance, and that they were certainly not inhabitants of Paradise. We of the north may dispute this piece of theology; but on the other hand, it is clear as the snow on the house-tops, that Adam was not under the necessity of shaving; and that when Eve walked out of her delicious bower, she did not step upon ice three inches thick.

Some people say it is a very easy thing to get up of a cold morning. You have only, they tell you, to take the resolution; and the thing is done. This may be very true; just as a boy at school has only to take a flogging, and the thing is over. But we have not at all made up our minds upon it; and we find it a very pleasant exercise to discuss the matter, candidly, before we get up. This at least is not idling, though it may be lying. It affords an excellent answer to those, who ask how lying in bed can be indulged in by a reasoning being, – a rational creature. How? Why, with the argument calmly at work in one's head, and the clothes over one's shoulder. Oh – it is a fine way of spending a sensible, impartial half-hour.

If these people would be more charitable, they would get on with their argument better. But they are apt to reason so ill, and to assert so dogmatically, that one could wish to have them stand round one's bed of a bitter morning, and lie before their faces. They ought to hear both sides of the bed, the inside and out. If they cannot entertain themselves with their own thoughts for half an hour or so, it is not the fault of those who can. If their will is never pulled aside by the enticing arms of imagination, so much the luckier for the stage-coachman.

Candid inquiries into one's decumbency, besides the greater or less privileges to be allowed a man in proportion to his ability of keeping early hours, the work given his faculties, etc., will at least concede their due merits to such representations as the following. In the first place, says the injured but calm appealer, I have been warm all night, and find my system in a state perfectly suitable to a warm-blooded animal. To get out of this state into the cold, besides the inharmonious and uncritical abruptness of the transition, is so unnatural to such a creature, that the poets, refining upon the tortures of the damned, make one of their greatest agonies consist in being suddenly transported from heat to cold, – from fire to ice. They are 'haled' out of their 'beds', says Milton, by 'harpy-footed furies', – fellows who come to call them. On my first movement towards the anticipation of getting up, I find that such parts of the sheets and bolster, as are exposed to the air of the room, are stone-cold. On opening my eyes, the first thing that meets them is my own breath rolling forth, as if in the open air, like smoke out of a cottage chimney. Think of this symptom. Then I turn my eyes sideways and see the window all frozen over. Think of that. Then the servant comes in. 'It is very cold this morning, is it not?' – 'Very cold, Sir.' – 'Very cold indeed, isn't it?' – 'Very cold indeed, Sir.' – 'More than usually so, isn't it, even for this weather?' (Here the servant's wit and good-nature are put to a considerable test, and the inquirer lies on thorns for the answer.) 'Why, Sir . . . I think it *is*.' (Good creature! There is not a better, or more truth-telling servant going.) 'I must rise, however, – get me some warm water.' – Here comes a fine interval between the departure of the servant and the arrival of the hot water; during which, of course, it is of 'no use' to get up. The hot water comes. 'Is it quite hot?' – 'Yes, Sir.' – 'Perhaps too hot for shaving: I must wait a little?' – 'No, Sir; it will just do.' (There is an over-nice propriety sometimes, an officious zeal of virtue, a little troublesome.) 'Oh – the shirt – you must air my clean shirt; – linen gets very damp this weather.' – 'Yes, Sir.' Here another delicious five minutes. A knock at the door. 'Oh, the shirt – very well. My stockings – I think the stockings had better be aired too.' – 'Very well, Sir.' – Here another interval. At length everything is ready, except myself. I now, continues our incumbent (a happy word, by the bye, for a country vicar) – I now cannot help thinking a good deal – who can? – upon the unnecessary and villainous custom of shaving: it is a thing so unmanly (here I nestle closer) – so effeminate (here I recoil from an unlucky step into the colder part of the bed). – No wonder that the Queen of France took part with the rebels against the degenerate King, her husband, who first affronted her smooth visage with a face like her own. The Emperor Julian never showed the luxuriancy of his genius to better advantage than in reviving the flowing beard. Look at Cardinal Bembo's picture – at Michael Angelo's – at Titian's – at Shakespeare's – at Fletcher's – at Spenser's – at Chaucer's – at Alfred's – at Plato's – I could name a great man for every tick of my watch. – Look at the Turks, a grave and otiose people. – Think of Haroun Al Raschid and Bedridden Hassan. – Think of Wortley Montagu, the worthy son of his mother, a man above the prejudice of his time. – Look at the Persian gentlemen, whom one is ashamed of

meeting about the suburbs, their dress and appearance
are so much finer than our own. – Lastly, think of the
razor itself – how totally opposed to every sensation of
bed – how cold, how edgy, how hard! how utterly different
from anything like the warm and circling amplitude,
which

> *Sweetly recommends itself*
> *Unto our gentle senses.*

Add to this, benumbed fingers, which may help you to cut
yourself, a quivering body, a frozen towel, and a ewer full
of ice; and he that says there is nothing to oppose in all
this, only shows, at any rate, that he has no merit in
opposing it.

Thomson the poet, who exclaims in his Seasons –

> *Falsely luxurious! Will not man awake?*

used to lie in bed till noon, because he said he had no
motive in getting up. He could imagine the good of rising;
but then he could also imagine the good of lying still; and
his exclamation, it must be allowed, was made upon
summer-time, not winter. We must proportion the argument to the individual character. A money-getter may be
drawn out of his bed by three and four pence; but this
will not suffice for a student. A proud man may say, 'What
shall I think of myself, if I don't get up?' but the more
humble one will be content to waive his prodigious notion
of himself, out of respect to his kindly bed. The mechanical
man shall get up without any ado at all; and so shall the
barometer. An ingenious lier in bed will find hard matter
of discussion even on the score of health and longevity.
He will ask us for our proofs and precedents of the ill
effects of lying later in cold weather; and sophisticate
much on the advantages of an even temperature of body;
of the natural propensity (pretty universal) to have one's

way; and of the animals that roll themselves up, and sleep all the winter. As to longevity, he will ask whether the longest life is of necessity the best; and whether Holborn is the handsomest street in London.

We only know of one confounding, not to say confounded argument, fit to overturn the huge luxury, the 'enormous bliss' – of the vice in question. A lier in bed may be allowed to profess a disinterested indifference for his health or longevity; but while he is showing the reasonableness of consulting his own or one person's comfort, he must admit the proportionate claim of more than one; and the best way to deal with him is this, especially for a lady; for we earnestly recommend the use of that sex on such occasions, if not somewhat *over*-persuasive; since extremes have an awkward knack of meeting. First then, admit all the ingeniousness of what he says, telling him that the bar has been deprived of an excellent lawyer. Then look at him in the most good-natured manner in the world, with a mixture of assent and appeal in your countenance, and tell him that you are waiting breakfast for him; that you never like to breakfast without him; that you really want it too; that the servants want theirs; that you shall not know how to get the house into order, unless he rises; and that you are sure he would do things twenty times worse, even than getting out of his warm bed, to put them all into good humour and a state of comfort. Then, after having said this, throw in the comparatively indifferent matter, to *him,* about his health; but tell him that it is no indifferent matter to you; that the sight of his illness makes more people suffer than one; but that if, nevertheless, he really does feel so very sleepy and so very much refreshed by – Yet stay; we hardly know whether the frailty of a – Yes, yes; say that too, especially if you say it with sincerity;

for if the weakness of human nature on the one hand and the *vis inertiae* on the other, should lead him to take advantage of it once or twice, good-humour and sincerity form an irresistible junction at last; and are still better and warmer things than pillows and blankets.

Other little helps of appeal may be thrown in, as occasion requires. You may tell a lover, for instance, that lying in bed makes people corpulent; a father, that you wish him to complete the fine manly example he sets his children; a lady, that she will injure her bloom or her shape, which M. or W. admires so much; and a student or artist, that he is always so glad to have done a good day's work, in his best manner.

Reader. And pray, Mr Indicator, how do *you* behave yourself in this respect?

Indic. Oh, Madam, perfectly, of course; like all advisers.

Reader. Nay, I allow that your mode of argument does not look quite so suspicious as the old way of sermonizing and severity, but I have my doubts, especially from that laugh of yours. If I should look in to-morrow morning –

Indic. Ah, Madam, the look in of a face like yours does anything with me. It shall fetch me up at nine, if you please – *six*, I meant to say.

A Few Thoughts on Sleep

THIS is an article for the reader to think of when he or she is warm in bed, a little before he goes to sleep, the clothes at his ear, and the wind moaning in some distant crevice.

'Blessings,' exclaimed Sancho, 'on him that first invented sleep! It wraps a man all round like a cloak.' It is a delicious moment certainly – that of being well

nestled in bed, and feeling that you shall drop gently to
sleep. The good is to come, not past: the limbs have been
just tired enough to render the remaining in one posture
delightful: the labour of the day is done. A gentle failure
of the perceptions comes creeping over one: – the spirit of
consciousness disengages itself more and more, with slow
and hushing degrees like a mother detaching her hand
from that of her sleeping child; – the mind seems to have
a balmy lid closing over it, like the eye; – 'tis closing;
– 'tis more closing; – 'tis closed. The mysterious spirit has
gone to take its airy rounds.

It is said that sleep is best before midnight: and Nature
herself, with her darkness and chilling dews, informs us
so. There is another reason for going to bed betimes; for
it is universally acknowledged that lying late in the
morning is a great shortener of life. At least, it is never
found in company with longevity. It also tends to make
people corpulent. But these matters belong rather to the
subject of early rising than of sleep.

Sleep at a late hour in the morning is not half so pleasant
as the more timely one. It is sometimes, however, excu-
sable, especially to a watchful or overworked head;
neither can we deny the seducing merits of 't' other doze',
– the pleasing wilfulness of nestling in a new posture, when
you know you ought to be up, like the rest of the house.
But then you cut up the day, and your sleep the next
night.

In the course of the day few people think of sleeping,
except after dinner; and then it is often rather a hovering
and nodding on the borders of sleep than sleep itself.
This is a privilege allowable, we think, to none but the
old, or the sickly, or the very tired and care-worn, and it
should be well understood before it is exercised in company. To escape into slumber from an argument; or to

take it as an affair of course, only between you and your biliary duct; or to assent with involuntary nods to all that you have just been disputing, is not so well; much less, to sit nodding and tottering beside a lady; or to be in danger of dropping your head into the fruit-plate or your host's face; or of waking up, and saying 'Just so' to the bark of a dog; or 'Yes, Madam,' to the black at your elbow.

Care-worn people, however, might refresh themselves oftener with day-sleep than they do; if their bodily state is such as to dispose them to it. It is a mistake to suppose that all care is wakeful. People sometimes sleep, as well as wake, by reason of their sorrow. The difference seems to depend upon the nature of their temperament; though in the *most* excessive cases, sleep is perhaps Nature's never-failing relief, as swooning is upon the rack. A person with jaundice in his blood shall lie down and go to sleep at noonday, when another of a different complexion shall find his eyes as uncloseable as a statue's, though he has had no sleep for nights together. Without meaning to lessen the dignity of suffering, which has quite enough to do with its waking hours, it is this that may often account for the profound sleeps enjoyed the night before hazardous battles, executions, and other demands upon an over-excited spirit.

The most complete and healthy sleep that can be taken in the day is in summer-time, out in a field. There is, perhaps, no solitary sensation so exquisite as that of slumbering on the grass or hay, shaded from the hot sun by a tree, with the consciousness of a fresh but light air running through the wide atmosphere, and the sky stretching far overhead upon all sides. Earth, and heaven, and a placid humanity seem to have the creation to themselves. There is nothing between the slumberer and the naked and glad innocence of nature.

Next to this, but at a long interval, the most relishing
snatch of slumber out of bed is the one which a tired person takes before he retires for the night, while lingering in
his sitting-room. The consciousness of being very sleepy,
and of having the power to go to bed immediately, gives
zest to the unwillingness to move. Sometimes he sits nodding in his chair; but the sudden and leaden jerks of the
head, to which a state of great sleepiness renders him
liable, are generally too painful for so luxurious a moment;
and he gets into a more legitimate posture, sitting sideways
with his head on the chairback, or throwing his legs up at
once on another chair, and half reclining. It is curious,
however, to find how long an inconvenient posture will
be borne for the sake of this foretaste of repose. The worst
of it is, that on going to bed the charm sometimes vanishes;
perhaps from the colder temperature of the chamber; for
a fireside is a great opiate.

Speaking of the painful positions into which a sleepy
lounger will get himself, it is amusing to think of the more
fantastic attitudes that so often take place in bed. If we
could add anything to the numberless things that have
been said about sleep by the poets, it would be upon this
point. Sleep ever shows himself a greater leveller. A man
in his waking moments may look as proud and self-
possessed as he pleases. He may walk proudly, he may sit
proudly, he may eat his dinner proudly; he may shave
himself with an air of infinite superiority; in a word, he
may show himself grand and absurd upon the most trifling occasions. But Sleep plays the petrifying magician.
He arrests the proudest lord as well as the humblest clown
in the most ridiculous postures: so that if you would draw
a grandee from his bed without waking him, no limb-
twisting fool in a pantomime should create wilder laughter. The toy with the string between its legs is hardly a

posture-master more extravagant. Imagine a despot lifted
up to the gaze of his valets, with his eyes shut, his mouth
open, his left hand under his right ear, his other twisted
and hanging helplessly before him like an idiot's, one knee
lifted up, and the other leg stretched out, or both knees
huddled up together: – what a scarecrow to lodge majestic
power in!

But Sleep is kindly even in his tricks; and the poets have
treated him with proper reverence. According to the
ancient mythologists he had even one of the Graces to
wife. He had a thousand sons, of whom the chief were
Morpheus, or the Shaper; Icelos, or the Likely; Phantasus,
and Fancy; and Phobetor, the Terror. His dwelling some
writers place in a dull and darkling part of the earth;
others, with greater compliment, in heaven; and others,
with another kind of propriety, by the sea-shore. There is a
good description of it in Ovid; but in these abstracted
tasks of poetry the moderns outvie the ancients; and there
is nobody who has built his bower for him so finely as
Spenser. Archimago, in the first book of the *Faerie Queene*
(canto I, st. 39), sends a little spirit down to Morpheus
to fetch him a Dream:

> *He, making speedy way through spersed ayre,*
> *And through the world of waters, wide and deepe,*
> *To Morpheus' house doth hastily repaire.*
>
> *Amid the bowels of the earth full steepe*
> *And low, where dawning day doth never peepe,*
> *His dwelling is. There, Tethys his wet bed*
> *Doth ever wash; and Cynthia still doth steepe*
> *In silver dew his ever-drooping head,*
> *Whiles sad Night over him her mantle black doth spred.*
>
> *And more to lull him in his slumber soft*
> *A trickling streame from high rocke tumbling downe,*

And ever-drizzling rain upon the loft,
Mixed with a murmuring winde, much like the soune
Of swarming bees, did cast him in a swoone.
No other noise, nor people's troublous cryes,
As still are wont to annoy the walled towne,
Might there be heard; but careless Quiet lyes,
Wrapt in eternall silence, far from enimyes.

Chaucer has drawn the cave of the same god with greater simplicity; but nothing can have a more deep and sullen effect than his cliffs and cold running waters. It seems as real as an actual solitude, or some quaint old picture in a book of travels in Tartary. He is telling the story of Ceyx and Alcyone in the poem called his Dream. Juno tells a messenger to go to Morpheus and 'bid him creep into the body' of the drowned king, to let his wife know the fatal event by his apparition.

This messenger took leave, and went
Upon his way; and never he stent
Till he came to the dark valley,
That stant betweene rockes twey.
There never yet grew corne, ne gras.
Ne tree, ne nought that aught was.
Beast, ne man, ne naught else;
Save that there were a few wells
Came running fro the cliffs adowne,
That made a deadly sleeping soune,
And runnen downe right by a cave,
That was under a rocky grave,
Amid the valley, wonder-deepe.
There these goddis lay asleepe,
Morpheus and Eclympasteire,
That was the god of Sleepis heire,
That slept and did none other worke.

Where the credentials of this new son and heir, Eclympas-teire, are to be found, we know not; but he acts very much, it must be allowed, like an heir presumptive, in sleeping and doing 'none other work'.

We dare not trust ourselves with many quotations upon sleep from the poets; they are so numerous as well as beautiful. We must content ourselves with mentioning that our two most favourite passages are one in the *Philoctetes* of Sophocles, admirable for its contrast to a scene of terrible agony, which it closes; and the other the following address in Beaumont and Fletcher's tragedy of *Valentinian*, the hero of which is also a sufferer under bodily torment. He is in a chair, slumbering; and these most exquisite lines are gently sung with music: —

> *Care-charming Sleep, thou easer of all woes,*
> *Brother to Death, sweetly thyself dispose*
> *On this afflicted prince. Fall like a cloud*
> *In gentle showers; give nothing that is loud*
> *Or painful to his slumbers; easy, sweet,*
> *And as a purling stream, thou son of Night,*
> *Pass by his troubled senses; sing his pain*
> *Like hollow murmuring wind, or silver rain;*
> *Into this prince, gently, oh gently slide,*
> *And kiss him into slumbers, like a bride.*

How earnest and prayer-like are these pauses! How lightly sprinkled, and yet how deeply settling, like rain, the fancy! How quiet, affectionate, and perfect the conclusion!

Sleep is most graceful in an infant; soundest, in one who has been tired in the open air; completest, to the seaman after a hard voyage; most welcome, to the mind haunted with one idea; most touching to look at, in the parent that has wept; lightest, in the playful child; proudest, in the bride adored.

ROBERT LOUIS STEVENSON

Walking Tours

IT must not be imagined that a walking tour, as some would have us fancy, is merely a better or worse way of seeing the country. There are many ways of seeing landscape quite as good; and none more vivid, in spite of canting dilettantes, than from a railway train. But landscape on a walking tour is quite accessory. He who is indeed of the brotherhood does not voyage in quest of the picturesque, but of certain jolly humours – of the hope and spirit with which the march begins at morning, and the peace and spiritual repletion of the evening's rest. He cannot tell whether he puts his knapsack on, or takes it off, with more delight. The excitement of the departure puts him in key for that of the arrival. Whatever he does is not only a reward in itself, but will be further rewarded in the sequel; and so pleasure leads on to pleasure in an endless chain. It is this that so few can understand; they will either be always lounging or always at five miles an hour; they do not play off the one against the other, prepare all day for the evening, and all evening for the next day. And, above all, it is here that your overwalker fails of comprehension. His heart rises against those who drink their curaçoa in liqueur glasses, when he himself can swill it in a brown john. He will not believe that the flavour is more delicate in the smaller dose. He will not believe that to walk this unconscionable distance is merely to stupefy and brutalize himself, and come to his inn, at night, with a sort of frost on his five wits, and a starless night of darkness in his spirit. Not for him the mild luminous evening of the temperate walker! He has nothing left of man but a physical need for bedtime and a double nightcap; and even his pipe, if he be a smoker, will be savourless and disenchanted. It is the fate of such an one to take twice as much trouble as is needed to obtain happiness, and miss the happiness in the end; he is the man of the proverb, in short, who goes further and fares worse.

Now, to be properly enjoyed, a walking tour should be gone upon alone. If you go in a company, or even in pairs, it is no longer a walking tour in anything but name; it is something else, and more in the nature of a picnic. A walking tour should be gone upon alone, because freedom is of the essence; because you should be able to stop and go on, and follow this way or that, as the freak takes you; and because you must have your own pace, and neither trot alongside a champion walker, nor mince in time with a girl. And then you must be open to all impressions and let your thoughts take colour from what you see. You should be as a pipe for any wind to play upon. 'I cannot see the wit', says Hazlitt, 'of walking and talking at the same time. When I am in the country, I wish to vegetate like the country', which is the gist of all that can be said upon the matter. There should be no cackle of voices at your elbow, to jar on the meditative silence of the morning. And so long as a man is reasoning he cannot surrender himself to that fine intoxication that comes of much motion in the open air, that begins in a sort of dazzle and sluggishness of the brain, and ends in a peace that passes comprehension.

During the first day or so of any tour there are moments of bitterness, when the traveller feels more than coldly towards his knapsack, when he is half in a mind to throw it bodily over the hedge and, like Christian on a similar

occasion, 'give three leaps and go on singing.' And yet it
soon acquires a property of easiness. It becomes magnetic;
the spirit of the journey enters into it. And no sooner have
you passed the straps over your shoulder than the lees of
sleep are cleared from you, you pull yourself together with
a shake, and fall at once into your stride. And surely, of
all possible moods, this, in which a man takes the road, is
the best. Of course, if he *will* keep thinking of his anxieties,
if he *will* open the merchant Abudah's chest and walk arm
in arm with the hag – why, wherever he is, and whether
he walk fast or slow, the chances are that he will not be
happy. And so much the more shame to himself! There
are perhaps thirty men setting forth at that same hour, and
I would lay a large wager there is not another dull face
among the thirty. It would be a fine thing to follow, in a
coat of darkness, one after another of these wayfarers,
some summer morning, for the first few miles upon the
road. This one, who walks fast, with a keen look in his
eyes, is all concentrated in his own mind; he is up at his
loom, weaving and weaving, to set the landscape to words.
This one peers about, as he goes, among the grasses; he
waits by the canal to watch the dragon-flies; he leans on
the gate of the pasture, and cannot look enough upon the
complacent kine. And here comes another talking, laughing, and gesticulating to himself. His face changes from
time to time, as indignation flashes from his eyes or anger
clouds his forehead. He is composing articles, delivering
oration, and conducting the most impassioned interviews, by the way. A little farther on, and it is as like as
not he will begin to sing. And well for him, supposing him
to be no great master in that art, if he stumble across no
stolid peasant at a corner; for on such an occasion, I
scarcely know which is the more troubled, or whether it is
worse to suffer the confusion of your troubadour or the

unfeigned alarm of your clown. A sedentary population, accustomed, besides, to the strange mechanical bearing of the common tramp, can in no wise explain to itself the gaiety of these passers-by. I knew one man who was arrested as a runaway lunatic because, although a full-grown person with a red beard, he skipped as he went like a child. And you would be astonished if I were to tell you all the grave and learned heads who have confessed to me that, when on walking tours, they sang – and sang very ill – and had a pair of red ears when, as described above, the inauspicious peasant plumped into their arms from round a corner. And here, lest you should think I am exaggerating, is Hazlitt's own confession, from his essay *On going a Journey*, which is so good that there should be a tax levied on all who have not read it: –

'Give me the clear blue sky over my head', says he, 'and the green turf beneath my feet, a winding road before me, and a three hours' march to dinner – and then to thinking! It is hard if I cannot start some game on these lone heaths. I laugh, I run, I leap, I sing for joy.'

Bravo! After that adventure of my friend with the policeman, you would not have cared, would you, to publish that in the first person? But we have no bravery nowadays, and, even in books, must all pretend to be as dull and foolish as our neighbours. It was not so with Hazlitt. And notice how learned he is (as, indeed, throughout the essay) in the theory of walking tours. He is none of your athletic men in purple stockings, who walk their fifty miles a day: three hours' march is his ideal. And then he must have a winding road, the epicure!

Yet there is one thing I object to in these words of his, one thing in the great master's practice that seems to me not wholly wise. I do not approve of that leaping and running. Both of these hurry the respiration; they both shake up the brain out of its glorious open-air confusion; and they both break the pace. Uneven walking is not so agreeable to the body, and it distracts and irritates the mind. Whereas, when once you have fallen into an equable stride, it requires no conscious thought from you to keep it up, and yet it prevents you from thinking earnestly of anything else. Like knitting, like the work of a copying clerk, it gradually neutralizes and sets to sleep the serious activity of the mind. We can think of this or that, lightly and laughingly, as a child thinks, or as we think in a morning doze; we can make puns or puzzle out acrostics, and trifle in a thousand ways with words and rhymes; but when it comes to honest work, when we come to gather ourselves together for an effort, we may sound the trumpet as loud and long as we please; the great barons of the mind will not rally to the standard, but sit, each one, at home, warming his hands over his own fire and brooding on his own private thought!

In the course of a day's walk, you see, there is much variance in the mood. From the exhilaration of the start, to the happy phlegm of the arrival, the change is certainly great. As the day goes on, the traveller moves from the one extreme towards the other. He becomes more and more incorporated with the material landscape, and the open-air drunkenness grows upon him with great strides, until he posts along the road, and sees everything about him, as in a cheerful dream. The first is certainly brighter, but the second stage is the more peaceful. A man does not make so many articles towards the end, nor does he laugh aloud; but the purely animal pleasures, the sense of physical well-being, the delight of every inhalation, of every time the muscles tighten down the thigh, console him for the absence of the others, and bring him to his destination still content.

Nor must I forget to say a word on bivouacs. You come to a milestone on a hill, or some place where deep ways meet under trees; and off goes the knapsack, and down you sit to smoke a pipe in the shade. You sink into yourself, and the birds come round and look at you, and your smoke dissipates upon the afternoon under the blue dome of heaven; and the sun lies warm upon your feet, and the cool air visits your neck and turns aside your open shirt. If you are not happy, you must have an evil conscience. You may dally as long as you like by the roadside. It is almost as if the millennium were arrived, when we shall throw our clocks and watches over the house-top, and remember time and seasons no more. Not to keep hours for a lifetime is, I was going to say, to live for ever. You have no idea, unless you have tried it, how endlessly long is a summer's day, that you measure out only by hunger, and bring to an end only when you are drowsy. I know a village where there are hardly any clocks, where no one knows more of the days of the week than by a sort of instinct for the *fête* on Sundays, and where only one person can tell you the day of the month, and she is generally wrong; and if people were aware how slow Time journeyed in that village, and what armfuls of spare hours he gives, over and above the bargain, to its wise inhabitants, I believe there would be a stampede out of London, Liverpool, Paris, and a variety of large towns, where the clocks lose their heads, and shake the hours out each one faster than the other, as though they were all in a wager. And all these foolish pilgrims would each bring his own misery along with him, in a watch-pocket! It is to be noticed, there were no clocks and watches in the much-vaunted days before the flood. It follows, of course, there were no appointments, and punctuality was not yet thought upon. 'Though ye take from a covetous man all his treasure,' says Milton, 'he has yet one jewel left; ye cannot deprive him of his covetousness.' And so I would say of a modern man of business, you may do what you will for him, put him in Eden, give him the elixir of life – he has still a flaw at heart, he still has his business habits. Now, there is no time when business habits are more mitigated than on a walking tour. And so during these halts, as I say, you will feel almost free.

But it is at night, and after dinner, that the best hour comes. There are no such pipes to be smoked as those that follow a good day's march; the flavour of the tobacco is a thing to be remembered, it is so dry and aromatic, so full and so fine. If you wind up the evening with grog, you will own there was never such grog; at every sip a jocund tranquillity spreads about your limbs, and sits easily in your heart. If you read a book – and you will never do so save by fits and starts – you find the language strangely racy and harmonious; words take a new meaning; single sentences possess the ear for half an hour together; and the writer endears himself to you, at every page, by the nicest coincidence of sentiment. It seems as if it were a book you had written yourself in a dream. To all we have read on such occasions we look back with special favour. 'It was on the 10th of April 1798,' says Hazlitt, with amorous precision, 'that I sat down to a volume of the new *Héloïse*, at the Inn at Llangollen, over a bottle of sherry and a cold chicken.' I should wish to quote more, for though we are mighty fine fellows nowadays we cannot write like Hazlitt. And talking of that, a volume of Hazlitt's essays would be a capital pocket-book on such a journey; so would a volume of Heine's songs; and for *Tristram Shandy* I can pledge a fair experience.

If the evening be fine and warm, there is nothing better in life than to lounge before the inn door in the sunset, or

lean over the parapet of the bridge, to watch the weeds
and the quick fishes. It is then, if ever, that you taste
joviality to the full significance of that audacious word.
Your muscles are so agreeably slack, you feel so clean and
so strong and so idle that whether you move or sit still,
whatever you do is done with pride and a kingly sort of
pleasure. You fall in talk with anyone, wise or foolish,
drunk or sober. And it seems as if a hot walk purged you,
more than of anything else, of all narrowness and pride,
and left curiosity to play its part freely, as in a child or a
man of science. You lay aside all your own hobbies, to
watch provincial humours develop themselves before you,
now as a laughable farce, and now grave and beautiful
like an old tale.

Or perhaps you are left to your own company for the
night, and surly weather imprisons you by the fire. You
may remember how Burns, numbering past pleasures,
dwells upon the hours when he had been 'happy thinking'.
It is a phrase that may well perplex a poor modern girt
about on every side by clocks and chimes, and haunted,
even at night, by flaming dial-plates. For we are all so
busy, and have so many far-off projects to realize, and
castles in the fire to turn into solid, habitable mansions on
a gravel soil, that we can find no time for pleasure trips
into the Land of Thought and among the Hills of Vanity.
Changed times, indeed, when we must sit all night, beside
the fire, with folded hands; and a changed world for most
of us, when we find we can pass the hours without discontent, and be happy thinking. We are in such haste to be
doing, to be writing, to be gathering gear, to make our
voice audible a moment in the derisive silence of eternity,
that we forget that one thing, of which these are but the
parts – namely to live. We fall in love, we drink hard, we
run to and fro upon the earth like frightened sheep. And

now you are to ask yourself if, when all is done, you would not have been better to sit by the fire at home, and be happy thinking. To sit still and contemplate, – to remember the faces of women without desire, to be pleased by the great deeds of men without envy, to be everything and everywhere in sympathy, and yet content to remain where and what you are – is not this to know both wisdom and virtue, and to dwell with happiness? After all, it is not they who carry flags, but they who look upon it from a private chamber who have the fun of the procession. And once you are at that, you are in the very humour of all social heresy. It is no time for shuffling, or for big empty words. If you ask yourself what you mean by fame, riches, or learning, the answer is far to seek; and you go back into that kingdom of light imaginations, which seem so vain in the eyes of Philistines perspiring after wealth, and so momentous to those who are stricken with the disproportions of the world, and in the face of the gigantic stars, cannot stop to split differences between two degrees of the infinitesimally small, such as a tobacco pipe or the Roman Empire, a million of money or a fiddlestick's end.

You lean from the window, your last pipe reeking whitely into the darkness, your body full of delicious pains, your mind enthroned in the seventh circle of content; when suddenly the mood changes, the weather-cock goes about, and you ask yourself one question more: whether, for the interval, you have been the wisest philosopher or the most egregious of donkeys? Human experience is not yet able to reply; but at least you have had a fine moment, and looked down upon all the kingdoms of the earth. And whether it was wise or foolish, to-morrow's travel will carry you, body and mind, into some different parish of the infinite.

An Apology for Idlers

BOSWELL: We grow weary when idle.
JOHNSON: That is, sir, because others being busy, we want company; but if we were all idle, there would be no growing weary; we should all entertain one another.

JUST now, when every one is bound, under pain of a decree in absence convicting them of *lèse*-respectability, to enter on some lucrative profession, and labour therein with something not far short of enthusiasm, a cry from the opposite party, who are content when they have enough, and like to look on and enjoy in the meanwhile, savours a little of bravado and gasconade. And yet this should not be. Idleness so called, which does not consist in doing nothing, but in doing a great deal not recognized in the dogmatic formularies of the ruling class, has as good a right to state its position as industry itself. It is admitted that the presence of people who refuse to enter in the great handicap race for sixpenny pieces, is at once an insult and a disenchantment for those who do. A fine fellow (as we see so many) takes his determination, votes for sixpences, and in the emphatic Americanism 'goes for' them. And while such an one is ploughing distressfully up the road, it is not hard to understand his resentment, when he perceives cool persons in the meadows by the wayside, lying with a handkerchief over their ears and a glass at their elbow. Alexander is touched in a very delicate place by the disregard to Diogenes. Where was the glory of having taken Rome for those tumultuous barbarians, who poured into the Senate-house, and found the Fathers sitting silent and unmoved by their success? It is a sore thing to have laboured along and scaled the arduous hilltops, and when all is done find humanity indifferent to your achievement. Hence physicists condemn the unphysical; financiers have only a superficial toleration for those who know little of stocks; literary persons despise the unlettered; and people of all pursuits combine to disparage those who have none.

But though this is one difficulty of the subject it is not the greatest. You could not be put in prison for speaking against industry, but you can be sent to Coventry for speaking like a fool. The greatest difficulty with most subjects is to do them well; therefore, please to remember this is an apology. It is certain that much may be judiciously argued in favour of diligence; only there is something to be said against it, and that is what, on the present occasion, I have to say. To state one argument is not necessarily to be deaf to all others, and that a man has written a book of travels in Montenegro, is no reason why he should never have been to Richmond.

It is surely beyond a doubt that people should be a good deal idle in youth. For though here and there a Lord Macaulay may escape from school honours with all his wits about him, most boys pay so dear for their medals that they never afterwards have a shot in their locker, and begin the world bankrupt. And the same holds true during all the time a lad is educating himself, or suffering others to educate him. It must have been a very foolish old gentleman who addressed Johnson at Oxford in these words: 'Young man, ply your book diligently now, and acquire a stock of knowledge; for when years come upon you, you will find that poring upon books will be but an irksome task.' The old gentleman seems to have been unaware that many other things besides reading grow irksome, and not a few become impossible, by the time a man has to use spectacles and cannot walk without a stick. Books are good enough in their own way, but they are a mighty bloodless substitute for life. It seems a pity to sit like the Lady of Shalott, peering into a mirror, with your back turned on all the bustle and glamour of reality. And if a man reads very hard, as the old anecdote reminds us, he will have little time for thought.

If you look back on your own education, I am sure it will not be the full, vivid, instructive hours of truantry that you regret; you would rather cancel some lack-lustre periods between sleep and waking in the class. For my own part, I have attended a good many lectures in my time. I still remember that the spinning of a top is a case of Kinetic Stability. I still remember that Emphyteusis is not a disease, nor Stillicide a crime. But though I would not willingly part with such scraps of science, I do not set the same store by them as by certain other odds and ends that I came by in the open street while I was playing truant. This is not the moment to dilate on that mighty place of education, which was the favourite school of Dickens and of Balzac, and turns out yearly many inglorious masters in the Science of the Aspects of Life. Suffice it to say this: if a lad does not learn in the streets, it is because he has no faculty of learning. Nor is the truant always in the streets, for if he prefers, he may go out by the gardened suburbs into the country. He may pitch on some tuft of lilacs over a burn, and smoke innumerable pipes to the tune of the water on the stones. A bird will sing in the thicket. And there he may fall into a vein of kindly thought, and see things in a new perspective. Why, if this be not education, what is? We may conceive Mr Worldly Wiseman accosting such an one, and the conversation that should thereupon ensue:

'How now, young fellow, what dost thou here?'

'Truly, sir, I take mine ease.'

'Is not this the hour of the class? and should'st thou not

be plying thy Book with diligence, to the end thou mayest obtain knowledge?'

'Nay, but thus also I follow after Learning, by your leave.'

'Learning, quotha! After what fashion, I pray thee? Is it mathematics?'

'No, to be sure.'

'Is it metaphysics?'

'Nor that.'

'Is it some language?'

'Nay, it is no language.'

'Is it a trade?'

'Nor a trade neither.'

'Why, then, what is't?'

'Indeed, sir, as time may soon come for me to go upon Pilgrimage, I am desirous to note what is commonly done by persons in my case, and where are the ugliest Sloughs and Thickets on the Road; as also, what manner of staff is of the best service. Moreover, I lie here, by this water, to learn by root-of-heart a lesson which my master teaches me to call Peace, or Contentment.'

Hereupon Mr Worldly Wiseman was much commoved with passion, and shaking his cane with a very threatful countenance, broke forth upon this wise: 'Learning, quotha!' said he: 'I would have all such rogues scourged by the Hangman!'

And so he would go his way, ruffling out his cravat with a crackle of starch, like turkey when it spreads its feathers.

Now this, of Mr Wiseman's, is the common opinion. A fact is not called a fact, but a piece of gossip, if it does not fall into one of your scholastic categories. An inquiry must be in some acknowledged direction, with a name to go by; or else you are not inquiring at all, only lounging; and the workhouse is too good for you. It is supposed that all knowledge is at the bottom of a well, or the far end of a telescope. Sainte-Beuve, as he grew older, came to regard all experience as a single great book, in which to study for a few years ere we go hence; and it seemed all one to him whether you should read in chapter xx, which is the differential calculus, or in chapter xxxix, which is hearing the band play in the gardens. As a matter of fact, an intelligent person, looking out of his eyes and hearkening in his ears, with a smile on his face all the time, will get more true education than many another in a life of heroic vigils. There is certainly some chill and arid knowledge to be found upon the summits of formal and laborious science; but it is all round about you, and for the trouble of looking, that you will acquire the warm and palpitating facts of life. While others are filling their memory with a lumber of words, one-half of which they will forget before the week be out, your truant may learn some really useful art: to play the fiddle, to know a good cigar, or to speak with ease and opportunity to all varieties of men. Many who have 'plied their book diligently', and know all about some one branch or another of accepted lore, come out of the study with an ancient and owl-like demeanour, and prove dry, stockish, and dyspeptic in all the better and brighter parts of life. Many make a large fortune, who remain underbred and pathetically stupid to the last. And meanwhile there goes the idler, who began life along with them – by your leave, a different picture. He has had time to take care of his health and his spirits; he has been a great deal in the open air, which is the most salutary of all things for both body and mind; and if he has never read the great Book in very recondite places, he has dipped into it and skimmed it over to excellent purpose. Might not the student afford some Hebrew roots, and the business man some of his half-crowns, for a share of the idler's knowledge of life at large, and Art of Living? Nay, and the idler has another and more important quality than these. I mean his wisdom. He who has much looked on at the childish satisfaction of other people in their hobbies, will regard his own with only a very ironical indulgence. He will not be heard among the dogmatists. He will have a great and cool allowance for all sorts of people and opinions. If he finds no out-of-the-way truths, he will identify himself with no very burning falsehood. His way takes him along a by-road, not much frequented, but very even and pleasant, which is called Common-place Lane and leads to the Belvedere of Common-sense. Thence he shall command an agreeable, if no very noble prospect; and while others behold the East and West, the Devil and the Sunrise, he will be contentedly aware of a sort of morning hour upon all sublunary things, with an army of shadows running speedily and in many different directions into the great daylight of Eternity. The shadows and the generations, the shrill doctors and the plangent wars, go by into ultimate silence and emptiness; but underneath all this, a man may see, out of the Belvedere windows, much green and peaceful landscape; many firelit parlours; good people laughing, drinking, and making love as they did before the Flood or the French Revolution; and the old shepherd telling his tale under the hawthorn.

Extreme *busyness,* whether at school or college, kirk or market, is a symptom of deficient vitality; and a faculty for idleness implies a catholic appetite and a strong sense of personal identity. There is a sort of dead-alive, hackneyed people about, who are scarcely conscious of living except in the exercise of some conventional occupation. Bring these fellows into the country or set them aboard ship, and you will see how they pine for their desk or their study. They have no curiosity; they cannot give themselves over to random provocations; they do not take pleasure in the exercise of their faculties for its own sake; and unless Necessity lays about them with a stick, they will even stand still. It is no good speaking to such folk: they *cannot* be idle, their nature is not generous enough: and they pass those hours in a sort of coma, which are not dedicated to furious moiling in the gold-mill. When they do not require to go to office, when they are not hungry and have no mind to drink, the whole breathing world is a blank to them. If they have to wait an hour or so for a train, they fall into a stupid trance with their eyes open. To see them, you would suppose there was nothing to look at and no one to speak with; you would imagine they were paralysed or alienated: and yet very possibly they are hard workers in their own way, and have good eyesight for a flaw in a deed or a turn of the market. They have been to school and college, but all the time they had their eye on the medal; they have gone about in the world and mixed with clever people, but all the time they were thinking of their own affairs. As if a man's soul were not too small to begin with, they have dwarfed and narrowed theirs by a life of all work and no play; until here they are at forty, with a listless attention, a mind vacant of all material of amusement, and not one thought to rub against another, while they wait for the train. Before he was breeched, he might have clambered on the boxes; when he was twenty, he would have stared at the girls; but now the pipe is smoked out, the snuff-box empty, and my gentleman sits bolt upright upon a bench, with lamentable eyes. This does not appeal to me as being Success in Life.

But it is not only the person himself who suffers from his busy habits, but his wife and children, his friends and relations, and down to the very people he sits with in a railway-carriage or an omnibus. Perpetual devotion to what a man calls his business, is only to be sustained by perpetual neglect of many other things. And it is not by any means certain that a man's business is the most important thing he has to do. To an impartial estimate it will seem clear that many of the wisest, most virtuous, and most beneficent parts that are to be played upon the Theatre of Life are filled by gratuitous performers, and pass, among the world at large, as phases of idleness. For in that Theatre, not only the walking gentlemen, singing chambermaids, and diligent fiddlers in the orchestra, but those who look on and clap their hands from the benches, do really play a part and fulfil important offices towards the general result.

You are no doubt very dependent on the care of your lawyer and stockbroker, of the guards and signalmen who convey you rapidly from place to place, and the policemen who walk the streets for your protection; but is there not a thought of gratitude in your heart for certain other benefactors who set you smiling when they fall in your way, or season your dinner with good company? Colonel Newcome helped to lose his friend's money; Fred Bayham had an ugly trick of borrowing shirts; and yet they were better people to fall among than Mr Barnes. And though Falstaff was neither sober nor very honest, I think I could name one or two long-faced Barabbases whom the world could better have done without. Hazlitt mentions that he was more sensible of obligation to Northcote, who had never done him anything he could call a service, than to his whole circle of ostentatious friends; for he thought a good companion emphatically the greatest benefactor. I know there are people in the world who cannot feel grateful unless the favour has been done them at the cost of pain and difficulty. But this is a churlish disposition. A man may send you six sheets of letter-paper covered with the most entertaining gossip, or you may pass half an hour pleasantly, perhaps profitably, over an article of his; do you think the service would be greater if he had made the manuscript in his heart's blood, like a compact with the devil? Do you really fancy you should be more beholden to your correspondent, if he had been damning you all the while for your importunity? Pleasures are more beneficial than duties because, like the quality of mercy, they are not strained, and they are twice blest. There must always be two to a kiss, and there may be a score in a jest; but wherever there is an element of sacrifice, the favour is conferred with pain, and, among generous people, received with confusion.

There is no duty we so much underrate as the duty of being happy. By being happy we sow anonymous benefits upon the world, which remain unknown even to ourselves, or when they are disclosed, surprise nobody so much as the benefactor. The other day, a ragged, barefoot boy ran down the street after a marble, with so jolly an air that he set every one he passed into a good humour; one of these persons, who had been delivered from more than usually black thoughts, stopped the little fellow and gave him some money with this remark: 'You see what sometimes comes of looking pleased.' If he had looked pleased before he had now to look both pleased and mystified. For my part, I justify this encouragement of smiling rather than tearful children; I do not wish to pay for tears anywhere but upon the stage; but I am prepared to deal largely in the opposite commodity. A happy man or woman is a better thing to find than a five-pound note. He or she is a radiating focus of goodwill; and their entrance into a room is as though another candle had been lighted. We need not care whether they could prove the forty-seventh proposition; they do a better thing than that, they practically demonstrate the great Theorem of the Liveableness of Life. Consequently, if a person cannot be happy without remaining idle, idle he should remain. It is a revolutionary precept; but, thanks to hunger and the workhouse, one not easily to be abused; and within practical limits, it is one of the most incontestable truths in the whole Body of Morality. Look at one of your industrious fellows for a moment, I beseech you. He sows hurry and reaps indigestion; he puts a vast deal of activity out to interest, and receives a large measure of nervous derangement in return. Either he absents himself entirely from all fellowship, and lives a recluse in a garret, with carpet slippers and a leaden inkpot; or he comes among people swiftly and bitterly, in a contraction of his whole nervous system, to discharge some temper before he returns to work. I do not care how much or how well he works, this fellow is an evil feature in other people's lives. They would be happier if he were dead. They could easier do without his services in the Circumlocution Office, than they can tolerate his fractious spirits. He poisons life at the well-head. It is better to be beggared out of hand by a scapegrace nephew, than daily hag-ridden by a peevish uncle.

And what, in God's name, is all this pother about? For what cause do they embitter their own and other people's lives? That a man should publish three or thirty articles a year, that he should finish or not finish his great allegorical picture, are questions of little interest to the world. The ranks of life are full; and although a thousand fall, there are always some to go into the breach. When they told Joan of Arc she should be at home minding women's work, she answered there were plenty to spin and wash. And so, even with your own rare gifts! When nature is 'so careless of the single life', why should we coddle ourselves into the fancy that our own is of exceptional importance?

Suppose Shakespeare had been knocked on the head some
dark night in Sir Thomas Lucy's preserves, the world
would have wagged on better or worse, the pitcher gone
to the well, the scythe to the corn, and the student to his
book; and no one been any the wiser of the loss. There are
not many works extant, if you look the alternative all over,
which are worth the price of a pound of tobacco to a man
of limited means. This is a sobering reflexion for the
proudest of our earthly vanities. Even a tobacconist may,
upon consideration, find not great cause for personal vain-
glory in the phrase; for although tobacco is an admirable
sedative, the qualities necessary for retailing it are neither
rare nor precious in themselves. Alas and alas! you may
take it how you will, but the services of no single individual are indispensable. Atlas was just a gentleman with a
protracted nightmare! And yet you see merchants who go
and labour themselves into a great fortune, and thence
into the bankruptcy court; scribblers who keep scribbling
at little articles until their temper is a cross to all who come
about them, as though Pharaoh should set the Israelites
to make a pin instead of a pyramid; and fine young men
who work themselves into a decline, and are driven off in a
hearse with white plumes upon it. Would you not suppose
these persons had been whispered, by the Master of the
Ceremonies, the promise of some momentous destiny?
and that this lukewarm bullet on which they play their
farces was the bull's-eye and centre-point of all the universe? And yet it is not so. The ends for which they gave
away their priceless youth, for all they know, may be
chimerical or hurtful; the glory and riches they expect
may never come, or may find them indifferent; and they
and the world they inhabit are so inconsiderable that the
mind freezes at the thought.

A Plea for Gas Lamps

CITIES given, the problem was to light them. How to conduct individual citizens about the burgess-warren, when once heaven had withdrawn its leading luminary? or – since we live in a scientific age – when once our spinning planet has turned its back upon the sun? The moon, from time to time, was doubtless very helpful; the stars had a cheery look among the chimney-pots; and a cresset here and there, on church or citadel, produced a fine pictorial effect, and, in places where the ground lay unevenly, held out the right hand of conduct to the benighted. But sun, moon, and stars abstracted or concealed, the nightfaring inhabitant had to fall back – we speak on the authority of old prints – upon stable lanthorns two stories in height. Many holes, drilled in the conical turret-roof of this vagabond Pharos, let up spouts of dazzlement into the bearer's eyes; and as he paced forth in the ghostly darkness, carrying his own sun by a ring about his finger, day and night swung to and fro and up and down about his footsteps. Blackness haunted his path; he was beleaguered by goblins as he went; and, curfew being struck, he found no light but that he travelled in throughout the township.

Closely following on this epoch of migratory lanthorns in a world of extinction, came the era of oil-lights, hard to kindle, easy to extinguish, pale and wavering in the hour of their endurance. Rudely puffed the winds of heaven; roguishly clomb up the all-destructive urchin; and, lo! in a moment night re-established her void empire, and the city groped along the wall, suppered but bedless, occult from guidance, and sorrily wading in the kennels. As if gamesome winds and gamesome youths were not sufficient, it was the habit to sling these fable luminaries from house to house above the fairway. There, on invisible cordage, let them swing! And suppose some crane-necked general to go speeding by on a tall charger, spurring the destiny of nations, red-hot in expedition, there would indubitably be some effusion of military blood, and oaths, and a certain crash of glass; and while the chieftain rode forward with a purple coxcomb, the street would be left to original darkness, unpiloted, unvoyageable, a province of the desert night.

The conservative, looking before and after, draws from each contemplation the matter for content. Out of the age of gas lamps he glances back slightingly at the mirk and glimmer in which his ancestors wandered; his heart waxes jocund at the contrast; nor do his lips refrain from a stave, in the highest style of poetry, lauding progress and the golden mean. When gas first spread along a city, mapping it forth about evenfall for the eye of observant birds, a new age had begun for sociality and corporate pleasure-seeking, and begun with proper circumstance, becoming its own birthright. The work of Prometheus had advanced by another stride. Mankind and its supper parties were no longer at the mercy of a few miles of sea-fog; sundown no longer emptied the promenade; and the day was length-ened out to every man's fancy. The cityfolk had stars of their own; biddable domesticated stars.

It is true that these were not so steady, nor yet so clear, as their originals; nor indeed was their lustre so elegant as that of the best wax candles. But then the gas stars, being nearer at hand, were more practically efficacious than Jupiter himself. It is true, again, that they did not unfold their rays with the appropriate spontaneity of the planets, coming out along the firmament one after another, as the need arises. But the lamplighters took to their heels every evening, and ran with a good heart. It was pretty to see man thus emulating the punctuality of heaven's orbs; and though perfection was not absolutely reached, and now and then an individual may have been knocked on the head by the ladder of the flying functionary, yet people commended his zeal in a proverb, and taught their children to say, 'God bless the lamplighter!' And since his passage was a piece of the day's programme, the children were well pleased to repeat the benediction, not, of course, in so many words, which would have been improper, but in some chaste circumlocution, suitable for infant lips.

God bless him, indeed! For the term of his twilight diligence is near at hand; and for not much longer shall we watch him speeding up the street, and, at measured intervals, knocking another luminous hole into the dusk. The Greeks would have made a noble myth of such an one; how he distributed starlight, and, as soon as the need was over, re-collected it; and the little bull's-eye, which was his instrument, and held enough fire to kindle a whole parish, would have been fitly commemorated in the legend. Now, like all heroic tasks, his labours draw towards apotheosis, and in the light of victory himself shall disappear. For another advance has been effected. Our tame stars are to come out in future, not one by one, but all in a body and at once. A sedate electrician somewhere in a back office touches a spring – and behold! from one end to another of the city, from east to west, from the Alexandra to the Crystal Palace, there is light! *Fiat Lux,* says the sedate electrician. What a spectacle, on some clear, dark nightfall, from the edge of Hampstead Hill, when in a moment, in the twinkling of an eye, the design of the monstrous city flashes into vision – a glittering hieroglyph many square miles in extent; and when, to borrow and debase an image, all the evening street lamps burst together into

song! Such is the spectacle of the future, preluded the
other day by the experiment in Pall Mall. Star-rise by
electricity, the most romantic flight of civilization; the
compensatory benefit for an innumerable array of fac-
tories and bankers' clerks. To the artistic spirit exercised about Thirlmere, here is a crumb of consolation;
consolatory, at least, to such of them as look out upon the
world through seeing eyes, and contentedly accept beauty
where it comes.

But the conservative, while lauding progress, is ever
timid of innovation; his is the hand upheld to counsel
pause; his is the signal advising slow advance. The word
electricity now stands the note of danger. In Paris, at the
mouth of the Passage des Princes, in the place before the
Opera portico, and in the Rue Drouot at the *Figaro*
office, a new sort of urban star now shines out nightly,
horrible, unearthly, obnoxious to the human eye; a lamp
for a nightmare! Such a light as this should shine only on
murders and public crime, or along the corridors of lunatic
asylums, a horror to heighten horror. To look at it only
once is to fall in love with gas, which gives a warm domestic radiance fit to eat by. Mankind, you would have
thought, might have remained content with what Prometheus stole for them and not gone fishing the profound
heaven with kites to catch and domesticate the wildfire
of the storm. Yet here we have the levin brand at our
doors, and it is proposed that we should henceforward take
our walks abroad in the glare of permanent lightning. A
man need not be very superstitious if he scruple to follow
his pleasures by the light of the Terror that Flieth, nor
very epicurean if he prefer to see the face of beauty more
becomingly displayed. That ugly blinding glare may not
improperly advertise the home of slanderous *Figaro,* which
is a back-shop to the infernal regions; but where soft joys

prevail, where people are convoked to pleasure and the philosopher looks on smiling and silent, where love and laughter and deifying wine abound, there, at least, let the old mild lustre shine upon the ways of man.

G. K. CHESTERTON

A Defence of Nonsense

THERE are two equal and eternal ways of looking at this twilight world of ours; we may see it as the twilight of evening or the twilight of morning; we may think of anything, down to a fallen acorn, as a descendant or as an ancestor. There are times when we are almost crushed, not so much with the load of the evil as with the load of the goodness of humanity, when we feel that we are nothing but the inheritors of a humiliating splendour. But there are other times when everything seems primitive, when the ancient stars are only sparks blown from a boy's bonfire, when the whole earth seems so young and experimental that even the white hair of the aged, in the fine biblical phrase, is like almond-trees that blossom, like the white hawthorn grown in May. That it is good for a man to realize that he is 'the heir of all the ages' is pretty commonly admitted; it is a less popular but equally important point that it is good for him sometimes to realize that he is not only an ancestor, but an ancestor of primal antiquity; it is good for him to wonder whether he is not a hero, and to experience ennobling doubts as to whether he is not a solar myth.

The matters which most thoroughly evoke this sense of the abiding childhood of the world are those which are really fresh, abrupt and inventive in any age; and if we were asked what was the best proof of this adventurous youth in the nineteenth century we should say, with all respect to its portentous sciences and philosophies, that it was to be found in the rhymes of Mr Edward Lear and in the literature of nonsense. 'The Dong with the Luminous Nose', at least, is original, as the first ship and the first plough were original.

It is true in a certain sense that some of the greatest writers the world has seen – Aristophanes, Rabelais, and Sterne – have written nonsense; but unless we are mistaken, it is in a widely different sense. The nonsense of these men was satiric – that is to say, symbolic; it was a kind of exuberant capering round a discovered truth. There is all the difference in the world between the instinct of satire, which seeing in the Kaiser's moustaches something typical of him, draws them continually larger and larger; and the instinct of nonsense which, for no reason whatever, imagines what those moustaches would look like on the present Archbishop of Canterbury if he grew them in a fit of absence of mind. We incline to think that no age except our own could have understood that the Quangle-Wangle meant absolutely nothing, and the Lands of the Jumblies were absolutely nowhere. We fancy that if the account of the knave's trial in *Alice in Wonderland* had been published in the seventeenth century it would have been bracketed with Bunyan's *Trial of Faithful* as a parody on the State prosecutions of the time. We fancy that if 'The Dong with the Luminous Nose' had appeared in the same period every one would have called it a dull satire on Oliver Cromwell.

It is altogether advisedly that we quote chiefly from Mr Lear's *Nonsense Rhymes*. To our mind he is both chronologically and essentially the father of nonsense; we think him superior to Lewis Carroll. In one sense, indeed, Lewis Carroll has a great advantage. We know what Lewis Carroll was in daily life: he was a singularly serious and conventional don, universally respected, but very much of a pedant and something of a Philistine. Thus his strange double life in earth and in dreamland emphasizes the idea that lies at the back of nonsense – the idea of *escape*, of escape into a world where things are not fixed horribly in an eternal appropriateness, where apples grow on pear-trees, and any odd man you meet may have three legs. Lewis Carroll, living one life in which he would have thundered morally against any one who walked on the wrong plot of grass, and another life in which he would cheerfully call the sun green and the moon blue, was, by his very divided nature, his one foot on both worlds, a per-fect type of the position of modern nonsense. His Wonder-land is a country populated by insane mathematicians. We feel the whole is an escape into a world of masquerade; we feel that if we could pierce their disguises, we might discover that Humpty Dumpty and the March Hare were Professors and Doctors of Divinity enjoying a mental holi-day. This sense of escape is certainly less emphatic in Edward Lear, because of the completeness of his citizen-ship in the world of unreason. We do not know his prosaic biography as we know Lewis Carroll's. We accept him as a purely fabulous figure, on his own description of himself:

> *His body is perfectly spherical,*
> *He weareth a runcible hat.*

While Lewis Carroll's Wonderland is purely intellectual, Lear introduces quite another element – the element of the poetical and even emotional. Carroll's works by the pure reason, but this is not so strong a contrast; for, after all, mankind in the main has always regarded reason as a bit of a joke. Lear introduces his unmeaning words and his amorphous creatures not with the pomp of reason, but with the romantic prelude of rich hues and haunting rhythms.

> *Far and few, far and few,*
> *Are the lands where the Jumblies live,*

is an entirely different type of poetry to that exhibited in 'Jabberwocky'. Carroll, with a sense of mathematical neatness, makes his whole poem a mosaic of new and mysterious words. But Edward Lear, with more subtle and placid effrontery, is always introducing scraps of his own elvish dialect into the middle of simple and rational statements, until we are almost stunned into admitting that we know what they mean. There is a genial ring of common sense about such lines as

> *For his aunt Jobiska said 'Every one knows*
> *That a Pobble is better without his toes,'*

which is beyond the reach of Carroll. The poet seems so easy on the matter that we are almost driven to pretend that we see his meaning, that we know the peculiar difficulties of a Pobble, that we are as old travellers in the 'Gromboolian Plain' as he is.

Our claim that nonsense is a new literature (we might almost say a new sense) would be quite indefensible if nonsense were nothing more than a mere aesthetic fancy. Nothing sublimely artistic has ever arisen out of mere art, any more than anything essentially reasonable has ever risen out of the pure reason. There must always be a rich moral soil for any great aesthetic growth. The principle of *art for art's sake* is a very good principle if it means that there is a vital distinction between the earth and the tree that has its roots in the earth; but it is a very bad principle if it means that the tree could grow just as well with its roots in the air. Every great literature has always been allegorical – allegorical of some view of the whole universe. The 'Iliad' is only great because all life is a battle, the 'Odyssey' because all life is a journey, the Book of Job because all life is a riddle. There is one attitude in which we think that all existence is summed up in the word 'ghosts'; another, and somewhat better one, in which we think it is summed up in the words 'A Midsummer Night's Dream'. Even the vulgarest melodrama or detective story can be good if it expresses something of the delight in sinister possibilities – the healthy lust for darkness and terror which may come on us any night in walking down a dark lane. If, therefore, nonsense is really to be the literature of the future, it must have its own version of the Cosmos to offer; the world must not only be tragic, romantic, and religious, it must be nonsensical also. And here we fancy that nonsense will, in a very unexpected way, come to the aid of the spiritual view of things. Religion has for centuries been trying to make men exult in the 'wonders' of creation, but it has forgotten that a thing cannot be completely wonderful so long as it remains sensible. So long as we regard a tree as an obvious thing, naturally and reasonably created for a giraffe to eat, we cannot properly wonder at it. It is when we consider it as a prodigious wave of the living soil sprawling up to the skies for no reason in particular that we take off our hats, to the astonishment of the park-keeper. Everything has in fact another side to it like the moon, the patroness of nonsense. Viewed from that other side, a bird is a blossom broken loose from its chain of stalk, a man a quadruped begging on its hind legs, a house a gigantesque hat to cover a man from the sun, a chair an apparatus of four wooden legs for a cripple with only two.

This is the side of things which tends most truly to spiritual wonder. It is significant that in the greatest religious poem existent, the Book of Job, the argument which convinces the infidel is not (as has been represented by the merely rational religionism of the eighteenth century) a picture of the ordered beneficence of the Creation; but, on the contrary, a picture of the huge and undecipherable unreason of it. 'Hast Thou sent the rain upon the desert where no man is?' This simple sense of wonder at the shape of things, and at their exuberant independence of our intellectual standards and our trivial definitions, is the basis of spirituality as it is the basis of nonsense. Nonsense and faith (strange as the conjunction may seem) are the two supreme symbolic assertions of the truth that to draw out the soul of things with a syllogism is as impossible as to draw out Leviathan with a hook. The well-meaning person who, by merely studying the logical side of things, has decided that 'faith is nonsense', does not know how truly he speaks; later it may come back to him in the form that nonsense is faith.

A Piece of Chalk

I REMEMBER one splendid morning, all blue and silver, in the summer holidays, when I reluctantly tore myself away from the task of doing nothing in particular, and put on a hat of some sort and picked up a walking-stick, and put six very bright-coloured chalks in my pocket. I then went into the kitchen (which, along with the rest of the house, belonged to a very square and sensible old woman in a Sussex village), and asked the owner and occupant of the kitchen if she had any brown paper. She had a great deal; in fact, she had too much; and she mistook the purpose and the rationale of the existence of brown paper. She seemed to have an idea that if a person wanted brown paper he must be wanting to tie up parcels; which was the last thing I wanted to do; indeed, it is a thing which I have found to be beyond my mental capacity. Hence she dwelt very much on the varying qualities of toughness and endurance in the material. I explained to her that I only wanted to draw pictures on it, and that I did not want them to endure in the least; and that from my point of view, therefore, it was a question not of tough consistency, but of responsive surface, a thing comparatively irrelevant in a parcel. When she understood that I wanted to draw she offered to overwhelm me with note-paper, apparently supposing that I did my notes and correspondence on old brown paper wrappers from motives of economy.

I then tried to explain the rather delicate logical shade, that I not only liked brown paper, but liked the quality of brownness in paper, just as I liked the quality of brownness in October woods, or in beer, or in the peat-streams of the North. Brown paper represents the primal twilight of the first toil of creation, and with a bright-coloured chalk or two you can pick out points of fire in it, sparks of gold, and blood-red, and sea-green, like the first fierce stars that sprang out of divine darkness. All this I said (in an off-hand way) to the old woman; and I put the brown paper in my pocket along with the chalks, and possibly other things. I suppose every one must have reflected how primeval and how poetical are the things that one carries in one's pocket; the pocket-knife, for instance, the type of all human tools, the infant of the sword. Once I planned to write a book of poems entirely about the things in my pocket. But I found it would be too long; and the age of the great epics is past.

*

With my stick and my knife, my chalks and my brown paper, I went out on to the great downs. I crawled across those colossal contours that express the best quality of England, because they are at the same time soft and strong. The smoothness of them has the same meaning as the smoothness of great cart-horses, or the smoothness of the beech-tree; it declares in the teeth of our timid and cruel theories that the mighty are merciful. As my eye swept the landscape, the landscape was as kindly as any of its cottages, but for power it was like an earthquake. The villages in the immense valley were safe, one could see, for centuries; yet the lifting of the whole land was like the lifting of one enormous wave to wash them all away.

I crossed one swell of living turf after another, looking for a place to sit down and draw. Do not, for heaven's sake, imagine I was going to sketch from Nature. I was going to draw devils and seraphim, and blind old gods that men worshipped before the dawn of right, and saints in robes of angry crimson, and seas of strange green, and all the sacred or monstrous symbols that look so well in bright colours on brown paper. They are much better worth drawing than Nature; also they are much easier to draw. When a cow came slouching by in the field next to me, a mere artist might have drawn it; but I always get wrong in the hind legs of quadrupeds. So I drew the soul of the cow; which I saw there plainly walking before me in the sunlight; and the soul was all purple and silver, and had seven horns and the mystery that belongs to all the beasts. But though I could not with a crayon get the best out of the landscape, it does not follow that the landscape was not getting the best out of me. And this, I think, is the mistake that people make about the old poets who lived before Wordsworth, and were supposed not to care very much about Nature because they did not describe it much.

They preferred writing about great men to writing about great hills; but they sat on the great hills to write it.

They gave out much less about Nature, but they drank in, perhaps, much more. They painted the white robes of their holy virgins with the blinding snow, at which they had stared all day. They blazoned the shields of their paladins with the purple and gold of many heraldic sunsets. The greenness of a thousand green leaves clustered into the live green figure of Robin Hood. The blueness of a score of forgotten skies became the blue robes of the Virgin. The inspiration went in like sunbeams and came out like Apollo.

*

But as I sat scrawling these silly figures on the brown paper, it began to dawn on me, to my great disgust, that I had left one chalk, and that a most exquisite and essential chalk, behind. I searched all my pockets, but I could not find any white chalk. Now, those who are acquainted with all the philosophy (nay, religion) which is typified in the art of drawing on brown paper, know that white is positive and essential. I cannot avoid remarking here upon a moral significance. One of the wise and awful truths which this brown-paper art reveals, is that, that white is a colour. It is not a mere absence of colour; it is a shining and affirmative thing, as fierce as red, as definite as black. When (so to speak) your pencil grows red-hot, it draws roses; when it grows white-hot, it draws stars. And one of the two or three defiant verities of the best religious morality, of real Christianity for example, is exactly the same thing; the chief assertion of religious morality is that white is a colour. Virtue is not the absence of vices or the avoidance of moral dangers; virtue is a vivid and separate thing, like pain or a particular smell. Mercy does not mean not being cruel or sparing people revenge or punishment; it means a plain and positive thing like the sun, which one has either seen or not seen. Chastity does not mean abstention from sexual wrong; it means something flaming, like Joan of Arc. In a word, God paints in many colours; but He never paints so gorgeously, I had almost said so gaudily, as when He paints in white. In a sense our age has realized this fact, and expressed it in our sullen costume. For if it were really true that white was a blank and colourless thing, negative and non-committal, then white would be used instead of black and grey for the funeral dress of this pessimistic period. We should see city gentlemen in frock coats of spotless silver satin, with top hats as white as wonderful arum lilies. Which is not the case.

Meanwhile I could not find my chalk.

*

I sat on the hill in a sort of despair. There was no town nearer than Chichester at which it was even remotely probable that there would be such a thing as an artist's colourman. And yet, without white, my absurd little pictures would be as pointless as the world would be if there were no good people in it. I stared stupidly round, racking my brain for expedients. Then I suddenly stood up and roared with laughter, again and again, so that the cows stared at me and called a committee. Imagine a man in the Sahara regretting that he had no sand for his hourglass. Imagine a gentleman in mid-ocean wishing that he had brought some salt water with him for his chemical experiments. I was sitting on an immense warehouse of white chalk. The landscape was made entirely out of white chalk. White chalk was piled mere miles until it met the sky. I stooped and broke a piece off the rock I sat on: it did not mark so well as the shop chalks do; but it gave the effect. And I stood there in a trance of pleasure, realizing that this Southern England is not only a grand peninsula, and a tradition and a civilization; it is something even more admirable. It is a piece of chalk.

A Defence of Penny Dreadfuls

ONE of the strangest examples of the degree to which ordinary life is undervalued is the example of popular literature, the vast mass of which we contentedly describe as vulgar. The boy's novelette may be ignorant in a literary sense, which is only like saying that a modern novel is ignorant in the chemical sense, or the economic sense, or the astronomical sense; but it is not vulgar intrinsically – it is the actual centre of a million flaming imaginations.

In former centuries the educated class ignored the ruck of vulgar literature. They ignored, and therefore did not, properly speaking, despise it. Simple ignorance and indifference does not inflate the character with pride. A man does not walk down the street giving a haughty twirl to his moustaches at the thought of his superiority to some variety of deep-sea fishes. The old scholars left the whole under-world of popular compositions in a similar darkness.

Today, however, we have reversed this principle. We do despise vulgar compositions, and we do not ignore them. We are in some danger of becoming petty in our study of pettiness; there is a terrible Circean law in the background that if the soul stoops too ostentatiously to examine anything it never gets up again. There is no class of vulgar publications about which there is, to my mind, more utterly ridiculous exaggeration and misconception than the current boys' literature of the lowest stratum.

This class of composition has presumably always existed, and must exist. It has no more claim to be good literature than the daily conversation of its readers to be fine oratory, or the lodging-houses and tenements they inhabit to be sublime architecture. But people must have conversation, they must have houses, and they must have stories. The simple need for some kind of ideal world in which fictitious persons play an unhampered part is infinitely deeper and older than the rules of good art, and much more important. Every one of us in childhood has constructed such an invisible *dramatis personae*; but it never occurred to our nurses to correct the composition by careful comparison with Balzac. In the East the professional story-teller goes from village to village with a small carpet; and I wish sincerely that any one had the moral courage to spread that carpet and sit on it in Ludgate Circus. But it is not probable that all the tales of the carpet-bearer are little gems of original artistic workmanship. Literature and fiction are two entirely different things. Literature is a luxury; fiction is a necessity. A work of art can hardly be too short, for its climax is its merit. A story can never be too long, for its conclusion is merely to be deplored, like the last halfpenny or the last pipelight. And so, while the increase of the artistic conscience tends in more ambitious works to brevity and impressionism, voluminous industry still marks the producer of the true romantic trash. There was no end to the ballads of Robin Hood; there is no end to the volumes about Dick Deadshot and the Avenging Nine. These two heroes are deliberately conceived as immortal.

But instead of basing all discussion of the problem upon the common-sense recognition of this fact – that the youth of the lower orders always has had and always must have formless and endless romantic reading of some kind, and

then going on to make provision for its wholesomeness –
we begin, generally speaking, by fantastic abuse of this
reading as a whole and indignant surprise that the errand-
boys under discussion do not read *The Egoist* and *The
Master Builder*. It is the custom, particularly among
magistrates, to attribute half the crimes of the Metropolis
to cheap novelettes. If some grimy urchin runs away with
an apple, the magistrate shrewdly points out that the
child's knowledge that apples appease hunger is traceable
to some curious literary researches. The boys themselves,
when penitent, frequently accuse the novelettes with great
bitterness, which is only to be expected from young people
possessed of no little native humour. If I had forged a will,
and could obtain sympathy by tracing the incident to the
influence of Mr George Moore's novels, I should find the
greatest entertainment in the diversion. At any rate, it is
firmly fixed in the minds of most people that gutter-boys,
unlike everybody else in the community, find their
principal motives for conduct in printed books.

Now it is quite clear that this objection, the objection
brought by magistrates, has nothing to do with literary
merit. Bad story writing is not a crime. Mr Hall Caine
walks the streets openly, and cannot be put in prison for
an anti-climax. The objection rests upon the theory that
the tone of the mass of boys' novelettes is criminal and
degraded, appealing to low cupidity and low cruelty.
This is the magisterial theory, and this is rubbish.

So far as I have seen them, in connexion with the
dirtiest bookstalls in the poorest districts, the facts are
simply these: The whole bewildering mass of vulgar
juvenile literature is concerned with adventures, rambling,
disconnected, and endless. It does not express any passion
of any sort, for there is no human character of any sort.
It runs eternally in certain grooves of local and historical

type: the medieval knight, the eighteenth-century duellist, and the modern cowboy recur with the same stiff simplicity as the conventional human figures in an Oriental pattern. I can quite as easily imagine a human being kindling wild appetites by the contemplation of his Turkey carpet as by such dehumanized and naked narrative as this.

Among these stories there are a certain number which deal sympathetically with the adventures of robbers, outlaws, and pirates, which present in a dignified and romantic light thieves and murderers like Dick Turpin and Claude Duval. That is to say, they do precisely the same thing as Scott's *Ivanhoe*, Scott's *Rob Roy*, Scott's *Lady of the Lake*, Byron's *Corsair*, Wordsworth's *Rob Roy's Grave*, Stevenson's *Macaire*, Mr Max Pemberton's *Iron Pirate*, and a thousand more works distributed systematically as prizes and Christmas presents. Nobody imagines that an admiration of Locksley in *Ivanhoe* will lead a boy to shoot Japanese arrows at the deer in Richmond Park; no one thinks that the incautious opening of Wordsworth at the poem on Rob Roy will set him up for life as a blackmailer. In the case of our own class, we recognize that this wild life is contemplated with pleasure by the young, not because it is like their own life, but because it is different from it. It might at least cross our minds that, for whatever other reason the errand-boy reads *The Red Revenge*, it really is not because he is dripping with the gore of his own friends and relatives.

In this matter, as in all such matters, we lose our bearings entirely by speaking of the 'lower classes' when we mean humanity minus ourselves. This trivial romantic literature is not specially plebeian: it is simply human. The philanthropist can never forget classes and callings. He says, with a modest swagger, 'I have invited twenty-five factory hands to tea.' If he said, 'I have invited twenty-five chartered accountants to tea', every one would see the humour of so simple a classification. But this is what we have done with this lumberland of foolish writing: we have probed, as if it were some monstrous new disease, what is, in fact, nothing but the foolish and valiant heart of man. Ordinary men will always be sentimentalists: for a sentimentalist is simply a man who has feelings and does not trouble to invent a new way of expressing them. These common and current publications have nothing essentially evil about them. They express the sanguine and heroic truisms on which civilization is built; for it is clear that unless civilization is built on truisms, it is not built at all. Clearly, there could be no safety for a society in which the remark by the Chief Justice that murder was wrong was regarded as an original and dazzling epigram.

If the authors and publishers of *Dick Deadshot*, and such remarkable works, were suddenly to make a raid upon the educated class, were to take down the names of every man, however distinguished, who was caught at a University Extension Lecture, were to confiscate all our novels and warn us all to correct our lives, we should be seriously annoyed. Yet they have far more right to do so than we; for they, with all their idiocy, are normal and we are abnormal. It is the modern literature of the educated, not of the uneducated, which is avowedly and aggressively criminal. Books recommending profligacy and pessimism, at which the high-souled errand-boy would shudder, lie upon all our drawing-room tables. If the dirtiest old owner of the dirtiest old bookstall in Whitechapel dared to display works really recommending polygamy or suicide, his stock would be seized by the police. These things are our luxuries. And with a hypocrisy so ludicrous as to be almost unparalleled in history, we rate the gutter-boys for their immorality at the very time that we are discussing (with equivocal German professors) whether morality is valid at all. At the very instant that we curse the Penny Dreadful for encouraging thefts upon property, we canvass the proposition that all property is theft. At the very instant we accuse it (quite unjustly) of lubricity and indecency, we are cheerfully reading philosophies which glory in lubricity and indecency. At the very instant that we charge it with encouraging the young to destroy life, we are placidly discussing whether life is worth preserving.

But it is we who are the morbid exceptions; it is we who are the criminal class. This should be our great comfort. The vast mass of humanity, with their vast mass of idle books and idle words, have never doubted and never will doubt that courage is splendid, that fidelity is noble, that distressed ladies should be rescued, and vanquished enemies spared. There are a large number of cultivated persons who doubt these maxims of daily life, just as there are a large number of persons who believe they are the Prince of Wales; and I am told that both classes of people are entertaining conversationalists. But the average man or boy writes daily in these great gaudy diaries of his soul, which we call Penny Dreadfuls, a plainer and better gospel than any of those iridescent ethical paradoxes that the fashionable change as often as their bonnets. It may be a very limited aim in morality to shoot a 'many-faced and fickle traitor', but at least it is a better aim than to be a many-faced and fickle traitor, which is a simple summary of a good many modern systems from Mr d'Annunzio's downwards. So long as the coarse and thin texture of mere current popular romance is not touched by a paltry culture it will never be vitally immoral. It is always on the side of life. The poor – the slaves who really stoop under the burden of life – have often been mad, scatter-brained, and cruel, but never hopeless. That is a class privilege, like cigars. Their drivelling literature will always be a 'blood and thunder' literature, as simple as the thunder of heaven and the blood of men.

HILAIRE BELLOC

The Crooked Streets

WHY do they pull down and do away with the Crooked
Streets, I wonder, which are my delight, and hurt no
man living?

Every day the wealthier nations are pulling down one or
another in their capitals and their great towns: they do
not know why they do it; neither do I.

It ought to be enough, surely, to drive the great broad
ways which commerce needs and which are the life-
channels of a modern city, without destroying all the
history and all the humanity in between: the islands of
the past. For, note you, the Crooked Streets are packed
with human experience and reflect in a lively manner all
the chances and misfortunes and expectations and do-
mesticity and wonderment of men. One marks a boundary,
another the kennel of an ancient stream, a third the track
some animal took to cross a field hundreds upon hundreds
of years ago; another is the line of an old defence, another
shows where a rich man's garden stopped long before the
first ancestor one's family can trace was born; a garden
now all houses, and its owner who took delight in it
turned to be a printed name.

Leave men alone in their cities, pester them not with
futilities of great governments, nor with the fads of
too powerful men, and they will build you Crooked Streets
of their very nature as moles throw up the little mounds
or bees construct their combs. There is no ancient city
but glories, or has gloried, in a whole foison and multitude

of Crooked Streets. There is none, however, wasted and
swept by power, which, if you leave it alone to natural
things, will not breed Crooked Streets in less than a
hundred years and keep them for a thousand more.

I know a dead city called Timgad, which the sand or
the barbarians of the Atlas overwhelmed fourteen centuries ago. It lies between the desert and the Algerian
fields, high up upon a mountain-side. Its columns stand.
Even its fountains are apparent, though their water-
ways are choked. It has a great forum or market-place,
all flagged and even, and the ruined walls of its houses
mark its emplacement on every side. All its streets are
straight, set out with a line, and by this you may judge
how a Roman town lay when the last order of Rome sank
into darkness.

Well, take any other town which has not thus been
mummified and preserved but has lived through the
intervening time, and you will find that man, active,
curious, intense, in all the fruitful centuries of Christian
time has endowed them with Crooked Streets, which kind
of streets are the most native to Christian men. So it is
with Arles, so it is with Nîmes, so it is with old Rome
itself, and so it is with the City of London, on which by a
special Providence the curse of the Straight Street has
never fallen, so that it is to this day a labyrinth of little
lanes. It was intended after the Great Fire to set it all
out in order with 'piazzas' and boulevards and the rest –
but the English temper was too strong for any such
nonsense, and the streets and the courts took to the
natural lines which suit us best.

The Renaissance indeed everywhere began this plague
of vistas and of avenues. It was determined three centuries
ago to rebuild Paris as regular as a chessboard, and nothing
but money saved the town – or rather the lack of money.

You may to this day see in a square called the 'Place des Vosges' what was intended. But when they had driven their Straight Street two hundred yards or so the exchequer ran dry, and thus was old Paris saved. But in the last seventy years they have hurt it badly again. I have no quarrel with what is regal and magnificent, with splendid ways of a hundred feet or more, with great avenues and lines of palaces; but why should they pull down my nest beyond the river – Straw Street and Rat Street and all those winding belts round the little Church of St Julien the Poor, where they say that Dante studied and where Danton in the madness of his grief dug up his dead love from the earth on his returning from the wars?

Crooked Streets will never tire a man, and each will have its character, and each will have a soul of its own. To proceed from one to another is like travelling in a multitude or mixing with a number of friends. In a town of Crooked Streets it is natural that one should be the Moneylender's Street and another that of the Burglars, and a third that of the Politicians, and so forth through all the trades and professions.

Then also, how much better are not the beauties of a town seen from Crooked Streets! Consider those old Dutch towns where you suddenly come round a corner upon great stretches of salt water, or those towns of Central France which from one street and then another show you the Gothic in a hundred ways.

It is as it should be when you have the back of Chartres Cathedral towering up above you from between and above two houses gabled and almost meeting. It is what the builders meant when one comes out from such fissures into the great Place, the parvis of the cathedral, like a sailor from a river into the sea. Not that certain buildings were not made particularly for wide approaches and splendid roads, but that these, when they are the rule, sterilize and kill a town. Napoleon was wise enough when he designed that there should lead up all beyond the Tiber to St Peter's a vast imperial way. But the modern nondescript horde, which has made Rome its prey, is very ill advised to drive those new Straight Streets foolishly, emptily, with mean façades of plaster and great gaps that will not fill.

You will have noted in your travels how the Crooked Streets gather names to themselves which are as individual as they, and which are bound up with them as our names are with all our own human reality and humour. Thus I bear in mind certain streets of the town where I served as a soldier. There was the Street of the Three Little Heaps of Wheat, the Street of the Trumpeting Moor, the Street of the False Heart, and an exceedingly pleasant street called 'Who Grumbles at It?' and another short one called 'The Street of the Devil in his Haste', and many others.

From time to time those modern town councillors from whom Heaven has wisely withdrawn all immoderate sums of money, and who therefore have not the power to take away my Crooked Streets and put Straight ones in their places, change old names to new ones. Every such change indicates some snobbery of the time: some little battle exaggerated to be a great thing; some public fellow or other in Parliament or what not; some fad of the learned or of the important in their day.

Once I remember seeing in an obscure corner a twist of dear old houses built before George III was king, and on the corner of this row was painted 'Kipling Street: late Nelson Street'.

Upon another occasion I went to a little Norman market

town up among the hills, where one of the smaller squares was called 'The Place of the Three Mad Nuns', and when I got there after so many years and was beginning to renew my youth I was struck all of a heap to see a great enamelled blue and white affair upon the walls. They had renamed the triangle. They had called it 'The Place Victor Hugo'!

However, all you who love Crooked Streets, I bid you lift up your hearts. There is no power on earth that can make man build Straight Streets for long. It is a bad thing, as a general rule, to prophesy good or to make men feel comfortable with the vision of a pleasant future; but in this case I am right enough. The Crooked Streets will certainly return.

Let me boldly borrow a quotation which I never saw until the other day, and that in another man's work, but which having once seen it, I shall retain all the days of my life.

'*O passi graviora, dabit Deus his quoque finem*', or words to that effect. I can never be sure of a quotation, still less of scansion, and anyhow, as I am deliberately stealing it from another man, **if** I have changed it so much the better.

A Conversation with a Cat

THE other day I went into the bar of a railway station and, taking a glass of beer, I sat down at a little table by myself to meditate upon the necessary but tragic isolation of the human soul. I began my meditation by consoling myself with the truth that something in common runs through all nature, but I went on to consider that this cut no ice, and that the heart needed something more. I might by long research have discovered some third term a little less hackneyed than these two, when fate, or some fostering star, sent me a tawny, silky, long-haired cat.

If it be true that nations have the cats they deserve, then the English people deserve well in cats, for there are none so prosperous or so friendly in the world. But even for an English cat this cat was exceptionally friendly and fine – especially friendly. It leapt at one graceful bound into my lap, nestled there, put out an engaging right front paw to touch my arm with a pretty timidity by way of introduction, rolled up at me an eye of bright but innocent affection, and then smiled a secret smile of approval.

No man could be so timid after such an approach as not to make some manner of response. So did I. I even took the liberty of stroking Amathea (for by that name did I receive this vision), and though I began this gesture in a respectful fashion, after the best models of polite deportment with strangers, I was soon lending it some warmth, for I was touched to find that I had a friend; yes, even here, at the ends of the tubes in S.W.99. I proceeded (as is right) from caress to speech, and said, 'Amathea, most beautiful of cats, why have you deigned to single me out for so much favour? Did you recognize in me a friend to all that breathes, or were you yourself suffering from loneliness (though I take it you are near your own dear home), or is there pity in the hearts of animals as there is in the hearts of some humans? What, then, was your motive? Or am I, indeed, foolish to ask, and not rather to take whatever good comes to me in whatever way from the gods?'

To these questions Amathea answered with a loud purring noise, expressing with closed eyes of ecstasy her delight in the encounter.

'I am more than flattered, Amathea,' said I, by way

of answer; 'I am consoled. I did not know that there was in the world anything breathing and moving, let alone so tawny-perfect, who would give companionship for its own sake and seek out, through deep feeling, some one companion out of all living kind. If you do not address me in words I know the reason and I commend it; for in words lie the seeds of all dissension, and love at its most profound is silent. At least, I read that in a book, Amathea; yes, only the other day. But I confess that the book told me nothing of those gestures which are better than words, or of that caress which I continue to bestow upon you with all the gratitude of my poor heart.'

To this Amathea made a slight gesture of acknowledgement – not disdainful – wagging her head a little, and then settling it down in deep content.

'Oh, beautiful-haired Amathea, many have praised you before you found me to praise you, and many will praise you, some in your own tongue, when I am no longer held in the bonds of your presence. But none will praise you more sincerely. For there is not a man living who knows better than I that the four charms of a cat lie in its closed eyes, its long and lovely hair, its silence, and even its affected love.'

But at the word affected Amathea raised her head, looked up at me tenderly, once more put forth her paw to touch my arm, and then settled down again to a purring beatitude.

'You are secure,' said I sadly; 'mortality is not before you. There is in your complacency no foreknowledge of death nor even of separation. And for that reason, Cat, I welcome you the more. For if there has been given to your kind this repose in common living, why, then, we men also may find it by following your example and not considering too much what may be to come and not remembering too much what has been and will never return. Also, I thank

you, for this, Amathea, my sweet Euplokamos' (for I was
becoming a little familiar through an acquaintance of a
full five minutes and from the absence of all recalcitrance),
'that you have reminded me of my youth, and in a sort of
shadowy way, a momentary way, have restored it to me.
For there is an age, a blessed youthful age (O my Cat)
even with the miserable race of men, when all things are
consonant with the life of the body, when sleep is regular
and long and deep, when enmities are either unknown or
a subject for rejoicing and when the whole of being is
lapped in hope as you are now lapped on my lap, Amathea.
Yes, we also, we of the doomed race, know peace. But
whereas you possess it from blind kittenhood to that last
dark day so mercifully short with you, we grasp it only
for a very little while. But I would not sadden you by the
mortal plaint. That would be treason indeed, and a vile
return for your goodness. What! When you have chosen
me out of seven London millions upon whom to confer
the tender solace of the heart, when you have proclaimed
yourself so suddenly to be my dear, shall I introduce you
to the sufferings of those of whom you know nothing save
that they feed you, house you and pass you by? At least
you do not take us for gods, as do the dogs, and the more
am I humbly beholden to you for this little service of
recognition – and something more.'

Amathea slowly raised herself upon her four feet, arched
her back, yawned, looked up at me with a smile sweeter
than ever and then went round and round, preparing for
herself a new couch upon my coat, whereon she settled
and began once more to purr in settled ecstasy.

Already had I made sure that a rooted and anchored
affection had come to me from out the emptiness and
nothingness of the world and was to feed my soul henceforward; already had I changed the mood of long years

and felt a conversion towards the life of things, an appreciation, a cousinship with the created light – and all that through one new link of loving kindness – when whatever it is that dashes the cup of bliss from the lips of mortal man (Tupper) up and dashed it good and hard. It was the Ancient Enemy who put the fatal sentence into my heart, for we are the playthings of the greater powers, and surely some of them are evil.

'You will never leave me, Amathea,' I said; 'I will respect your sleep and we will sit here together through all uncounted time, I holding you in my arms and you dreaming of the fields of Paradise. Nor shall anything part us, Amathea; you are my cat and I am your human. Now and onwards into the fullness of peace.'

Then it was that Amathea lifted herself once more, and with delicate, discreet, unweighted movement of perfect limbs leapt lightly to the floor as lovely as a wave. She walked slowly away from me without so much as looking back over her shoulder; she had another purpose in her mind; and as she so gracefully and so majestically neared the door which she was seeking, a short, unpleasant man standing at the bar said 'Puss, Puss, Puss!' and stooped to scratch her gently behind the ear. With what a wealth of singular affection, pure and profound, did she not gaze up at him, and then rub herself against his leg in token and external expression of a sacramental friendship that should never die.

MAURICE HEWLETT

The Maypole and the Column

IN days of more single purpose than these, young men and maidens, in the first flush of summer, set up a maypole on the green; but before they joined hands and danced round about it they had done honour to what it stood for by draping it with swags of flowers and green-stuff, hanging it with streamers of divers colours, and sticking it with as many gilt hearts as there were hearts among them of votive inclination. So they transfigured the thing signified, and turned a shaven tree-trunk from a very crude emblem into a thing of happy fantasy. That will serve me for a figure of how the poet deals with his little idea, or great one; and in his more sober mood it is open to the essayist so to deal with his, supposing he have one. He must hang his pole, or concept, not with rhyme but with wise or witty talk. He must turn it about and about, not to set the ornaments jingling, or little bells ringing; rather that you may see its shapeliness enhanced, its proportions emphasized, and in all the shifting lights and shadows of its ornamentation discern it still for the notion that it is. That at least is my own notion of what the essayist should do, though I am aware that very distinguished practitioners have not agreed with me and do not agree at this hour. The modern essayist, for reasons which I shall try to expound, has been driven from the maypole to the column.

Certainly, the parent of the Essay draped no maypoles with speech. Montaigne was a sedentary philosopher, of the order of the post-prandials; a wine-and-walnuts man. One thing would open out into another, and one seem better than the other, at the time of hearing. 'Je n'enseigne point; je raconte,' he tells you of himself; and it is true. To listen to him is a liberal education; yet you can hardly think of Montaigne footing it on the green. Bacon's line, again, was the aphoristic. He shreds off his maypole rather than clothes it: but he has one set up. He can give his argument as witty a turn as the Frenchman when he pleases – 'There is no man doth a wrong for the wrong's sake, but thereby to purchase himself profit, or pleasure, or honour, or the like. Therefore why should I be angry with a man for loving himself better than me?' That is the turn his thoughts take upon Revenge, and a fair sample of his way with an abstract idea – shredding off it all the time, getting down to the pith. But he can be very obscure: 'A single life doth well with Churchmen; for charity will hardly water the ground where it must first fill a pool.' That is proleptic reasoning. We are to caper about the pole before the ornaments are on.

But since his time the Maypole has gone out of use. The modern essayist has had a column reared for him instead, which he is required, not to drape, but to fill. That kind of column is no symbol of the earth's fertility, but too often the grave of it. It has been, however, the opportunity of the babbler, the prater, the prattler, and the agreeable rattle: all's one to the Column so that it be filled. You may write on something, or nothing; you may grind axes on your column, or roll logs on it. But you must fill it. To be too long for it is nothing. There is the Procrustean sword. To be too short – Minotaur will howl for more.

Hazlitt is the typical journalist-essayist. He could fill a column with any man born, yet not with pure gain to literature. He makes an ungracious figure in history, un-social and anti-social too, with his blundering, uncouth loves, his undignified quarrels, and insatiable hatreds. His spleen engulfed him, and I have often wondered what our Wiltshire shepherds made of him, lowering like a storm about the coombes of Winterslow. None of the 'pastoral melancholy' of that grassy solitude shows in his writing, whose zest is that of hunger rather than whole-some appetite. Indeed, I don't think he was a tolerable essayist. He was too eager to destroy, and the very moral of his own John Bull who would sooner, any day, give up an estate than a bugbear. How many people he hated, and how much! Whole nations at once – such as the French. He hated Southey and Gifford, and for their sakes the *Quarterly*, Pitt and Castlereagh, Byron and Coleridge. He was a fierce lover, too, but not comfortable in his loves. Sometimes he knew both passions for the same person. Burke, for instance: *Odi et amo*, he said of him. He had that bad symptom of the violent lover, that he could only honour his love at another's expense. So Racine and Walter Scott must be trampled under foot before Shakespeare can be duly esteemed. There is con-sequently a sense of strain in reading Hazlitt which his fine raptures (and no writer soared more rapturously) can only overcome on select occasions. His account of Ca-vanagh the fives player is one, his essay on John Buncle another. For once, for twice, he was single-minded, and forgot to hurt anybody.

He learned length from the Reviews, which encouraged the essay to be a treatise, and have many a tedious page, Illustrations press upon him and cannot be refused. He has that trick of saying the same thing several times in slightly different ways which was common to all the essayists of his time, doomed to fill their columns. Procter,

Leigh Hunt, and Lamb all did that – Lamb less tiresomely than any; for Lamb enhanced the image, or shifted it into happier view, with every addition. But Hazlitt left it where it was, or hid it.

Lamb was essayist first, and journalist with what remained over. A column was set up: he made it a maypole. No craftsman has draped his idea, or capered about it as Lamb did. He transfigures whatever he touches; more, he transmutes it. His seventeenth-century jargon, which you may find tiresome, is part of the fun. It is, so to speak, joco-serious with him. He is generally better without it, as in 'Blakesmoor' or 'Barbara S—' or 'Dream-Children'; yet of all Elia the most beautiful thing to me is one which has Burton and Sir Thomas Browne all over it, 'A Quakers' Meeting'. There you have exactly what I mean by my overworked figure of the Maypole. A theme set up, and hung with loving art; then round about it a measure trodden, sedately for the most part, but with involuntary skips aside as the whim takes him. Lamb could not spare a joke even at a funeral; but this is sheer beauty, a serene and lovely close:

The very garments of a Quaker seem incapable of receiving a soil; and cleanliness in them to be something more than the absence of its contrary. Every Quakeress is a lily; and when they come up in bands to their Whitsun conferences, whitening the easterly streets of the metropolis, from all parts of the United Kingdom, they show like troops of the Shining Ones.

That is to do more than dance about a maypole. It is to dance before the Lord.

All the pieces which follow* were written for and published in daily newspaper or weekly or monthly review: *The Times* and *Manchester Guardian, Nation* and *Outlook, Nineteenth Century and After, London Mercury, Cornhill.*

* This was originally written as a preface to a volume of essays.

Well or ill, they were intended to deck their column as if it had been a maypole. Rightly or wrongly, they were to be literature as well as journalism. Journalism loves the particular, but literature must hold fast to the general. Journalism accepts the ephemeral, gives you its daily screed in exchange for its daily bread; but literature has its eye on posterity, expresses the spirit of fact rather than the body of it; and its servants, if not exacting a monument more perdurable than brass, wish that they may get, and try to deserve it. Genius does what it must, and need not concern us here. Shakespeare wrote *Hamlet* for hire, and Walter Scott *The Bride of Lammermoor*, that he might add field to field by Tweedside. They had their monument without a thought thrown that way. And Keats, who said that his name was writ in water? Did he not know that it was writ in ink, which grows blacker with age? But let the smaller man do consciously and with premeditation what his betters did by the Grace of God. No man needs be the worse journalist for taking immense pains to be something beside.

It is hard work. 'I never have a holiday. On Monday towards noon I lift up my head, and breathe for about an hour; after that the wicket shuts again and I am in my prison cell for seven days.' So said Sainte-Beuve; and Matthew Arnold comments upon the saying, 'The *causeries* were at this price.' Hard work – but the only way to serve your two masters, turn your column into a maypole and pace out your dedicatory dance.

E. V. LUCAS

A Funeral

IT was in a Surrey churchyard on a grey, damp afternoon – all very solitary and quiet with no alien spectators and only a very few mourners; and no desolating sense of loss, although a very true and kindly friend was passing from us. A football match was in progress in a field adjoining the churchyard, and I wondered, as I stood by the grave, if, were I the schoolmaster, I would stop the game just for a few minutes during which a body was committed to the earth; and I decided that I would not. In the midst of death we are in life just as in the midst of life we are in death; it is all as it should be in this bizarre, jostling world. And he whom we had come to bury would have been the first to wish the boys to go on with their sport.

He was an old scholar – not so very old, either – whom I had known for some five years, and had many a long walk with: a short and sturdy Irish gentleman, with a large, genial grey head stored with odd lore and the best literature; and the heart of a child. I never knew a man of so transparent a character. He showed you all his thoughts: as some one once said, his brain was like a beehive under glass – you could watch all its workings. And the honey in it! To walk with him at any season of the year was to be reminded or newly told of the best that the English poets have said on all the phenomena of wood and hedgerow, meadow and sky. He had the more lyrical passages of Shakespeare at his tongue's end, and all he had read everything that has the true rapturous note, and had forgotten none of its spirit.

His life was divided between his books, his friends, and long walks. A solitary man, he worked at all hours without much method, and probably courted his fatal illness in this way. To his own name there is not much to show; but such was his liberality that he was continually helping others, and the fruits of his erudition are widely scattered, and have gone to increase many a comparative stranger's reputation. His own *magnum opus* he left unfinished; he had worked at it for years, until to his friends it had come to be something of a joke. But though still shapeless, it was a great feast, as the world, I hope, will one day know. If, however, this treasure does not reach the world, it will not be because its worth was insufficient, but because no one can be found to decipher the manuscript; for I may say incidentally that our old friend wrote the worst hand in London, and it was not an uncommon experience of his correspondents to carry his missives from one pair of eyes to another, seeking a clue; and I remember on one occasion two such inquirers meeting unexpectedly, and each simultaneously drawing a letter from his pocket and uttering the request that the other should put everything else on one side in order to solve the enigma.

Lack of method and a haphazard and unlimited generosity were not his only Irish qualities. He had a quick, chivalrous temper, too, and I remember the difficulty I once had in restraining him from leaping the counter of a small tobacconist's in Great Portland Street, to give the man a good dressing for an imagined rudeness – not to himself, but to me. And there is more than one bus conductor in London who has cause to remember this sturdy Quixotic passenger's championship of a poor woman to whom insufficient courtesy seemed to him to have been shown. Normally kindly and tolerant, his indignation on hearing of injustice was red hot. He burned at a story of meanness. It would haunt him all the evening. 'Can it really be true?' he would ask, and burst forth again to flame.

Abstemious himself in all things, save reading and writing and helping his friends and correspondents, he mixed excellent whisky punch, as he called it. He brought to this office all the concentration which he lacked in his literary labours. It was a ritual with him; nothing might be hurried or left undone, and the result, I might say, justified the means. His death reduces the number of such convivial alchemists to one only, and he is in Tasmania, and, so far as I am concerned, useless.

His avidity as a reader – his desire to master his subject – led to some charming eccentricities, as when, for a daily journey between Earl's Court Road and Addison Road stations, he would carry a heavy hand-bag filled with books, 'to read in the train'. This was no satire on the railway system, but pure zeal. He had indeed no satire in him; he spoke his mind and it was over.

It was a curious little company that assembled to do honour to this old kindly bachelor – the two or three relatives that he possessed, and eight of his literary friends, most of them of a good age, and for the most part men of intellect, and in one or two cases of world-wide reputation, and all a little uncomfortable in unwonted formal black. We were very grave and thoughtful, but it was not exactly a sad funeral, for we knew that had he lived longer – he was sixty-three – he would certainly have been an invalid, which would have irked his active, restless mind and body almost unbearably; and we knew, also, that he had died in his first real illness after a very happy life. Since we knew this, and also that he was a bachelor and almost alone, those of us who were not his kin were not melted and unstrung by that poignant sense of untimely loss and irreparable removal that makes some funerals so tragic; but death, however it come, is a mystery before which one cannot stand unmoved and unregretful; and I, for one, as I stood there, remembered how easy it would have been oftener to have ascended to his eyrie and lured him out into Hertfordshire or his beloved Epping, or even have dragged him away to dinner and whisky punch; and I found myself meditating, too, as the profoundly impressive service rolled on, how melancholy it was that all that storied brain, with its thousands of exquisite phrases and its perhaps unrivalled knowledge of Shakespearean philology, should have ceased to be. For such a cessation, at any rate, say what one will of immortality, is part of the sting of death, part of the victory of the grave, which St Paul denied with such magnificent irony.

And then we filed out into the churchyard, which is a new and very large one, although the church is old, and at a snail's pace, led by the clergyman, we crept along, a little black company, for, I suppose, nearly a quarter of a mile, under the cold grey sky. As I said, many of us were old, and most of us were indoor men, and I was amused to see how close to the head some of us held our hats – the merest barleycorn of interval being maintained for reverence' sake; whereas the sexton and the clergyman had slipped on those black velvet skull-caps which God, in His infinite mercy, either completely overlooks, or seeing, smiles at. And there our old friend was committed to the earth, amid the contending shouts of the football players, and then we all clapped our hats on our heads with firmness (as he would have wished us to do long before), and returned to the town to drink tea in an ancient hostelry, and exchange memories, quaint, and humorous, and touching, and beautiful, of the dead.

The Town Week

IT is odd that 'Mondayish' is the only word which the days
of the week have given us; since Monday is not alone in
possessing a positive and peculiar character. Why not
'Tuesdayish' or 'Wednesdayish'? Each word would convey as much meaning to me, 'Tuesdayish' in particular, for
Monday's cardinal and reprehensible error of beginning
the business week seems to me almost a virtue compared
with Tuesday's utter flatness. To begin a new week is no
fault at all, though tradition has branded it as one. To
begin is a noble accomplishment; but to continue dully,
to be the tame follower of a courageous beginner, to be
the second day in a week of action, as in Tuesday's case –
that is deplorable, if you like.

Monday can be flat enough, but in a different way from
Tuesday. Monday is flat because one has been idling,
perhaps unconsciously absorbing notions of living like the
lilies; because so many days must pass before the week
ends; because yesterday is no more. But Tuesday has the
sheer essential flatness of nonentity; Tuesday is nothing.
If you would know how absolutely nothing it is, go to a
week-end hotel at, say Brighton, and stay on after the
Saturday-to-Monday population has flitted. On Tuesday
you touch the depths. So does the menu – no *chef* ever
exerted himself for a Tuesday guest. Tuesday is also very
difficult to spell, many otherwise cultured ladies putting
the *e* before the *u*: and why not? What right has Tuesday
to any preference?

With all its faults, Monday has a positive character.
Monday brings a feeling of revolt; Tuesday, the base
craven, reconciles us to the machine. I am not surprised
that the recent American revivalists held no meetings on

Mondays. It was a mark of their astuteness; they knew that the wear and tear of overcoming the Monday feeling of the greater part of their audience would exhaust them before their magnetism began to have play; while a similarly stubborn difficulty would confront them in the remaining portion sunk in apathy by the thought that to-morrow would be Tuesday. It is this presage of certain tedium which has robbed Monday evening of its 'glittering star'. Yet since nothing so becomes a flat day as the death of it, Tuesday evening's glittering star (it is Wordsworth's phrase) is of the brightest – for is not the dreary day nearly done, and is not to-morrow Wednesday the bland?

With Wednesday, the week stirs itself, turns over, begins to wake. There are matinées on Wednesday; on Wednesdays some of the more genial weekly papers come out. The very word has a good honest round air – Wednesday. Things, adventures, might happen very naturally on Wednesday; but that nothing ever happened on a Tuesday I am convinced. In summer Wednesday has often close finishes at Lord's, and it is a day on which one's friends are pretty sure to be accessible. On Monday they may not have returned from the country; on Friday they have begun to go out of town again; but on Wednesday they are here, at home – are solid. I am sure it is my favourite day.

(Even politicians, so slow as a rule to recognize the kindlier, more generous, side of life, realized for many years that Wednesday was a day on which they had no right to conduct their acrimonious business for more than an hour or so. Much of the failure of the last Government may be traced to their atheistical decision no longer to remember Wednesday to keep it holy.)

On Thursday the week falls back a little; the stirring of Wednesday is forgotten; there is a return to the folding of the hands. I am not sure that Thursday has not become the real day of rest. That it is a good honest day is the most that can be said for it. It is certainly not Thor's day any longer – if my reading of the character of the black-smith-god is true. There is nothing strong and downright and fine about it. Compared with Tuesday's small beer, Thursday is almost champagne; but none the less they are related. One can group them together. If I were a business man, I should, I am certain, sell my shares at a loss on Monday and at a profit on Wednesday and Friday, but on Tuesday and Thursday I should get for them exactly what I gave.

I group Friday with Wednesday as a day that can be friendly to me, but it has not Wednesday's quality. Wednesday is calm, assured, urbane; Friday allows itself to be a little flurried and excited. Wednesday stands alone; Friday to some extent throws in its lot with Saturday. Friday is too busy. Too many papers come out, too many bags are packed, on Friday. But herein, of course, is some of its virtue; it is the beginning of the end, the forerunner of Saturday and Sunday. If anticipation, as the moralists say, is better than the realization, Friday is perhaps the best day of the week, for one spends much of it in thinking of the morrow and what of good it should bring forth. Friday's greatest merit is perhaps that it paves the way to Saturday and the cessation of work. That it ever was really unlucky I greatly doubt.

And so we come to Saturday and Sunday. But here the analyst falters, for Saturday and Sunday pass from the region of definable days. Monday and Tuesday, Wednesday and Thursday and Friday, these are days with a character fixed more or less for all. But Saturday and Sunday are what we individually make of them. In one family they are friends, associates; in another as ill-assorted as Socrates and Xantippe. For most of us

Saturday is not exactly a day at all, it is a collection of hours, part work, part pleasure, and all restlessness. It is a day that we plan for, and therefore it is often a failure. I have no distinct and unvarying impression of Saturday, except that trains are full and late and shops shut too early.

Sunday even more than Saturday is different as people are different. To the godly it is a day of low tones, its minutes go by muffled; to the children of the godly it is eternity. To the ungodly it is a day jeopardized by an interest in barometers that is almost too poignant. To one man it is an interruption of the week; to another it is the week itself, and all the rest of the days are but preparations for it. One cannot analyse Saturday and Sunday.

But Monday? There we are on solid ground again. Monday – but I have discussed Monday already: that is one of its principal characteristics, that it is always coming round again, pretending to be new. It is always the same in reality.

A Door-Plate

BUT for having lived in London long enough to know the rules, or, in other words, to be aware that nothing is out of place there, I should have thought the door-plate which, in Fetter Lane, suddenly caught my eye an incongruity. But no; I am inured, and therefore I merely looked at it twice instead of only once, and passed on with a head full of mental and intensely uncivic pictures of undauntable men, identical in patience and hopefulness, standing hour after hour at the ends of piers all round our coasts, watching their lines. For the words on the door-plate were these: 'British Sea Anglers' Society'.

I shall continue to deny that the notice was out of place, but a certain oddity (not uncommon in London) may be conceded, for Fetter Lane otherwise has less marine association than any street that one could name; and angling is too placid, too philosophic, too reclusive a sport to be represented by an office absolutely on the fringe of that half-square mile of the largest city in the world given over to fierce, feverish activity; where printing presses are at their thickest, busy and clattering, day and night, in the task of providing this nation with all – and a little more – of the news, and a fresh sensation for every breakfast table. Except that upon the breakfast table is often to be found the herring in one or other of its posthumous metamorphoses, there is no connecting link whatever. And why one has to belong to a society with a doorplate in Fetter Lane before drawing mackerel from Pevensey Bay, or whiting from the Solent, is a question to answer which is beside the mark; although that fish can be caught from the sea without membership of this fraternity I myself can testify – for was I not once in the English Channel in a small boat in the company of two conger eels and a dogfish, whose noisy and acrobatic reluctance to die turned what ought to have been a party of pleasure into misery and shame; and shall I ever forget the look of dismay (a little touched by triumph) on the face of a humane English girl visiting Ireland, when, after she had pulled in an unresisting pollock at the end of a trawl line and the boatman had taken it from the hook and had beaten it sickeningly to death with an iron thole pin, she heard him say, as, later, he handed the fish to a colleague on the landing-stage, 'The young lady killed it'?

But this is not London – far, indeed, from it! – although an excellent example of London's peculiar and precious gift of starting the mind on extra-mural adventures.

The sea, however, is, in reality too, very near the city, and the closeness of London's relations with it can be tested in many delightful ways. Although, for example, the natural meeting-place of those two old cronies, Father Thames and Neptune, is somewhere about Gravesend, Neptune, as a matter of fact, comes for a friendly glass with Gog (I almost wrote Grog) and Magog right up to town. If you lean over the eastern parapet of London Bridge (just under the clock which has letters instead of numerals) you will see the stevedores unloading all kinds of wonderful seaborne exotic merchandise. The other morning I was the guest of a skipper of one of these vessels, and sat in his cabin (which smelt authentically of tobacco smoke, as only a cabin can) with his first engineer, and ate ship's biscuits and heard first-hand stories of the sinking of the *Titanic*, together with details of a romance in the European quarter of a certain African port all ready to the magic hand of Mr Conrad. Twelve minutes later I was in a club in Pall Mall!

But there is no need to enter a cabin, although that is, of course, the pleasantest way, and I am sure Captain Potter (as we will call him) would be glad to see you, for if you wander down to the Tower you can sit on an old cannon on the quay and have the music of cordage in your ears, and if you climb to the top of the Tower Bridge the scene below you has the elements of a thousand yarns. And there are streets near the docks which might have been cut out of Plymouth or Bristol. Now and then, indeed, London may be said to be actually on the sea.

Such excursions are for the hours of light. In the hours of darkness I used to have, before the war, a favourite river-side refuge. At that far-off time, when cabmen asked for custom instead of repulsing it, and public-houses remained open until half-past 12 a.m., I had for fine summer nights, after a dull play or dinner, a diversion that never failed; and this was to make my way – if possible with a stranger to such sights and scenes, and an impressionable one – to the Angel at Rotherhithe and watch the shipping for an hour. The Angel is difficult of access, but once there you might be at Valparaiso. It is a quarter of a mile below the Tower Bridge on the South bank, with a wooden balcony overhanging the water, and a mass of dark creeping barges moored below. Here on the balcony we used to sit, while the great ships stole by at quarter speed, groping for their moorings, and strange lights appeared and disappeared, and voices hailed each other and were answered, and little sinister rowing boats moved here and there on unknown missions, and perhaps an excursion steamer, back very late from Margate, with its saloon all lighted and a banjo bravely making merry to the bitter end, would glide past towards London Bridge; and such is the enchantment of ships and shipping that not even she could break the spell.

May the Angel survive the deluge! If not, I must carry out the dream of my life and make friends with the captain of a Thames tug.

ARTHUR CLUTTON-BROCK

The Defects of English Prose

I cannot read Mr Pearsall Smith's anthology of English Prose without thinking of the anthology I would make myself and wondering all the while why his differs from mine. Why, among writers of the past, does he omit Shaftesbury and give but one passage from Johnson, when he gives so many from Sir Thomas Browne? Why is there not more of Gibbon's wit, and why not his great passage upon the funeral and character of Julian the Apostate? Why so many short, laboured, and not profound sentences from Carlyle, followed by but one extract from Newman? Why the Gioconda passage from Pater, which has the defect that it is false? Why no Dickens at all, and no William Morris, and no W. H. Hudson? The answer is that Mr Pearsall Smith lays his own emphasis in this anthology and I should lay another. For him our prose is greatest when it is nearest to poetry; it is overshadowed by our poetry and almost its poor relation. A Frenchman reading his anthology might say: 'All this is magnificent, but it is hardly prose. This is the literature of a people that can sing and preach, but cannot converse. I listen with amazement to all these prophets, but I should not care to talk with them; for, to tell the truth, they are not civilized. They do not seem to be men like myself, only abler; they are chiefs or elders at a tribal gathering, practising the eloquence of barbarians.'

Yet there is another side to English prose which Mr Pearsall Smith almost ignores: perhaps because he is making an anthology and that other side cannot easily be exhibited in extracts. Prose of its very nature is longer than verse, and the virtues peculiar to it manifest themselves gradually. If the cardinal virtue of poetry is love, the cardinal virtue of prose is justice; and, whereas love makes you act and speak on the spur of the moment, justice needs inquiry, patience, and a control even of the noblest passions. But English Prose, as Mr Pearsall Smith presents it, is at the mercy of its passions and just only by accident. By justice here I do not mean justice only to particular people or ideas, but a habit of justice in all the processes of thought, a style tranquillized and a form moulded by that habit. The master of prose is not cold, but he will not let any word or image inflame him with a heat irrelevant to his purpose. Unhasting, unresting, he pursues it, subduing all the riches of his mind to it, rejecting all beauties that are not germane to it; making his own beauty out of the very accomplishment of it, out of the whole work and its proportions, so that you must read to the end before you know that it is beautiful. But he has his reward, for he is trusted and convinces, as those who are at the mercy of their own eloquence do not; and he gives a pleasure all the greater for being hardly noticed. In the best prose, whether narrative or argument, we are so led on as we read, that we do not stop to applaud the writer: nor do we stop to question him. But we stop, whether to applaud or to question, at a sentence such as this, which Mr Pearsall Smith gives us from Carlyle:

Brave Sea captain, Norse Sea-king Columbus, my hero, royalist Sea-king of all! it is no friendly environment this of thine, in the waste deep waters: round thee mutinous discouraged souls, behind thee disgrace and ruin, before thee the unpenetrated veil of Night.

If a writer continues long in this style, he wearies us like a man talking at the top of his voice; and if he does not continue, the passage distracts us with its incongruity, like a sudden shouting. Carlyle here, and often, yields to a habit of excitement as if he had a right to be indulged in it. He is like a man who will make speeches at the dinner-table to show the force of his convictions. These are the manners of egotism, and egotism is the worst of all faults in prose.

For prose is the achievement of civilization, of people who have learned to discuss without blows or invective, who know that truth is hard to find and worth finding, who do not begin by accusing an opponent of wickedness, but elicit reason and patience by displaying them. You cannot say in poetry what the best prose says, or accomplish what the best prose accomplishes. Civilization may not surpass a primitive society in heights of rapture or heroism, but it is, if it be civilization, better for everyday life, kinder, more rational, more sustained in effort; and this kindness and reason and sustained effort are expressed and encouraged in the masterpieces of prose. The French understood this long ago, because they prize civilization and enjoy it. Pascal, writing his *Provincial Letters* in 1656 upon a subject obscured by medieval subtleties and distorted by party passions, is already just, polite, and lucid; he does not even affect the magnificent disdain of Gibbon, but is a civilized man talking to other civilized men, and therefore all the more deadly in debate. But it is fallacies that he would kill, not those who maintain them. He knows that the art of controversy is, not to begin with invective, but to state your case in such a way that those who like invective will supply it themselves against your adversary.

So we read Milton's controversy for its accidents,

splendid as they are, but Pascal's still for the controversy itself. Though he is not clothed in shining armour, he fights for the children of light in all ages, with no pretence of being an angel or a dervish, but quietly appealing to the everlasting reason from whence comes his help. In this book of Mr Pearsall Smith's, with its array of great names and great passages, we notice how his moderns seem to archaize when they would soar, as if they must pretend to be of the giant race before the flood so as to believe in their own greatness. Emerson says:

Our friendships hurry to short and poor conclusions, because we have made them a texture of wine and dreams, instead of the tough fibre of the human heart.

Ruskin, even in *Praeterita*, writes thus of his first sight of the Alps:

Infinitely beyond all that we had ever thought or dreamed – the seen walls of lost Eden could not have been more beautiful to us; not more awful round Heaven, the walls of sacred Death.

Pater begins a paragraph:

I have remarked how in the process of our brain-building, as the house of thought in which we live gets itself together like some airy bird's nest of floating thistledown and chance straws, compact at last, little accidents have their consequence.

Stevenson, in a letter, and talking of familiar things, says:

Methought you asked me – frankly, was I happy? Happy (said I); I was happy only once; that was at Hyères; it came to an end from a variety of reasons, decline of health, change of place, increase of money, age with his stealing steps; since then, as before then, I know not what it means.

It is always finely, but not naturally, said.
Each writer seems to have a model not quite suited to

the matter or the occasion, and makes us think of this model when we should be thinking only of what he has to say. But the prose which interests us most, and persuades us unconsciously to go on reading it, seems to be made by the matter and the occasion; it is like talk between intimates, and the writer draws us into intimacy by his manner of address, which assumes that we do not wish to be tricked or dazzled, that, if he has anything worth saying, we shall listen to it for its own sake.

There is less of this prose in our literature than we could wish, but more than we should gather from Mr Pearsall Smith's anthology. It began to be written about the time of the Restoration by Cowley, Halifax, and Dryden among others. Mr Pearsall Smith gives one short passage from Cowley, one from Halifax, and none from Dryden – perhaps he thinks that the best of Dryden's prose is in his verse. But the first easy master of it is Shaftesbury, especially in his *Letter concerning Enthusiasm*. Here the case is all the more remarkable because he is talking of religion and saying things both novel and profound about it. His plea is for good humour in controversy, and he gives an example of it in his own letter. He begins lightly enough, and then, with a humane and natural art, leads us into seriousness:

This, my Lord, is the security against superstition: To remember that there is nothing in God but what is God-like; and that He is either not at all or truly and perfectly good. But when we are afraid to use our reason freely, even on that very question, 'Whether He really be, or not'; we then actually presume Him bad, and flatly contradict that pretended character of goodness and greatness, whilst we discover this mistrust of His temper, and fear His anger and resentment in the case of this freedom of inquiry.

But though this is just and even now fresh, we cannot

deny that it lacks the music and images of Jeremy Taylor or Milton; and they are absent from the prose of Johnson and all the eighteenth century. For that reason the Romantics despised even its virtues; for them, again, prose became the poor relation of poetry, and must wear its cast-off clothes; or else they wrote like orators addressing a crowd with repetitions and loud emphasis, abrupt transitions and noisy images. Hazlitt is more eloquent than scrupulous; he never seems to be alone with you as you read him, but rather speaking to catch votes, even though it be for the best writers or painters; and Macaulay, ignored by Mr Pearsall Smith, is worse. His prose has all the defects of a nation political rather than social, he is incapable of meditation or even of converse, but lectures always; while Burke writes of the Sublime and Beautiful like an orator.

So, but for a few shy, never enough honoured writers, there is one whole province of the English mind left out of our prose, for we are capable of meditation and intimate talk; we are more civilized than our manners or our style. Mr W. H. Hudson, for instance, seems always to be meditating or remembering; writing for him is a means of saying what he would never say aloud. He makes his dearest friend of the reader, and confides in him with speech that has the beauty of a wild animal's eyes. And Mark Rutherford, with a different kind of matter but the same shyness and melancholy faith, arouses a like confidence in us. These writers seldom say much in a single sentence or even paragraph, but they have a cumulative power that cannot be proved by quotation, a wandering music that blows where it lists, because they never force their inspiration or tell you what they have not got to say. Their peculiar quality is justice; they describe without a laboured eagerness or momentum, and

without vivid words, just what they have seen and felt.
They do not exploit their loves or their hatreds, and it is
wonderful that you should remember so well what is said
with so little emphasis or apparent skill of words. Yet it
is remembered, like a thought that does not need saying;
it sinks deep into the mind, beyond language, like an
actual experience, and, if you read their books with care,
you are changed as if by an event.

But such writers are likely to remain few, for they are
little encouraged. We are not yet a public of readers
civilized enough to demand the highest virtues of prose;
we prefer 'clamorous sublimities' and phrases that ask to
be noticed; we must be urged through a book by the
crack of the writer's whip. Yet still one dreams of a prose
that has never yet been written in English, though the
language is made for it and there are minds not incapable
of it, a prose dealing with the greatest things quietly and
justly as men deal with them in their secret meditations,
seeming perhaps to wander, but always advancing in an
unbroken sequence of thought, with a controlled ardour
of discovery and the natural beauties of a religious mind.
Johnson might have written it, if he had had a stronger
sense of beauty and more faith in the flights of reason;
Newman if he had been a greater master of words and
less afraid of his own questioning; Henry James if he had
exercised his subtlety on larger things. But the best of our
prose writers, living or dead, are not civilized enough, or
too much in love with something else, or not enough in
love with anything, to write the prose we dream of. The
English Plato is still to be.

EDWARD THOMAS

Broken Memories

'Mr —, the well-known merchant, is building a fine house, half a mile from the — Road. Close upon two acres of woodland have been felled, where, by the way, the largest and juiciest blackberries I know used to be found.'

London Local Newspaper.

AND in this way many suburbans have seen the paradise of their boyhood effaced. The building rises during some long farewell, and steals away a fraction of the very sky in which once we beheld Orion sink down like a falling sword into the west and its line of battlemented woods. Only here and there a coppice will survive, blockaded by houses a-row. Sometimes a well-beloved pleasaunce is left almost as it was; the trees are the same; the voices are the same; a silence is there still; but there is a caret somewhere – in ourselves or in the place. In childhood we went there as often as our legs could bear us so far; often yet in youth; but less and less with time. Then, perhaps, we travel – anyway we live feverishly and variously; and only think of the old places when the fire is tranquil and lights are out, and 'each into himself descends', or when we meet one who was once a friend, or when we lay open a forgotten drawer. A very slender chain only binds us to the gods of forest and field – but binds us nevertheless. Then we take the old walk, it may be, in a walking suit of the best; fearful of mire; carrying a field-glass too; and smoking the pipe that used to seem an insult so intolerable in the great woods. We take the old walk, and it seems shorter than before, a walk not formidable at all, as it was in the years when the end used to find us testy with fatigue and overpowered by tumultuous impressions; when we ourselves thought the sea itself could not be far, and the names of village and hill we visited were unknown.

A railway bisects the common we cross. Everything is haggard and stale; the horizon is gone; and the spirit chafes and suffocates for lack of it. (But the gorse is in flower still.) Then the feet weary on gravel paths downhill. On either side are fields, edged by flaccid suburban grass, with an odour as of tombs – as though nothing fair could blossom in a soil that must be the sepulchre of many divinities. And again the pathway is dogged by houses, interrupting the fields. The former sanity and amenity of air is gone. We can no longer shorten the way to the next houses by a path from the willowy riverside over fields, for the willows are down, the fields heavily burdened with streets. Another length of mean houses, neither urban nor rustic, but both, where I remembered the wretched children's discordant admiration of the abounding gold hair of a passer-by; and soon the bridge over a railway gives a view across plantations of cabbage, etc. But the view is comforting – there is an horizon! There is an horizon barred with poplar trees to the south; the streets are behind, in the north. The horizon is dear to us yet, as the possible home of the unknown and the greatly desired, as the apparent birthplace and tomb of setting and rising suns; from under it the clouds mount, and under it again they return after crossing the sky. A mystery is about it as when we were children playing upon a broad, treeless common, and actually long continued running in pursuit of the horizon.

After three miles in all we leave the turnpike, to follow

a new but grassy road out among the fields, under lines of acacia and poplar and horse-chestnut last. Once more the ploughland shows us the twinkling flight of peewits; the well, and the quaking water uplifted in a shining band where it touches the stones; the voices of sparrows while the trees are dripping in the dawn; and overhead the pompous mobilization of cloud armadas, so imposing in a country where they tilt against ebony boughs ... In a thicket some gipsies have encamped, and two of them – superb youths, with favours of raven hair blowing across the dusky roses of their cheeks – have jumped from their labour to hear the postman reading their letters. Several pipe-sucking bird-catchers are at watch over an expanse of nets. We cross a ploughland half within the sovereignty of the forest shadow. Here is the wood!

The big wood we called it. So well we knew it, and for so many years – wandered here with weeping like Imogen's, and with laughter like Yorick's laughter – that when past years bulk into the likeness of a forest through which the memory takes its pleasure at eventide,

> *Or in clear dream or solemn vision,*

it is really this wood that we see, under a halcyon sky.

It covered two acres in the midst of ploughland; but we thought of it as enormous, because in it we often lost one another; it had such diversity; it made so genuine a solitude. The straight oaks rising branchless for many feet expanded and then united boughs in a firmament of leaves. It seemed far enough from London for feelings of security. But even of that our thoughts have changed; for the houses are fearfully close – a recollection of them lingers in the heart of the wood; and perhaps they will devour it also ... Who shall measure the sorrow of him that hath set his heart upon that which the world hath power to destroy and hath destroyed? Even to-day the circuit of a cemetery is cutting into the field where we gathered buttercups before the dignity of knickerbockers. ... And here was a solitude. We cannot summon up any thought or reverie which had not in this wood its nativity. 'Tis we have changed! And if we could paint, and wished to make a picture of our youth with its seriousness and its folly, we should paint in this wood, instead of in a hostel-yard, another Don Quixote watching his armour all night after the false accolade.

The dark earth itself was pleasant to handle – earth one might wish to be buried in – and had the healthy and special quality of wild earth: upon it you could rest deliciously. (Compare the artificial soil of a London common with it!) Out of this rose up trees that preserved their wild attitudes. The age-fallen or tempest-uprooted oak tree lay where it dropped, or hung balanced in the boughs of others. Tenderest bramble spray or feeler of honeysuckle bridged those gaps in the underwood that served as paths. And the winds were husbandmen, reapers and sowers thereof. Though, indeed, the trees were ordered with an incongruous juxtaposition of birch and oak and elm, it seemed to us a fragment of the primeval forest left by a possible good fortune at the city verge. But it was more than this. With its lofty roof and the mysterious flashes of light in the foliaged clerestory, with its shapely boles in cluster and colonnade, and the glimpses of bright white sky that came and went among the leaves, the forest had a real likeness to a temple. Shelley's 'Ode to the West Wind' and passages of Adonais were the *ediscenda* of our devotions.

Here we saw the grim jewellery of winter on fallen leaf and bow of grass; gold and purple colouring inseparable from the snow upon boughs overhead; the hills far away

sombre and yet white with snow; and on the last of the
icy mornings, the sward beaming with melted frost, and
the frost only persisting on the ample shadows with which
the trees stamp the grass. Here we saw the coming of
spring, when the liquid-orbed leaves of toad-flax crept
out of a barren stone. Full of joy we watched here the
'sweet and twenty' of perfect summer, when the matin
shadows were once deleted, and the dew-globes evaporated
from the harebell among the fern, or twinkled as they fell
silently underfoot. But the favourite of memory is a
certain flower-shadowing tree whose branches had been
earthbent by the swinging of boyish generations. Foliage
and shadow muffled the sight, and seated there in profound emerald moss, the utmost you achieved was to find
a name for each of the little thicket flowers. If you raised
your head you would have seen in a tumultuous spasm of
sunshine – say at mid March – the blue smoke upcoiling
between the boughs of overhanging trees far off and
dissipated in the dashing air; the trees shining in their
leaflessness like amber and dark agate; above that the
woodland seared in black upon the heated horizon blue;
– but you never raised your head. For hours you could
here have peace, among the shadows embroidered with
flowers of the colour of gold. All which tantalizes – sun and
clouds and forever inaccessible horizon – was locked out;
only (like a golden bar across a gloomy coat of arms) one
sunbeam across the brown wood; thrushes and blackbirds
warbled unseen. The soul – this made a cage bird of it.
The eagle's apotheosis in the fires of the sun was envied
not. What a subtle diversity of needled herbs and grass
there is in the plainest field carpet! all miniature after
close cropping of rabbit and sheep; auriferous dande-
lion, plumed self-heal, dainty trefoil, plantain, delicate
feathered grasses, starry blossomed heather, illuminations

of tormentil, unsearchable moss forests, and there jewelled insects, rosy centaury; nearly all in flower together, and the whole not deep enough to hide a field-mouse.

A dim solitude thus circumscribed liked us hugely. We loved not the insolent and importunate splendours of perfect light. Cobwebs and wholesome dust – we needed some of both in the corners of our minds. They mature the wine of the spirit perhaps. We would always have had, as it were, a topmost and nearly inaccessible file of tomes, which we never read, but often planned to read – records peradventure of unvictorious alchymist and astrologer. Thither a sunbeam never penetrated and unmasked. The savour of paraffin and brick-dust should never cling about it. Unfortunate (we thought) is he who has no dusty and never-explored recesses in his mind!

JAMES AGATE

Likes and Dislikes

THESE are my likings.

An old park in our middle England, dripping trees, undergrowth, decay, a lady many years disconsolate; bleak pinches, moors and winding roads; old inns, coffee rooms, and faded prints; high noon in market squares, the roguery of dealers, Hodge's reverence to parson and bank manager; all that England which lies between Hogarth and Trollope; the placidity which is content with Rydal Water and the glory of Wordsworth; the eaves and the thatches of Hertfordshire; Surrey's imitation of Corot; the apple-sense of Somerset; the mothy coombes of Devon.

And then the reflex sentimentality of those direct emotions and the play Stevenson would have made of them; the Wardour Street glamour of such words as 'sundial' and 'curfew', the Victorian lilt and cadence of that perfect *raser* King Arthur; the saturated melancholy of headstones. The sentimentality of parchments; old brocades, fans that have not fluttered and lace that has not stirred for a generation; the *mouches* and petulance of *petites marquises*; the painter's sense of great ladies.

I could tease myself that these emotions are so general as not to be worth setting down, were it not that strong affection loses nothing by being shared with the whole world. Sealing wax and sailing ships fascinate me none the less for having appealed to another. Yet there are certain intimate appreciations, discoveries of one's own, to be hugged exultingly. Such the homely lilt of ballads, the crinolined grace of *She Wore a Wreath of Roses*, the faded propriety of *My Mother Bids me Bind my Hair*. I sometimes think they have missed the better half of life who do not know *Claribel*, stern mistress of our tender youth, inexorable guide to wayward fingers. Well do I remember the tone of ivory keys deepening through saffron to rich brown, the nubbly, polished ebonies, the puckered rose-coloured silk lining, the fretted walnut front, the fantastic scroll-work of the maker's name. Collard and Collard – how many hours did my childish soul ponder over all the possible combinations of father and son, uncle and nephew, brothers it may be. I often find myself wondering what has become of the old piano over which half my childhood was wept away. I believe I should know it again by its fragrance, the fragrance of my mother's fingers. As I write the perfume steals across me.

I adore all acting, all masks and subterfuges, all cloaks and garbs of respectability, the obsequiousness of head waiters and the civility of underlings, all rogues and vagabonds soever, the leer of the pavement and the wit of the gutter. I love Bond Street at eleven in the morning, Scott's at noon, some *matinée* at which there shall be question of faded emotion – say, the old retainer's. And then sunset, red as a guardsman's tunic, gilding the front of the westward-going bus, a music-hall, enough money in my pocket to pay the small-hours' supper bill, the lights extinguished and by the butt of a glowing cigar, a last florin for its fellow, a last sixpence for human *débris* insistent with pitiful whine. I love the mystery and peril of the streets. I love to lie lazily in London, to loop my curtains and surrender myself to the hypnotic effect of the one hundred and sixty-three stags and two thousand two hundred and eighty-two hounds in full cry which I must presume to have been my landlord's taste in wall-paper some lustres ago. I like to gaze at framed elevens and fifteens, at the jumble of racquets and clubs, the jowl of a prize-fighter, Vardon at the top of his swing, Miss Letty Lind ineffably graceful in some Chinese fantasy. I like to look down on Regent Street – my rooms are at the top of a nest of actors' clubs, registry offices, shady money-lenders, and still shadier solicitors – and watch the late last loiterer. I love to lie and think of the world as my own, my very own, in which, though I earn a living by rule and in tune with the common whim, I may by the grace of God think what I like and choose the friends who shall make me laugh and the books which shall make me cry. Every man leads a double life in this most precious of senses. In this world of my own I am supreme lord and master, and may shatter and rebuild according to my proper desire. Events in the tangible universe do not as events interest me at all. Kings may die, and empires fade away, but until these happenings are presented in some saturated phrase my consciousness is unaffected. A new planet is of less moment to me than a new reading of an old line. It needed the Shakespearean echo of some journalist's 'Now is England to be tested to her marrow' to move me to the full responsibility of our pledge to Belgium.

I love the vanity of artists stretching their sad fastidious-ness on the rack till perfection be found; the martyr's egotism which will sacrifice health and life itself, not that we may read, but that he may write. So the pride of the soldier, caring less for the cause than that he shall die worthily. I love words for their own sake. I love the words 'hyacinth', 'narcissus', 'daffodil', 'dog-rose'; their very look on the page enchants me; they smell more

sweetly in the writer's garden than in Nature's rank
parterre. I have never seen a trumpet-orchid, yet I know
that when I read:

> Fly forward, O my heart, from the Foreland to the Start —
>   We're steaming all too slow,
> And it's twenty thousand mile to our little lazy isle
>   Where the trumpet-orchids blow,

the word conjures up the nostalgia of far-off seas. I love
the tinkle of 'onyx', 'chalcedony', 'beryl', more than the
trumpery gauds themselves. I love the word 'must-
stained' without desire to gaze upon the feet of the treader
of grapes; the words 'spikenard' and 'alabaster' without
longing for pot or jar. I am crazy for 'jasmine' and for
'jade', and were I a French writer you would find *jadis*
on every page. I would give the million I do not possess
to flaunt a scutcheon with the device *Désormais!* But if I
am in love with words, it must not be supposed that I
have no affection for the idea also. Though I would insist
that the idea shall emerge from the foam and tumble of
its wrappings glorious as any goddess from the sea, yet
do I not disdain to disentangle the writer from his own
enmeshings, to lie in wait for him, to detect him in his
style. I like to hear in the slipshod cadence of Dickens
the beating of his great untidy heart; to trace in the
lowering of beautiful words to unromantic purpose the
infinite common sense of his latter-day successor; to nose
the corruption of the decadent in the paint and powder
of his prose. Words for me are not the grace-notes of
existence, but the very stuff and texture of life. This may
be madness, but it is an honest frenzy, and remember
that in your own kingdom you have a right to be mad. I
like to think of Piccadilly as it must have been in those
early days which saw me mewed up in our provinces of

sterling worth. Of the *coudoiement* of notabilities. Of the days when Ellen Terry brought a new morning to the jaded world and Irving sent us shuddering to bed; when, touchingly, at eleven-thirty, Mr and Mrs Kendal would make it up again. When Mr Beerbohm Tree was a rising actor and Mr George confesses he was young. When those tremendous initials G. B. S. first growled and thundered in the pages of *The Saturday Review*, Wilde had not tired of confounding peacockery with prose, and the giant Wells was stirring in his sleep. When Rudyard Kipling was a power in the land, Lord Rosebery a Liberal-Imperialist hope, and it seemed as though the Prince would never be king.

I am a good lover, but an even better hater. I have an unparalleled zest for the most moderate of dislikes. I mislike – to put it no more strongly – a great many women and nearly all men, with a special aversion for the type of man adored by women, mincing-mouthed, luxuriant-polled *genre coiffeur*. I mislike the purist who claims that one language should be enough for any writer and secretly begrudges Caesar his dying Latinism; and I mislike all those honest folk who insist upon taking you at the foot of the letter instead of at the top, or at least half-way down. I dislike all aldermen, mayors, beadles, janitors, pew-openers, the whole bag of officialdom; all sham repentances and most sincere ones; all those to whom the night brings counsel, the *oncle à succession*, and the pliant inheritor; the little ninny who insists that the *Moonlight Sonata* is by Mendelssohn. I have a contempt for the Christian who looks down upon the Jew, the white man who animadverts against the black. I have a horror of the Freemason in his cups; of the players of solo-whist; of the actor with pretensions towards edification claiming to raddle his face that ultimately fewer women may raddle

theirs, who 'asks a blessing' on his Hamlet. I hate the
commonplaces of the train, the street, and the market.
I abhor the belly of the successful man and the swelling
paunch of the Justice. But my particular loathing is
reserved for the unknowledgeable fool who says in his
heart: 'These things are not within my experience; therefore they cannot be true.'

What a plague is *ennui*! To have been everywhere, seen
everything, done everything, to have used up the senses
and let slip the supreme boon, is of all moral diseases the
last incurable. To be tired of oneself and one's proficiencies,
of the feel of a cue, the whip of a club, the way the racquet
comes up in the hand, the touch of reins, the 'handle' of
your favourite book, all this is indeed to find the world
flat and unprofitable. Nothing remains, says your quack,
but to take his pills. Nothing remains but to follow my
system of exercises, declares some frock-coated Hercules.

There is, we have often been told, valour and to spare
in the spirit's triumph over the flesh. But there is ignominy,
I take it, in a romantic spleen giving way to massage, in a
fine frenzy of melancholy yielding before a system of
exercises. I know nothing more humiliating than this
o'ercrowing of the spirit by the body. Hamlet himself
had done less girding at the world if he had not been, as
Gertrude remarks, in poor condition. That the world is
out of joint is an old cry. It belongs to our day to advertise
all that loss of figure and excess of flesh, baldness and
superfluous hair, tuberculosis, which are our inheritance.
I have never been able to fathom the delicate arts' survival
of these natural shocks. Greatly in their favour has been
the lateness of the world's discovery of electricity, X-rays,
Swedish drills, and physical exercises. A Musset the picture
of rude health, a Chopin who should dedicate a nocturne
to Mr Sandow, a Shelley *père de famille*, a Baudelaire who

should be an inside right to be reckoned with – these
were unthinkable. But it is no part of the story-teller's
business to argue, especially when he is not too sure of his
case, and you could shatter mine by citing the admirable
boxer who is responsible for *Pelléas and Mélisande*.

What I am driving at is that life is never as exquisite
nor as tragic as it appears on the surface. I am plagued
with the keen appreciation of the tendency of things to
find their own level, and I see the world through common-
sense spectacles. With me the exquisite moment is of short
duration; subsidence is always at hand. Grief is tragic,
but its expression, except in the hands of the trained
actor, grotesque. A woman in tears is the most monstrous
of spectacles, birth as lamentable as death, the terror of
many an honest execution marred by the vulgarity of the
hangman and our vision of the glass which is to refresh
him. What, we ask, remains, for the fellow in the evening
of his days save the decline to some bar-parlour? Life is
always taking the edge off things, and it is become the
fashion to scoff at the monster and the grand *détraqué*. One
laughs them out of existence, poor souls. Life is reasonable
and sane; your true realist should have nothing to do with
bravura. Life is exactly like a common-sensical novel by –
never mind whom, and I fear sometimes lest the Ultimate
Cause be made after that author's image. And yet the
most modern writers have their cowardices. Which of
them dares portray a murderer *bored* with the imbecile
chunnerings, the senile irrelevancies of his judge? Which
of them will attribute the clear eye and healthy appetite
of the released convict less to the joy of freedom than to
a *régime* of regular hours and enforced abstinences? They
are afraid of their readers, and rightly. What reader would
tolerate that I should set down my real feelings on nearing
discharge? From me is expected relief from the intermittent

panic, the perpetual dread, the nameless horror, whereas all I have to tell is of escape from an ecstasy of boredom. The truth is that even fear cannot endure for ever; the human mechanism has its limits. Soldiers have told of the power at the long last to put fear behind, not that desperate fear which is the moment of valour's catch in the throat, but the more serious dread, the dull foreboding of inaction. Man cannot keep his mind for ever on the rack; God is to be thanked that we have not complete control of our mentality. I have to reason myself to consciousness of the great deeds which are afoot; I have come to feel intuitively that death is cheapening and that it has become a little thing to die.

A little thing in one sense, how tremendous in another! My reverence for the common soldier exceeds all bounds. Even more vital than the compulsion to mete out to hellish torturers the measure they meted out to their helpless victims is the obligation of this country to see that no common soldier who has served in France shall ever know the meaning of want. It is for the nation to adopt its cripples and its maimed, to exact from the poor man his contribution of work and from the rich man even to one hundred per cent of that which he hath, rather than that a single one of these unmurmuring brave should starve. Yesterday a man died in my ward whom in ordinary times one would have dismissed as a drunkard and a lecher. I am not content with these old classifications; I am not content with the future life for this soldier which shall be all Michael Angelo and Sebastian Bach. There must be a paradise for the simpletons as for the picked spirits. I am not content with a roll-call of the illustrious dead who shall arise to greet the coming of our latter-day heroes – great Edward and great Harry, the swinging Elizabethan blade, businesslike Roundhead and inefficient Cavalier. Marlborough, Wellington, Napier, Nicholson, Havelock, Gordon – the shining list does not suffice. I am not content though Nelson return a million-told the kiss he received from Hardy. I want a Valhalla which shall not be a palace, but a home. I think I could trust Lamb to make a sufficient welcome, though it is to Falstaff I should look to discourse of honour in a strain bearable to soldier ears. Nectar and ambrosia may be good taking, but there must be a familiar grog and laughter and good-fellowship. I want a heaven in which horses shall be run, and the laying of odds allowed a sinless occupation. I want to see Sayers and Heenan fight it out again, to roar at Dan Leno, to watch old Grace till the shadows grow long.

The most bizarre conceptions assail me. I do not despair of finding a good terrier, a sufficiency of rats, and an unoccupied corner of the marble floor. I want not only the best the celestial architects may contrive in the way of saloons, but I want the atmosphere of bar-parlours; I want pipes of clay and pint-pots of jasper, common briars and spittoons of jade. Out of doors, playing-fields with well-matched teams, keen-eyed umpires, hysterical sup-porters, and tapering goal-posts – chrysoprase if you insist, but common deal will do – and a feeling that once a week it will be Saturday afternoon.

I remember reading in some exquisite diary of the War this letter of a soldier:

DEAR MUM, AND DAD, AND LOVING SISTERS, ROSE, MABEL, AND OUR GLADYS,

I am very pleased to write you another welcome letter as this leaves me at present. Dear Mum and Dad and loving sisters, keep the homes-fires burning. Not arf! The boys are in the pink. Not arf! Dear loving sisters, Rose, Mabel, and our Gladys, keep merry and bright. Not arf!

I place this amongst the most pathetic and most beautiful of the world's letters. It brings tears, and the refrain 'Rose, Mabel, and our Gladys' has the plaintiveness of a litany.

I want a heaven for this writer that shall please him.

ROBERT LYND

The Darkness

IT was common enough during the first year of the war to meet people who took an aesthetic pleasure in the darkness of the streets at night. It gave them *un nouveau frisson*. They said that never had London been so beautiful. It was hardly a gracious thing to say about London. And it was not entirely true. The hill of Piccadilly has always been beautiful, with its lamps suspended above it like strange fruits. The Thames between Westminster Bridge and Blackfriars has always been beautiful at night, pouring its brown waters along in a dusk of light and shadow. And have we not always had Hyde Park like a little dark forest full of lamps, with the gold of the lamps shaken into long Chinese alphabets in the windy waters of the Serpentine? There was Chelsea, too. Surely, even before the war, Chelsea by night lay in darkness like a town forgotten and derelict in the snug gloom of an earlier century. And if Chelsea was pitchy, St George's-in-the-East and London of the docks were pitchier. There we seemed already to be living underground. The very lamps, yellow as a hag's skin with snuff in every wrinkle, seemed scarcely to give enough light to enable one to see the world of rags and blackness which one was visiting like a stranger from another planet. One finds it so difficult to conjure up the appearance of London in the time before the war that one may be exaggerating. But, so far as one can remember, night in London was even then something of an enchantment and London the land of an enchantress. Her palace lights, her dungeon darkness, her snoring suburbs tucked away into bed after a surfeit of the piano and the gramophone – here, even in days of peace, was an infinite variety of spectacle. Not that I will pretend that the suburbs were ever beautiful. They are more depressing than a heap of old tins, than a field of bricks, than slob-lands, than vineyards in early summer. They are more commonplace than the misuse of the word 'phenomenal' or the jargon of house-agents. They do not possess enough character even to be called ugly. They are the expression in brick of the sin of the Laodiceans. Neither the light of peace nor the Tartarus of war can awaken them out of their bad prose. One thinks of them as the commodious slave-quarters of modern civilization. The human race has yet to learn, or to re-learn, how to build suburbs. It is a proof of our immorality that we cannot do so. Well, the darkness has at least hidden the face of the suburbs. It has changed long rows of houses into little cottages, and monotonous avenues into country lanes down which cautious figures make their way with torches. Sometimes in these circumstances, the dullest street becomes like a parade of will-o'-the-wisps. The post-girl alone, with her larger lamp, is impressive as a motor-car or a policeman. She steps with the self-assurance of an institution past the images of lost souls looking for Paradise by candlelight . . .

Certainly, the first searchlight that waved above London like a sword was wonderful. That made the darkness – and Charing Cross – beautiful. The lovers of darkness were right when they praised searchlights. Probably the first of them was but a tiny affair compared to those that now lie thick as post-offices between the hills of north and south London; but it impressed the imagination as an adventurer among the stars. One would not have been unduly surprised if one had caught sight of the prince of the powers of the air making his way on black wings from star to star at the end of its long beam. Later on, London sent forth a hundred such lights. She spent her evenings like a mathematician drawing weird geometrical figures on the darkness. She became the greatest of the Futurists, all cubes and angles. Sometimes she seemed like a crab lying on its back and waving a multitude of inevitable pincers. Sometimes she seemed to be fishing in the sky with an immense drag-net of light. Sometimes, on misty-moisty nights, the searchlights lit up the sluggish clouds with smudges of gold. It was like a decoration of water-lilies on long stems of light. On nights on which a Zeppelin raid was in progress one has seen the distant sky filled, as it were, with lilies, east and west, north and south. And, for many people, the Zeppelins themselves seemed to have beautified the night. For my part, I confess I cannot regard the Zeppelin without prejudice as a spectacle. That it is beautiful as a silver fish, as the lights play on it, I will not deny. Nor can one remain unmoved by the sight as shells burst about it with little sputters, like fireworks on a wet night. But, even as a pyrotechnic display, the Zeppelin raid has, in my opinion, been overestimated. They could do better at the Crystal Palace. As soon as the first novelty of the Zeppelins had worn off, it was their beastliness rather than their beauty that impressed itself upon those with the most persistent passion for sight-seeing. Even the sight of a Zeppelin in flames, awe-inspiring though it was, soon ceased to be a novelty calling for superlatives. All the same, London of the searchlights and the Zeppelins will not be forgotten in sixty years. Men and women now living will relate to their grandchildren how they saw a ship in the sky in a tangle of gold lights, and how the ship was then swallowed up in darkness, and how, after a space of darkness and echoes, the sky suddenly purpled into a

false dawn and opened into a rose of light. Then, hung in
the air for a moment, was a little ball of flame, and then
the darkness again, and only a broken rope of gold hur-
riedly dropped down the sky to announce the ultimate
horror of disaster. Those who had a nearer view of the
affair will have their own variant of the story. They, too,
will tell how the sky was suddenly flooded with monstrous tides of light at midnight, and how the wonders of
morning and sunset were mingled, and how the sunset
began to move towards them with its red eye, with its red
mouth, a vast furnace ship, an enemy of the world, increasing, lengthening, a doom impending till once more,
darkness and foolish cheers, and laughter and anecdotes in
the streets. Assuredly, the darkness of London has had its
interesting moment ...

One has to admit the attractions even of the common
darkness of the streets. Perhaps it has become, from an
aesthetic point of view, excessive in recent months, and,
except on moonlight nights, we have too much the air of
shadowy creatures of the Brocken as we make our way
about in the dimness. The tram that used to sail along like
a ship with all its lights burning was certainly a prettier
thing to see than the dismal bus of these days, packed like
a doss-house, charging into obscurity. A long line of taxi-
cabs can still give a street in a busy hour the appearance of
a stream of stars, and on a wet evening even a procession
of vans with their red lights reflected in the pavement can
impart to the commonest road the magic of a Venetian
canal. But the darkness is by no means so beautiful now as
it was when a few windows were still left lighted. At the
time of the first lighting regulations, we were given a
subdued light instead of a glare. Buildings with every
feature a misunderstanding revealed themselves as impressive masses; illuminated advertisements disappeared;

and we could still see to read the evening paper in a bus, so that we were rather gratified, or at least disinclined to grumble. Now, however, we have reached the stage of real darkness. To go out in it is, as I heard a servant remark, like going into the coal-hole without a candle. There are parts of the town in which even the soberest man may walk into a tree or a lamp-post, and there is almost no part of the town in which during the dark of the moon a man may not fall down a flight of stone steps – and will not, if he does not carry an electric torch. Perhaps the best compensation Londoners have been given for the darkness is the pleasing variety of the means by which the lights have been dimmed in different neighbourhoods. In some suburbs the lamps look as though they had been dirtied like a slut's face. Elsewhere they wear masks pierced with holes, and are terrible and black like inquisitors or medieval executioners. Some of them are blue, some green, some brown, some flamingo-coloured. London, that lawless city, was never more admirably lawless than in this. Light falls from many of them like the veils that little children wear in Catholic countries on taking their first communion. From others it falls like the garment of a ghost. Other lights give the effect of a row of Chinese lanterns hung high above a high street. But there is no sense of merriment amid all these fantastic odds and ends of lights. The light regulations have manifestly muted the life of London. Even the Australian and Canadian soldiers who pace so determinedly up and down the Strand and hang in groups round every corner, have an elfin un-substantial appearance among the shadows. Men not in khaki look black as Hamlets. Girls of the plainest are mysteries till one hears their voices. The porches of theatres are filled with a blue mystic light that would make one speak in whispers. Night certainly falls on London like a blanket. Perhaps it is mostly illusion. There is, as they say, all the fun of the fair going on for those who are young and giddy of heart, and London is not without laughter and loud voices and reeling figures. But the effect is, undoubtedly, depressing. Public-houses, darkened like prisons, no longer invite the mob with bright and vulgar windows. Cinematograph theatres are as gloomy-fronted as though over their doors they bore the motto: 'Abandon hope, all ye who enter here.' Rather than venture into such a wilderness of joylessness, many people prefer to sit at home and play tiddleywinks. Or argue. How they argue!

Luckily, in the beginning, there were created, along with the earth, a sun and a moon, and neither policeman nor magistrate nor any other creature has any power over them of regulation or control. It is the moon that makes London by night beautiful in war-time. It is the moon that makes the north side of Trafalgar Square white with romance like a Moorish city, and makes the South Kensington Museum itself appear as though it had been built to music. London under the moon is a city of wonder, a city of fair streets and fair citizens. Under the moon the arc-lamps in their cowls no longer affect us like sentinel killjoys. They seem feeble and insignificant as dying torches when the moonlight performs her miracles and exalts this city of mean dwellings into a beauty equal to that of the restless sea.

On Not Being a Philosopher

'HAVE you read Epictetus lately?' 'No, not lately.' 'Oh, you ought to read him. Tommy's been reading him for the first time, and is fearfully excited.' I caught this scrap of dialogue from the next table in the lounge of an hotel. I became interested, curious, for I had never read Epictetus, though I had often looked at his works on the shelf – perhaps I had even quoted him – and I wondered if here at last was the book of wisdom that I had been looking for at intervals ever since I was at school. Never have I lost my early faith that wisdom is to be found somewhere in a book – to be picked up as easily as a shell from the sand. I desire wisdom as keenly as Solomon did, but it must be wisdom that can be obtained with very little effort – wisdom that can be caught almost by infection. I have no time or energy for the laborious quest of philosophy. I wish the philosophers to perform the laborious quest and, at the end of it, to feed me with the fruits of their labours; just as I get eggs from the farmer, apples from the fruit-grower, medicines from the chemist, so do I expect the philosopher to provide me with wisdom at the cost of a few shillings. That is why at one time I read Emerson and, at another, Marcus Aurelius. To read them, I hoped, was to become wise by reading. But I did not become wise. I agreed with them while I read them, but, when I had finished reading, I was still much the same man that I had been before, incapable of concentrating on the things on which they said I should concentrate or of not being indifferent to the things to which they said I should not be indifferent. Still, I have never lost faith in books, believing that somewhere printed matter exists from which I shall be able to absorb philosophy and strength of character while smoking in an armchair. It was in this mood that I took down Epictetus after hearing the conversation in the hotel lounge.

I read him, I confess with considerable excitement. He is the kind of philosopher I like, not treating life as if at its finest it were an argument conducted in difficult jargon, but discussing, among other things, how men should behave in the affairs of ordinary life. Also, I agreed with nearly everything he said. Indifference to pain, death, poverty – yes, that is eminently desirable. Not to be troubled about anything over which one has no control, whether the oppression of tyrants or the peril of earth-quakes – on the necessity of this also, Epictetus and I are as one. Yet, close as is the resemblance between our opinions, I could not help feeling, as I read, that Epictetus was wise in holding his opinions and that I, though holding the same opinions, was far from wise. For, indeed though I held the same opinions for purposes of theory, I could not entertain them for a moment for purposes of conduct. Death, pain, and poverty are to me very real evils, except when I am in an armchair reading a book by a philosopher. If an earthquake happened while I was reading a book of philosophy, I should forget the book of philosophy and think only of the earthquake and how to avoid tumbling walls and chimneys. This, though I am the staunchest possible admirer of Socrates, Pliny, and people of that sort. Sound though I am as an armchair philoso-pher, at a crisis I find that both the spirit and the flesh are weak.

Even in the small things of life I cannot comfort myself like a philosopher of the school of Epictetus. Thus, for example, when he advises us how to 'eat acceptably to the gods' and bids us to this end to be patient even under the most incompetent service at our meals, he commands a spiritual attitude of which my nature is incapable. 'When you have asked for warm water,' he says, 'and the slave does not heed you; or if he does heed you but brings tepid water; or if he is not even to be found in the house, then to refrain from anger and not to explode, is not this acceptable to the gods?... Do you not remember over whom you rule – that they are kinsmen, that they are brothers by nature, and they are the offspring of Zeus?' That is all perfectly true, and I should like very much to be a man who could sit in a restaurant, smiling patiently and philosophically while the waiter brought all the wrong things or forgot to bring anything at all. But in point of fact bad waiting irritates me. I dislike having to ask three times for the wine-list. I am annoyed when, after a quarter of an hour's delay, I am told that there is no celery. It is true that I do not make a scene on such occasions. I have not enough courage for that. I am as sparing of objurgations as a philosopher, but I suspect that the scowling spirit within me must show itself in my features. Certainly, I do not think of telling myself: 'This waiter is my kinsman; he is the offspring of Zeus.' Besides, even if he were, why should the offspring of Zeus wait so badly? Epictetus never dined at the — Restaurant. And yet his patience might have served him even there. If so, what a difference between Epictetus and me! And, if I cannot achieve his imperturbability in so small affairs as I have mentioned, what hope is there of my being able to play the philosopher in presence of tyrants and earthquakes?

Again, when Epictetus expresses his opinions on material possessions and counsels us to be so indifferent to them that we should not object to their being stolen, I agree with him in theory and yet in practice I know I should be unable to obey him. There is nothing more certain than that a man whose happiness depends on his possessions is not happy. I am sure a wise man can be happy on a pittance. Not that happiness should be the aim of life, according to Epictetus or myself. But Epictetus at least holds up an ideal of imperturbability, and he assures us that we shall achieve this if we care so little for material

things that it does not matter to us whether somebody
steals them or not. 'Stop admiring your clothes,' he bids
us, 'and you are not angry at the man who steals them.'
And he goes on persuasively concerning the thief: '*He*
does not know wherein the true good of man consists, but
fancies that it consists in having fine clothes, the very same
fancy that you also entertain. Shall he not come, then, and
carry them off?' Yes, logically I suppose he should, and
yet I cannot feel so at the moment at which I find that a
guest at a party has taken my new hat and left his old one
in its place. It gives me no comfort to say to myself
'*He* does not know wherein the true good of man consists,:
but fancies that it consists in having my hat.' Nor should
I dream of attempting to console a guest at a party in my
own house with such philosophy in similar circumstances.
It is very irritating to lose a new hat. It is very irritating
to lose anything at all, especially if one thinks it has been
taken on purpose. I feel that I could imitate Epictetus if I
lived in a world in which nothing happened. But in a world
in which things disappear through loss, theft, and 'pinch-
ing', and in which bad meals are served by bad waiters
in many of the restaurants, and a thousand other disagreeable things happen, an ordinary man might as well
set out to climb the Himalayas in walking shoes as
attempt to live the life of a philosopher at all hours.

In spite of this, however, most of us cannot help
believing that the philosophers were right – right when
they proclaimed, amid all their differences, that most of
the things we bother about are not worth bothering about.
It is easier to believe that oneself is a fool than that
Socrates was a fool, and yet, if he was not right, he must
have been the greatest fool who ever lived. The truth is,
nearly everybody is agreed that such men as Socrates and
Epictetus were right in their indifference to external

things. Even men earning £10,000 a year and working for
more would admit this. Yet, while admitting it, most of us
would be alarmed if one of our dearest friends began to
put the philosophy of Epictetus into practice too literally.
What we regard as wisdom in Epictetus we should look on
as insanity in an acquaintance. Or, perhaps, not in an
acquaintance, but at least in a near relation. I am sure that
if I became as indifferent to money and comfort and all
external things as Epictetus, and reasoned in his fashion
with a happy smile about property and thieves, my relations would become more perturbed than if I became a
successful company promoter with the most materialistic
philosophy conceivable. Think, for example, of the reasoning of Epictetus over the thief who stole his iron lamp:

He bought a lamp for a very high price; for a lamp he became
a thief, for a lamp he became faithless, for a lamp he became
bestial. This is what seemed to him to be profitable!

The reasoning is sound, yet neither individually nor as a
society do we live in that contempt of property on which
it is based. A few saints do, but even they are at first a
cause of great concern to their friends. When the world
is normally cheerful and comfortable, we hold the para-
doxical belief that the philosophers were wise men, but
that we should be fools to imitate them. We are convinced
that, while philosophers are worth reading, material
things are worth bothering about. It is as though we
enjoyed wisdom as a spectacle – a delightful spectacle on a
stage which it would be unseemly for the audience to
attempt to invade. Were the Greeks and the Romans made
differently? Did the admirers of Socrates and Epictetus
really attempt to become philosophers, or were they like
ourselves, hopeful of achieving wisdom, not by practice
but through a magic potion administered by a wiser man
than they? To become wise without effort – by listening

to a voice, by reading a book – it is at once the most exciting and the most soothing of dreams. In such a dream I took down Epictetus. And, behold, it was only a dream.

Why We Hate Insects

IT has been said that the characteristic sound of summer is the hum of insects, as the characteristic sound of spring is the singing of birds. It is all the more curious that the word 'insect' conveys to us an implication of ugliness. We think of spiders, of which many people are more afraid than of Germans. We think of bugs and fleas, which seem so indecent in their lives that they are made a jest by the vulgar, and the nice people do their best to avoid mentioning them. We think of blackbeetles scurrying into safety as the kitchen light is suddenly turned on – blackbeetles which (so we are told) in the first place are not beetles, and in the second place are not black. There are women who will make a face at the mere name of any of these creatures. Those of us who have never felt this repulsion – at least, against spiders and blackbeetles – cannot but wonder how far it is natural. Is it born in certain people, or is it acquired like the old-fashioned habit of swooning and the fear of mice? The nearest I have come to it is a feeling of disgust when I have seen a cat retrieving a blackbeetle just about to escape under a wall and making a dish of it. There are also certain crawling creatures which are so notoriously the children of filth and so threatening in their touch that we naturally shrink from them. Burns may make merry over a louse crawling in a lady's hair, but few of us can regard its kind with equanimity even on the backs of swine. Men of science deny that

the louse is actually engendered by dirt, but it undoubtedly thrives on it. Our anger against the flea also arises
from the fact that we associate it with dirt. Donne once
wrote a poem to a lady who had been bitten by the same
flea as himself, arguing that this was a good reason why
she should allow him to make love to her. It is, and was
bound to be, a dirty poem. Love, even of the wandering
and polygynous kind, does not express itself in such
images. Only while under the dominion of the youthful
heresy of ugliness could a poet pretend that it did. The
flea, according to the authorities, is 'remarkable for its
powers of leaping, and nearly cosmopolitan'. Even so, it
has found no place in the heart or fancy of man. There
have been men who were indifferent to fleas, but there
have been none who loved them, though if my memory
does not betray me, there was a famous French prisoner
some years ago who beguiled the tedium of his cell by
making a pet and a performer of a flea. For the world at
large, the flea represents merely hateful irritation. Mr
W. B. Yeats has introduced it into poetry in this sense in
an epigram addressed 'to a poet who would have me
praise certain bad poets, imitators of his and of mine':

> *You say as I have often given tongue*
> *In praise of what another's said or sung,*
> *'Twere politic to do the like by these,*
> *But where's the wild dog that has praised his fleas?*

When we think of the sufferings of human beings and
animals at the hands – if that is the right word – of insects,
we feel that it is pardonable enough to make faces at
creatures so inconsiderate. But what strikes one as remarkable is that the insects that do man most harm are not
those that horrify him most. A lady who will sit bravely
while a wasp hangs in the air and inspects first her right
and then her left temple will run a mile from a harmless

spider. Another will remain collected (though murderous) in presence of a horse-fly, but will shudder at sight of a moth that is innocent of blood. Our fears, it is evident, do not march in all respects with our sense of physical danger. There are insects that make us feel that we are in the presence of the uncanny. Many of us have this feeling about moths. Moths are the ghosts of the insect world. It may be the manner in which they flutter in unheralded out of the night that terrifies us. They seem to tap against our lighted windows as though the outer darkness had a message for us. And their persistence helps to terrify. They are more troublesome than a subject nation. They are more importunate than the importunate widow. But they are most terrifying of all if one suddenly sees their eyes blazing crimson as they catch the light. One thinks of nocturnal rites in an African forest temple and of terrible jewels blazing in the head of an evil goddess – jewels to be stolen, we realize, by a foolish white man, thereafter to be the object of a vendetta in a sensational novel. One feels that one's hair would be justified in standing on end, only that hair does not do such things. The sight of a moth's eye is, I fancy, a rare one for most people. It is a sight one can no more forget than a house on fire. Our feelings towards moths being what they are, it is all the more surprising that superstition should connect the moth so much less than the butterfly with the world of the dead. Who says a cabbage-grower has any feeling against butterflies? And yet in folk-lore it is to the butterfly rather than to the moth that is assigned the ghostly part. In Ireland they have a legend about a priest who had not believed that men had souls, but, on being converted, announced that a living thing would be seen soaring up from his body when he died – in proof that his earlier scepticism had been wrong. Sure enough, when he lay dead, a beautiful creature 'with

four snow-white wings' rose from his body and fluttered
round his head. 'And this', we are told, 'was the first
butterfly that was ever seen in Ireland; and now all men
know that the butterflies are the souls of the dead waiting
for the moment when they may enter Purgatory.' In the
Solomon Islands, they say, it used to be the custom, when a
man was about to die, for him to announce that he was
about to transmigrate into a butterfly or some other
creature. The members of his family, on meeting a
butterfly afterwards, would explain: 'This is papa', and
offer him a coconut. The members of an English family
in like circumstances would probably say: 'Have a
banana'. In certain tribes of Assam the dead are believed
to return in the shape of butterflies or house-flies, and for
this reason no one will kill them. On the other hand, in
Westphalia the butterfly plays the part given to the scape-
goat in other countries, and on St Peter's Day, in Febru-
ary, it is publicly expelled with rhyme and ritual. Elsewhere, as in Samoa – I do not know where I found all these
facts – probably in *The Golden Bough* – the butterfly has
been feared as a god, and to catch a butterfly was to run
the risk of being struck dead. The moth, for all I know,
may be the centre of as many legends, but I have not met
them. It may be, however, that in many of the legends the
moth and the butterfly are not very clearly distinguished.
To most of us it seems easy enough to distinguish between
them; the English butterfly can always be known, for instance, by his clubbed horns. But this distinction does not
hold with regard to the entire world of butterflies – a
world so populous and varied that thirteen thousand
species have already been discovered, and entomologists
hope one day to classify twice as many more. Even in these
islands, indeed, most of us do not judge a moth chiefly by
its lack of clubbed horns. It is for us the thing that flies by

night and eats holes in our clothes. We are not even afraid
of it in all circumstances. Our terror is an indoor terror.
We are on good terms with it in poetry, and play with the
thought of

> *The desire of the moth for the star.*

We remember that it is for the moths that the pallid
jasmine smells so sweetly by night. There is no shudder in
our minds when we read:

> *And when white moths were on the wing,*
> *And moth-like stars were flickering out,*
> *I dropped the berry in a stream,*
> *And caught a little silver trout.*

No man has ever sung of spiders or earwigs or any other
of our pet antipathies among the insects like that. The
moth is the only one of the insects that fascinates us with
both its beauty and its terror.

I doubt if there have ever been greater hordes of insects
in this country than during the past spring. It is the only
complaint one has to make against the sun. He is a
desperate breeder of insects. And he breeds them not in
families like a Christian but in plagues. The thought of the
insects alone keeps us from envying the tropics their blue
skies and hot suns. Better the North Pole than a plague of
locusts. We fear the tarantula and have no love for the
tse-tse fly. The insects of our own climate are bad enough
in all conscience. The grasshopper, they say, is a murderer,
and, though the earwig is a perfect mother, other insects
such as the burying-beetle have the reputation of parri-
cides. But, dangerous or not, the insects are for the most
part teasers and destroyers. The greenfly makes its
colonies in the rose, a purple fellow swarms under the
leaves of the apples, and another scoundrel, black as the

night, swarms over the beans. There are scarcely more diseases in the human body than there are kinds of insects in a single fruit tree. The apple that is rotten before it is ripe is an insect's victim, and, if the plums fall green and untimely in scores upon the ground, once more it is an insect that has been at work among them. Talk about German spies! Had German spies gone to the insect world for a lesson, they might not have been the inefficient bunglers they showed themselves to be. At the same time, most of us hate spies and insects for the same reason. We regard them as noxious creatures intruding where they have no right to be, preying upon us and giving us nothing but evil in return. Hence our ruthlessness. We say: 'Vermin', and destroy them. To regard a human being as an insect is always the first step in treating him without remorse. It is a perilous attitude and in general is more likely to beget crime than justice. There has never, I believe, been an empire built in which, at some stage or other, a massacre of children among a revolting population has not been excused on the ground that 'nits make lice'. 'Swot that Bolshevik' no doubt, seems to many reactionaries as sanitary a counsel as 'Swot that fly'. Even in regard to flies, however, most of us can only swot with scruple. Hate flies we may, and wish them in perdition as we may, we could not slowly pull them to pieces, wing after wing, and leg after leg, as thoughtless children are said to do. Many of us cannot endure to see them slowly done to death on those long strips of sticky paper on which the flies drag their legs and their lives out – as it seems to me, a vile cruelty. A distinguished novelist has said that to watch flies trying to tug their legs off the paper one after another till they are twice their natural length is one of his favourite amusements. I have never found any difficulty in believing it of him. It is an odd fact that considerateness, if not actually kindness, to flies has been made one of the tests of gentleness in popular speech. How often has one heard it said in praise of a dead man: 'He wouldn't have hurt a fly!' As for those who do hurt flies, we pillory them in history. We have never forgotten the cruelty of Domitian. 'At the beginning of his reign,' Suetonius tells us, 'he used to spend hours in seclusion every day, doing nothing but catch flies and stab them with a keenly sharpened stylus. Consequently, when someone once asked whether anyone was in there with Caesar, Vibius Crispus made the witty reply: "Not even a fly."' And just as most of us are on the side of the fly against Domitian, so are most of us on the side of the fly against the spider. We pity the fly as (if the image is permissible) the underdog. One of the most agonizing of the minor dilemmas in which a too sensitive humanitarian ever finds himself is whether he should destroy a spider's web, and so, perhaps, starve the spider to death, or whether he should leave the web, and so connive at the death of a multitude of flies. I have long been content to leave Nature to her own ways in such matters. I cannot say that I like her in all her processes, but I am content to believe that this may be owing to my ignorance of some of the facts of the case. There are, on the other hand, two acts of destruction in Nature which leave me unprotesting and pleased. One of these occurs when a thrush eats a snail, banging the shell repeatedly against a stone. I have never thought of the incident from the snail's point of view. I find myself listening to the tap-tap of the shell on the stone as though it were music. I felt the same sort of mild thrill of pleasure the other day when I found a beautiful spotted ladybird squeezing itself between two apples and settling down to feed on some kind of aphides that were eating into the fruit. The ladybird, the butterfly, and the bee – who would put chains upon such creatures?

These are insects which must have been in Eden before the snake. Beelzebub, the god of the other insects, had not yet any endangering power on the earth in those days, when all the flowers were as strange as insects and all the insects were as beautiful as flowers.

The Pleasures of Ignorance

IT is impossible to take a walk in the country with an average townsman – especially, perhaps, in April or May – without being amazed at the vast continent of his ignorance. It is impossible to take a walk in the country oneself without being amazed at the vast continent of one's own ignorance. Thousands of men and women live and die without knowing the difference between a beech and an elm, between the song of a thrush and the song of a blackbird. Probably in a modern city the man who can distinguish between a thrush's and a blackbird's song is the exception. It is not that we have not seen the birds. It is simply that we have not noticed them. We have been surrounded by birds all our lives, yet so feeble is our observation that many of us could not tell whether or not the chaffinch sings, or the colour of the cuckoo. We argue like small boys as to whether the cuckoo always sings as he flies or sometimes in the branches of a tree – whether Chapman drew on his fancy or his knowledge of nature in the lines:

> *When in the oak's green arms the cuckoo sings,*
> *And first delights men in the lovely springs.*

This ignorance, however, is not altogether miserable. Out of it we get the constant pleasure of discovery. Every fact of nature comes to us each spring, if only we are sufficiently ignorant, with the dew still on it. If we have lived half a lifetime without having ever seen a cuckoo, and know it only as a wandering voice, we are all the more delighted at the spectacle of its runaway flight as it hurries from wood to wood conscious of its crimes and at the way in which it halts hawk-like in the wind, its long tail quivering, before it dares descend on a hill-side of fir-trees where avenging presences may lurk. It would be absurd to pretend that the naturalist does not also find pleasure in observing the life of the birds, but his is a steady pleasure, almost a sober and plodding occupation, compared to the morning enthusiasm of the man who sees a cuckoo for the first time, and, behold, the world is made new.

And, as to that, the happiness even of the naturalist depends in some measure upon his ignorance, which still leaves him new worlds of this kind to conquer. He may have reached the very Z of knowledge in the books, but he still feels half ignorant until he has confirmed each bright particular with his eyes. He wishes with his own eyes to see the female cuckoo – rare spectacle! – as she lays her egg on the ground and takes it in her bill to the nest in which it is destined to breed infanticide. He would sit day after day with a field-glass against his eyes in order personally to endorse or refute the evidence suggesting that the cuckoo *does* lay on the ground and not in a nest. And, if he is so far fortunate as to discover this most secretive of birds in the very act of laying, there still remain for him other fields to conquer in a multitude of such disputed questions as whether the cuckoo's egg is always of the same colour as the other eggs in the nest in which she abandons it. Assuredly the men of science have no reason as yet to weep over their lost ignorance. If they seem to know everything, it is only because you and I know almost nothing. There will always be a fortune of ignorance waiting for them under every fact they turn up. They will never know what song the Sirens sang to Ulysses any more than Sir Thomas Browne did.

If I have called in the cuckoo to illustrate the ordinary man's ignorance, it is not because I can speak with authority on that bird. It is simply because, passing the spring in a parish that seemed to have been invaded by all the cuckoos of Africa, I realized how exceedingly little I, or anybody else I met, knew about them. But your and my ignorance is not confined to cuckoos. It dabbles in all created things, from the sun and moon down to the names of the flowers. I once heard a clever lady asking whether the new moon always appears on the same day of the week. She added that perhaps it is better not to know, because, if one does not know when or in what part of the sky to expect it, its appearance is always a pleasant surprise. I fancy, however, the new moon always comes as a surprise even to those who are familiar with her time-tables. And it is the same with the coming-in of spring and the waves of the flowers. We are not the less delighted to find an early primrose because we are sufficiently learned in the services of the year to look for it in March or April rather than in October. We know, again, that the blossom precedes and not succeeds the fruit of the apple-tree, but this does not lessen our amazement at the beautiful holiday of a May orchard.

At the same time there is, perhaps, a special pleasure in re-learning the names of many of the flowers every spring. It is like re-reading a book that one has almost forgotten. Montaigne tells us that he had so bad a memory that he could always read an old book as though he had never read it before. I have myself a capricious and leaking memory. I can read *Hamlet* itself and *The Pickwick Papers* as though they were the work of new authors and had come wet from the press, so much of them fades between one reading and another. There are occasions on which a memory of this kind is an affliction, especially if one has a passion for accuracy. But this is only when life has an object beyond entertainment. In respect of mere luxury, it may be doubted whether there is not as much to be said for a bad memory as for a good one. With a bad memory one can go on reading Plutarch and *The Arabian Nights* all one's life. Little shreds and tags, it is probable, will stick even in the worst memory, just as a succession of sheep cannot leap through a gap in a hedge without leaving a few wisps of wool on the thorns. But the sheep themselves escape, and the great authors leap in the same way out of an idle memory and leave little enough behind.

And, if we can forget books, it is as easy to forget the months and what they showed us, when once they are gone. Just for a moment I tell myself that I know May like the multiplication table and could pass an examination on its flowers, their appearance and their order. To-day I can affirm confidently that the buttercup has five petals. (Or is it six? I knew for certain last week.) But next year I shall probably have forgotten my arithmetic, and may have to learn once more not to confuse the buttercup with the celandine. Once more I shall see the world as a garden through the eyes of a stranger, my breath taken away with surprise by the painted fields. I shall find myself wondering whether it is science or ignorance which affirms that the swift (that black exaggeration of the swallow and yet a kinsman of the humming-bird) never settles even on a nest, but disappears at night into the heights of the air. I shall learn with fresh astonishment that it is the male, and not the female, cuckoo that sings. I may have to learn again not to call the campion a wild geranium, and to

rediscover whether the ash comes early or late in the etiquette of the trees. A contemporary English novelist was
once asked by a foreigner what was the most important
crop in England. He answered without a moment's
hesitation: 'Rye'. Ignorance so complete as this seems
to me to be touched with magnificence; but the ignorance
even of illiterate persons is enormous. The average man
who uses a telephone could not explain how a telephone
works. He takes for granted the telephone, the railway
train, the linotype, the aeroplane, as our grandfathers took
for granted the miracles of the gospels. He neither questions nor understands them. It is as though each of us
investigated and made his own only a tiny circle of facts.
Knowledge outside the day's work is regarded by most
men as a gewgaw. Still we are constantly in reaction
against our ignorance. We rouse ourselves at intervals and
speculate. We revel in speculations about anything at all –
about life after death or about such questions as that which
is said to have puzzled Aristotle, 'why sneezing from noon
to midnight was good, but from night to noon unlucky.'
One of the greatest joys known to man is to take such a
flight into ignorance in search of knowledge. The great
pleasure of ignorance is, after all, the pleasure of asking
questions. The man who has lost this pleasure or exchanged it for the pleasure of dogma, which is the pleasure
of answering, is already beginning to stiffen. One envies
so inquisitive a man as Jowett, who sat down to the study
of physiology in his sixties. Most of us have lost the sense
of our ignorance long before that age. We even become
vain of our squirrel's hoard of knowledge and regard
increasing age itself as a school of omniscience. We forget
that Socrates was famed for wisdom not because he was
omniscient but because he realized at the age of seventy
that he still knew nothing.

A. A. MILNE

A Village Celebration

ALTHOUGH our village is a very small one, we had fifteen men serving in the Forces before the war was over. Fortunately, as the Vicar well said, 'we were wonderfully blessed in that none of us was called upon to make the great sacrifice'. Indeed, with the exception of Charlie Rudd, of the Army Service Corps, who was called upon to be kicked by a horse, the village did not even suffer any casualties. Our rejoicings at the conclusion of Peace were wholehearted.

Naturally, when we met to discuss the best way in which to give expression to our joy, our first thoughts were with our returned heroes. Miss Travers, who plays the organ with considerable expression on Sundays, suggested that a drinking fountain erected on the village green would be a pleasing memorial of their valour, if suitably inscribed. For instance, it might say, 'In gratitude to our brave defenders who leaped to answer their country's call', followed by their names. Embury, the cobbler, who is always a wet blanket on these occasions, asked if 'leaping' was the exact word for a young fellow who got into khaki in 1918, and then only in answer to his country's police. The meeting was more lively after this, and Mr Bates, of Hill Farm, had to be personally assured by the Vicar that for his part he quite understood how it was that young Robert Bates had been unable to leave the farm before, and he was sure that our good friend Embury meant nothing personal by his, if he might say so, perhaps somewhat untimely observation. He would suggest himself that some such phrase as 'who gallantly answered' would be more in keeping with Miss Travers' beautiful idea. He would venture to put it to the meeting that the inscription should be amended in this sense.

Mr Clayton, the grocer and draper, interrupted to say that they were getting on too fast. Supposing they agreed upon a drinking fountain, who was going to do it? Was it going to be done in the village, or were they going to get sculptors and architects and such-like people from London? And if so – The Vicar caught the eye of Miss Travers, and signalled her to proceed; whereupon she explained that, as she had already told the Vicar in private, her nephew was studying art in London, and she was sure he would be only too glad to get Augustus James or one of those Academy artists to think of something really beautiful.

At this moment Embury said that he would like to ask two questions. First question – In what order were the names of our gallant defenders to be inscribed? The Vicar said that, speaking entirely without preparation and on the spur of the moment, he would imagine that an alphabetical order would be the most satisfactory. There was a general 'Hear, hear', led by the Squire, who thus made his first contribution to the debate. 'That's what I thought,' said Embury. 'Well, then, second question – What's coming out of the fountain?' The Vicar, a little surprised, said that presumably, my dear Embury, the fountain would give forth water. 'Ah!' said Embury with great significance, and sat down.

Our village is a little slow at getting on to things; 'leaping' is not the exact word for our movements at any time, either of brain or body. It is not surprising, therefore, that even Bates failed to realize for a moment that his son's name was to have precedence on a water fountain. But when once he realized it, he refused to be pacified by the cobbler's explanation that he had only said 'Ah!' Let those who had anything to say, he observed, speak out openly, and then we should know where we were. Embury's answer, that one could generally guess where some people were, and not be far wrong, was drowned in the ecclesiastical applause which greeted the rising of the Squire.

The Squire said that he – er – hadn't – er – intended – er – to say anything. But he thought – er if he might – er – intervene – to – er say something on the matter of – er – a matter which – er – well, they all knew what it was – in short – er – money. Because until they knew how they – er – stood, it was obvious that – it was obvious – well, it was a question of how they stood. Whereupon he sat down.

The Vicar said that as had often happened before, the sound common-sense of Sir John had saved them from undue rashness and precipitancy. They were getting on a little too fast. Their valued friend Miss Travers had made what he was not ashamed to call a suggestion both rare and beautiful, but alas! in these prosaic modern days the sordid question of pounds, shillings, and pence could not be wholly disregarded. How much money would they have?

Everybody looked at Sir John. There was an awkward silence, in which the Squire joined . . .

Amid pushings and whisperings from his corner of the room, Charlie Rudd said that he would just like to say a few words for the boys, if all were willing. The Vicar said that certainly, certainly he might, my dear Rudd. So Charlie said that he would just like to say that with all respect to Miss Travers, who was a real lady, and many was the packet of fags he'd had from her out there, and all the other boys could say the same, and if some of them joined up sooner than others, well perhaps they did, but they all tried to do their bit, just like those who stayed at home, and they'd thrashed Jerry, and glad of it, fountains or no fountains, and pleased to be back again and see them all, just the same as ever, Mr Bates and Mr Embury and all of them, which was all he wanted to say, and the other boys would say the same, hoping no offence was meant, and that was all he wanted to say.

When the applause had died down, Mr Clayton said that, in his opinion, as he had said before, they were getting on too fast. Did they want a fountain, that was the question. Who wanted it? The Vicar replied that it would be a beautiful memento for their children of the stirring times through which their country had passed. Embury asked if Mr Bates' child wanted a memento of – 'This is a general question, my dear Embury,' said the Vicar.

There rose slowly to his feet the landlord of the Dog and Duck. Celebrations he said. We were celebrating this here peace. Now, as man to man, what did celebrations mean? He asked any of them. What did it mean? Celebrations meant celebrating, meant sitting down hearty-like, sitting down like Englishmen and – and celebrating. First, find how much money they'd got, same as Sir John said; that was right and proper. Then if so be as they wanted to leave the rest to him, well, he'd be proud to do his best for them. They knew him. Do fair by him and he'd do fair by them. Soon as he knew how much money they'd got, and how many were going to sit down, then he could get to work. That was all he'd got to say about celebrations.

The enthusiasm was tremendous. But the Vicar looked anxious, and whispered to the Squire. The Squire shrugged his shoulders and murmured something, and the Vicar rose. They would all be glad to hear, he said, glad but not surprised, that with his customary generosity the Squire had decided to throw open his own beautiful gardens and pleasure-grounds to them on Peace Day and to take upon his own shoulders the burden of entertaining them. He would suggest that they now give Sir John three hearty cheers. This was done, and the proceedings closed.

Golden Fruit

OF the fruits of the year I give my vote to the orange. In the first place it is a perennial – if not in actual fact, at least in the greengrocer's shop. On the days when dessert is a name given to a handful of chocolates and a little preserved ginger, when *macedoine de fruits* is the title bestowed on two prunes and a piece of rhubarb, then the orange, however sour, comes nobly to the rescue; and on those other days of plenty when cherries and strawberries and raspberries and gooseberries riot together upon the table, the orange, sweeter than ever, is still there to hold its own. Bread and butter, beef and mutton, eggs and bacon, are not more necessary to an ordered existence than the orange.

It is well that the commonest fruits should be also the best. Of the virtues of the orange I have not room fully to speak. It has properties of health-giving, as that it cures influenza and establishes the complexion. It is clean, for whoever handles it on its way to your table, but handles its outer covering, its top coat, which is left in the hall. It is round, and forms an excellent substitute with the young for a cricket ball. The pips can be flicked at your enemies, and quite a small piece of peel makes a slide for an old gentleman.

But all this would count nothing had not the orange such delightful qualities of taste. I dare not let myself go upon this subject. I am a slave to its sweetness. I grudge every marriage in that it means a fresh supply of orange blossom, the promise of so much golden fruit cut short. However, the world must go on.

Next to the orange I place the cherry. The cherry is a companionable fruit. You can eat it while you are reading or talking, and you can go on and on, absent-mindedly as it were, though you must mind not to swallow the stone. The trouble of disengaging this from the fruit is just sufficient to make the fruit taste sweeter for the labour. The stalk keeps you from soiling your fingers; it enables you also to play bob cherry. Lastly it is by means of cherries that one penetrates the great mysteries of life – when and whom you will marry, and whether she really loves you or is taking you for your worldly prospects. (I may add here that I know a girl who can tie a knot in the stalk of a cherry with her tongue. It is a tricky business, and I am doubtful whether to add it to the virtues of the cherry or not.)

There are only two ways of eating strawberries. One is neat in the strawberry bed, and the other is mashed on the plate. The first method generally requires us to take up a bent position under a net – in a hot sun very uncomfortable, and at any time fatal to the hair. The second method takes us into the privacy of the home, for it demands a dressing-gown and no spectators. For these reasons I think the strawberry an overrated fruit. Yet I must say that I like to see one floating in cider cup. It gives a note of richness to the affair, and excuses any shortcomings in the lunch itself.

Raspberries are a good fruit gone wrong. A raspberry by itself might indeed be the best fruit of all; but it is almost impossible to find it alone. I do not refer to its attachment to the red currant; rather to the attachment to it of so many of our dumb little friends. The instinct of the lower creatures for the best is well shown in the case of the raspberry. If it is to be eaten it must be picked by the hand, well shaken, and then taken.

When you engage a gardener, the first thing to do is to come to an understanding with him about the peaches. The best way of settling the matter is to give him the carrots and the black currants and the rhubarb for himself, to allow him a free hand with the groundsel and the walnut trees, and to insist in return for this that you should pick the peaches when and how you like. If he is a gentleman he will consent. Supposing that some satisfactory arrangement were come to, and supposing also that you had a silver-bladed pocket-knife with which you could peel them in the open air, then peaches would come very high in the list of fruits. But the conditions are difficult.

Gooseberries burst at the wrong end and smother you; melons – as the nigger boy discovered – make your ears sticky; currants, when you have removed the skin and extracted the seeds, are unsatisfying; blackberries have the faults of raspberries without their virtues; plums are never ripe. Yet all these fruits are excellent in their season. Their faults are faults which we can forgive during a slight acquaintance, which indeed seem but pleasant little idiosyncrasies in the stranger. But we could not live with them.

Yet with the orange we do live year in and year out. That speaks well for the orange. The fact is that there is an honesty about the orange which appeals to all of us-

If it is going to be bad – for the best of us are bad sometimes – it begins to be bad from the outside, not from the inside. How many a pear which presents a blooming face to the world is rotten at the core. How many an innocent-looking apple is harbouring a worm in the bud. But the orange has no secret faults. Its outside is a mirror of its inside, and if you are quick you can tell the shopman so before he slips it into the bag.

HAROLD NICOLSON

A Defence of Shyness

IT is surely discreditable, under the age of thirty, not to be shy. Self-assurance in the young betokens a lack of sensibility: the boy or girl who is not shy at twenty-two will at forty-two become a bore. 'I may be wrong, of course' – thus will he or she gabble at forty-two, 'but what I always say is . . .'

No, let us educate the younger generation to be shy in and out of season: to edge behind the furniture: to say spasmodic and ill-digested things: to twist their feet round the protective feet of sofas and armchairs; to feel that their hands belong to someone else – that they are objects, which they long to put down on some table away from themselves.

For shyness is the protective fluid within which our personalities are able to develop into natural shapes. Without this fluid the character becomes merely standardized or imitative: it is within the tender velvet sheath of shyness that the full flower of idiosyncrasy is nurtured: it is from this sheath alone that it can eventually unfold itself, coloured and undamaged. Let the shy understand, therefore, that their disability is not merely an inconvenience, but also a privilege. Let them regard their shyness as a gift rather than as an affliction. Let them consider how intolerable are those of their contemporaries who are not also shy.

There was a boy once who lived near my grandmother in Ireland. He was fourteen at the time and I was twelve.

His name – and it was well chosen – was Everard. I loathed that boy. My grandmother was in the habit of giving tea-parties, at which there were hot tea-cakes in an inimical little dish with a cover. I was told that it was my duty to hand round this hostile dish to the assembled ladies, and that to do this elegantly, I should hold the dish in my right hand and raise the cover successively, when offering the tea-cakes, with my left. To me this process was a physical impossibility: it was as irksome as those excruciating exercises which entail having to rub with one hand and pat simultaneously with the other. I would pass from old lady to old lady – (that feeling about one's boots being untidy and loose, that feeling of the sock descending) – and I would hold the lid open widely when crossing carefully from group to group, and close it firmly when offering it to my grandmother's guests. Never could I achieve the right combination: never could I manage to close the dish protectively when walking about, or open it hospitably when offering its contents. On one occasion I placed the lid upon a side-table, hoping to be unobserved. I was not unobserved. 'What', my grandmother exclaimed 'have you done with the dish-cover?' Unfortunately I had placed it, not on a table, but upon a leather album containing photographs of Pompeii, and, if I remember rightly, of Paestum. The dish-cover left a neat circle of grease upon that album. I was sharply reproved. I was told that Everard was not so clumsy: that Everard was already a perfect little gentleman: that next time it should be Everard who would hand the cakes. He did so. An ingratiating but deft manner was his, such as I have observed in the more expensive class of hairdressers.

My grandmother kept on casting glances at me where I hid in the corner, glances exhorting me to observe, to draw comparisons, to profit from the egregious example of

Everard. And yet to-day I am convinced that in comparison to that trim little poodle I was (I repeat, in comparison) a nice little boy. A little soiled, perhaps, and apt
to stumble, but still, in comparison, nice. I tell this story
in order that those of my dear readers who are shy and
awkward may realize that the advice I give them comes
from the heart.

This advice, I fear, is somewhat worldly, or let us call it
realistic. I do not think that shyness can be kept within
bounds by any ethical arguments. I used to tell myself,
for instance, at those moments outside the doorways of the
great when shyness becomes a laughing monster with its
fangs already at one's heart – I used to tell myself that I
was as good, as powerful, as rich, as beautiful, and as
magnificent as any of those I was about to meet. This was
not a good system. It made me pert. I would bounce into
the room gaily, as if I were the Marquis de Soveral; be
somewhat impudent to my hostess, cut my host dead,
show undue familiarity towards the distinguished author
who had once lectured to us at Balliol, and fling myself
noisily, completely at my ease, into an armchair. The
chair would recede at this impact and upset a little table
on which were displayed a bottle of smelling-salts, a little
silver cart from Rome, a Persian pen-box, a photograph of
the Grand Duchess of Saxe-Meiningen, and a bowl of
anemones. These objects would rattle loudly to the floor,
and with them would tumble my assertiveness. Such de-
ductive systems invariably fail. Fatal also is the reverse
process of behaving like the worm one feels. 'Remember,'
I have said to myself on giving my hat and coat to the
footman, 'remember that you are a worm upon this earth.
These people have only asked you because they met your
aunt at St Jean de Luz. They do not wish to see you, still
less do they wish to hear you speak. You may say good

evening to your hostess, and then you must retreat behind a sofa and remain unobserved. There is no need for you, when in your retreat, to behave self-consciously – to examine the French engravings on the wall, or the lacquer of the incised screen. You can put both your hands upon the back of the chair and then just look (without blinking) in front of you. If addressed, you will reply with modesty and politeness. If not addressed, you will not speak at all.' Things do not work out that way. The place behind the sofa is, when you get there, fully occupied by an easel containing a picture by Carolus Duran; and then one falls over the dog. No – shyness must be controlled and conquered by more scientific methods.

In the first place, you must diagnose the type of shyness from which you suffer. There are two main divisions of the disease: the physical type and the mental type. The physical type are shy about their limbs – their arms and legs make jerky automatic movements which cause breakages and embarrassment. The mental type are shy about what they say or where they look. It is the latter who are most to be pitied. For whereas the physical sufferer can generally, by using great circumspection, avoid the worst consequences of his affliction, and can in the end sit down and sit even upon his heated hands, the mental type is not released until he finds him or herself alone again within the motor, homeward bound. It is upon the latter type that I desire to concentrate.

The first rule is to make it perfectly clear to one's parents before arriving at the party that one is to remain unnoticed. One's mother, sitting next to the host, should not be allowed to make gestures at one – down the table – of encouragement and love. One's father, sitting next to the hostess, should be forbidden to confide in her that this is the first time that you have worn an evening suit or a low-necked dress – should be forbidden to cast sly paternal glances at one, or to observe whether one does, or does not, enjoy oneself. All parental responsibility or interference must be excluded from the beginning. One must be left alone with one's shyness as with some secret possession.

The second rule is to determine from the outset that one does not desire to shine either socially or intellectually. Nor should one attempt to appear older than one actually is. These things do not carry conviction. You will find yourself, if you give way to these ambitions, slipping into phrases which are not your own phrases and of which, once they have escaped the barrier of your lips, you will feel ashamed. You may be calling, for instance, upon the wife of a neighbour: you will find her sitting on the veranda in a green deck chair: if you are wise, you will have the modesty to say merely 'How are you, Mrs Maple?': but if you are unwise, and wish to appear at your ease as you come into the room, you will exclaim, 'Please don't get up!' Having said this, you will reflect that Mrs Maple had no idea of getting out of her deck chair for such a worm as you: and you will be mortified by this reflection. Do not, therefore, adopt or even adapt the phrases of your elders. Above all, do not break into conversations. It may well be that the Primavera is a picture painted, not by Cimabue, but by Botticelli. But it is not for you, when others attribute the painting to an earlier artist, either to interfere or to correct. A slight pursing of the lips is all that you may allow yourself. The only justification for being shy is to be shy to all the people all the time. You must avoid being pert to governesses and polite to bishops. But if you are always shy, people will end by imagining that you have a modest nature: and that, since it will flatter their own self-esteem, will make you extremely popular. Only when you have become

popular can you afford to be interesting, intelligent or
impressive. It is a great mistake to endeavour to awake
admiration before you have stilled envy; it is only when
people have started by ignoring the young that they end
by liking the young. It may be a comfort to you therefore
to consider that it is an excellent thing, at first, to be
regarded as being of no importance. You can hide behind
your chair.

There are certain more practical hints which I should
wish to furnish to the youthful shy. It is essential, for
instance, to have quite clear in your mind what are to be
the opening words which you will address to your hostess.
Unless you have prepared these words, other words may
come skipping into their place, and instead of saying,
'How are you, Mrs Maple? It was too kind of you to let
me come,' you will say, 'Your butler has got the largest
carbuncle I have ever seen.' Then there is that business
about the palm of the hand. When I was a young man
women wore long kid gloves which were particularly
sensitive to any humidity of the palm. 'POP!' they went
as one shook hands, and they came away stickily after the
explosion. To-day, this particular terror is diminished. It
is a fact, however, that damp palms are things that go
with shyness. My own palm, at the age of 18, was as firm
and dry as the desert of Takla Makan. But at the slightest
menace of a hostess it became moist, and at the thought of
that impending kid glove this moisture oozed. I am sorry
to become unpleasant about it, but my sufferings were so
acute that I wish to impart to others the cure which I
discovered. It was called 'Papier Poudré' and took the
form of a neat little book of which the pages were tissue
paper, backed by a thin layer of powder. By passing
successive sheets of this paper, one at a time, over the
palm of the hand all moisture disappeared.

Then there was that business about saying goodbye. I became quite good at what we might call 'set' goodbyes – the ones, that is, for which I was prepared in advance. It was the unexpected greetings and farewells that I failed, for so long, to manage. The meeting with one's schoolmaster in Regent Street. The few minutes' conversation – the terror of how to get away. One cannot swing round on those occasions and walk off briskly in the opposite direction. The dodge is to begin to move while still speaking. 'Well, don't forget to ring me up,' one says – walking backwards and away from the man, 'Central 4689,' one shouts at a receding figure. Having thus increased the distance between your schoolmaster and yourself, it is possible without abruptness to turn round and walk down Regent Street. But there must in all such cases be an interval in which, while still facing him, you walk, like the Lord Chamberlain, away.

I mention this point in social difficulty since it is illustrative of a method which has cured me of the malady and rendered me a sturdy, though amiable, lump of self-assurance. It is only when the unexpected happens that I to-day am shy. I then – for why deny it? – lose my head. I blush and wobble and my throat becomes slightly dry. Generally, however, it is the expected which happens in life, and for the expected I am now magnificently prepared. It is a question of industry and experience. It is also a question of forethought. One should be prepared for all eventualities. One should be prepared, for instance, for one's hostess to ask after one's grandfather when the only honest answer to such a question is that one's grandfather is dead. An awkward pause will follow, and one should have ready some quip or quotation by which that pause can be filled. If taken unawares one may stumble: but if fore-armed one can play with the situation as

Rubinstein with his submerged sevenths. But then, to do this, one must already be middle-aged. And I for one would rather be shy, to the point even of shaking hands with the butler, than be middle-aged.

Then there are those of course who are shy for life. Such people suffer the pangs both of bashfulness and of being no longer very young. This malady is one that at times afflicts successful writers. Oliver Goldsmith and Charles Lamb were shy: Mr E. M. Forster and Virginia Woolf are shy to the point even of appearing rude: I have seen Mr Lytton Strachey hiding in agony behind a door, Mr Arnold Bennett struck dumb, Mr Sassoon writhing, Mr Hugh Walpole (yes, even Mr Hugh Walpole) dither. And yet other writers are not shy. I should not describe Mr Sinclair Lewis as a shy man, nor have I often observed the blush of shame mantling in the cheek either of Michael Arlen or Philip Guedalla. One can never tell.

Perhaps shyness is a purely Anglo-Saxon failing. I doubt whether even the tenderest of the Roman poets, whether Virgil even, was shy. Horace, as we know, was one large lump of bounce. Nor was Dante shy – disagreeable was Dante, but never shy. Ah, yes – there is Racine. He at least was so shy that he ran away and hid himself at Port-Royal. But then Racine, as M. Lemaître has remarked, stands apart. Yes, I think shyness is an Anglo-Saxon quality. And as such it should be honoured as a bond between the English-speaking nations.

Food

I ONCE knew a man who was inordinately greedy. He was also inordinately rich. The combination of these two

qualities had rendered him fussy and asthmatic: he was
always suffering either from repletion or hunger: his
eyes goggled, at one moment with expectation, at another
with satiety: he was not a very happy man. Lonely and
expectant, he lived in a large untenanted house, and the
pleasures which graced his solitary life were in their
nature transitory: a spring chicken, the first asparagus, a
new salad – but, then, how quickly do such things pass
out of our lives! Even love, politics even, afford more
durable stimulants.

My millionaire had in his time experienced both these
things and found them hollow; he had retired from public
and even from civic life; he lived in a large house packed
with expensive and curious purchases and surrounded by
intricate gardens. In the centre of his house stood his
kitchen, and a *chef* from Dijon, and a *patissier* from Nancy.
The essential meal occurred in the middle of the day; a
peach only for breakfast; and for dinner, only a little
broth. Then there was his Swedish masseur, who created
an appetite by banging and beating the old gentleman
across the stomach from eleven till eleven-thirty; a little
turn in the Dutch garden; and then, breathless with lust,
rolling large ogre eyes, smacking ogre chops, the old man
would stump into the enormous dining-room, and there,
beneath the Gobelins, he would sit (fee-fi-fo-fum) in an
Italian brocade chair; waiting for his soup.

Yes, he had soup at luncheon. But not as you or I
would taste this scrannel beverage. The ceremony which
amended its preparation recalled the age of Hadrian, the
age, at moments, of Trimalchio. There was, in the first
place, an object which, for want of a better name, I shall
call a tureen. It arrived in a vehicle, or to be more exact
it was wheeled up to him on a little table fitted with india-
rubber tyres. In appearance it was like a large silver

cauldron, fixed on heavy silver claws, and warmed from underneath by a lamp which belched flames. Another servant then arrived with a further table, similarly propelled, which contained two tiers laden with a varied assortment of condiments and viands. The first table was placed at his right side, the second at his left. The ceremony had begun.

Upon the second table was a lobster, rather shattered and dissected, but still a lobster. There was a large dish of black potatoes, which were in fact truffles, the very largest truffles which the most expert of the Perigord trufflers had been able to unearth. Pink hog-like noses rootling for truffles: careful and experienced Perigourdins selecting the ones, those round bumpy ones, which my particular millionaire was known to like. Then there were scarlet pepperheads from Thessaly, and pickled cucumbers from the Ukraine, spices from Bali and Sumatra, a little silver nutmeg-grater, a little gold instrument for crushing picatilloes, a little crystal mortar for grinding those locarto beans which come from Marakesh; the roots of a palmetto mush; olives from Ithaca.

I exaggerate a little, but I do not exaggerate very much. My host, breathing heavily, would goggle from left to right, stirring the cauldron on his one side, transfixing pimentos from the assortment on his other side, transferring them to the cauldron, letting them drop (fee-fi-fo-fum) slowly into the seething, anxious soup.

The guests meanwhile would sit silently in their places, as if children at a school-feast, watching this strange alchemy, wishing that the old man would hurry up. This moment, we may presume, was for him the culmination of his orgies; anticipation and desire mingled their agonizing tension within his soul; satisfaction, to be snatched when the suspense became intolerable, could be held for the

moment, for a series of delicious suspended moments, at
arm's length. His guests, who could not understand these
sensual subtleties, merely sat there silently, hungry,
annoyed, and with eyes which in their turn became
protuberant. Fee, Fi, Fo, Fum. The lobster would be
raised, an articulated corpse, above the cauldron; those
fat and trembling fingers would hold it there gloatingly,
disentangling its nakedness from the shell; flakes of lobster
would detach themselves and splash into the seething lava
below them: and then the claws of the beast would be
twisted deftly sideways till they snapped: the claws
dropped into the soup shell and all.

This was the penultimate ceremony. A footman would
stand there with a golden bowl of warm water scented with
peppermint or verbena. The ogre washed his hands. The
steam from the cauldron eddied across the table, bringing
with it memories of Marseilles fish-taverns, and spirits of
wine. Thereat the host – a final libation – would raise
in his right hand a bottle of Veuve Clicquot, and in his
left a bottle of Amontillado, their twin amber streams
mingling as they hissed into the steam below.

We were given our soup. It was very hot indeed. It had
a distinct taste of lobster mixed with cloves. It was like
some very hot cough-mixture drunk with shrimp paste.
But our host would lap and guzzle there, unconscious of
the tentative and disappointed sips of those around him.
After luncheon (he called it luncheon), he would go to his
room and sleep. But his guests, who had had breakfast
that morning but had not had the masseur, would walk,
thoughtful and blear-eyed, along the herbaceous border.

Here you have a picture, more accurate than you
suppose, of gargantuan rather than lucullan greediness.
On me these luncheons (I must have attended four or five)
made a deep and lasting impression. Those meals, that

soup, convinced me that one can have too great a quantity
of quality. The healthiest appetite, the most sensitive
palate, the greatest previous abstinence, the most expert
masseur, would not have made me really like that soup. I
had always been told that the sure sign of an indifferent
cook is the presence of sherry in the food. My old friend,
however, had poured a whole bottle of the best Amontillado into his concoction, had added thereto a bottle of excellent champagne, and yet it tasted only of cloves, as
might be an apple tart, of those four cloves which, in a
moment of fussy carelessness, he had allowed to degrade
the whole.

Even on an empty stomach, even amid the snow and ice
of the Italian Riviera, the memory of that cauldron turns
me a little sick. I think of other meals; of that salmon-
trout at San Vigilio; of the day when, all ravenous, I ate
a little partridge in triumph at Persepolis. For in food, as
in many things (I quote – and why shouldn't I? – from
Aristotle), the surprising is delightful, provided that it is
not overdone. Good food should thus come upon the eater
with a shock of surprised delight: but the surprises leave
behind them only a faint nausea and the scent of cloves.
The surprise, though startling, should not moreover be
entirely incongruous: a short sharp anchovy hidden in a
strawberry ice would make any man jump: but he would
not thereafter think of the meal lovingly, as I today of
San Vigilio.

No; food is not a thing to treat with flippancy. Like all
events which gratify the senses, it should be approached
anxiously though calmly, and with what Mr John Drink-
water would call 'a fine thoughtfulness'. Above all,
patriotism is not enough. It is indeed very foolish, if one is
English, or even American, to be unduly patriotic about
one's food. We have our virtues. The English have their

bacon and their beef. The Americans have their salads and those crisp but flabby things one eats with treacle. But we have also our failures. It would be mere jingoism to contend that the halibut of the English dining-car is anything more than a dead and sodden fish. One would have to be 102 per cent American to defend those sickly and gaseous beverages with which, so I am told, the most powerful nation of the twentieth century destroys its teeth and its digestion.

And yet this regionalism, nay this nationalism, in regard to food is a most common and distressing feature of modern life. I have heard Parisians rejecting, with that un-hesitating insularity which so hampers the full charm of the French character, ravioli. I have seen Englishmen addressing sole marguéry in terms of undisguised and terribly erring contempt. I have heard Americans, when confronted by a fricandeau, exclaim 'And so this is this!'

Such an attitude of scepticism towards the food of other nations is not merely ill-mannered: it is a rejection of ex-perience. And, as I hope one day to establish, the only form of vulgarity which really matters is that form which leads its victims to reject experience. Eat your frogs, therefore, eat your scampi, your snails and your octopuses, with gentle and interested forbearance; do not laugh at what you do not understand; and, if you are rendered seriously ill thereby, recollect that you have enlarged your experience, that you have refused, once again, to surrender to vulgarity. In fact, you will have done more than this. You will, by your fine thoughtfulness, have advanced the cause of international understanding. For it may be remarked that there is nothing which leads to such sus-picion and evil thought among nations (as indeed between individualists) as this very question of national foods and dishes.

Americans, it is true, generally concentrate their criticism of foreign civilizations on points of plumbing. Often have I been wounded to the quick by their complaints of having found no bathroom handy in the inn at Warwick, or of the water having been tepid when they got to Stratford. I have pointed out that hot water is an indulgence of a spoilt and arrogant plutocracy, and that if Americans choose to visit our impoverished and backward Island they must expect, in the smaller inns which they desire, to soak only in the vapour of non-contiguous bathrooms. Besides, it isn't true. I suspect, indeed, that by 'plumbing' Americans mean something even more intimate and essential than mere baths; and my suspicion is confirmed by the fact that the most refined among them, those who come from Virginia or New England, adopt, when using the word, a downward and deprecatory look, as is suitable for indelicacies.

Such differences in stages of civilization, the mere presence or absence of adjoining bathrooms, can only be superficial. Hands will, in spite of their insults on the subject and our wounds, still stretch across the sea. Food, if I may employ so light a play upon the words, plumbs depths. I do not, for instance, care for our national habit of cooking Brussels sprouts in water, but when I find a foreigner who shares my disinclination and comments thereon, I am inflamed by defensive patriotism and I say sharp things about 'grease' and about 'oil'. I do not, moreover, feel that English coffee, as ladled out to the public, is as good as that obtained in Austria or in France; but should a foreigner himself make such a suggestion, I smile at him aloof, I assure him that our coffee, as our climate, is an acquired taste.

Such instinctive gestures of defence and protection are but symbols of a deeper nationalist arrogance which I am not alone in feeling. Observe, for instance, how wide-spread and how popular are the gibes directed at those countries who do not predominantly eat the things that we do. The Old Testament bristles with prejudices of this nature, and so, for that matter, does the New. History bears upon its disfigured face the scars and weals of controversies which have been born merely from dis-agreement about food. The dislike which France, until, let us say, 1909, bore for England, was summed up in two words of withering reproach, 'Roast beef'. The con-tempt which, until 1909, every healthy Englishman felt for French superiority in art, literature, and music, found its outlet, and perhaps its appeasement, by shouting 'frogs' at them, by shouting 'snails'. 'Sausage', and for the more expert 'sauerkraut', became the watchwords with which the soul of England expressed and eased the pain caused to it by the success, between 1870 and 1914, of the German Empire. It is pleasant to reflect that there are as yet no such opprobrious words which England or America can sling at each other cross the Atlantic. The word 'plumb-ing' will not, today, raise a flush of fury on any English cheek; nor I presume would even the best American be really indignant were we to make jokes about corn or candy or the other thing. Chewing-gum, after all, is only inadvertently swallowed.

This is a pleasant reflection. Until some such acute and poignant difference arises, our relations with America are safe. Nor do I overstress the point. Observe the effect of food-differences upon your personal relations. The man who doesn't like oysters, the woman who cannot abide sardines. We know the type. For food, we are told, is the staple of life. In later life it becomes one of our rarest enjoyments. But it carries with it the germs of external as well as internal disorder; it carries with it the seeds of quarrels, violence, and misunderstanding. It is not a thing of which to think lightly, as of daily recurrence. It is a thing about which you must soberly think. Sit down and think. But be careful not to think too much.

And yet – for I feel obliged to recur to the subject – it is really very odd that the Anglo-Saxon race, so enterprising and so self-indulgent, should be indifferent to the manner in which their food is cooked. The basis of all cooking is butter, and we in England possess the best butter in the world. The average Englishman, however, spurns lubricants in his food, preferring that all flavour should be boiled out of things, that his vegetables should taste of straw and water, that his sauces should taste of nothing at all. It all comes from our having a large breakfast. This we do well. The fact remains, however, that races which have a good breakfast have a bad luncheon and a bad dinner. Then we have buns for tea. Hot buttered buns and sometimes muffins.

There will be no hope for Anglo-Saxon cooking until we train ourselves to have rusks and coffee for breakfast and no tea at all.

Men's Clothes

It is related of Mr Herbert Spencer that he possessed a suit which had been specially made for him. He only wore this suit when he was feeling irritable, but he sometimes wore it for weeks at a time. It was made all in one piece and of a soft soothing Jaeger sort of texture. He entered the suit from the middle, huddling his angry legs into the lower part, as if he were putting on bed-socks; working his impatient head into the upper part, as if entering a

bathing-dress. Then down the front was an arrangement
for lacing the thing together. Today that arrangement
would run on a ratchet on what I believe is called the Zip
method. In one would get, and then Zip . . . one would be
dressed with no greater effort than is required to close
a tobacco pouch. In the evening one would reverse this
process and tumble quickly into bed as a banana released
from its sheath.

Clearly such a system would be soothing to the nerves.
But it was not aesthetic. The members of Mr Herbert
Spencer's household, seeing him descend to breakfast in
what had come to be known as 'his angry suit', would
quail, would bend apprehensive ringlets over their bacon
and their eggs. And then these ringlets would begin to
shake with what (although nervous laughter) was still
laughter. Mr Spencer, it must be confessed, looked very
odd in his combination suit. Those fierce and prominent
eyes would glare out above the Jaeger wrappings, too
proud to ask why all those bent ringlets should be shaking
(with suppressed merriment, but still with merriment)
above their bacon and their eggs.

Mr Spencer was an obstinate as well as an egoistic man.
Still dressed in his angry suit, he would take his daily
drive down Bond Street, and so round the Green and then
St James's Park. Angrier and still angrier would he
become as people stared at this odd old man enveloped
like Dr Peary or Doctor Cook upon a June morning. The
angry suit ceased to soothe; it irritated gratuitously; it
became a shirt of Nessus excruciating to its wearer. Mr
Spencer would stop the carriage and feel his pulse,
holding a large gold watch in his veined and bony hand.
His pulse would be fast that morning, and the carriage
would thus lumber back up Bond Street, flop, flop, flop
from the single horse, and an indignant philosopher

would be returned to Park Terrace, or to Hanover Row. (For I forget at this moment what was Mr Spencer's address.) He would sit upstairs in his angry overalls, too angry to come down to luncheon. And next morning he would dress in a neat suit of grey tweed, and be again his bright and petulant self.

These facts are historical, but, as with so much of history, they have not been digested. Why was it that the Jaeger combinations invented by Mr Herbert Spencer failed, when put to it, to soothe his nerves? Why was it that 'his angry suit' made him angrier still? Carlyle, who wrote much turgid nonsense upon the philosophy of clothes, makes no contribution to this problem. Carlyle, poor ignoramus, knew nothing of Mr Spencer's suit. But the problem, as a problem, existed before Mr Spencer, and persists after his death. It is the problem of how to reconcile comfort with decency. It is the problem of how to steer between the rocks of discomfort and the sand-banks of looking a joke. It is the problem of how to be individual without being funny.

Other people in their time have worn odd clothes. Lord Byron, when he proceeded to liberate Greece, designed for himself a little Hussar uniform of green cloth with white frogs and tags. On the top of his fussy little jacket he had meant to wear a huge helmet with a horsehair plume, such as one sees in heroic representations of the siege of Troy. But people laughed at this hat, and he put it back again in its pink bandbox. It can be seen today in his bedroom at Newstead.

Leigh Hunt for his part dressed, when over sixty, like little Lord Fauntleroy. But then Leigh Hunt, in later life, became very odd indeed. And Lord Salisbury, and Lord Beaconsfield, and the late Lord Astor – these each in his own way were either dirty or strange. And yet they all took trouble about their clothes. There must have been moments, let us say in January and June, when Lord Salisbury stood in his shirt sleeves in Arlington Street, while deferential tailors stretched measuring tapes around his frame. There must have been moments when similar tailors were summoned to Cliveden or to Hever and pinned upon Lord Astor the scaffoldings of those smart alpaca jackets in which, together with a boiled shirt and tie, he would walk majestically among his Italian gardens, Even Mussolini must sometimes be tried on.

It is a little painful to picture our heroes at such moments. Not merely is it disgraceful to visualize such vital and important beings submitting to the fingering and fussing of persons who, if they will forgive my saying so, evoke no very romantic image; not merely is it unpleasant to envisage them as standing there, turning round when told to, raising their arms like zanies. ('A little higher, My Lord, *if* you please. 49.3, Mr Burkinshaw!' '49.3,' repeats the subservient Mr Burkinshaw, scribbling in his note-book); not merely is it humiliating to conceive of a mere tailor making chalk-marks upon the backs of statesmen rounded with the weight of half the world; nay, the impression created is more profound than any pain evoked by the picture of the magnificent in humiliation, it is an impression which derives its deep poignancy from the realization that even the most majestic among us wear two buttons on the back of a tail coat. Why do we do this thing? Both these particular buttons are otiose. And yet even the most liberated among us would miss these buttons if they failed to appear.

It is well enough for the fashionable and the slim. Their bodies fall naturally into the shape of their clothes, their waistcoats sit lightly, concavely, upon their adolescent frames. Couth and gainly they rise in the morning, couth and gainly they don their silken pyjamas for the night. Buttons for them are mere finishing touches to a lineal design, mere points of break in the monotony of what might otherwise appear too rigidly perpendicular. A button more, a button less, what matters it to those whose bodies are encased *in* but not *by* their clothes? It is only for those whose buttons are things which are apt to bulge and burst that this clothes question assumes the proportions of a deep human drama. It is for such people that I write these words of encouragement. I write for men. I do not write for boys and maidens. I write for men who, though still young in conscience, are yet not slim in shape. I do not write for women. It is not necessary, it would in fact be a mistake, to give women any gratuitous encouragement about their clothes.

It is thus for convex males that I write, and above all for those among them who are not exuberantly young. There comes a time, there comes, alas, a moment, when men of this type are apt to feel a sudden self-consciousness in regard to their pockets. A day in their life arrives when they hesitate, as never before, to cram that passport, that book of railway tickets, that diary and that letter-case into their breast pocket. They find themselves dividing so bulky a bundle, distributing its contents among pockets that hang at the sides of one, placing the lot in some separate bag. That is the first stage.

The second stage centres round the strap which sustains, maintains, and retains the waistcoat at the back. With the slim and the adolescent, this strap is a static object; it is just a strap; it is just there. But after the age, let us say, of twenty-seven, there are times when that strap, by a deft backward movement of the hands, is released or loosened. It is a terrible moment for any man when he

catches himself loosening his strap. It marks the second
stage in the grim progress from elegance to comfort.

The third stage is reached (it would be idle to defend it)
when the top, and in extreme cases the two top, button
or buttons of the trousers are, after a heavy meal, undone.
By insensible degrees this third stage melts into one in
which Swedish exercises figure, and Turkish baths, and a
doubt whether waistcoats after all are a very sensible form
of wear. Better a pullover. Better, in summer at least, nothing at all.

Then, Americans, so I am told, do not wear braces.
They call them 'suspenders', a word applied, in our grey
and pitiful island, only to socks. Americans, so I am
assured, wear belts. I am sorry for them in this respect,
since belts are a cruel register of girth; one can count the
holes. That dark and glossy bar upon the leather which
marked the limit of 1937, is not by any means the bar on
which, in 1938, the buckle comes to its readiest repose.
In 1939, maybe, that bar may move a further fraction of
an inch along the leather scale of roundness. Very human
will be the expedients by which a man will try to hide
from himself the slow shifting of that mark upon the belt.
But shift it does. He will suddenly catch sight of himself
one evening at some night club: he may be laughing at the
moment, he may be smiling brightly, he may be feeling
at his best. Then suddenly, from some mirror opposite will
leer at him a stout though not wholly unfamiliar face and
form. His uncle in Texas? Not a bit of it. *Himself*. The
laughter, at that, will die in his throat, that bright smile
will fade upon his lips.

It will be then and not till then that the problem of
clothes will loom for him in its true significance: not as the
daily indulgence of the spring-time; but as some dour and

compelling necessity of the autumn months. It will be then
that he will think, with that exquisite sensibility which I
have above displayed, of Lords Salisbury and Astor. It will
be then, unless he be very wise or very lacking in all forms
of sensuousness, that he will decide that his style of
clothing must, and at once, be subjected to some radical
change.

He does not confess, of course, that this metamorphosis
is dictated by any desire to conceal the fading flower of his
youth. He discovers, as I have already indicated, that
waistcoats are but ungainly objects, devoid of real
backing. He begins, unless he be indeed the late Lord
Astor, to manifest an objection to stiff shirts, which indeed are apt to pop away from all but the slimmest frame,
and to bulge outwards, away from all restraining bands.
Stiff collars, also, are intolerable, intolerable to the
fattening neck. A certain Bohemianism thereafter descends
upon his vesture, and his clothes take on a tendency to
slop and flop. A velvet smoking-jacket is not recom-
mendable, but it will be tried. It is always tried. Then the
hats grow wider, the hair longer, the ties daily more large
and strange. Boots, during this Bohemian phase, remain
the same: it is only in the succeeding phase that they also
become challenging. For the succeeding phase is frequently very fierce indeed.

It comes upon vain and virile people who wish to hide
their middle-age by an appearance of violence. It is a
butcher phase. Essentially, if subconsciously, the impression which this phase is intended to convey is that
although there *has* been an increase, it has been an
increase of muscle rather than of flesh. Rough grey shirts
are much affected during such periods, and heavy
odorous tweed. Shoes, as I have stated, become arrogant,
assuming a St Moritz appearance, as if about to be

employed on winter sports. Fishing-hooks are worn in the hat, and in the breast pockets (which button outwards on a flap), silk handkerchiefs are carried, or any other object which occupies less space than would appear. This particular phase is both tiring and expensive. It leads rich people to take grouse-moors in Scotland, and poor people to go walking tours in the Adirondacks. A knapsack, if skilfully slung, can cover a multitude of sins. The phase, however, is not a long one. It is the last flicker of resistance before collapse.

Mr William James, if I recollect aright, has some very penetrating passages upon this collapse. He is speaking of false claims. He speaks of the great joy which comes to a man when he abandons all hope of not becoming fat. This, says Mr William James, is the last release. I am inclined to agree with him. I look forward to my own collapse, let us say (if God will) in 1949. A large and amiable old bumble bee in huge grey flannels. In a huge all-embracing belt. Puffing around. Then, and then only, shall I have solved the problem of clothes.

But meanwhile, some words of advice. (1) Never take any exercise. Exercise develops the muscles, and when once muscles have been developed, they have to be banged to prevent them turning into fat. It is extremely painful to be banged. (2) When young, always have your clothes made a little too large for you. This, as the real estate agents say, will give you a margin of development. (3) Concentrate on colour rather than on shape. Colour can be bought in any shop. (4) Cultivate an impression of vitality rather than of Bohemianism. This can be done by frequently slapping the thighs. It is curious how vital a man becomes if he frequently slaps his thighs. (5) Be very successful in your public life. Fame, more than anything else, enables one to wear comfortable and even becoming

clothes. (6) Avoid elegance in any form after the age of
twenty-five.

And yet, and yet ... It is all very difficult. You see, I
have said very little about clothes really because they do
not interest me. What does interest me is the inevitable
approach of the sit-and-grunt period of later middle-age.
Can clothes retard its approach, or disguise its advent?
They can do nothing of the kind. The worst thing, I fear,
about being no longer young is that one is no longer young.

'W. G.'

In the Memorial Biography of W. G. Grace are sung the praises of the greatest of all cricketers. Many famous men do homage to the Grand Old Man's mastery – some of those who played the game with him in his prime; some of them cricketers of the present day who, babes in swaddling clothes at the time he was hitting his mightiest centuries, yet found him still a power in the land when they themselves came to ripeness. And the testimony is not only from masters of W.G.'s own craft; an Anglican Canon vies with a Peer of the Realm in polishing the lustre of his name. Page after page the deep-chested unison goes, telling over again his processional motion from triumph to triumph. 'Had Grace been born in Ancient Greece,' the book concludes, in the Bishop of Hereford's words, 'the Iliad would have been different. Had he lived in the Middle Ages he would have been a Crusader, and would now have been lying with his legs crossed in some ancient abbey. As he was born when the world was older, he was the best-known of all Englishmen and king of cricket.'

Grace was certainly the most famous man of his day, if fame consists in being talked about by the largest number of perfect strangers. He was institutional; people regarded him and discussed him just as they regarded and discussed Mr Gladstone and the National Debt. It did not matter at all whether or not you yourself were interested in cricket, you came under a social obligation to say

something about him at dinner. You might even have been
a professor of economics, with marginal utility the main
thing on your mind, yet it was up to you to begin the
conversation by asking how many W.G. had made that
day. Grace was so famous indeed, that among public men
of his period he was the most readily recognized of them
all by the man in the street, no matter in what part of
the country he might travel. People actually crossed the
high seas to witness a century by Grace. A newspaper of
the day notes that as soon as the merest whisper of an
innings by Grace at Lord's was breathed in the City 'all
the Clubs emptied and a stream of cabs dashed towards
St John's Wood.' There was no end at all to his renown.
Children at school put down his name in all seriousness
amongst the seven wonders of the world, omitting, no
doubt, the Hanging Gardens of Babylon; he was in *Punch*
every week; the Royal Family was concerned about him
from time to time. He was the solitary subject of thought
with the great bowlers of the day; they even sat up late
at night, getting rather cross about him and exchanging
points of strategy. Tom Emmett used to have bad dreams
about him; the story goes that the Yorkshireman once
brought on a violent nightmare by falling asleep just as
he was forming a mental picture of the consequences to
him should W.G. some day hit back a slow ball straight.
There was no talk about 'brightening' cricket in Grace's
time. The crowds followed him everywhere. And on those
rare occasions when he failed! People rubbed their eyes;
it was as though something had gone awry with the proper
order and fitness of things. The bowler, no matter how
seasoned a veteran he might be, would throw his cap into
the air like a schoolboy. Then he would remember that
there was another innings tomorrow, and think better of
it, especially after that bodeful glance from glistening eyes

as the Old Man passed the wicket on his way back to the pavilion. Grace's mastery was so complete, indeed, that in 1871 it was proposed that the rules of cricket be altered that bowlers might the better cope with him. 'I puts the ball where I likes,' was the comment of J. C. Shaw, a master of his craft, 'but that beggar, he puts it where *he* likes.'

W. G.'s record in first-class cricket begins with seven completed innings in 1865, his age then being 17. It continues, without the break of a single summer, until 1908. In that time he scored 54,896 runs in 1,388 innings, average 39.55. He also captured 2,864 wickets at 17.97 each. These figures boggle the imagination, but they do not reveal the fundamental point of his greatness. For one thing, Grace, for the best part of his career, played on wickets the like of which are not known in these days of marl and the heavy roller. More important still is this fact; it is the great fact of Grace's fame. He invented modern batting. It is not sufficiently borne in mind even by W. G.'s most ardent worshippers that at the time he took to cricket, overarm bowling had been the fashion for only some thirty years. And the amount of cricket played in a summer in that age was so small that those thirty seasons could nowadays be rolled into a mere half-dozen. Grace thus came upon a batting technique developed out of an obsolete attack, and at once changed it into the fully orchestrated thing it is today. He took the best points of Fuller Pilch's forward method and combined them with a back-play all his own. He demonstrated to a rather scandalized cricket field that a straight ball, dead on the wicket, could be driven; he taught the cut; he managed the then new offbreak, even as Hobbs manages it today, by forcing it off his pads to the on-side. He invented the difficult science of placing the ball, and

out of this arose the mobile field instead of the fixed one.
He invented footwork. Cricketers before his coming played
forward well enough, but they rarely combined it with
back play. Grace brought his legs into action as a defensive
factor, only not in the decadent modern manner. He did
not jump in front of the wicket, leaving the ball alone,
with a divine trust in the umpire and the l.b.w. rule;
no batsman left fewer balls alone than Grace, as Lord
Harris points out in his biography. But Grace made the
left pad go out alongside the bat in forward play, and the
right leg go back with it in back play, so closely keeping the
two together in both movements that it was almost impossible
for the ball to get past the combination. The best thing ever
said about Grace's batting is written down with a dash of high
poetry, in Ranjitsinhi's *Jubilee Book of Cricket*. 'He turned
the single-stringed instrument into the many-chorded lyre.'

That W.G. worked his way each summer to a high
place in the bowling averages is the best indication possible
of his zeal for cricket. Really, he was not a bowler by
nature: his action was clumsy, without the free swing of
the man born to the work. There can be little doubt that
he took to bowling simply because he could not bear for a
solitary moment to be out of the picture. He could not
always be getting runs; the other side *had* to bat sooner or
later. Very well, then; he was the man to get them out.
A. G. Steel has left us the classic description of W.G. in
action as a bowler – '. . . an enormous man rushing up to
the wickets with both elbows out, a great black beard
blowing on both sides of him, a huge yellow cap on top of
a dark, swarthy face.' He was easily the most spectacular
man that ever played a game. He was shaggy and ponder-
ous, with muscular arms, capacious hands, and immense
feet. He ambled about the field rather than walked, and
as the players gathered together for conversation at the

fall of a wicket his giant dimensions overtopped them all, making everybody else seem mere children. He was the Dr Johnson of cricket – as full of his subject, as kindly and as irascible, and just as dogmatic in his dispensations of authority. It has been well said of him that on the field he took a second place to none, not even to the umpire. Even from his seat in the pavilion where, according to all the rules and procedure of cricket, he was 'out of play', he must needs dominate the scene. During a Surrey and Gloucestershire match at the Oval a favourite of W.G.'s was given out. Up rose the Old Man from the pavilion balcony and thundered over the ground: 'Shan't have it; can't have it; and I won't have it.' Though he be fielding at deep square leg he would appeal vociferously for 'l.b.w.', no matter how ill-placed such a position for making any sort of judgement on the point. C. I. Thornton tells a good story neatly quizzing this particular excess of zeal. W.G. was fielding at right angles to the wicket, and Roberts, the Gloucestershire fast bowler, hit a batsman plumb on the pad. At the end of the over W.G. said, 'Why didn't you appeal for that l.b.w.?' 'Well, sir,' the bowler replied, 'the truth is I was waiting for you to.' On another occasion a batsman disputed an l.b.w. decision on an appeal made by Grace, off his own bowling. The champion simply raised his head and thundered: 'Pavilion you.' The batsman retired instantly.

But when all has been said about W.G.'s skill as a cricketer, we are far enough from the secret of his power over countless thousands of his countrymen. The truth is that they found in him something closer to the common heart than immense science and prodigious energy. With the average man it was not Grace's hundreds alone that compelled devotion, not Grace's bowling and his fielding; it was just the Grand Old Man's zest, his perfectly English

zest, for a game. No man ever flung himself into a game
more passionately than W. G. With what scorn he would
have met Mr Shaw's taunt that the Englishman turns his
games into hard work. Grace, who knew cricket so
intimately, whose innermost nature responded swiftly to
every demand made upon it by cricket, understood well
that a great national game is not a mere plaything for
indolent men, but a perpetual test and challenge, to which
he might answer worthily only by giving up at once and
gladly all that was in him of patience, courage, watchfulness, endurance, and largeness of heart. There is no finer
praise to be offered to cricket than that for the complete
expression of its genius, through W. G. Grace, all these
attributes of character were sternly called for. And there
can be no better tribute to the Grand Old Man's memory
than this: that he was not found wanting in the test.

IVOR BROWN

A Sentimental Journey

A QUARTER of a century is a phrase with an epochal ring, and these last five and twenty years have altered the world more than most. Empires have waxed and waned; motorcars have altered the whole face of travel and the whole scale of British distances; a penny has become a halfpenny, and the char-à-banc has crashed its way through the silent austerities of the Scottish Sabbath. But much of Scotland stands exactly where it did. Here in the north-east, whither I have made my sentimental journey, the land and sea yield the old harvests of grain and herring. The plough that has not altered since Homer told its shape and motion is not to suffer change while a boy grows up. The sea shows more of steam and less of sail, but evolution has obliged Tennessee by signally failing to leave new marks on herring and haddock, rabbit and hare. Had I been a London boy, I could hardly go in search of my youth. For the horses of the green Atlas bus that took me to Lord's have vanished, and no more is the effortless beauty of J. T. Hearne's bowling to be observed. But here I can go to 'the games' last visited in 1900 and they will be held in the same 'haugh'; the same dancing master will sit on the judgement bench to nod gravely at the same flings and sword-dances. The pipes will be mournful and brisk with the same airs, and tea-time will bring the same neat bag of cakes. True, the programme hinted at the presence of the Abertochty 'jazz band'. But what's in a name? As of old there were fiddlers three.

The conditions, as they say, are eminently suitable. Here one may indeed go in search of one's youth and reconstruct in the tranquillity of a sunny afternoon the emotions of a very small boy. Of course it is all much smaller than one's memory. A mile has dwindled to a furlong, a forest to a copse, a torrent to a trickle. The trout that were Tritons are now to be seen as flickering minnows in the shallows under the bridge. A mountain has shrunk to a hillock. It doesn't do, this retracing of boyhood's steps. One knew, of course, that looking backward is like looking through an opera-glass reversed. But the distortion is worse than one imagined. One shouldn't have gone. The return has been a cowardly assault upon romance, a butchering of innocent memories. Far better have left the old house to be, in mind's eye, grandiose, mysterious, abounding in dark possibilities; in short, the half-menacing, half-entrancing monster that it used to be. Far better have left to the gardens their flattering spaciousness of boyhood's vision, to the wood its pristine mystery of cavernous and black allure.

But one has done the deed. There it all lies, plain-set in smiling sunlight, a diminished Paradise. It is just a piece of Eastern Scotland, that frank and self-explanatory countryside which rolls an open bosom to the plain, straightforward sea. No Celtic twilights, tortuous lochs, and peaks that stab the mist are here to make adult reason concede a tremor to romance. Good farming trims the landscape; grey, orderly walls keep watch over pasture, roots, and oats. Here and there the rising ground soars out of man's control and green fields admit their limitations and march peaceably with heather. Here the hillside turns to fir plantation, there to empty purple acres. But the wildness, the strangeness, the beckoning immensities of those old days have shrivelled and departed. Boyhood was too small for Ordnance maps and the withering accuracies of the measuring-rod. It made its own mileage, forged its own contours, made and named and ruled its mountain range. Compute it now coldly at 'one inch to a mile' and a kingdom turns to a crofter's holding. Yet within this nut-shell moved a king of infinite space. Perhaps not king; a princeling were more accurate.

The owls have gone from the quivering pinewood; no heron flaps its pondering course along the burn. The coneys we have always with us, and their tribe at least is slow to dwindle. The gamekeeper has gone from the lodge, and he who knew the haunts of beast and bird now peddles bull's-eyes and half-pounds of tea. He is an injured man. Somebody started a war, and there has been no need for small estates since then. A nice range of red deer, grouse, and salmon will fetch a doubled price from merchant princes, for we are not all paupers at holiday-time. But the solid 'mixed shooting' with nothing showy about it and a four-square chunk of masonry to maintain attracts no bidders now. The lawns grow weeds, and the gamekeeper digs potatoes until the shop bell rings, and then he must weigh out another quarter of sweeties. He knows it is all wrong, but he says very little. He never goes near the house from which he has been driven. For relaxation he has his parlour, and there he sits with all the immobility of the soil-bound peasant looking at nothing, unless it is the past. 'You'll notice the sea has worked in a lot,' he says. 'It's beating the land by the yard a year. It'll tak' a' the links. There's changes everywhere.'

Yet was this visitation altogether a blundering folly? Has the sentimental journey proved altogether a wanton outrage upon sentiment? No; it has its powers of re-assurance, its compensations, and its fair suggestions. The woods have lost their wonder, and their darkness is a plain, unghosted thing. But beauty has crept in. Boyhood never saw that. Boyhood never knew the exquisite proportion of this countryside in which the elements of sea, moor, tilth, pasture, and copse have been dispensed as though by some inspired chemist of landscape. The place does yield its reparations and pays them in the currency of the eye's delight. How fitly the house lifts up its native stone, grey, unassuming, comfortably set! How lightly the bridge jumps the burn and leads to the village and the mellow-gardened manse! The sense of a desert has departed and the sense of a civilization has come in. If one no longer looks for eagles in the skies or marauders in the glades, one can look for shapeliness in homes and handsomeness in everything. And it is a handsome country garnished by diligence and fruitful under discipline. The grey-beard who comes down from his farm to judge the piping and dancing at the village games will not whine to you about bad times. He has the measure of the soil and of his agrarian competitors; he has whipped his land into a clean prosperity, and his cattle are known and feared at the Royal Northern Show. His sons have gone to the university, but he is just a little doubtful about the teaching at the village academy. They want a better man, and, from the sound of his voice, they mean to get one. To judge the pibrochs is the limit of his surrender to Gaelic dreaming. His youngest boy is going to be as great a man of medicine as ever went south from Aberdeen. He goes on Sundays to the kirk, thinks little of the minister and has no qualms.

It was once a land of giants, black-bearded men, who came up from the coastal fisheries and sometimes took a small boy in their boat to see the odd harvest of their nets. It was full of dark pools and distant heights, of birds and animals, of hopes and panics and surprises. It is not at all like that now. Boy Scouts encamp themselves where once was desolation. The burn trills equably through small and genial copses. The fields run up to the heather, and the heather, a mere mile of it, runs down again to the fields. But the view is gracious, and the air earns all the compliments that Shakespeare paid to the less deserving climate of sluggish Inverness. The land breeds pensive but not ungenial men whose philosophy has hard, clear lines. Boyhood turned honest farms into its land of fancy-free, made every trout a salmon, and every cushat a capercailzie; other years see other things. It is not all loss.

All that has gone is quantity. Quality remains. No glory, save that of stature, has departed. Rather has glory increased. To go in search of one's youth is to have done with the nonsense preached with a sublime eloquence by Wordsworth in his *Ode on the Intimations of Immortality*. To grow up in body is to grow up in spirit. The eye develops with the frame, appreciation with the spread of limb. The shades of the prison house with which the poet threatened adolescence are indeed the fiction of brain-sickly brooding. Take the village. What was it to a boy but the goal of a morning journey? There were lessons waiting in the study at the manse; there was toffee at the village-shop. But now I can see that village and praise the wisdom that built it under the woods and above the burn, in as sweet a nook as Scotland can contain. I can praise the fitness of its shaping, and see that the houses of native stone have grown up like living things in perfect kinship with their landscape. The queer house that is half a fortress, the manse that is at once kindly and formal like a domesticated kirk, home of stern virtues and of gentle flowers and fruit, the twist and surge of the rambling street – all these were nothing then. They are much now. My boyhood, at least, had no vision splendid

to surround its practical journeying. It thought of guns,
fishing-rods, and sweetmeats. It breathed no larger air.

So there is good in growing up. The boy cannot see the
wood for the trees, the burn for the lurking trout, the
moor for the possible excitements of beast and bird. Now
beauty comes in, life's compensation for adventure. The
compensation outweighs the loss. The village takes its
place in the scheme of things; it is the work of generations
of living, labouring men: its crannied walls have the
flowers which you may search for the ultimate mysteries.
But the walls need not drive you so far into the byways
of reflection. They have their more obvious story and are
the testament of the grey, orderly, but not ungenial
culture of Eastern Scotland. So, at the end of a sentimental journey, one may bask without regrets. Wonder
has gone, but admiration remains. The meadow has lost
its mystery, but found its meaning, and takes its place in a
scheme of things far beyond the scope and range of
childish mind. The black wood that housed Jack Redskin
no longer enfolds imaginary denizens. Does it matter?
It is beautiful now as well as black. The house in which
I gladly lived has become the house at which I gladly
look. It is a generous exchange. It is indeed worth while
to go in search of one's youth. That is dead and may not
be discovered. But all the things that boyhood missed,
how excellent they are!

J. B. PRIESTLEY

On Doing Nothing

I HAD been staying with a friend of mine, an artist and delightfully lazy fellow, at his cottage among the Yorkshire fells, some ten miles from a railway-station; and as we had been fortunate enough to encounter a sudden spell of really warm weather, day after day we had set off in the morning, taken the nearest moorland track, climbed leisurely until we had reached somewhere about two thousand feet above sea-level, and had then spent long golden afternoons lying flat on our backs – doing nothing. There is no better lounging place than a moor. It is a kind of clean bare antechamber to heaven. Beneath its apparent monotony that offers no immediate excitements, no absorbing drama of sound and colour, there is a subtle variety in its slowly changing patterns of cloud and shadow and tinted horizons, sufficient to keep up a flicker of interest in the mind all day. With its velvety patches, no bigger than a drawing-room carpet, of fine moorland grass, its surfaces invite repose. Its remoteness, its permanence, its old and sprawling indifference to man and his concerns, rest and cleanse the mind. All the noises of the world are drowned in the one monotonous cry of the curlew.

Day after day, then, found us full-stretched upon the moor, looking up at the sky or gazing dreamily at the distant horizon. It is not strictly true, of course, to say that we did absolutely nothing, for we smoked great quantities of tobacco, ate sandwiches and little sticks of chocolate, drank from the cold bubbling streams that spring up from nowhere, gurgle for a few score yards, then disappear again. Occasionally we exchanged a remark or two. But we probably came as close to doing nothing as it is possible for two members of our race. We made nothing, not even any plans; not a single idea entered our heads; we did not even indulge in that genial boasting which is the usual pastime of two friendly males in conference. Somewhere, far away, our friends and relatives were humming and bustling, shaping and contriving, planning, disputing, getting, spending; but we were as gods, solidly occupied in doing nothing, our minds immaculate vacancies. But when our little hour of idling was done and we descended for the last time, as flushed as sunsets, we came down into this world of men and newspaper owners only to discover that we had just been denounced by Mr Gordon Selfridge.

When and where he had been denouncing us I do not know. Nor do I know what hilarious company had invited and received his confidences. Strange things happen at this season, when the unfamiliar sun ripens our eccentricities. It was only last year or the year before that some enterprising person who had organized a conducted tour to the Continent arranged, as a bait for the more intellectual holiday-makers, that a series of lectures should be given to the party by eminent authors at various places *en route*. The happy tourists set out, and their conductor was as good as his word, for behold – at the very first stopping-place Dean Inge gave them an address on the modern love of pleasure. But whether Mr Selfridge had been addressing a crowd of holiday-makers or a solemn conference of emporium owners, I do not know, but I do know that he said that he hated laziness more than anything else and held it the greatest of sins. I

believe too that he delivered some judgement on persons
who waste time, but I have forgotten his reasons and
instances and, to be frank, would count it a disgraceful
waste of time to discover again what they were. Mr
Selfridge did not mention us by name, but it is hardly
possible to doubt that he had us in mind throughout his
attack on idleness. Perhaps he had had a frantic vision of
the pair of us lying flat on our backs on the moor, wasting
time royally while the world's work waited to be done,
and, incidentally, to be afterwards bought and sold in
Mr Selfridge's store. I hope he had, for the sight should
have done him good; we are a pleasing spectacle at any
time, but when we are doing nothing it would do any
man's heart good to see us, even in the most fragmentary
and baffling vision. Unfortunately, Mr Selfridge had
probably already made up his mind about the sin, as he
would call it, of laziness, and so was not open to conviction, was not ready to be pleased. It is a pity, and all
the more so because his views seem to me to be wrong
and quite definitely harmful.

All the evil in this world is brought about by persons
who are always up and doing, but do not know when they
ought to be up nor what they ought to be doing. The
devil, I take it, is still the busiest creature in the universe,
and I can quite imagine him denouncing laziness and
becoming angry at the smallest waste of time. In his
kingdom, I will wager, nobody is allowed to do nothing,
not even for a single afternoon. The world, we all freely
admit, is in a muddle, but I for one do not think that it
is laziness that has brought it to such a pass. It is not the
active virtues that it lacks but the passive ones; it is
capable of anything but kindness and a little steady
thought. There is still plenty of energy in the world (there
never were more fussy people about), but most of it is

simply misdirected. If, for example, in July 1914, when
there was some capital idling weather, everybody, em-
perors, kings, archdukes, statesmen, generals, journalists,
had been suddenly smitten with an intense desire to do
nothing, just to hang about in the sunshine and consume
tobacco, then we should all have been much better off
than we are now. But no, the doctrine of the strenuous
life still went unchallenged; there must be no time wasted;
something must be done. And, as we know, something was
done. Again, suppose our statesmen, instead of rushing
off to Versailles with a bundle of ill-digested notions and
a great deal of energy to dissipate, had all taken a fortnight off, away from all correspondence and interviews
and what not, and had simply lounged about on some
hillside or other, apparently doing nothing for the first
time in their energetic lives, then they might have gone
to their so-called Peace Conference and come away again
with their reputations still unsoiled and the affairs of the
world in good trim. Even at the present time, if half the
politicians in Europe would relinquish the notion that
laziness is a crime and go away and do nothing for a little
space, we should certainly gain by it. Other examples
come crowding into the mind. Thus, every now and then,
certain religious sects hold conferences; but though there
are evils abroad that are mountains high, though the fate
of civilization is still doubtful, the members who attend
these conferences spend their time condemning the length
of ladies' skirts and the noisiness of dance bands. They
would all be better employed lying flat on their backs
somewhere, staring at the sky and recovering their mental
health.

The idea that laziness is the primary sin and the
accompanying doctrine of the strenuous life are very
prevalent in America, and we cannot escape the fact that

America is an amazingly prosperous country. But neither can we escape the fact that society there is in such a condition that all its best contemporary writers are satirists. Curiously enough, most of the great American writers have not hesitated to praise idleness, and it has often been their faculty for doing nothing and praising themselves for doing it, that has been their salvation. Thus, Thoreau, without his capacity for idling and doing nothing more than appreciate the Milky Way, would be a cold prig; and Whitman, robbed of his habit of lounging round with his hands in his pockets and his innocent delight in this pastime, would be merely a large-sized ass. Any fool can be fussy and rid himself of energy all over the place, but a man has to have something in him before he can settle down to do nothing. He must have reserves to draw upon, must be able to plunge into strange slow rivers of dream and reverie, must be at heart a poet. Wordsworth, to whom we go when most other poets fail us, knew the value of doing nothing; nobody, you may say, could do it better; and you may discover in his work the best account of the matter. He lived long enough to retract most of his youthful opinions, but I do not think that he ever went back on his youthful notion that a man could have no healthier and more spiritualizing employment than idling about and staring at Nature. (It is true that he is very angry in one poem with some gipsies because they had apparently done absolutely nothing from the time he passed them at the beginning of his walk to the time when he passed them again, twelve hours later. But this is racial prejudice, tinged, I suspect, with envy, for though he had not done much, they had done even less.) If he were alive today I have no doubt he would preach his doctrine more fervently and more frequently than ever, and he would probably attack Mr

Selfridge and defend us (beginning 'Last week they loitered on a lone wide moor') in a series of capital sonnets, which would not, by the way, attract the slightest attention. He would tell us that the whole world would be better off if it spent every possible moment it could, these next ten years, lying flat on its back on a moor, doing nothing. And he would be right.

My First Article

WHEN I was sixteen I was already writing articles and offering them to any kind of editor whose address I could discover. These articles were of two kinds. The first, which I signed portentously 'J. Boynton Priestley', were serious, very serious indeed, and were full of words like 'renaissance' and 'significance' and 'aftermath', and suggested that their author was about a hundred and fifty years old. And nobody wanted them. They could not be given away. No editor had a body of readers old enough for such articles. The other kind were skits and burlesques and general funny work, written from the grimly determined humorous standpoint of the school magazine. One of these was accepted, printed and paid for by a London humorous weekly. I had arrived. (And my father, not to be found wanting on such an occasion, presented me with one of his fourpenny cigars, with which, as I fancy he guessed, I had been secretly experimenting for some months.) The issue of the weekly containing my article burst upon the world. Riding inside a tram from Duckworth Lane to Godwin Street, Bradford, I saw a middle-aged woman opening this very copy of the weekly, little knowing, as I made haste to tell myself, that one of its

group of brilliant contributors was not two yards away.
I watched her turn the pages. She came to *the* page; she
hesitated; she stopped, she began to read my article. Ah –
what delight! But mine, of course, not hers. And not mine
for long, not more than a second, for then there settled
on her face an expression I have noticed ten thousand
times since, and have for years now tried not to notice –
the typical expression of the reader, the audience, the
customer, the patron. How shall I describe this curious
look? There is in it a kind of innocence – and otherwise
I think I would have stopped writing years ago – but
mixed a trifle sourly with this admirable innocence is a
flavouring of wariness, perhaps a touch of suspicion itself.
'Well, what have we here?' it inquires dubiously. And
then the proud and smirking Poet and Maker falls ten
thousand feet into dubiety. So ever since that tram ride I
have never caught a glimpse of the reader, the audience,
the customer, the patron, without instantly trying to
wedge myself into the rocks above the black tarn of doubt.
As I do this, there is the flash of a blue wing – and the bird
of delight has flown.

Seeing the Actors

WHEN I was a lad and regularly took my place in the
queue for the early door of the gallery in the old Theatre
Royal, Bradford, the actors on their way to the stage door
had to walk past us. I observed them with delight. In
those days, actors looked like actors and like nothing else
on earth. There was no mistaking them for wool merchants,
shipping clerks, and deacons of Baptist chapels, all those
familiar figures of my boyhood. They wore suits of startling

check pattern, outrageous ties, and preposterous overcoats reaching down to their ankles. They never seemed
to remove all their make-up as actors do now, and always
had a rim of blue-black round their eyelids. They did not
belong to our world and never for a moment pretended to
belong to it. They swept past us, fantastically overcoated,
with trilbies perched raffishly on brilliantined curls,
talking of incredible matters in high tones, merely casting
a few sparkling glances – all the more sparkling because
of that blue-black – in our direction; and then vanished
through the stage door, to reappear, but out of all recognition, in the wigs and knee-breeches of *David Garrick*, or
The Only Way. And my young heart, as innocent as an egg,
went out to these romantic beings; and, perhaps it was
then, although I have no recollection of it, that the desire
was born in me to write one day for the Theatre. Now,
after working on so many stages, I know all about actors,
and I doubt if the very least of their innumerable mad-
dening tricks and absurd egoisms has escaped my observation; but, quite apart from the work we do together and
without reference to the needs of my profession, I have a
soft spot for actors, and probably it is because of that old
delight I used to feel as they went swaggering past us on
their way to the stage door. And indeed I sometimes wish
they would swagger more now, buy bigger overcoats and
wilder hats, and retain those traces of make-up that put
them outside respectability and kept them rogues and
vagabonds, which is what at heart – bless 'em! – they are.

Money for Nothing

IN the early nineteen-twenties, when I first settled in London, I did a great deal of reviewing. (There was much more space then for book reviews than there is now.) I was ready to review anything, and often did columns of short notes on new books. The books themselves were then sold – fiction for a third of the publisher's price, non-fiction for about a half – to a certain shop not far from the Strand, a shop that specialized in the purchase and re-sale of review copies, a traffic that had a faintly piratical air. At this shop, where human nature was understood, one was always paid at once and paid in cash, generally in exquisite new pound notes. And of all the money I have ever handled, this gave me most delight. Money for Jam, Money for Old Rope, Money for Nothing. When we receive our wages, salaries or fees, we may be content, for this is what we have earned, but we are a long way from delight. It is money that we have not earned, the windfall, the magical bonus, that starts us capering. Many sociologists, who understand everything except their fellow creatures, are bewildered and saddened by the ubiquitous passion among the mob for betting and gambling. But the more we standardize wages, hours and prices, the more we insist upon social security for everybody, the more we compel two and two to make four everywhere, the more people will take to the greyhound tracks and the football pools. For it is when two and two miraculously make five that the heart leaps up at last. It is when money looks like manna that we truly delight in it. Since those days when I used to sell my review copies I have earned in one way or another very considerable sums of money indeed; but they have all been lost in a dreary maze of bank accounts, stocks and shares, tax certificates, cheques and bills and receipts. I have never felt rich and careless, like a man returning from a lucky day at the races or a sailor home from a long voyage. But when I used to hurry out of that shop with five or six new pound notes singing in my pocket, for quarter of an hour or so I felt like a tipsy millionaire or the man who broke the bank at Monte Carlo. Money to Burn! And the only comparable moments I have known since have been on certain very rare occasions when I happen to have been fortunate in playing those fruit machines, which were so popular in the American south-west when we were there. These machines are so rigged that the odds are monstrously against the customer. Nickels and quarters by the score could vanish as lemons tried to mate with plums. But the jackpot, which must surely have been the invention of some poet, more than compensated for all these losses. As the magic combination of symbols showed itself, the machine would first hesitate, then shiver and noisily gather its works together, and then, like an exasperated fairy godmother, would splutteringly hurl whole handfuls of coin at you so that below your waist it seemed to be raining nickels or quarters. This is acquisition lit with wonder and glory. We could do with more of it.

Quietly Malicious Chairmanship

QUIETLY malicious chairmanship. There is no sound excuse for this. It is deeply anti-social, and a sudden excess of it would tear great holes in our communal life. But a man can be asked once too often to act as chairman, and to such a man, despairing of his weakness and feeling a thousand miles from any delight, I can suggest a few devices. In introducing one or two of the chief speakers, grossly over-praise them but put no warmth into your voice, only a metallic flavour of irony. If you know what a speaker's main point is to be, then make it neatly in presenting him to the audience. During some tremendous peroration, which the chap has been working at for days, either begin whispering and passing notes to other speakers or give the appearance of falling asleep in spite of much effort to keep awake. If the funny man takes possession of the meeting and brings out the old jokes; either look melancholy or raise your eyebrows as high as they will go. Announce the fellow with the weak delivery in your loudest and clearest tones. For any timid speaker, officiously clear a space bang in the middle and offer him water, paper, pencil, a watch, anything. With noisy cheeky chaps on their feet, bustle about the platform, and if necessary give a mysterious little note to some member of the audience. If a man insists upon speaking from the floor of the hall, ask him for his name, pretend to be rather deaf, and then finally, announce his name with a marked air of surprise. After that you can have some trouble with a cigarette lighter and then take it to pieces. When they all go on and on, make no further pretence of paying any attention and settle down to drawing outrageous caricatures of the others on the platform, and then at last ask some man you particularly dislike to take over the chair, and stalk out, being careful to leave all your papers behind. And if all this fails to bring you any delight, it should at least help to protect you against further bouts of chairmanship.

Tragedy and the Whole Truth

THERE were six of them, the best and bravest of the hero's companions. Turning back from his post in the bows, Odysseus was in time to see them lifted, struggling, into the air, to hear their screams, the desperate repetition of his own name. The survivors could only look on, helplessly, while Scylla 'at the mouth of her cave devoured them, still screaming, still stretching out their hands to me in the frightful struggle.' And Odysseus adds that it was the most dreadful and lamentable sight he ever saw in all his 'explorings of the passes of the sea.' We can believe it; Homer's brief description (the too poetical simile is a later interpolation) convinces us.

Later, the danger passed, Odysseus and his men went ashore for the night, and, on the Sicilian beach, prepared their supper – prepared it, says Homer, 'expertly'. The Twelfth Book of the Odyssey concludes with these words: 'When they had satisfied their thirst and hunger, they thought of their dear companions and wept, and in the midst of their tears sleep came gently upon them.'

The truth, the whole truth and nothing but the truth – how rarely the older literatures ever told it! Bits of the truth, yes; every good book gives us bits of the truth, would not be a good book if it did not. But the whole truth, no. Of the great writers of the past incredibly few have given us that. Homer – the Homer of the *Odyssey* – is one of those few.

'Truth?' you question. 'For example, $2 + 2 = 4$? Or

Queen Victoria came to the throne in 1837? Or light travels at the rate of 187,000 miles a second?' No, obviously, you won't find much of that sort of thing in literature. The 'truth' of which I was speaking just now is in fact no more than an acceptable verisimilitude. When the experiences recorded in a piece of literature correspond fairly closely with our own actual experiences, or with what I may call our potential experiences – experiences, that is to say, which we feel (as the result of a more or less explicit process of inference from known facts) that we might have had – we say, inaccurately no doubt: 'This piece of writing is true.' But this, of course, is not the whole story. The record of a case in a textbook of psychology is scientifically true, in so far as it is an accurate account of particular events. But it might also strike the reader as being 'true' with regard to himself – that is to say, acceptable, probable, having a correspondence with his own actual or potential experiences. But a textbook of psychology is not a work of art – or only secondarily and incidentally a work of art. Mere verisimilitude, mere correspondence of experience recorded by the writer with experience remembered or imaginable by the reader, is not enough to make a work of art seem 'true'. Good art possesses a kind of super-truth – is more probable, more acceptable, more convincing than itself. Naturally; for the artist is endowed with a sensibility and a power of communication, a capacity to 'put things across', which events and the majority of people to whom events happen, do not possess. Experience teaches only the teachable, who are by no means as numerous as Mrs Micawber's papa's favourite proverb would lead us to suppose. Artists are eminently teachable and also eminently teachers. They receive from events much more than most men receive, and they can transmit what they have received with a peculiar penetrative force, which drives their communication deep into the reader's mind. One of our most ordinary reactions to a good piece of literary art is expressed in the formula: 'This is what I have always felt and thought, but have never been able to put clearly into words, even for myself.'

We are now in a position to explain what we mean when we say that Homer is a writer who tells the Whole Truth. We mean that the experiences he records correspond fairly closely with our own actual or potential experiences – and correspond with our experiences not on a single limited sector, but all along the line of our physical and spiritual being. And we also mean that Homer records these experiences with a penetrative artistic force that makes them seem peculiarly acceptable and convincing.

So much, then, for truth in literature. Homer's, I repeat, is the Whole Truth. Consider how almost any other of the great poets would have concluded the story of Scylla's attack on the passing ship. Six men, remember, have been taken and devoured before the eyes of their friends. In any other poem but the *Odyssey*, what would the survivors have done? They would, of course, have wept, even as Homer made them weep. But would they previously have cooked their supper, and cooked it, what's more, in a masterly fashion? Would they previously have drunk and eaten to satiety? And after weeping, or actually while weeping, would they have dropped quietly off to sleep? No, they most certainly would not have done any of these things. They would simply have wept, lamenting their own misfortune and the horrible fate of their companions, and the canto would have ended tragically on their tears.

Homer, however, preferred to tell the Whole Truth.

He knew that even the most cruelly bereaved must eat; that hunger is stronger than sorrow and that its satisfaction takes precedence even of tears. He knew that experts continue to act expertly and to find satisfaction in their accomplishment, even when friends have just been eaten, even when the accomplishment is only cooking the supper. He knew that, when the belly is full (and only when the belly is full) men can afford to grieve, and that sorrow after supper is almost a luxury. And finally he knew that, even as hunger takes precedence of grief, so fatigue, supervening, cuts short its career and drowns it in a sleep all the sweeter for bringing forgetfulness of bereavement. In a word, Homer refused to treat the theme tragically. He preferred to tell the Whole Truth.

Another author who preferred to tell the Whole Truth was Fielding. *Tom Jones* is one of the very few Odyssean books written in Europe between the time of Aeschylus and the present age; Odyssean, because never tragical; never – even when painful and disastrous, even when pathetic and beautiful things are happening. For they do happen; Fielding, like Homer, admits all the facts, shirks nothing. Indeed, it is precisely because these authors shirk nothing that their books are not tragical. For among the things they don't shirk are the irrelevancies which, in actual life, always temper the situations and characters that writers of tragedy insist on keeping chemically pure. Consider, for example, the case of Sophy Western, that most charming, most nearly perfect of young women. Fielding, it is obvious, adored her (she is said to have been created in the image of his first, much-loved wife). But in spite of his adoration, he refused to turn her into one of those chemically pure and, as it were, focused beings who do and suffer in the world of tragedy. That innkeeper who lifted the weary Sophia from her horse – what need had

he to fall? In no tragedy would he (nay, could he) have
collapsed beneath her weight. For, to begin with, in the
tragical context weight is an irrelevance; heroines should
be above the law of gravitation. But that is not all; let
the reader now remember what were the results of his fall.
Tumbling flat on his back, he pulled Sophia down on top
of him – his belly was a cushion, so that happily she came
to no bodily harm – pulled her down head first. But head
first is necessarily legs last; there was a momentary display
of the most ravishing charms; the bumpkins at the inn
door grinned or guffawed; poor Sophia, when they picked
her up, was blushing in an agony of embarrassment and
wounded modesty. There is nothing intrinsically im-
probable about this incident, which is stamped, indeed,
with all the marks of literary truth. But however true, it
is an incident which could never, never have happened
to a heroine of tragedy. It would never have been allowed
to happen. But Fielding refused to impose the tragedian's
veto; he shirked nothing – neither the intrusion of irrelevant absurdities into the midst of romance or disaster,
nor any of life's no less irrelevantly painful interruptions
of the course of happiness. He did not want to be a
tragedian. And, sure enough, that brief and pearly gleam
of Sophia's charming posterior was sufficient to scare the
Muse of Tragedy out of *Tom Jones* just as, more than five
and twenty centuries before, the sight of stricken men
first eating, then remembering to weep, then forgetting
their tears in slumber had scared her out of the *Odyssey*.

In his *Principles of Literary Criticism* Mr I. A. Richards
affirms that good tragedy is proof against irony and irrelevance – that it can absorb anything into itself and
still remain tragedy. Indeed, he seems to make of this
capacity to absorb the untragical and the anti-tragical a
touchstone of tragic merit. Thus tried, practically all

Greek, all French and most Elizabethan tragedies are found wanting. Only the best of Shakespeare can stand the test. So, at least, says Mr Richards. Is he right? I have often had my doubts. The tragedies of Shakespeare are veined, it is true, with irony and an often terrifying cynicism; but the cynicism is always heroic idealism turned neatly inside out, the irony is a kind of photographic negative of heroic romance. Turn Troilus's white into black and all his blacks into white and you have Thersites. Reversed, Othello and Desdemona become Iago. White Ophelia's negative is the irony of Hamlet, is the ingenuous bawdry of her own mad songs; just as the cynicism of mad King Lear is the black shadow-replica of Cordelia. Now, the shadow, the photographic negative of a thing, is in no sense irrelevant to it. Shakespeare's ironies and cynicisms serve to deepen his tragic world, but not to widen it. If they had widened it, as the Homeric irrelevancies widened out the universe of the *Odyssey* – why, then, the world of Shakespearean tragedy would automatically have ceased to exist. For example, a scene showing the bereaved Macduff eating his supper, growing melancholy over the whisky, with thoughts of his murdered wife and children, and then, with lashes still wet, dropping off to sleep, would be true enough to life; but it would not be true to tragic art. The introduction of such a scene would change the whole quality of the play; treated in this Odyssean style, *Macbeth* would cease to be a tragedy. Or take the case of Desdemona. Iago's bestially cynical remarks about her character are in no sense, as we have seen, irrelevant to the tragedy. They present us with negative images of her real nature and of the feelings she has for Othello. These negative images are always *hers*, are always recognizably the property of the heroine-victim of a tragedy. Whereas, if, springing ashore at Cyprus, she had tumbled, as the no less exquisite Sophia was to tumble, and revealed the inadequacies of sixteenth-century under-clothing, the play would no longer be the *Othello* we know. Iago might breed a family of little cynics and the existing dose of bitterness and savage negation be doubled and trebled; *Othello* would still remain fundamentally *Othello*. But a few Fieldingesque irrelevancies would destroy it – destroy it, that is to say, as a tragedy; for there would be nothing to prevent it from becoming a magnificent drama of some other kind. For the fact is that tragedy and what I have called the Whole Truth are not compatible; where one is, the other is not. There are certain things which even the best, even Shakespearean tragedy, cannot absorb into itself.

To make a tragedy the artist must isolate a single ele-ment out of the totality of human experience and use that exclusively as his material. Tragedy is something that is separated out from the Whole Truth, distilled from it, so to speak, as an essence is distilled from the living flower. Tragedy is chemically pure. Hence its power to act quickly and intensely on our feelings. All chemically pure art has this power to act upon us quickly and intensely. Thus, chemically pure pornography (on the rare occasions when it happens to be written convincingly, by some one who has the gift of 'putting things across') is a quick-acting emotional drug of incomparably greater power than the Whole Truth about sensuality, or even (for many people) than the tangible and carnal reality itself. It is because of its chemical purity that tragedy so effectively performs its functions of catharsis. It refines and corrects and gives a style to our emotional life, and does so swiftly, with power. Brought into contact with tragedy, the elements of our being fall, for the moment at any rate, into an ordered and beautiful pattern, as the iron filings arrange themselves

under the influence of the magnet. Through all its individual variations, this pattern is always fundamentally
of the same kind. From the reading or the hearing of a
tragedy we rise with the feeling that

> *Our friends are exultations, agonies,*
> *And love, and man's unconquerable mind;*

with the heroic conviction that we too would be unconquerable if subjected to the agonies, that in the midst
of the agonies we too should continue to love, might even
learn to exult. It is because it does these things to us that
tragedy is felt to be so valuable. What are the values of
Wholly-Truthful art? What does it do to us that seems
worth doing? Let us try to discover.

Wholly-Truthful art overflows the limits of tragedy and
shows us, if only by hints and implications, what happened
before the tragic story began, what will happen after it is
over, what is happening simultaneously elsewhere (and
'elsewhere' includes all those parts of the minds and bodies
of the protagonists not immediately engaged in the tragic
struggle). Tragedy is an arbitrarily isolated eddy on the
surface of a vast river that flows on majestically, irresistibly, around, beneath, and to either side of it. Wholly-
Truthful art contrives to imply the existence of the entire
river as well as of the eddy. It is quite different from
tragedy, even though it may contain, among other con-
stituents, all the elements from which tragedy is made.
(The 'same thing' placed in different contexts, loses its
identity and becomes, for the perceiving mind, a succession of different things. In Wholly-Truthful art the
agonies may be just as real, love and the unconquerable
mind just as admirable, just as important, as in tragedy.
Thus, Scylla's victims suffer as painfully as the monster-
devoured Hippolytus in *Phèdre*; the mental anguish of Tom

Jones when he thinks he has lost his Sophia, and lost her by his own fault, is hardly less than that of Othello after Desdemona's murder. (The fact that Fielding's power of 'putting things across' is by no means equal to Shakespeare's is, of course, merely an accident.) But the agonies and indomitabilities are placed by the Wholly-Truthful writer in another, wider context, with the result that they cease to be the same as the intrinsically identical agonies and indomitabilities of tragedy. Consequently, Wholly-Truthful art produces in us an effect quite different from that produced by tragedy. Our mood when we have read a Wholly-Truthful book is never one of heroic exultation; it is one of resignation, of acceptance. (Acceptance can also be heroic.) Being chemically impure, Wholly-Truthful literature cannot move us as quickly and intensely as tragedy or any other kind of chemically pure art. But I believe that its effects are more lasting. The exultations that follow the reading or hearing of a tragedy are in the nature of temporary inebriations. One being cannot long hold the pattern imposed by tragedy. Remove the magnet and the filings tend to fall back into confusion. But the pattern of acceptance and resignation imposed upon us by Wholly-Truthful literature, though perhaps less unexpectedly beautiful in design, is (for that very reason perhaps) more stable. The catharsis of tragedy is violent and apocalyptic; but the milder catharsis of Wholly-Truthful literature is lasting.

In recent times literature has become more and more acutely conscious of the Whole Truth – of the great oceans of irrelevant things, events and thoughts stretching endlessly away in every direction from whatever island point (a character, a story) the author may choose to contemplate. To impose the kind of arbitrary limitations, which must be imposed by any one who wants to write a tragedy, has become more and more difficult – is now indeed, for those who are at all sensitive to contemporaneity, almost impossible. This does not mean, of course, that the modern writer must confine himself to a merely naturalistic manner. One can imply the existence of the Whole Truth without laboriously cataloguing every object within sight. A book can be written in terms of pure phantasy and yet, by implication, tell the Whole Truth. Of all the important works of contemporary literature not one is a pure tragedy. There is no contemporary writer of significance who does not prefer to state or imply the Whole Truth. However different one from another in style, in ethical, philosophical and artistic intention, in the scales of values accepted, contemporary writers have this in common, that they are interested in the Whole Truth. Proust, D. H. Lawrence, André Gide, Kafka, Hemingway – here are five obviously significant and important contemporary writers. Five authors as remarkably unlike one another as they could well be. They are at one only in this: that none of them has written a pure tragedy, that all are concerned with the Whole Truth.

I have sometimes wondered whether tragedy, as a form of art, may not be doomed. But the fact that we are still profoundly moved by the tragic masterpieces of the past – that we can be moved, against our better judgement, even by the bad tragedies of the contemporary stage and film – makes me think that the day of chemically pure art is not over. Tragedy happens to be passing through a period of eclipse, because all the significant writers of our age are too busy exploring the newly discovered, or re-discovered world of the Whole Truth to be able to pay any attention to it. But there is no good reason to believe that this state of things will last for ever. Tragedy is too valuable to be allowed to die. There is no reason, after all, why the two kinds of literature – the Chemically Impure and the Chemically Pure, the literature of the Whole Truth and the literature of Partial Truth – should not exist simultaneously, each in its separate sphere. The human spirit has need of both.

Selected Snobberies

ALL men are snobs about something. One is almost tempted to add: There is nothing about which men cannot feel snobbish. But this would doubtless be an exaggeration. There are certain disfiguring and mortal diseases about which there has probably never been any snobbery. I cannot imagine, for example, that there are any leprosy snobs. More picturesque diseases, even when they are dangerous, and less dangerous diseases, particularly when they are the diseases of the rich, can be and very frequently are a source of snobbish self-importance. I have met several adolescent consumption-snobs, who thought that it would be romantic to fade away in the flower of youth, like Keats or Marie Bash-kirtseff. Alas, the final stages of the consumptive fading are generally a good deal less romantic than these ingenuous young tubercle-snobs seem to imagine. To any who has actually witnessed these final stages the complacent poeticizings of these adolescents must seem as exasperating as they are profoundly pathetic. In the case of those commoner disease-snobs, whose claim to distinction is that they suffer from one of the maladies of the rich, exasperation is not tempered by very much sympathy. People who possess sufficient leisure, sufficient wealth, not to mention sufficient health, to go travelling from spa to

spa, from doctor to fashionable doctor, in search of cures
from problematical diseases (which, in so far as they exist
at all, probably have their source in overeating) cannot
expect us to be very lavish in our solicitude and pity.

Disease-snobbery is only one out of a great multitude
of snobberies, of which now some, now others take pride
of place in general esteem. For snobberies ebb and flow;
their empire rises, declines, and falls in the most approved
historical manner. What were good snobberies a hundred
years ago are now out of fashion. Thus, the snobbery of
family is everywhere on the decline. The snobbery of
culture, still strong, has now to wrestle with an organized
and active low-browism, with a snobbery of ignorance and
stupidity unique, so far as I know, in the whole of history.
Hardly less characteristic of our age is that repulsive
booze-snobbery, born of American Prohibition. The
malefic influences of this snobbery are rapidly spreading
all over the world. Even in France, where the existence
of so many varieties of delicious wine has hitherto imposed
a judicious connoisseurship and has led to the branding
of mere drinking as a brutish solecism, even in France
the American booze-snobbery, with its odious accom-
paniments – a taste for hard drinks in general and for
cocktails in particular – is making headway among the
rich. Booze-snobbery has now made it socially permissible,
and in some circles even rather creditable, for well-brought-
up men and (this is the novelty) well-brought-up women of
all ages, from fifteen to seventy, to be seen drunk, if not
in public, at least in the very much tempered privacy
of a party.

Modernity-snobbery, though not exclusive to our age,
has come to assume an unprecedented importance. The
reasons for this are simple and of a strictly economic
character. Thanks to modern machinery, production is

outrunning consumption. Organized waste among con-
sumers is the first condition of our industrial prosperity.
The sooner a consumer throws away the object he has
bought and buys another, the better for the producer.
At the same time, of course, the producer must do his bit
by producing nothing but the most perishable articles.
'The man who builds a skyscraper to last for more than
forty years is a traitor to the building trade.' The words
are those of a great American contractor. Substitute
motor car, boot, suit of clothes, etc., for skyscraper, and
one year, three months, six months, and so on for forty
years, and you have the gospel of any leader of any
modern industry. The modernity-snob, it is obvious, is
this industrialist's best friend. For modernity-snobs naturally tend to throw away their old possessions and buy
new ones at a greater rate than those who are not
modernity-snobs. Therefore it is in the producer's interest
to encourage modernity-snobbery. Which in fact he does
do – on an enormous scale and to the tune of millions
and millions a year – by means of advertising. The
newspapers do their best to help those who help them;
and to the flood of advertisement is added a flood of less
directly paid-for propaganda in favour of modernity-
snobbery. The public is taught that up-to-dateness is one
of the first duties of man. Docile, it accepts the reiterated
suggestion. We are all modernity-snobs now.

Most of us are also art-snobs. There are two varieties of
art-snobbery – the platonic and the unplatonic. Platonic
art-snobs merely 'take an interest' in art. Unplatonic
art-snobs go further and actually buy art. Platonic art-
snobbery is a branch of culture-snobbery. Unplatonic
art-snobbery is a hybrid or mule; for it is simultaneously
a sub-species of culture-snobbery and of possession-
snobbery. A collection of works of art is a collection of

culture-symbols, and culture-symbols still carry social prestige. It is also a collection of wealth-symbols. For an art collection can represent money more effectively than a whole fleet of motor cars.

The value of art-snobbery to living artists is considerable. True, most art-snobs collect only the works of the dead; for an Old Master is both a safer investment and a holier culture-symbol than a living master. But some art-snobs are also modernity-snobs. There are enough of them, with the few eccentrics who like works of art for their own sake, to provide living artists with the means of subsistence.

The value of snobbery in general, its humanistic 'point', consists in its power to stimulate activity. A society with plenty of snobberies is like a dog with plenty of fleas: it is not likely to become comatose. Every snobbery demands of its devotees unceasing efforts, a succession of sacrifices. The society-snob must be perpetually lion-hunting; the modernity-snob can never rest from trying to be up-to-date. Swiss doctors and the Best that has been thought or said must be the daily and nightly preoccupation of all the snobs respectively of disease and culture.

If we regard activity as being in itself a good, then we must count all snobberies as good; for all provoke activity. If, with the Buddhists, we regard all activity in this world of illusion as bad, then we shall condemn all snobberies out of hand. Most of us, I suppose, take up our position somewhere between the two extremes. We regard some activities as good, others as indifferent or downright bad. Our approval will be given only to such snobberies as excite what we regard as the better activities; the others we shall either tolerate or detest. For example, most professional intellectuals will approve of culture-snobbery (even while intensely disliking most individual culture-snobs), because it compels the philistines to pay at least some slight tribute to the things of the mind and so helps to make the world less dangerously unsafe for ideas than it otherwise might have been. A manufacturer of motor cars, on the other hand, will rank the snobbery of possessions above culture-snobbery; he will do his best to persuade people that those who have fewer possessions, particularly possessions on four wheels, are inferior to those who have more possessions. And so on. Each hierarchy culminates in its own particular Pope.

V. S. PRITCHETT

The Dean

THE world would be poor without the antics of clergymen. The Dean, for example, wished he was a horse. A very Irish wish which a solid Englishwoman very properly came down on; Lady Mary Wortley Montagu was one of the few hostile critics of *Gulliver*:

> Great eloquence have (the authors) employed to prove themselves beasts and show such a veneration for horses, that, since the Essex Quaker nobody has appeared so passionately devoted to that species; and to say truth they talk of a stable with so much warmth and affection I cannot help suspecting some very powerful motive at the bottom of it.

It *was* odd that a man as clean as the Dean should find solace among the mangers; and there is a stable tip for psycho-analysts here. The function which he loathed in Celia and could never stop mentioning, had become unnoticeable at last. Shades of the Freudian Cloacina imprison the growing boy, but are guiltlessly charmed away when, pail and shovel in hand, we make our first, easy, hopeful acquaintance with the fragrant Houyhnhnms.

Dr Johnson was also hostile. *Gulliver* was written 'in defiance of truth and regularity'. Yet the Dean and the Doctor had much in common. They were both sensible men in a century devoted to the flightiness of Reason. What annoyed the Doctor was what enchanted the public; the *madness* of *Gulliver*. Very irregular. We see now that the Augustan prose was a madman's mask and that the age of Reason was also the age of witchcraft, hauntings,

corruption, and the first Gothic folly. History has confirmed Dr Johnson's judgement first by numbing the satire
– for who can be bothered to look up the digs at Walpole,
Newton and the rest? – and by giving the book a totally
different immortality. It is not an accident that *Gulliver*
has become a child's book; only a child could be so des-
tructive, so irresponsible and so cruel. Only a child has the
animal's eye; only a child, or the mad clergyman, can
manage that unhuman process of disassociation which is
the beginning of all satire from Aristophanes onwards;
only children (or the mad) have that monstrous and
infantile egotism which assumes everything is meaningless
and that, like children, we run the world on unenlightened
self-interest like a wagon-load of monkeys. What a relief
it is that the Dean's style is as lucid and plain as common
water; it runs like water off a duck's back. If *Gulliver* had
been written in the coloured prose of the Bible, bulging
with the prophetic attitudinisings of the Jews, the book
might have caused a revolution – there is some very
revolutionary stuff in Lilliput – but a moderate church
Tory like the Dean had no intention of doing that. There
must have been satisfaction in reminding a Queen in the
rational century that under her petticoat she was a Yahoo
and savage satisfaction in knowing she liked the idea. In
this she was a sensible woman; she had, like the rest of us,
been charmed back to the minute and monstrous remem-
brances of childhood, she had been captivated by the
plain, good and homely figure of Gulliver himself. She
picked out the topical bits and when the Dean waded into
his generalities about human nature, her eyes no doubt
wandered off that almost too easy page and examined her
finger-nails.

But there was a part of *Gulliver* which nobody liked or
which most people thought inferior. Laputa missed the

mark. Why? It was topical enough. The skit of science was
a good shot at the young Royal Society and the wave of
projects which obsessed the times. The highbrow is always
fair game. Visually and satirically Laputa is the most
delightful of the episodes. The magic island floats crystal-
line in the air, rising and falling to the whim of its ruler,
and its absent-minded philosophers are only tickled into
awareness by a fly-whisk. Laputa is the rationalist's day-
dream. Here is the unearthly paradise, an hydraulic and
attainable heaven. True, the philosophers were fools and
the scientists, with their attempts to get sunshine out of
cucumbers, cloth from spiders, food from dirt and panic
from astronomy, were ridiculous. The knowledge machine
was grotesque. But what was the matter with the men of
Newton's time that they could not appreciate Laputa?
The age of Reason enjoyed the infantile, the animal and
irrational in *Gulliver*; it rejected the satire on knowledge.

The only answer can be that the Augustans had not had
enough of science to know it was worth satirizing. The
Dean was before his time; and the world would have to
wait a hundred and fifty years for *Bouvard and Pécuchet* to
continue the unpopular game – the origins of *Bouvard* and
Gulliver are, incidentally, identical, and both Flaubert and
Swift spent ten years on and off writing the books – and
among ourselves, we have only Aldous Huxley's crib of
Laputa, *Brave New World*. Yet Laputa is the only part of
Gulliver which has not been eclipsed by subsequent
writing. Voltaire, Wells, Verne – to take names at random
– have all taken the freshness of Swift's idea; and what the
Utopians have left out has been surpassed by science
itself. The sinister functionalism of the termites, the pedes-
trian mysticism of the bee, the ribald melodramas of the
aquarium and the Grand Guignol of the insect house, have
all defeated human life and literature as material for the

political satirist. These things have put the date on Lilliput, but Laputa is untouched. It stands among us, miraculously contemporary.

It is the surrealist island. At least Laputa is to Lilliput what Alice in Wonderland is to surrealism. The sportively clinical and sinister succeed to the human and extra-ordinary. One cannot love Laputa as one loves Lilliput, but one *recognizes* Laputa. It is the clinic we have come to live in. It is the world of irresponsible intellect and irresponsible science which prepared the way for the present war. We enter at once into our inhumanity, into that glittering laboratory which is really a butcher's shop. What science does not dissect, it blows to pieces. The Dean, safe at the beginning of the period, did not foresee this – though he does note that, to crush rebellion, the King was in the habit of letting the island down bodily from the sky on the rebellious inhabitants.

We are also in the world of the cubist painters. The rhomboid joints, the triangular legs of mutton come out of Wyndham Lewis – has he illustrated Laputa? – those mathematicians take us to our Bertrand Russells. Among the astronomers, with their weakness for judicial astrology, does one not detect the philosophical speculations of Jeans and Eddington? Pure thought, moreover, led to a laxity of morals, for husbands devoted to the higher intellectual life were inclined either to be short-sighted or absent-minded, and the wives in Laputa found it necessary and simple to descend to coarser but more attentive lovers on the mainland below. In search perhaps of Gerald Heard's new mutation, the speculative despised sex or forgot about it; or having read their *Ends and Means*, thought of giving sex up. Yes, Laputa, the island of the non-attached, is topical.

Like all satirists, the Dean was, nevertheless, in a

vulnerable position. By temperament and in style he is one of the earliest scientific writers in modern literature. He delights, with a genuine anticipation of scientific method, in those measurements of hoofs, heads, and fingers, the calculated quantities of food, the inevitable observation on his bladder. One might be reading Malinowski or Dr Zuckermann. Yet when one puts the book down it is to realize that there is one more country in the story which is the counterblast to Laputa, Lilliput, and the whole list. This is Gulliver himself. The world is mad, grotesque, a misanthropic Irishman's self-destructive fantasy; but Gulliver is not. Gulliver is sane. He is good, homely, friendly, and decent. How he keeps himself to himself in his extraordinary adventures! No love affairs; Mrs Gulliver and family are waiting at home. Unlike the philosophers, he not a cuckold. One is sure he isn't.

'I have ever hated all nations, professions, and communities', the Dean wrote to Pope; 'and all my love is towards individuals; for instance I hate the tribe of lawyers, but I love Councillor Such a One and Judge Such a One; principally I hate and detest that animal called man, although I heartily love John, Peter, Thomas and so forth.'

A religious mind, even one as moderate in its religion as Swift's, must, in the end, be indifferent to material welfare, progress and hopes. Gulliver is simply John, Peter, or Thomas, the ordinary sensible man, and he stands alone against the mad laboratories of the floating island. Gulliver could not know that people would one day make a knowledge machine or invent sunshine substitutes (but not out of cucumbers), but he does know that it is folly to let the world be run by these people. They will turn it (as the visit to Lagado showed, or, shall we say, to a blitzed town) into a wilderness. The world, the mad

Dean says in the figure of Gulliver, must be run by John, Peter, Thomas, the sensible man.

The First Detective

THE time of the year and the year itself are unknown, but one day, well before the French Revolution, a tall, good-looking, fair-haired youth was hanging about dejectedly on the quay at Ostend seeking for a boat which would take him to America. Arras was his native town, but Arras could not hold him. His energy, his vitality, his hopes demanded a larger land. Unhappily the only boats going to America were far too expensive for him, and he stood on the quay lonely, homesick, and in despair. He was in this state when a stranger fell into conversation with him, a stranger who turned out to be a shipping agent and who explained that once you knew the ropes it was the simplest thing on earth to find a ship. He, personally, would see to it. The two men went off to an inn to discuss the matter further. What happened after that was never quite clear to the youth. There had been good food and drink; there appeared to have been some 'dames fort aimables' whose hospitality was of 'the antique kind' which did not stop at the table; he even had some recollection of being in a pleasant if rotating room and under the same eiderdown as one of the ladies. All the more astonishing therefore to wake up in the morning and find himself lying half-naked on a pile of ropes – the only ones he was to learn about – with only a couple of *écus* in his pockets. A sad story and, as the innkeeper said, he ought to be grateful that worse had not happened. But this was not the appropriate moral. The money with which Eugène-François Vidocq had planned to pay his fare to America had been stolen from his mother's baker's shop in Arras. The theft was the first major enterprise – hitherto he had only tickled pennies out of the slot in the counter with a feather dipped in glue – in a picaresque career which was to lead Eugène-François into the French, Austrian, and revolutionary armies, into the perpetual company of criminals, all over the roads of France and into most of the prisons, until at last, an artist in escape and quick changes, he arrived at the Sûreté in Paris not as a convict but as its Director. To his legend as a criminal was to be added a new legend as a detective. He was to be the first of the Big Four.

The astonishing story of the life of Vidocq can be read in two French biographies, notably one by Jagot published in 1928; a far fuller and livelier account, however, is contained in the four volumes of Vidocq's own *Mémoires* published in 1829, of which, as far as I know, no complete or reliable English translation exists. A French edition in two volumes is published by the Librairie Grund. The *Mémoires* are said not to be his own work, but, whoever wrote them, the book is enormously readable, especially the opening volume. This early narrative has the rapidity, the nonchalance, the variety and crude intrigue of the good picaresque novels; and in it Vidocq is a living man and not a mere first person singular. If he touched up his own past or if someone else touched it up for him introducing romantic coincidences – Vidocq was always running into his ex-wife, his discarded mistresses or ill-intentioned fellow prisoners, at the least desirable moments – the story gains in romance and ingenuity.

To describe Vidocq as a great criminal is inaccurate. Rather he was a reckless, adventurous young man with a gift for trouble, a true *tête brûleé*. The Revolution, the war

with Austria, the amateur and professional armies of the
period, were his environment; the armies were recruited,
dissolved, changed sides and, in default of pay, lived by
their wits. Brussels was a hive of this knavery and there
Vidocq found himself posing as an officer and plotting a
bigamous marriage with an elderly baroness. There is
some charm in his account of how his nerve went and of
how he confessed to the lady. After the Ostend episode he
had avoided theft and had tried to settle down with a
circus. His employer tried to make him into an acrobat
and failed; the alternative was the role of the noble savage,
but he found this uncongenial, indeed terrifying: he was
expected to eat birds alive and swallow stones. His next
master was a wandering quack and knave who swindled
farmers and who took Vidocq back to Arras, where his
adventures and an orgy of forgiveness by his parents at
once made him famous. Vidocq no doubt boasted. He was
a great talker and something of an actor. Soon he had
mistresses all over the town, was fighting duels or assaul-
ting those who refused to fight. He found himself at last in
prison.

Here one picks up the recurring pattern of Vidocq's life.
Gaoled because of one woman, he intrigues with another
to get him out – going this time to the length of marriage –
but once he is out, the jealousy or unfaithfulness of the
rescuing lady drives him again into hiding. It is a continually repeated story. Worse than his infidelity was
his lack of tact. A girl called Francine, for example, risked
everything to aid his escape from one gaol; yet, such was
his crassness or his ill-luck, he walked straight out of the
prison gates into the arms of an old mistress and unwisely
spent the night with her instead of going to the woman
who had rescued him. This was too much for the faithful,
or at least sacrificial, Francine. It seemed to her – and to

many others – that the best way to be assured of Vidocq was to get him back to prison as soon as possible. Vidocq made no pretence of virtue and delighted in the mystery which gradually grew around his character. He had the vanity of a child. Later on he was to describe with a proper sardonic agony how, when escaping from the public in Brittanny and disguised as a nun, he was obliged by a farmer and his wife to occupy the same bed as their daughters, in the interests of propriety. Such a trial by fire is the kind of thing picaresque literature enjoys.

The other element in the Vidocq pattern is his faculty for escape. Vidocq always held that his big conviction was unjust and that he was 'framed' by a fellow prisoner. To escape was therefore a matter of justice and duty. There is something moving in this very vital man's continual struggles for liberty. The fame of his escapes eclipsed whatever other notoriety he had. At Arras the disconsolate police were driven to put out the legend that he was a werewolf. One gendarme swore that, as he laid hands on him, Vidocq turned into a bale of straw.

Awaiting trial, for example, he simply picked up the coat and helmet of the guard, which had been put on a bench near by, and walked unmolested out of court. On another occasion he locked the police up in his room. Over and over again he enjoyed the comedy of leading an un-suspecting police officer on to saying what he would do with Vidocq when he caught him. Jumping out of cabs when under escort, leaving prison by a rope at the window, sawing through manacles, digging tunnels out of gaol or making guards drunk, became a routine. In Arras, where he was very much wanted, he lived for a year disguised as an Austrian officer and neither his family, the police, nor the girl he lived with, who had known him well before, discovered his true identity.

For twelve years, while he was supposedly serving a long sentence, Vidocq was more often out of prison than in it. But it was an exhausting life; freedom was constantly menaced by blackmailing associates, and just when he seemed to have settled down happily as a draper – such was his mild ambition – he met his divorced wife and found himself keeping her and her relatives in order to shut their mouths. The worm turned. He went to the Chief of Police and made him an offer. Pardon him, leave him in peace, Vidocq said, and he would help them to capture all the criminals they desired. It cannot be said that this second period of respectable fame makes entirely comfortable reading. He delivered 'the goods' of course; no one could approach his abilities as a detective, for no one else had his knowledge of the underworld. The vanity of criminals is as inexhaustible as their love of the great figure; a burglar or assassin, however great in his own esteem, was flattered if the great and mysterious Vidocq sat down with him at the table of some shabby *marchand de vin*. Vidocq decoyed them with charm or effrontery, as the case demanded. With a rather devilish gusto he will tell how, hearing So-and-so was wanted, he would go to the house of the man's mistress, announce her man had been caught, install himself with the lady for a few days and (his own mistress aiding him) would get to know the whole gang, and, at the right moment, strike. It is a little embarrassing. The authorities themselves became embarrassed. The law never feels very happy about the *agent provocateur*.

The *Mémoires* of Vidocq are by a man who was hugely proud of his life both as a fugitive and a pursuer of fugitives. He had an eye for character and there are some admirable farces of low life such as his adventures with the drunken colonial sergeant and their riotous visits to the brothels. The dialogue is racy and real. His portraits of the innumerable 'dames fort aimables' are very vivid. He is delighted with himself as a detective. There is a search, at one period, for a house where a hunchback girl lives in a quarter which at first seems to have no hunchbacks. Hunchbacks (Vidocq reasons) are natural gossips – especially about other people's love affairs; they are jealous and also very respectable. Where do the most respectable gossips meet? At the milk shops. Disguised as a respectable man of 60 he sets out to search the most popular creameries. Sure enough a hunchback appears, a very Venus of hunchbacks, of course, a great-eyed creature like a medieval fairy. Posing as a wronged husband, Vidocq soon discovers who is living in sin in the house and so traces his victims.

One can hardly call this subtle, but the methods of Vidocq were made for the chaotic period of the Napoleonic wars and their aftermath when France swarmed with criminals. Later on, more systematic and respectable means were wanted. His day came to an end and he had the mortification of seeing another reformed criminal, his secretary, one Coco Lacour, succeed him. Coco had reformed in earnest. He had gone to the Jesuits, who made him and his wife do public penance bare-footed in the streets. A coolness existed between Vidocq and Coco. Coco was a miserable man with no air of the gentleman about him and Vidocq had pointed out that a touch more polish in his conversation as a member of the Big Four would be an advantage. (After all, Vidocq had very nearly married a baroness, a Belgian baroness it is true, but still . . .) Coco resented his lessons in etiquette. Vidocq, in his jealousy, has drawn a very funny portrait of the little reformed sinner sitting all day by the Pont Neuf fishing while, at home, his wife is doing a good trade in clothes with prostitutes.

Once out of favour Vidocq is said to have faked a robbery and then to have made arrests to show how clever he was; but the trick was discovered and the words *agent provocateur* finally doomed him. He started a paper factory which failed, a detective agency which declined into triviality. He died at last in poverty. There is one sentence in the *Mémoires* which I like to think he really wrote:

Les voleurs de profession [it says] *sont tous ceux qui, volontairement ou non, ont contracté l'habitude de s'approprier le bien d'autrui.*

MORE ABOUT PENGUINS
AND PELICANS

For further information about books available from Penguins please write to Dept EP, Penguin Books Ltd, Harmondsworth, Middlesex UB7 0DA.

In the U.S.A.: For a complete list of books available from Penguins in the United States write to Dept CS, Penguin Books, 625 Madison Avenue, New York, New York 10022.

In Canada: For a complete list of books available from Penguins in Canada write to Penguin Books Canada Ltd, 2801 John Street, Markham, Ontario L3R 1B4.

In Australia: For a complete list of books available from Penguins in Australia write to the Marketing Department, Penguin Books Australia Ltd, P.O. Box 257, Ringwood, Victoria 3134.

The Penguin English Library

DANIEL DEFOE
MOLL FLANDERS
Edited by Juliet Mitchell

In Moll's self-interested and picaresque adventures Defoe creates a book of universal appeal. 'Defoe's excellence it is', observed Coleridge, 'to make me forget my specific class, character and circumstances, and to raise me, while I read him, into the universal man.'

also by Daniel Defoe

A JOURNAL OF THE PLAGUE YEAR
ROBINSON CRUSOE
A TOUR THROUGH THE WHOLE ISLAND
OF GREAT BRITAIN

HENRY FIELDING
TOM JONES
Edited by R. P. C. Mutter

This is one of the great comic novels of the English language, a vivid Hogarthian panorama of eighteenth-century life, with a plot which Coleridge described as one of the three most perfect ever planned. *Tom Jones* also has an underlying seriousness and all the rich and generous humanity of its author.

also by Henry Fielding:

JOSEPH ANDREWS

WILLIAM THACKERAY
VANITY FAIR
Edited by J. I. M. Stewart

Through the free-wheeling melée of early nineteenth-century English society sails Becky Sharp, one of literature's most resourceful, engaging and amoral characters, with Amelia Sedley, her less lustrous but more ambiguous foil. Their story is, in J. I. M. Stewart's words, 'a landmark in the history of English fiction.'

NATHANIEL HAWTHORNE
THE SCARLET LETTER
AND SELECTED TALES
Edited by Thomas E. Connolly

'He has the purest style, the finest taste, the most available scholarship, the most delicate humour, the most touching pathos, the most radiant imagination, the most consummate ingenuity,' wrote Poe of Hawthorne, whose novel, *The Scarlet Letter* (1850), is generally regarded as the first great work of American fiction. It is the story of a 'fallen woman' – fallen, that is, in the eyes of the Calvinist-Puritan society of Boston – and of her daughter and the unacknowledged father.

CHARLES MATURIN
MELMOTH THE WANDERER
Edited by Alethea Hayter

Melmoth the Wanderer, first published in 1820, is one of the masterpieces of the school of Terror Romance. The name 'Melmoth' itself has come to stand for that typically Romantic hero, the outsider who has voluntarily exchanged his salvation for the knowledge and power that come with prolonged life and who then desperately tries to lay his fearful burden on another victim.

THREE GOTHIC NOVELS

WALPOLE The Castle of Otranto

BECKFORD Vathek

MARY SHELLEY Frankenstein

With an introduction by Mario Praz

The Gothic novel, that curious literary genre which flourished from about 1765 until 1825, revels in the horrible and supernatural, in suspense and exotic settings. This volume presents three of the most celebrated Gothic novels: *The Castle of Otranto*, published pseudonymously in 1765, is one of the first of the genre and the most truly Gothic of the three. *Vathek* (1786), an oriental tale by an eccentric millionaire, exotically combines Gothic romanticism with the vivacity of *The Arabian Nights*. The story of *Frankenstein* (1818) and the monster he created is as spine-chilling today as it ever was; as in all Gothic novels, horror is the keynote.

THOMAS LOVE PEACOCK

NIGHTMARE ABBEY

and

CROTCHET CASTLE

Edited by Raymond Wright

A romantic in his youth and a friend of Shelley, Thomas Love Peacock happily made hay of the romantic movement in *Nightmare Abbey*, clamping Coleridge, Byron, and Shelley himself in a kind of painless pillory. And in *Crotchet Castle* he did no less for the political economists, pitting his gifts of exaggeration and ridicule against scientific progress and the March of Mind.

The Penguin English Library

This series covers classic works of English literature from the pre-Renaissance to the early twentieth century; from Malory's *Morte d'Arthur* to Samuel Butler's *Erewhon* and *The Way of All Flesh*. Here is a selection of recent titles.

George Eliot

ADAM BEDE

EDITED BY STEPHEN GILL

ROMOLA

EDITED BY ANDREW SANDERS

Benjamin Disraeli

SYBIL: THE TWO NATIONS

INTRODUCED BY R.A. BUTLER
AND EDITED BY THOM BRAUN

FOUR MORALITY PLAYS

The Castle of Perseverance/Magnyfycence/King Johan/Ane Satire of the Thrie Estaitis

EDITED BY PETER HAPPÉ

Robert Louis Stevenson

DR JEKYLL AND MR HYDE AND OTHER STORIES

EDITED BY JENNI CALDER

WEIR OF HERMISTON

EDITED BY PAUL BINDING

Charlotte Brontë

VILLETTE

EDITED BY MARK LILLY
WITH AN INTRODUCTION BY TONY TANNER